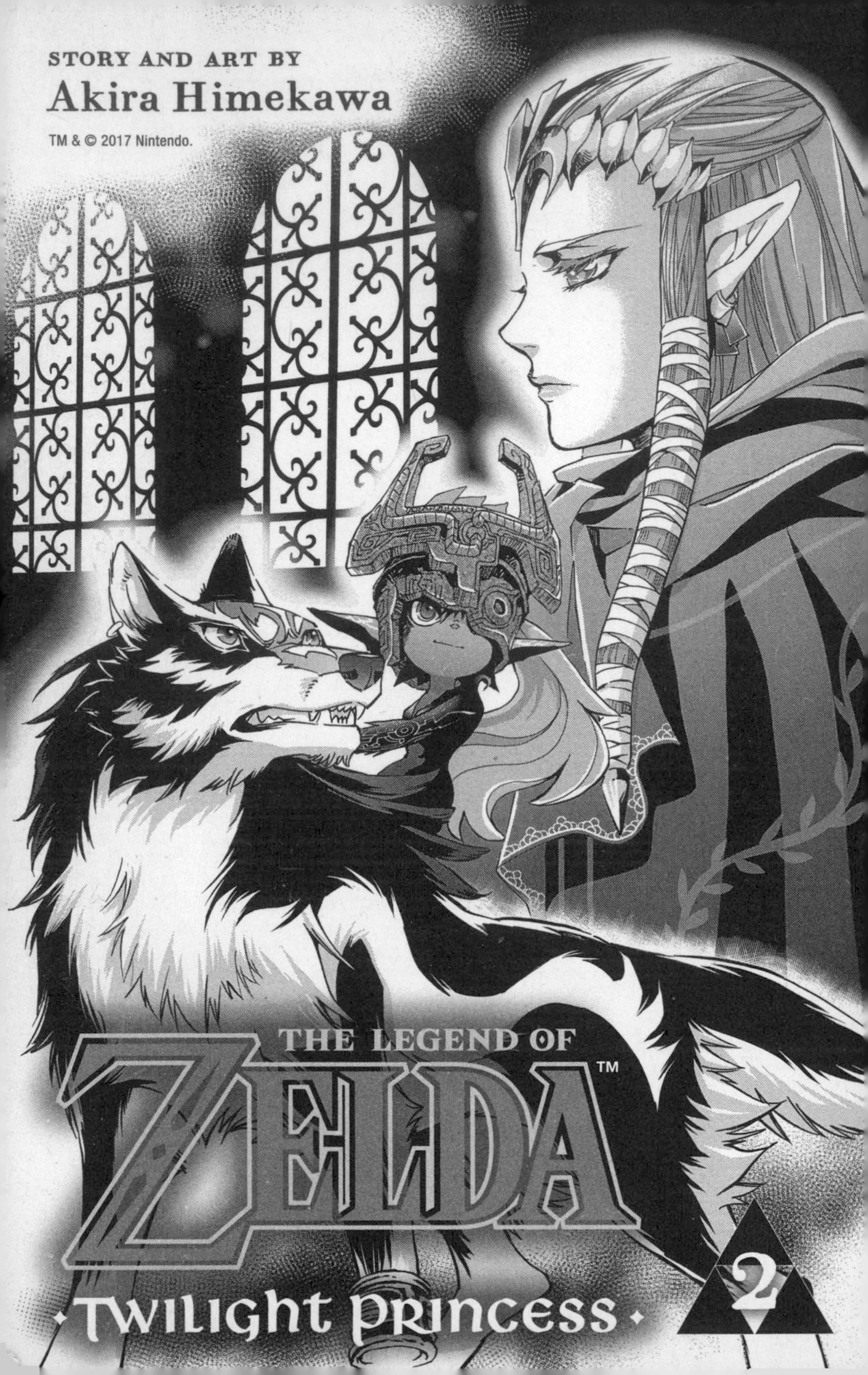
STORY AND ART BY
Akira Himekawa
TM & © 2017 Nintendo.
THE LEGEND OF
ZELDA™
·Twilight Princess·
2

THE LEGEND OF

ZELDA

·Twilight Princess·

2

CONTENTS

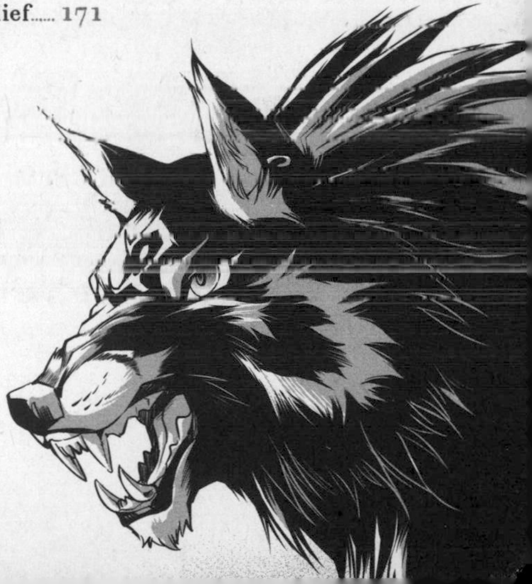

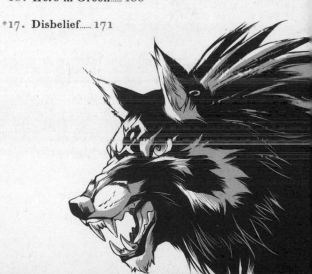

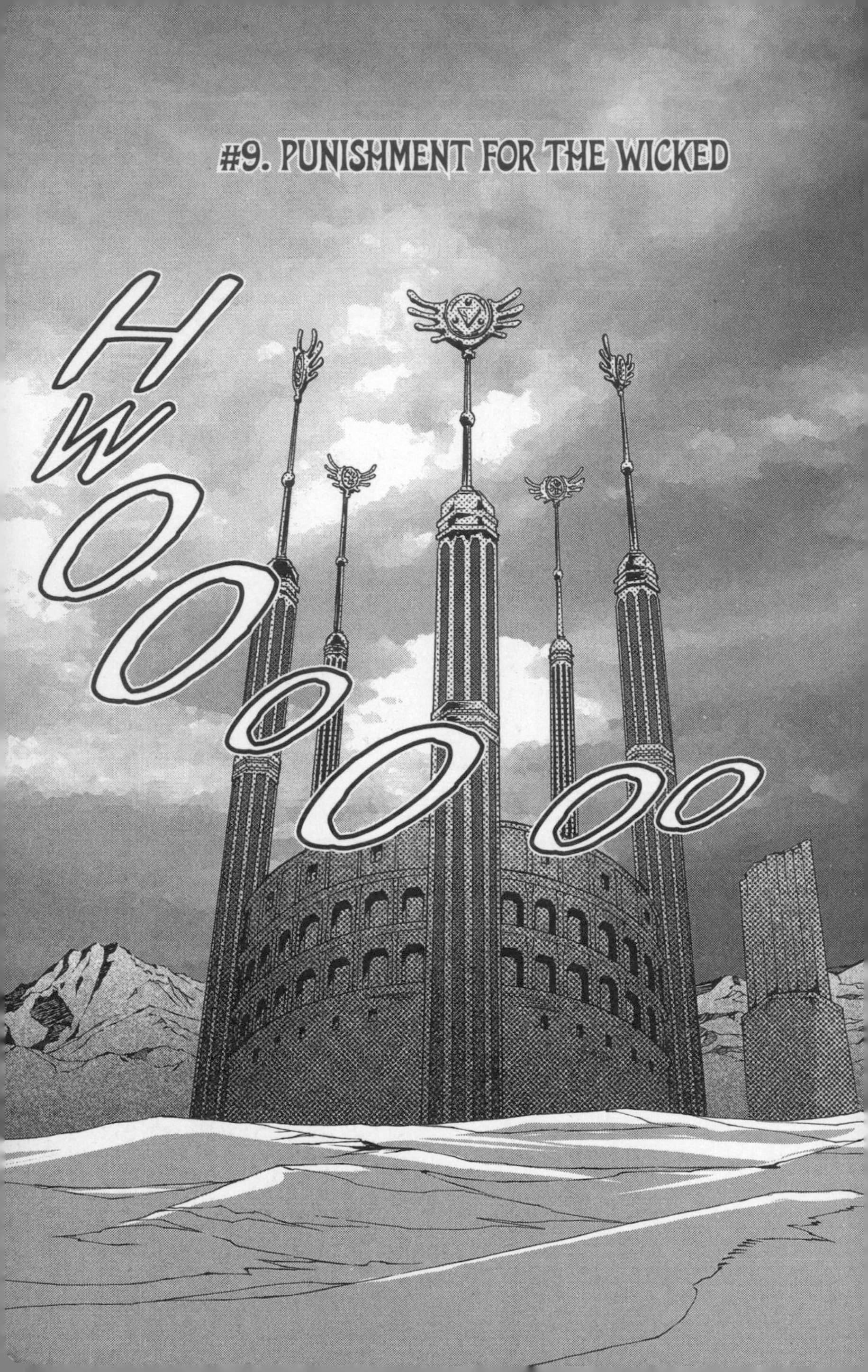
#9. PUNISHMENT FOR THE WICKED
HWOOOOOO

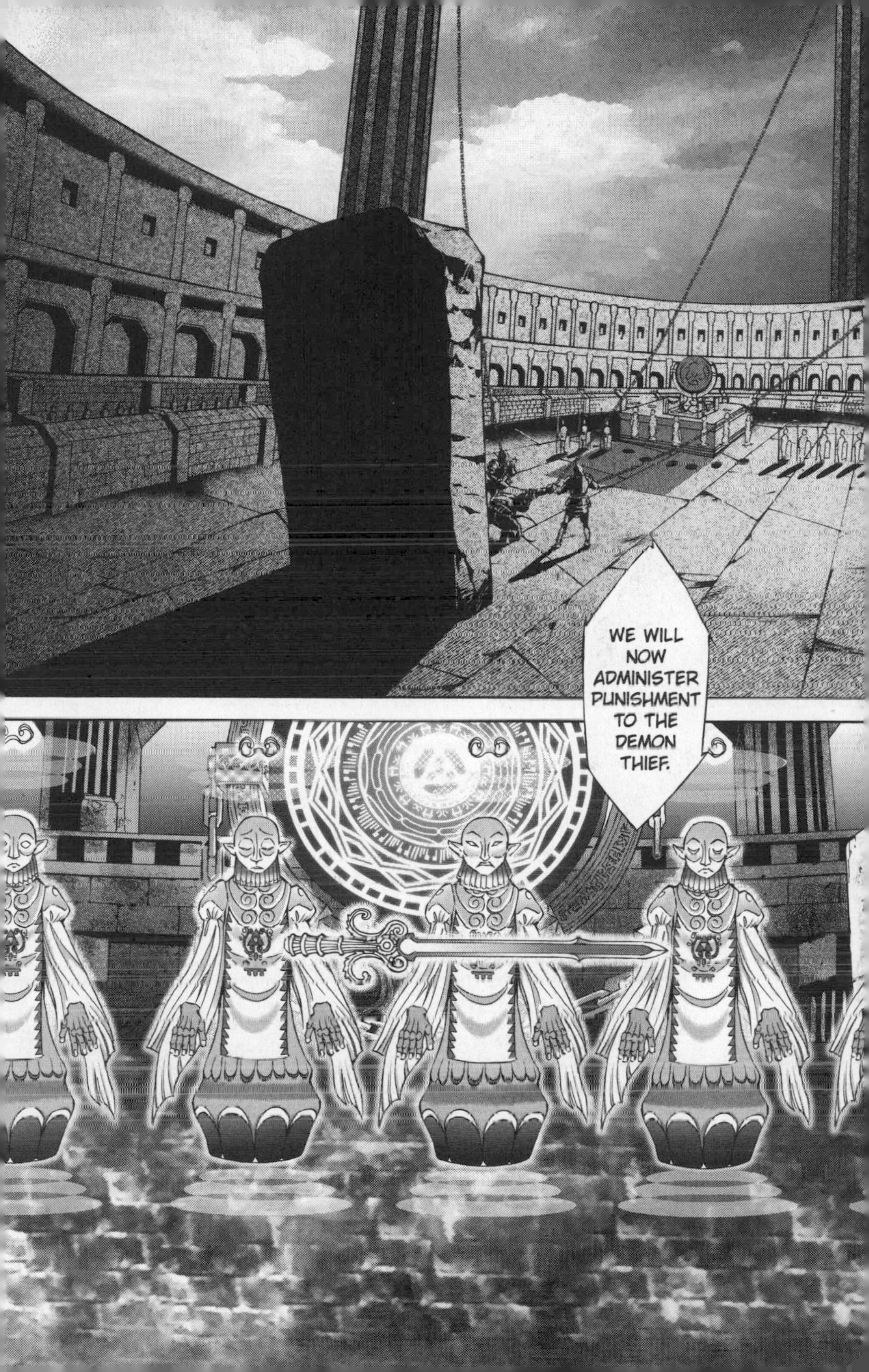
WE WILL NOW ADMINISTER PUNISHMENT TO THE DEMON THIEF.

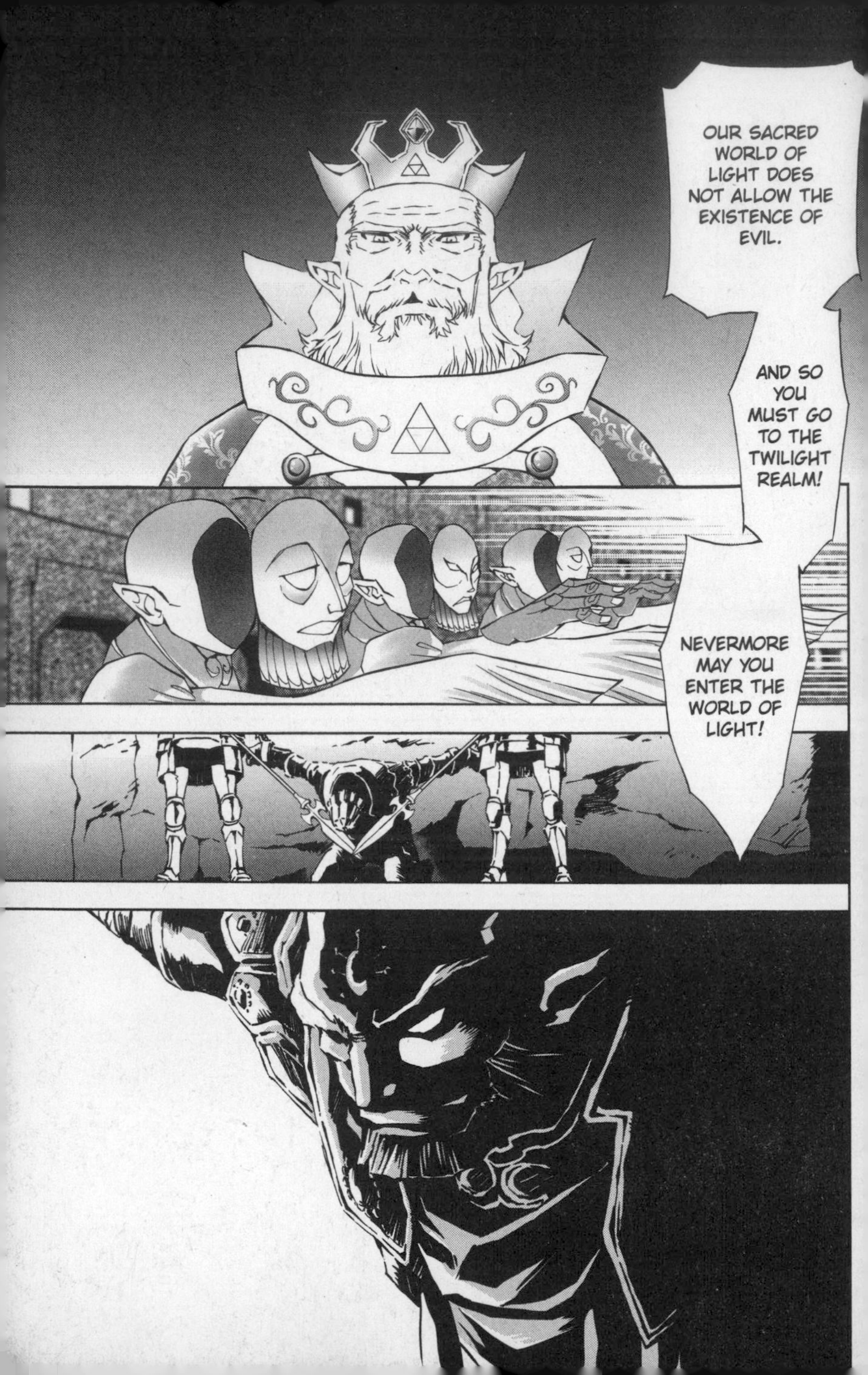
OUR SACRED WORLD OF LIGHT DOES NOT ALLOW THE EXISTENCE OF EVIL.
AND SO YOU MUST GO TO THE TWILIGHT REALM!
NEVERMORE MAY YOU ENTER THE WORLD OF LIGHT!

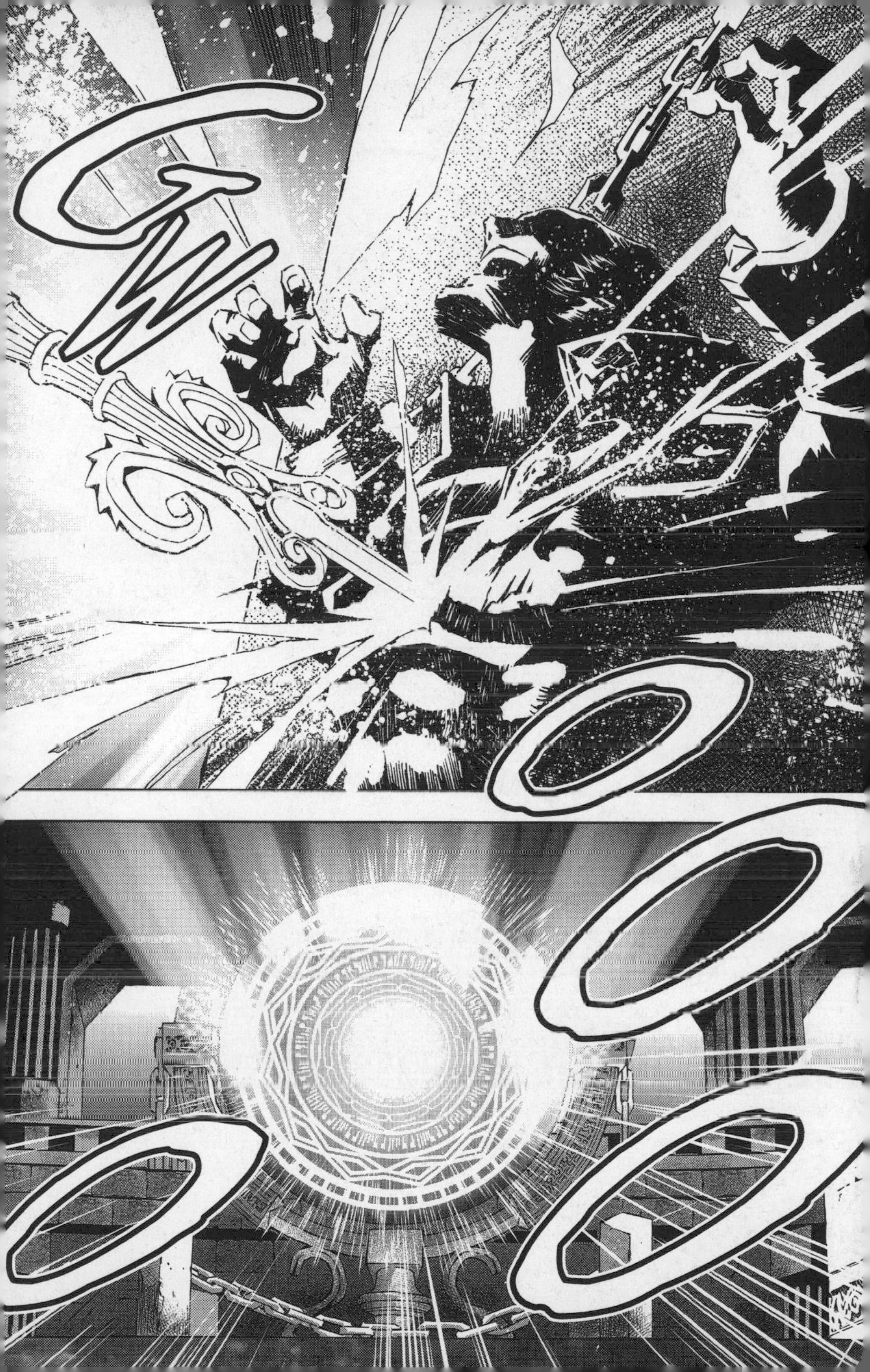
GWOOOO

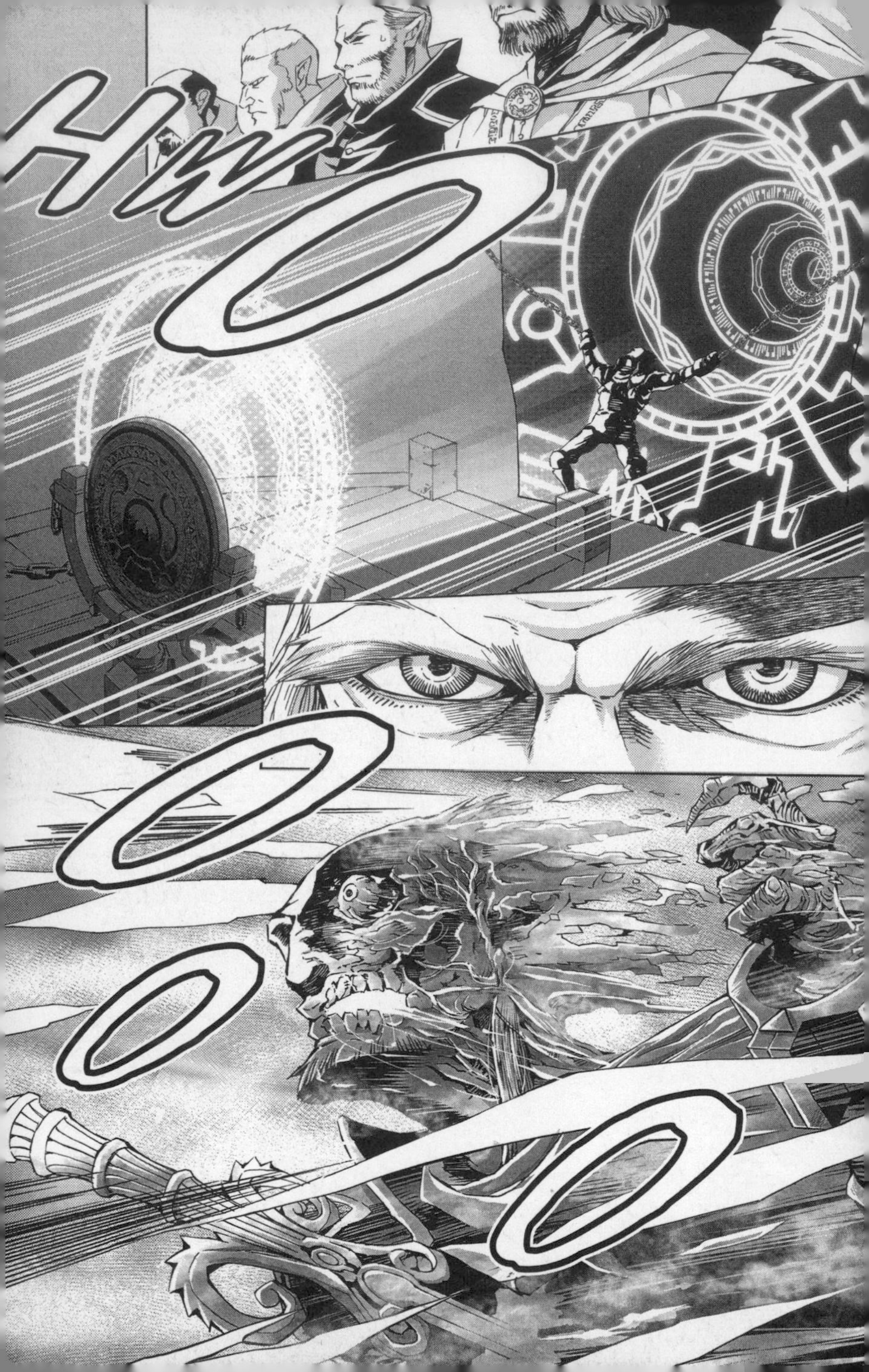
HWOOOO

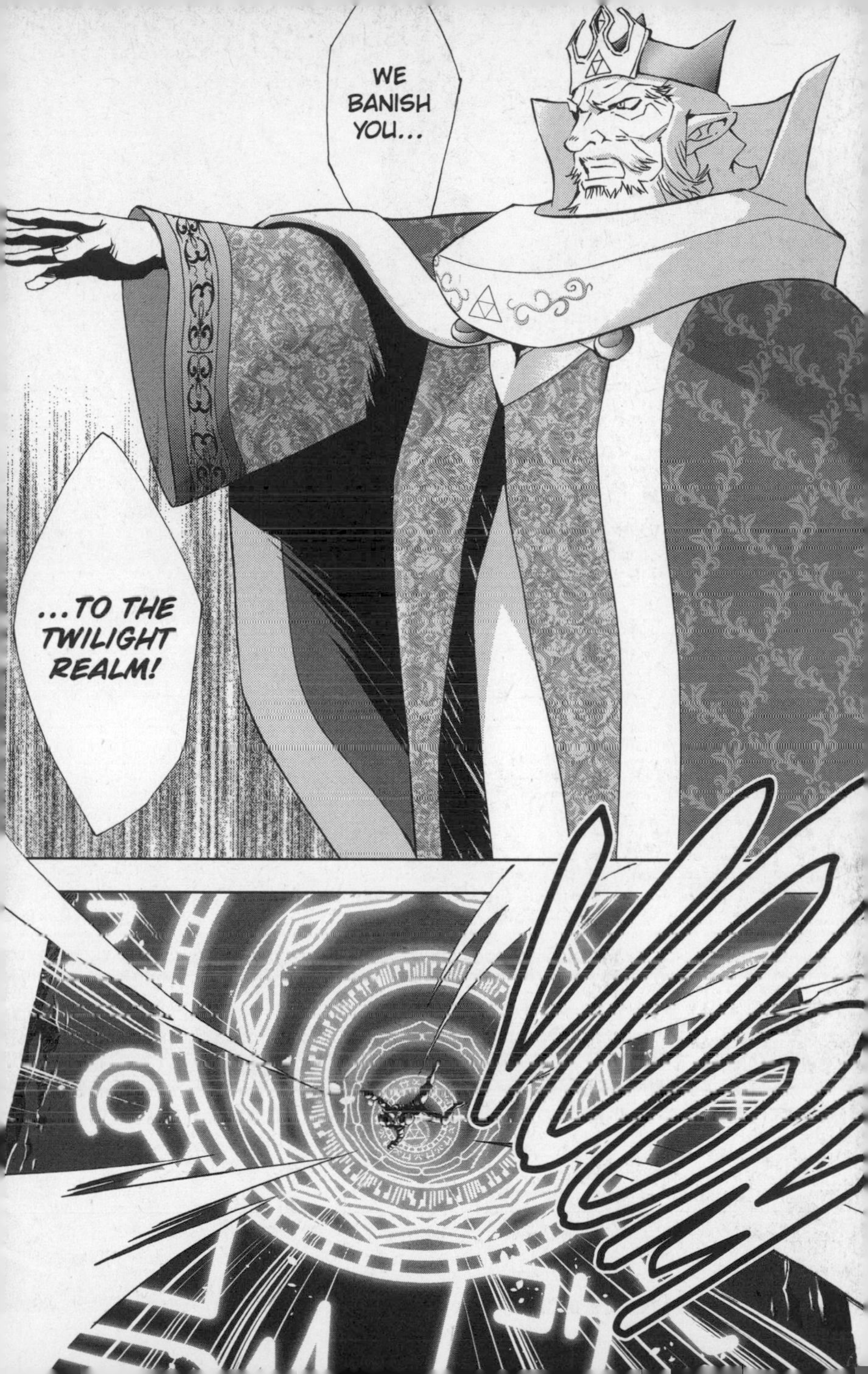
WE BANISH YOU...
...TO THE TWILIGHT REALM!

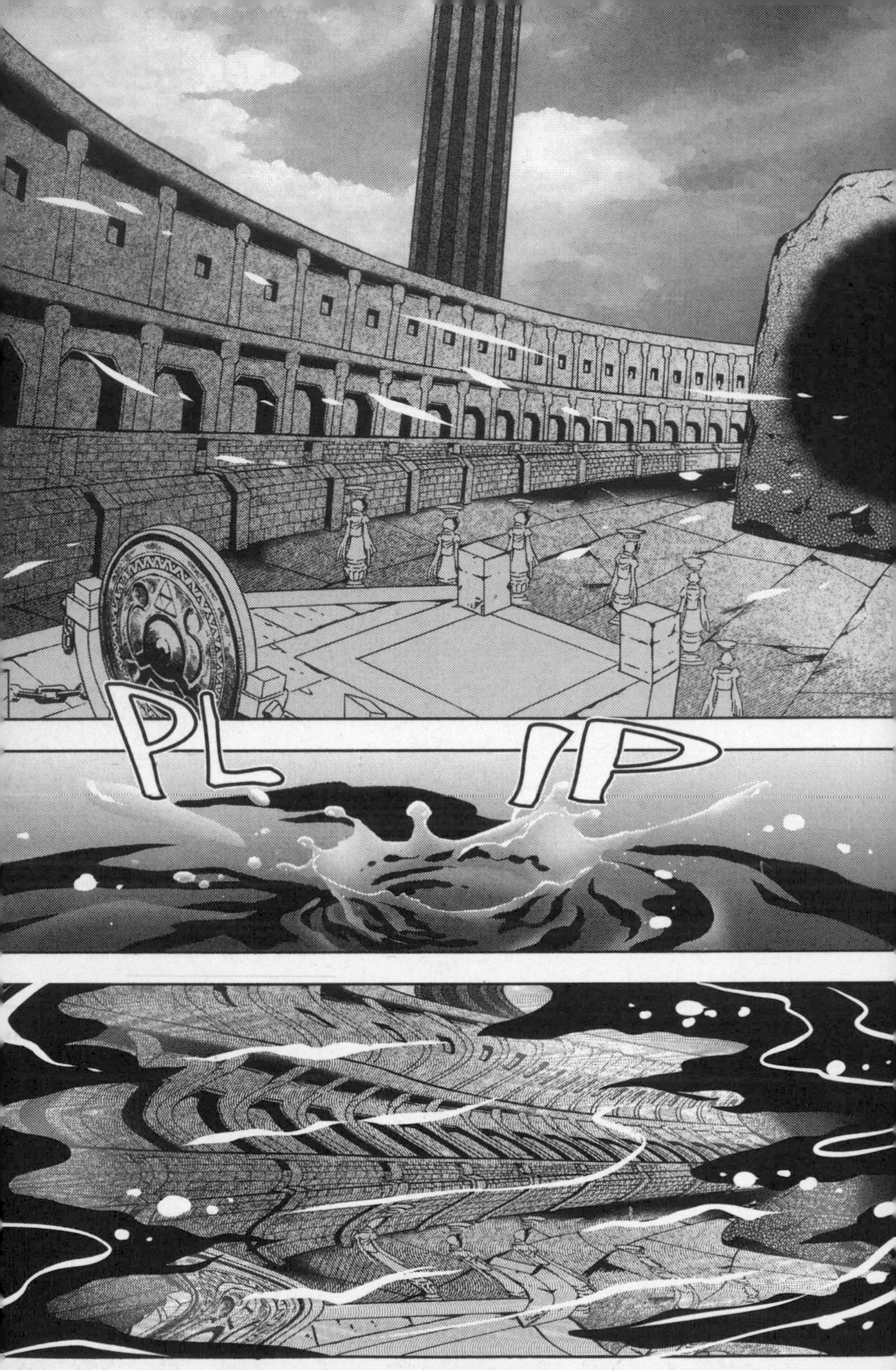
PLIP

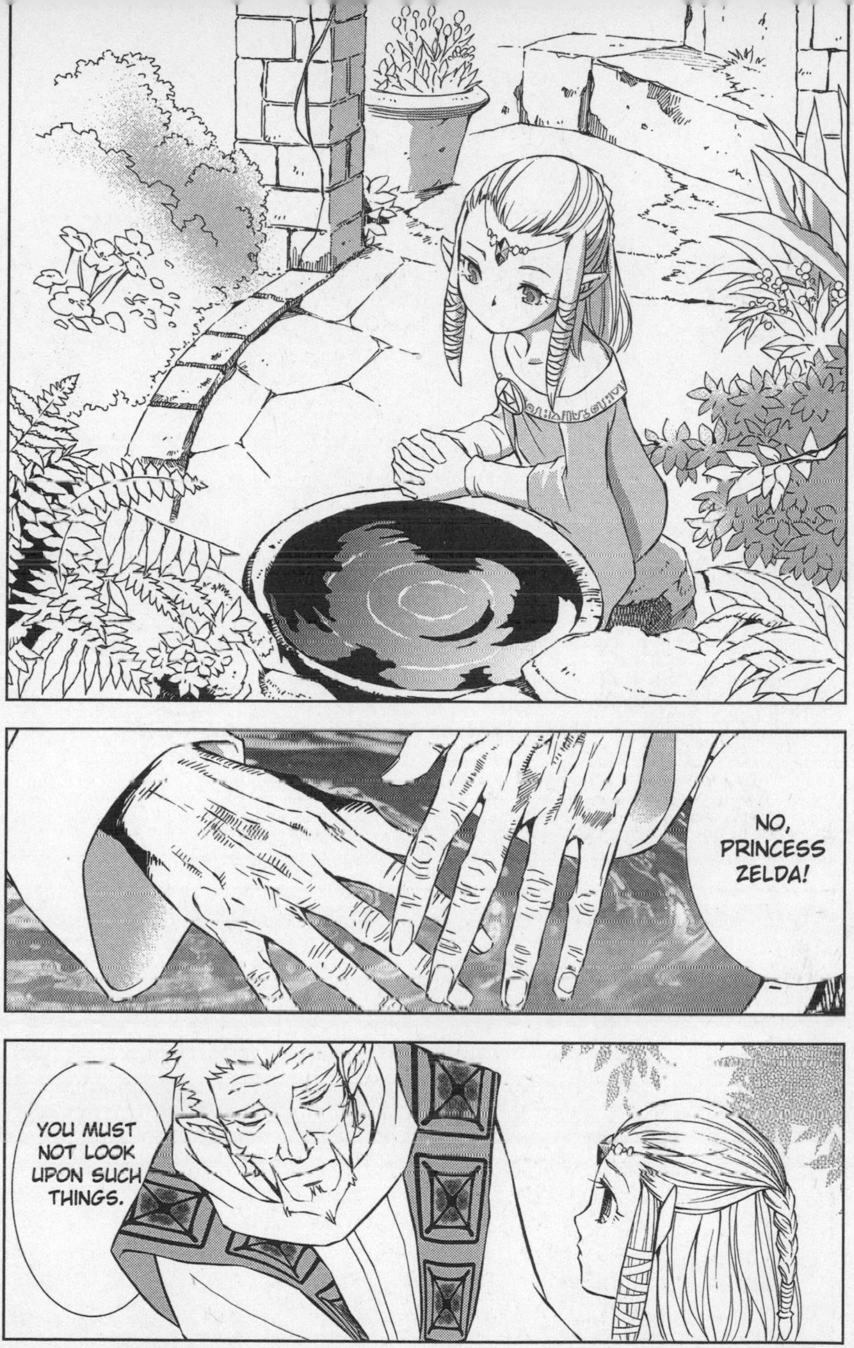
NO, PRINCESS ZELDA!
YOU MUST NOT LOOK UPON SUCH THINGS.

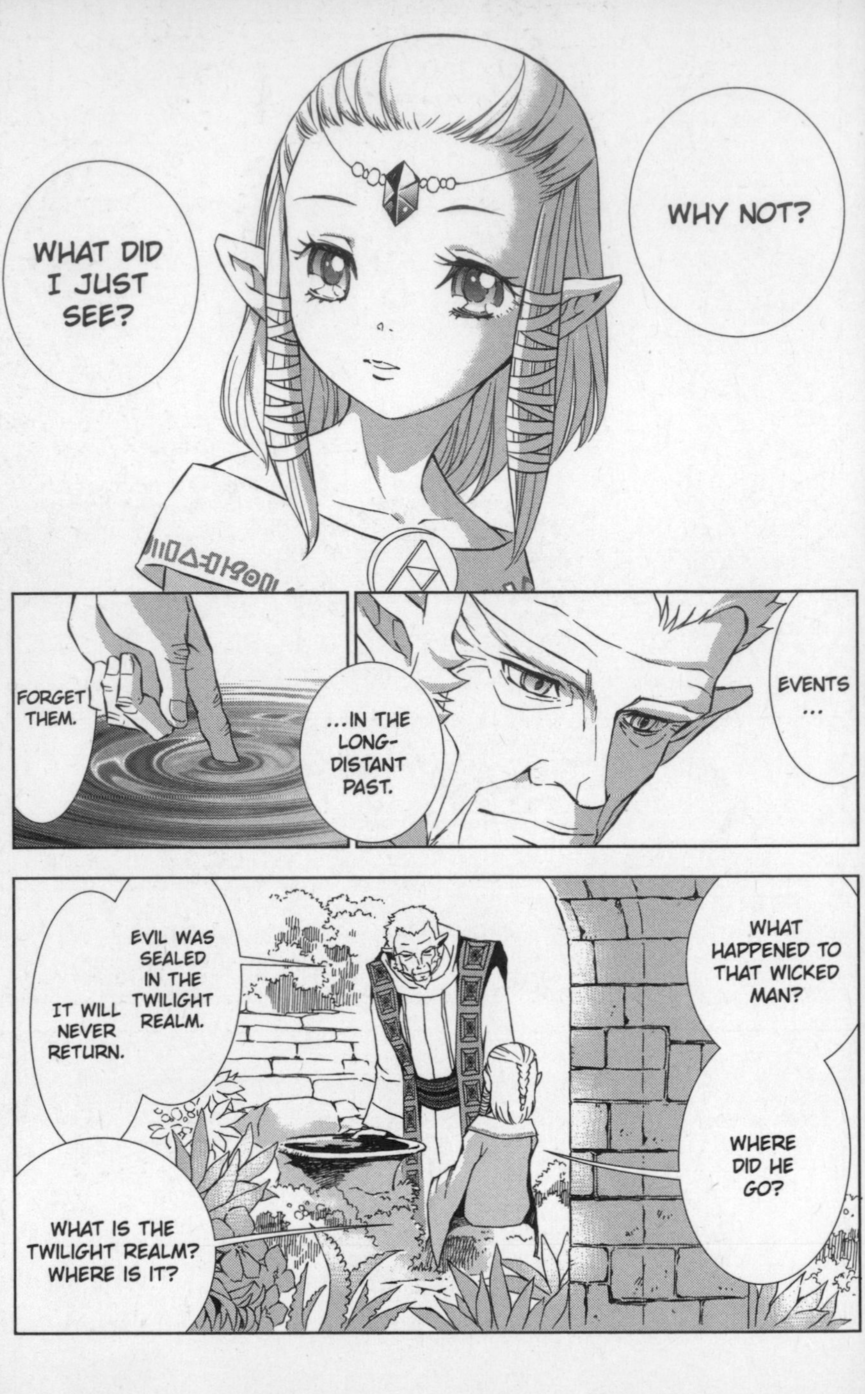
WHY NOT?
WHAT DID I JUST SEE?
EVENTS...
...IN THE LONG-DISTANT PAST.
FORGET THEM.
WHAT HAPPENED TO THAT WICKED MAN?
WHERE DID HE GO?
EVIL WAS SEALED IN THE TWILIGHT REALM.
IT WILL NEVER RETURN.
WHAT IS THE TWILIGHT REALM? WHERE IS IT?

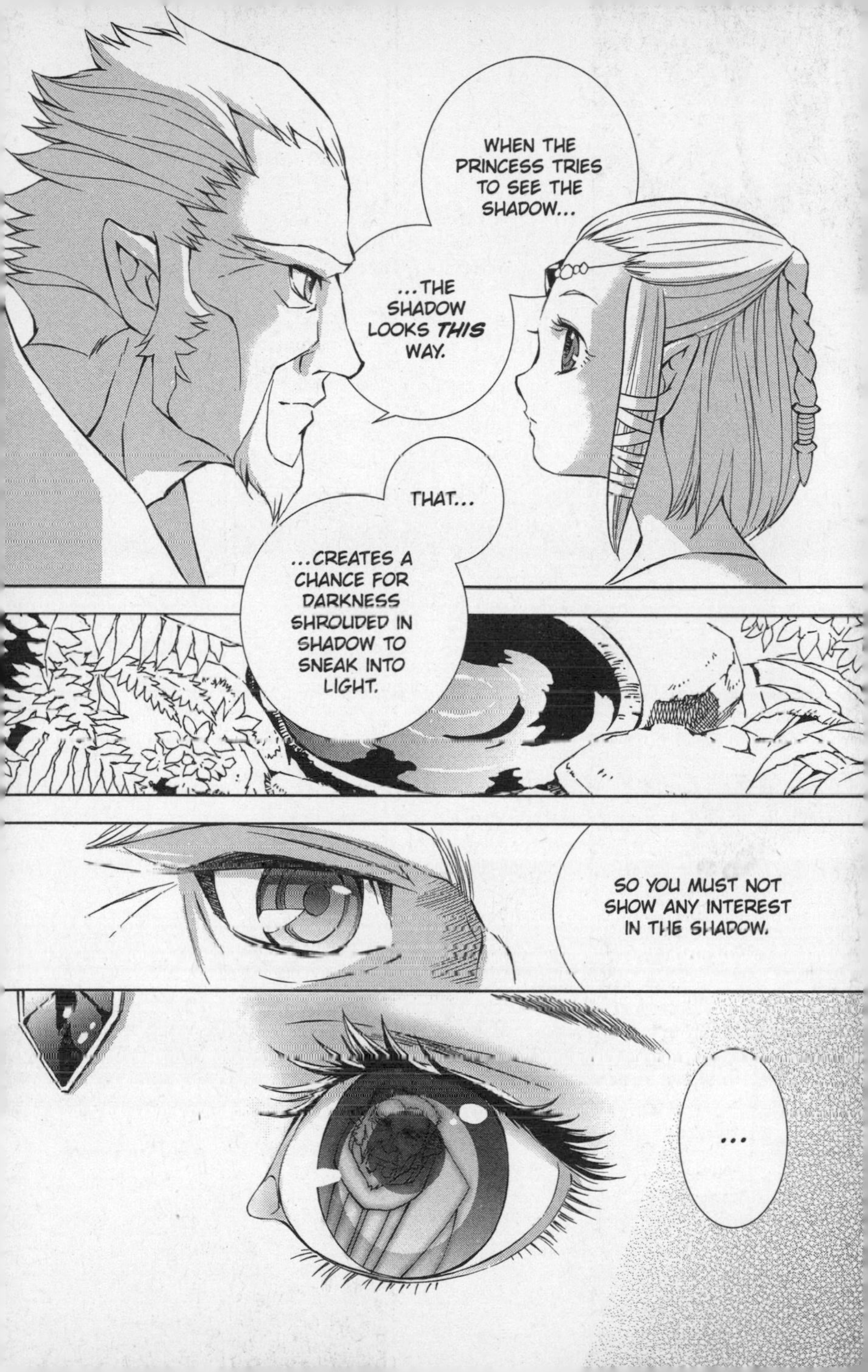
WHEN THE PRINCESS TRIES TO SEE THE SHADOW...
...THE SHADOW LOOKS *THIS* WAY.
THAT...
...CREATES A CHANCE FOR DARKNESS SHROUDED IN SHADOW TO SNEAK INTO LIGHT.
SO YOU MUST NOT SHOW ANY INTEREST IN THE SHADOW.
...

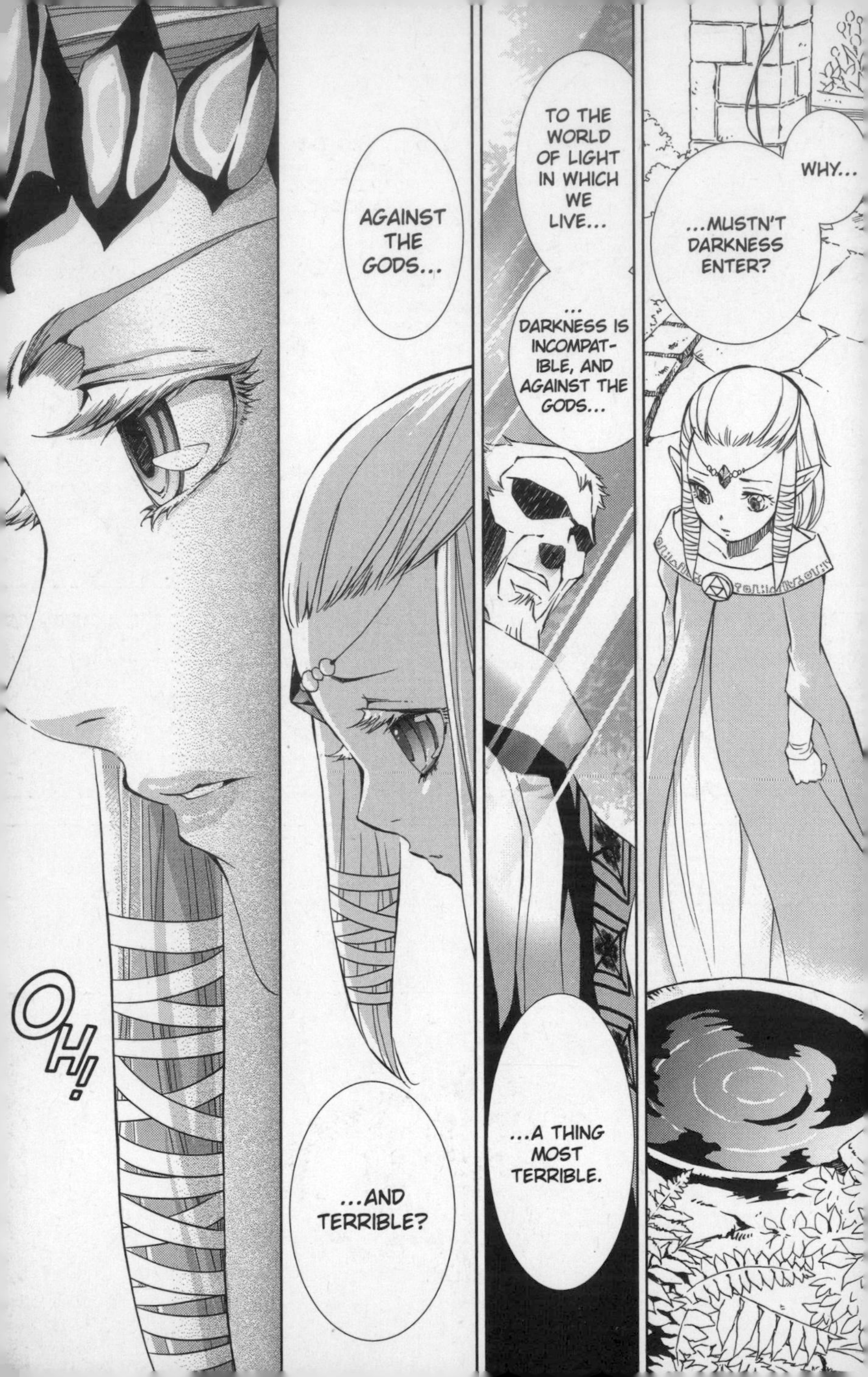
WHY...
...MUSTN'T DARKNESS ENTER?
TO THE WORLD OF LIGHT IN WHICH WE LIVE...
...DARKNESS IS INCOMPATIBLE, AND AGAINST THE GODS...
...A THING MOST TERRIBLE.
AGAINST THE GODS...
...AND TERRIBLE?
OH!

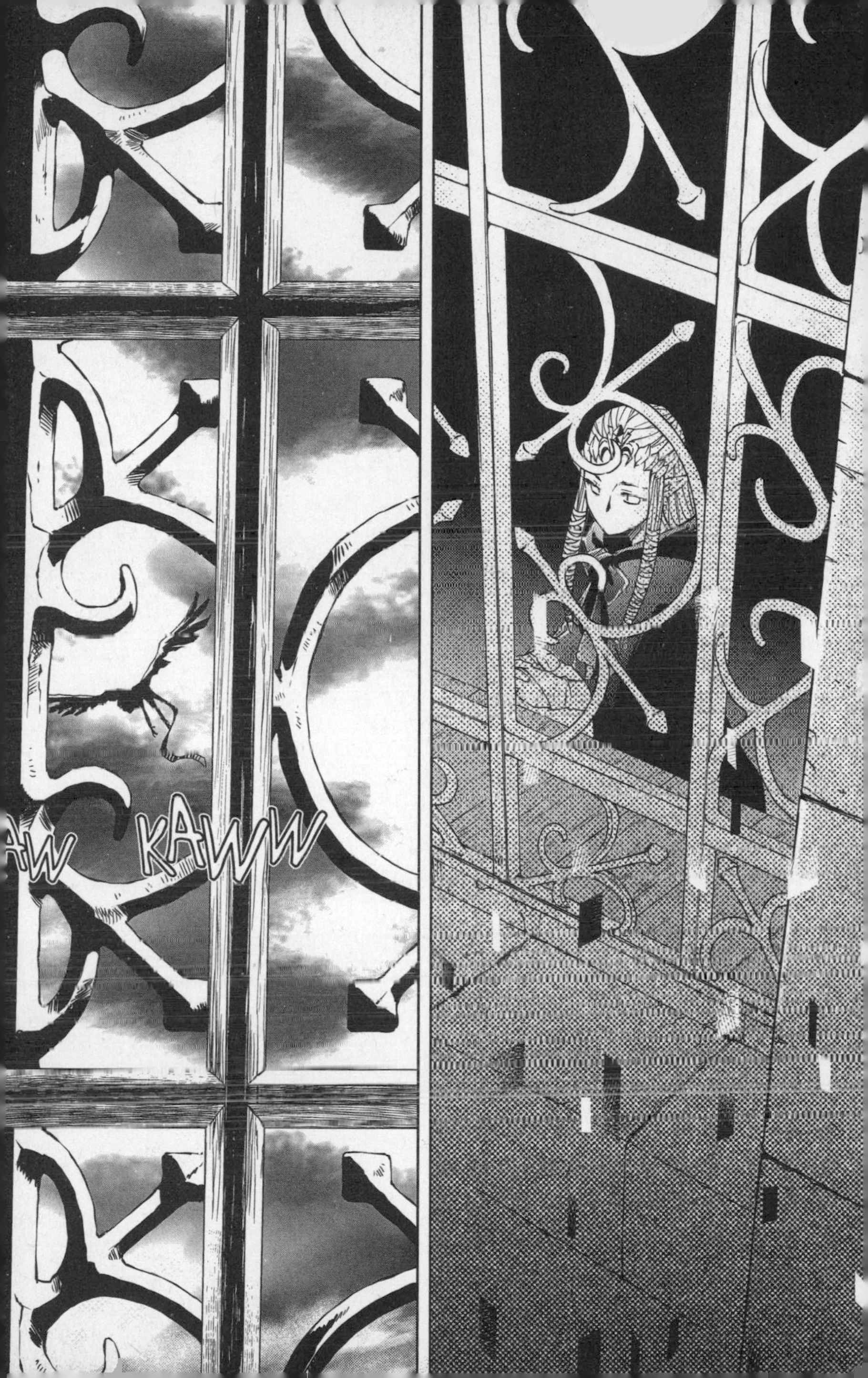
KAWW
AW

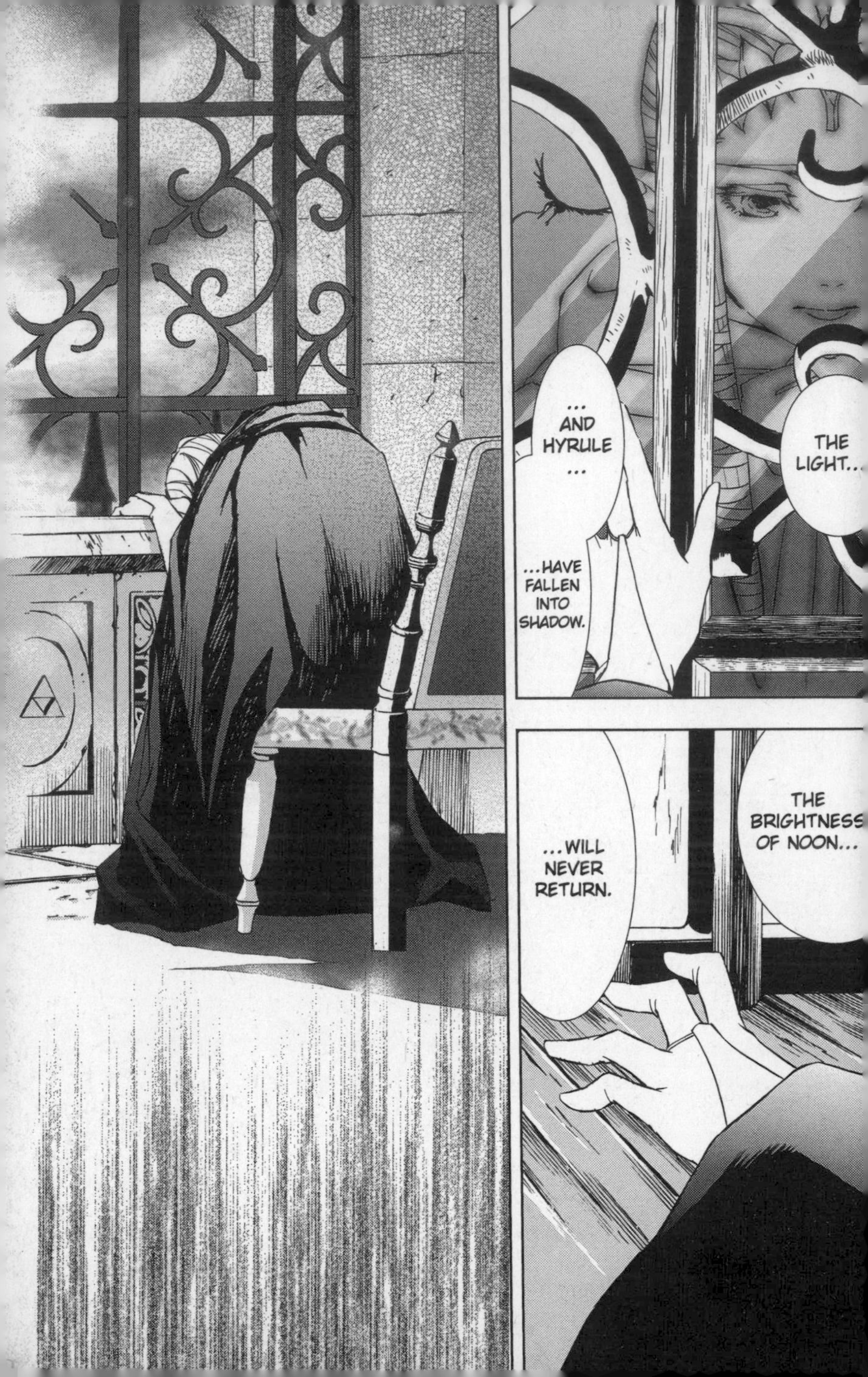
THE LIGHT...
... AND HYRULE ...
...HAVE FALLEN INTO SHADOW.
THE BRIGHTNESS OF NOON...
...WILL NEVER RETURN.

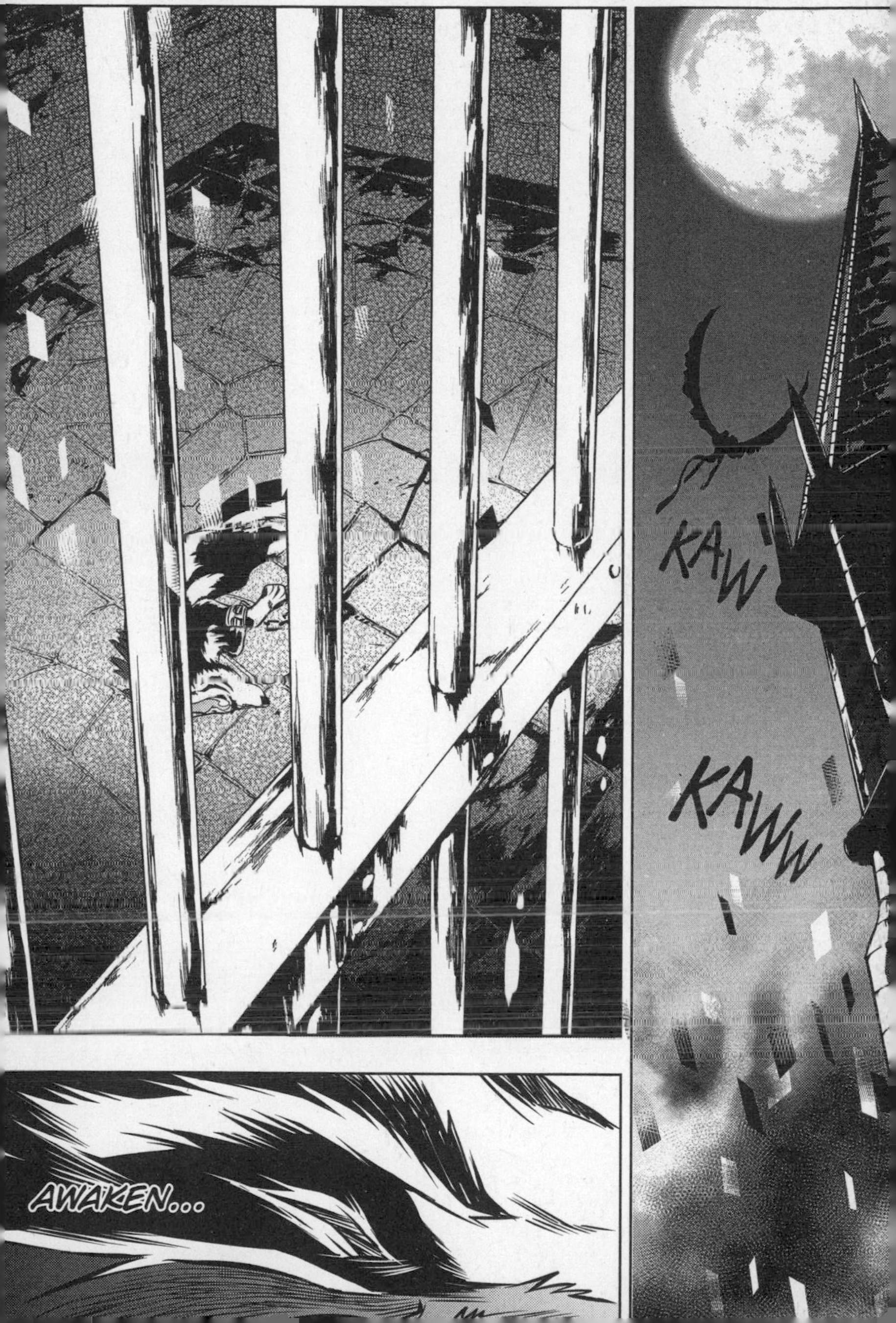
KAW
KAWW
AWAKEN...

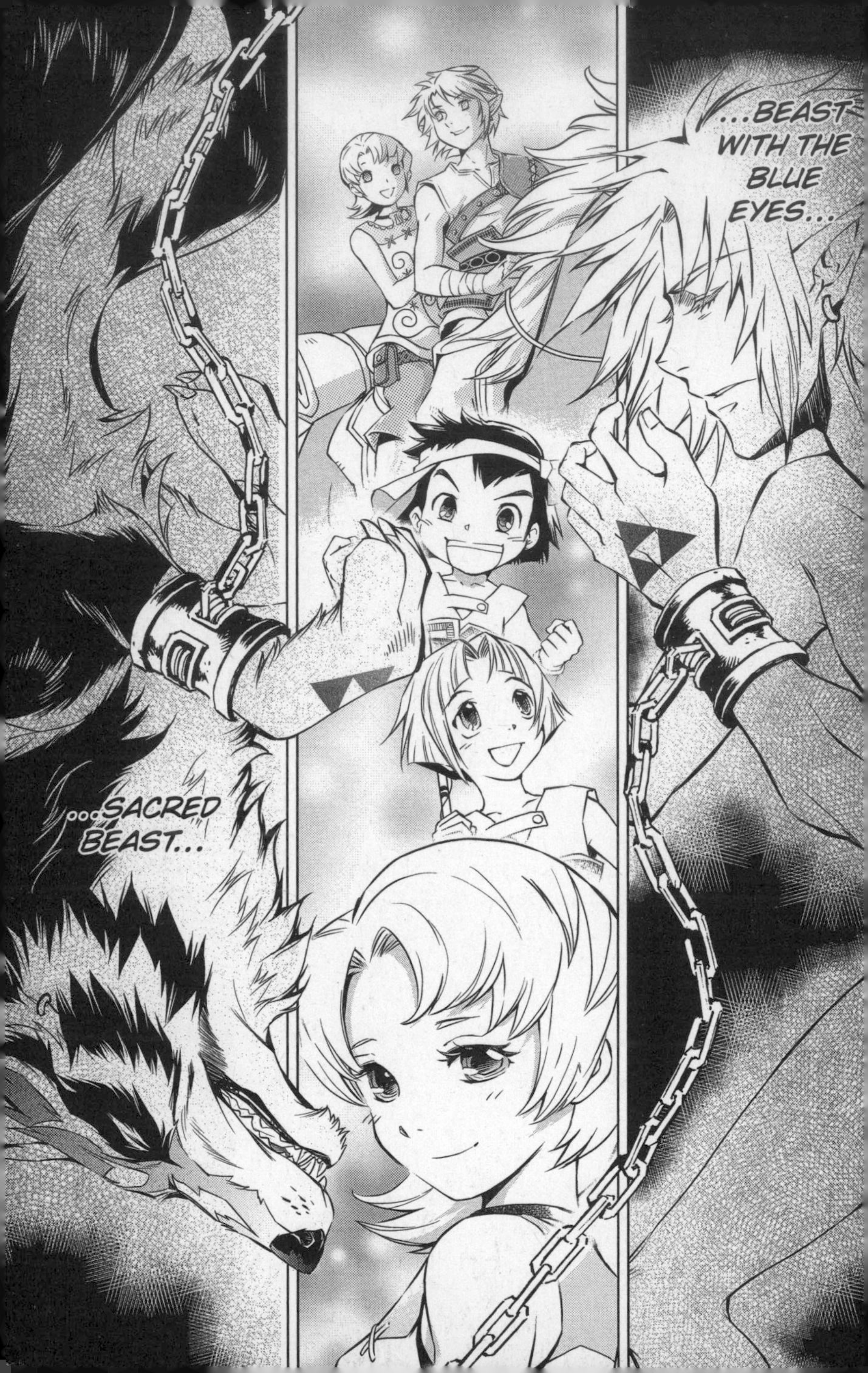
...BEAST WITH THE BLUE EYES...
...SACRED BEAST...

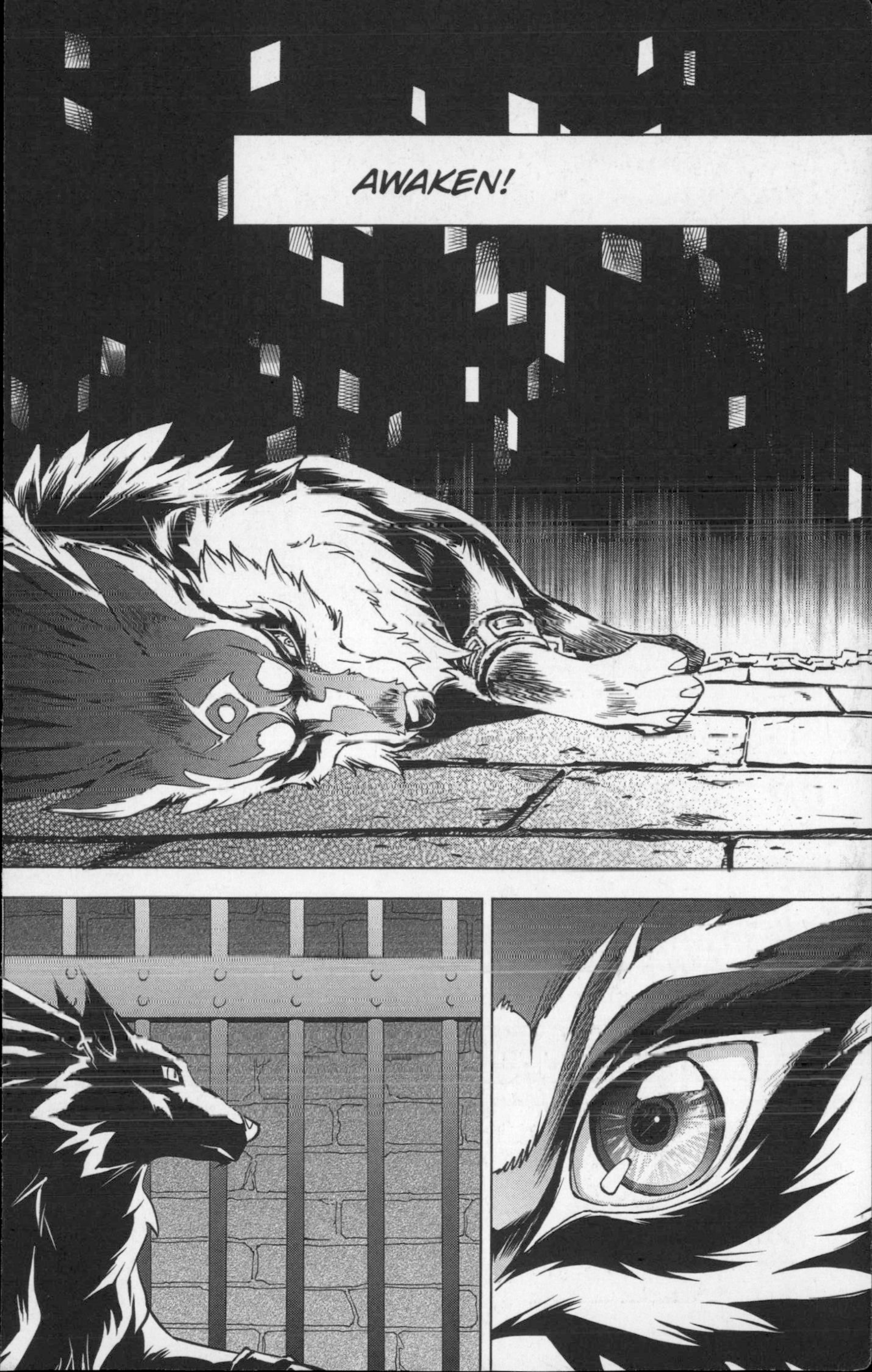
AWAKEN!

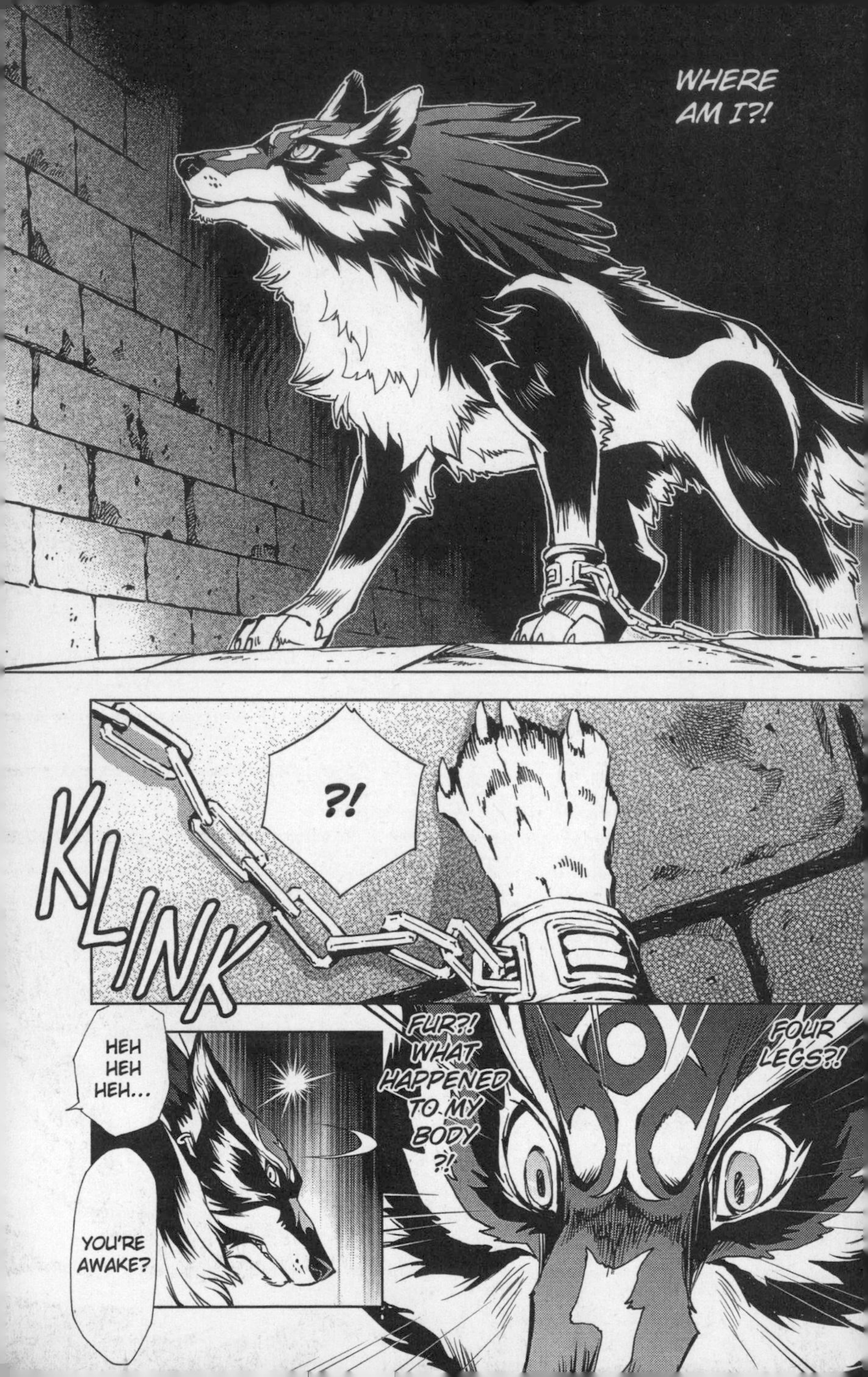
WHERE AM I?!
?!
KLINK
FOUR LEGS?!
FUR?! WHAT HAPPENED TO MY BODY ?!
HEH HEH HEH...
YOU'RE AWAKE?

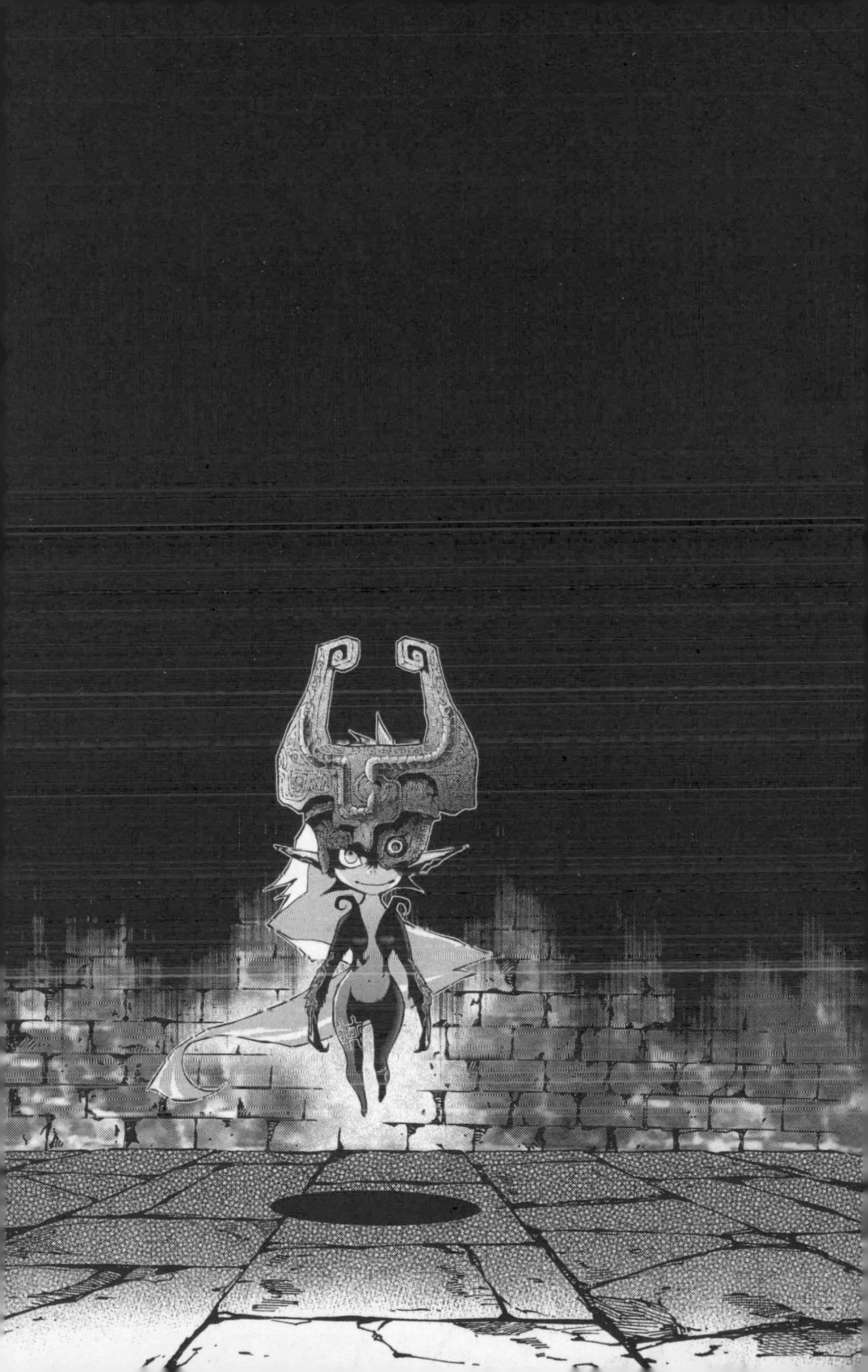

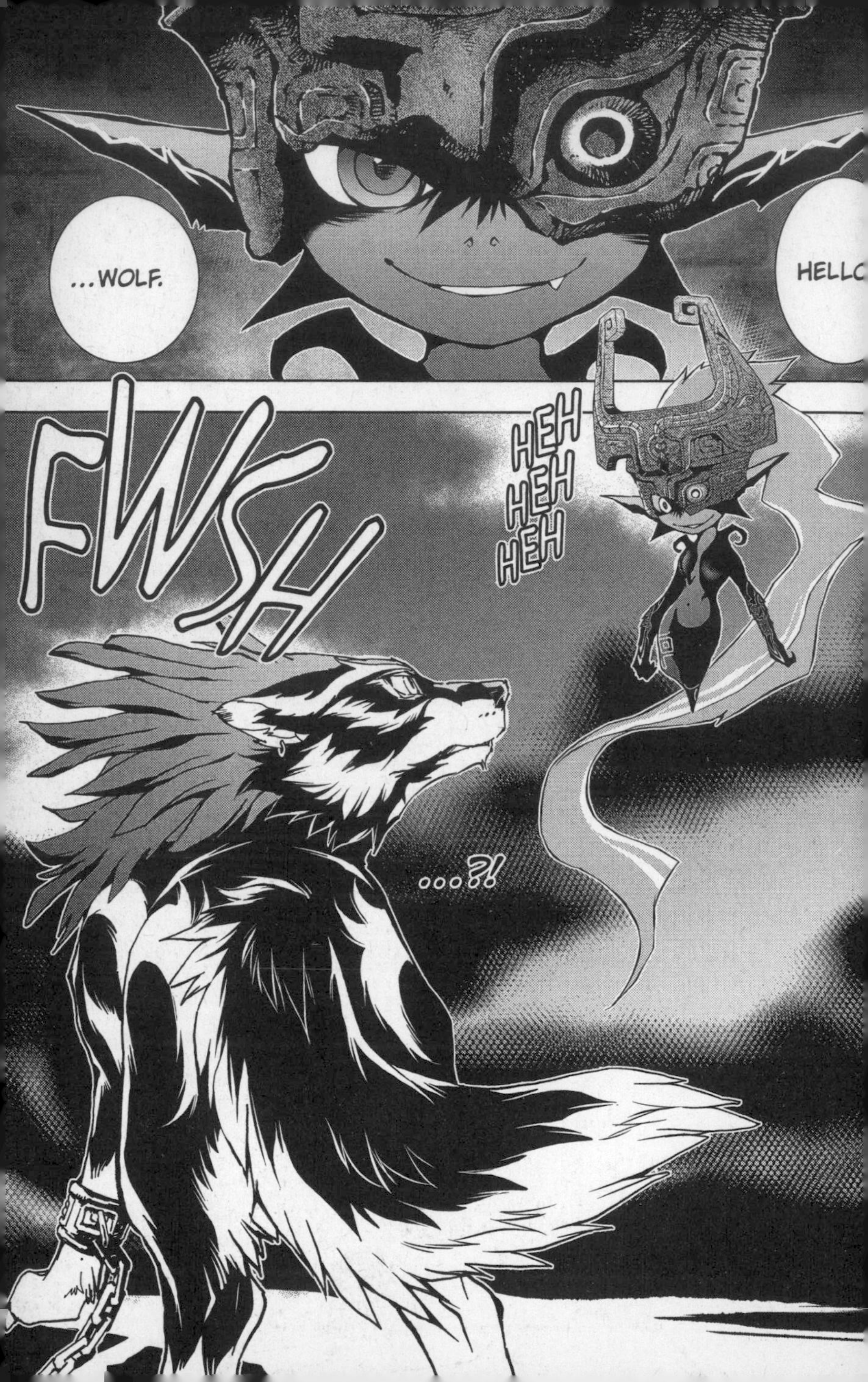
HELLO
...WOLF.
HEH HEH HEH HEH
FWSH
...?!

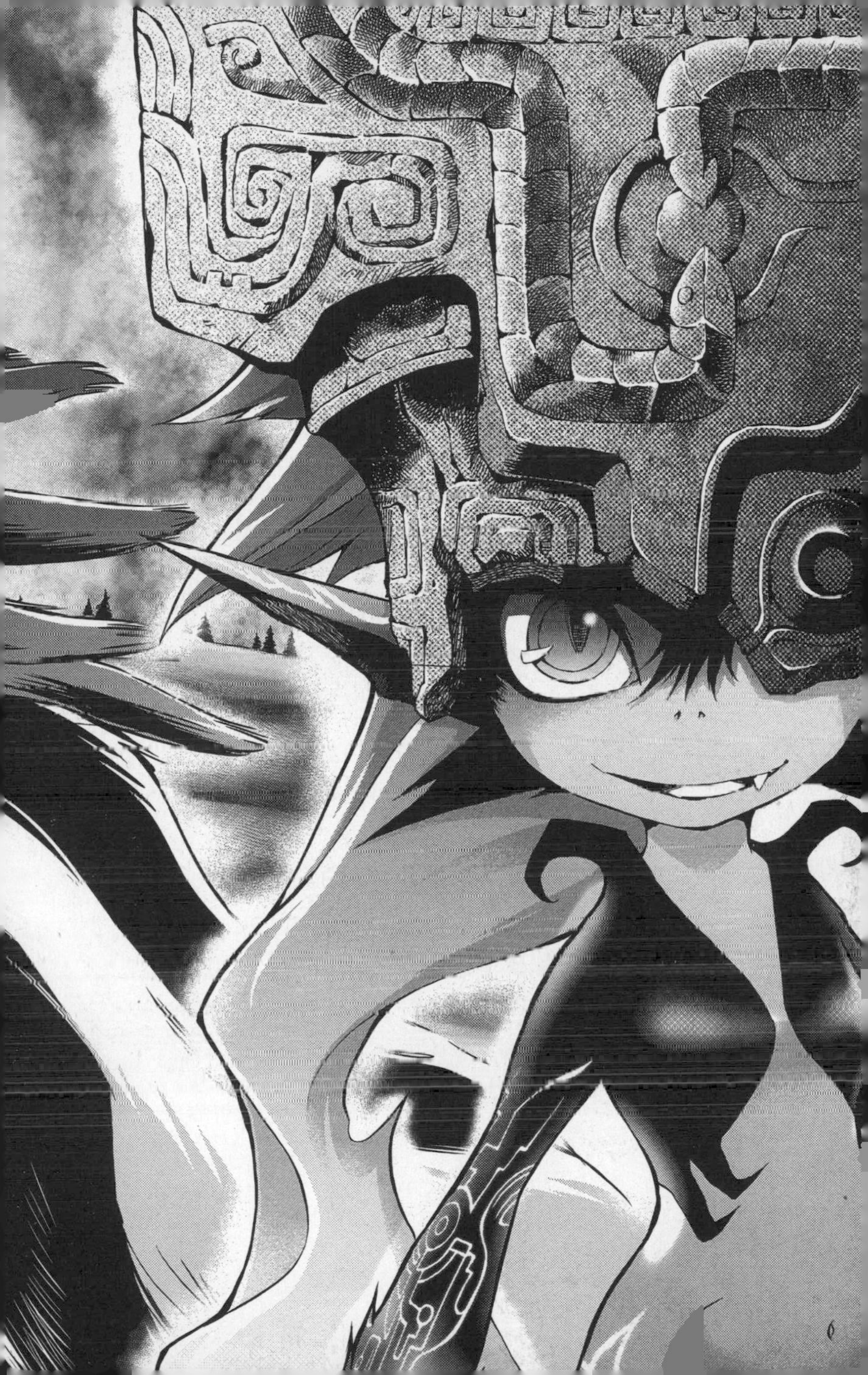

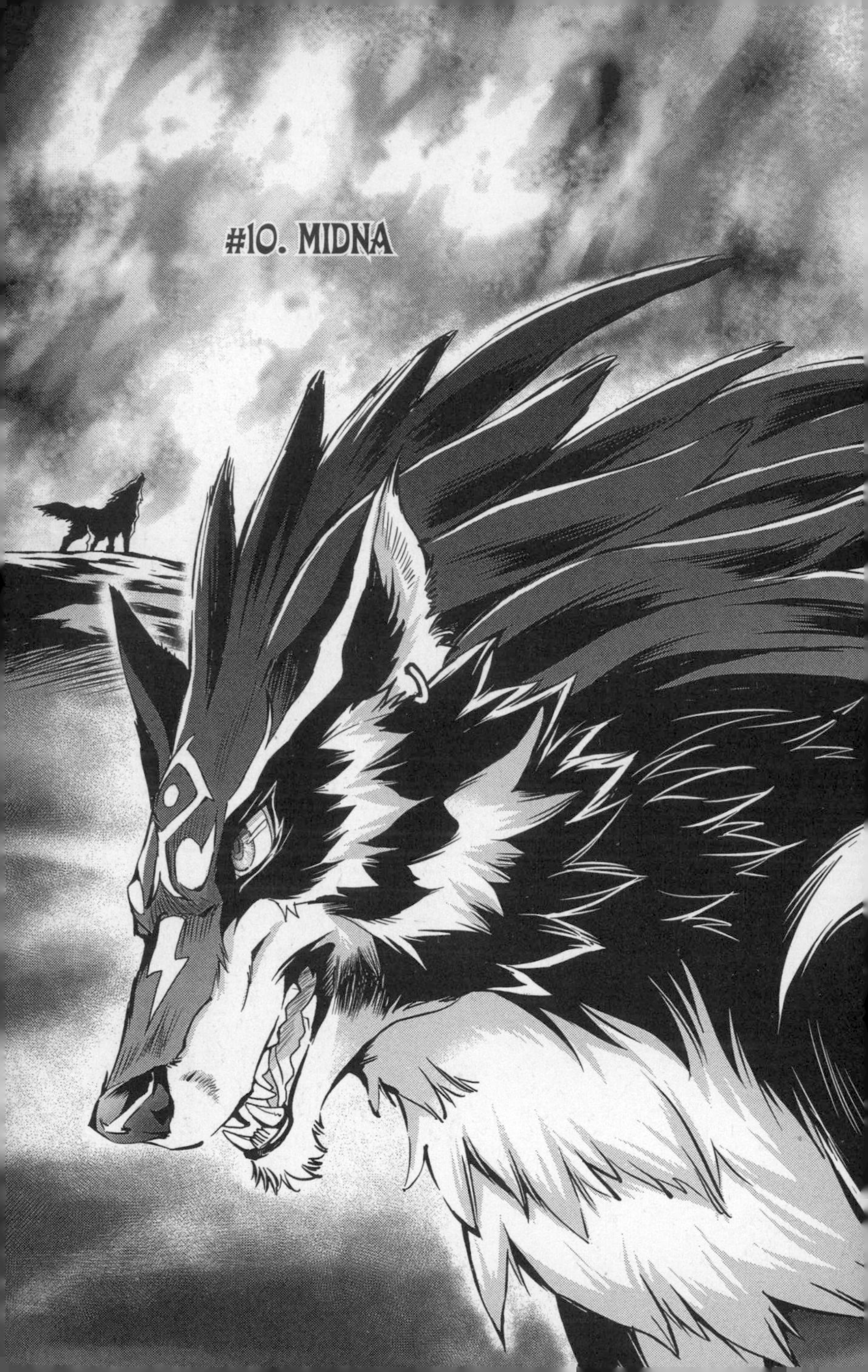
#10. MIDNA

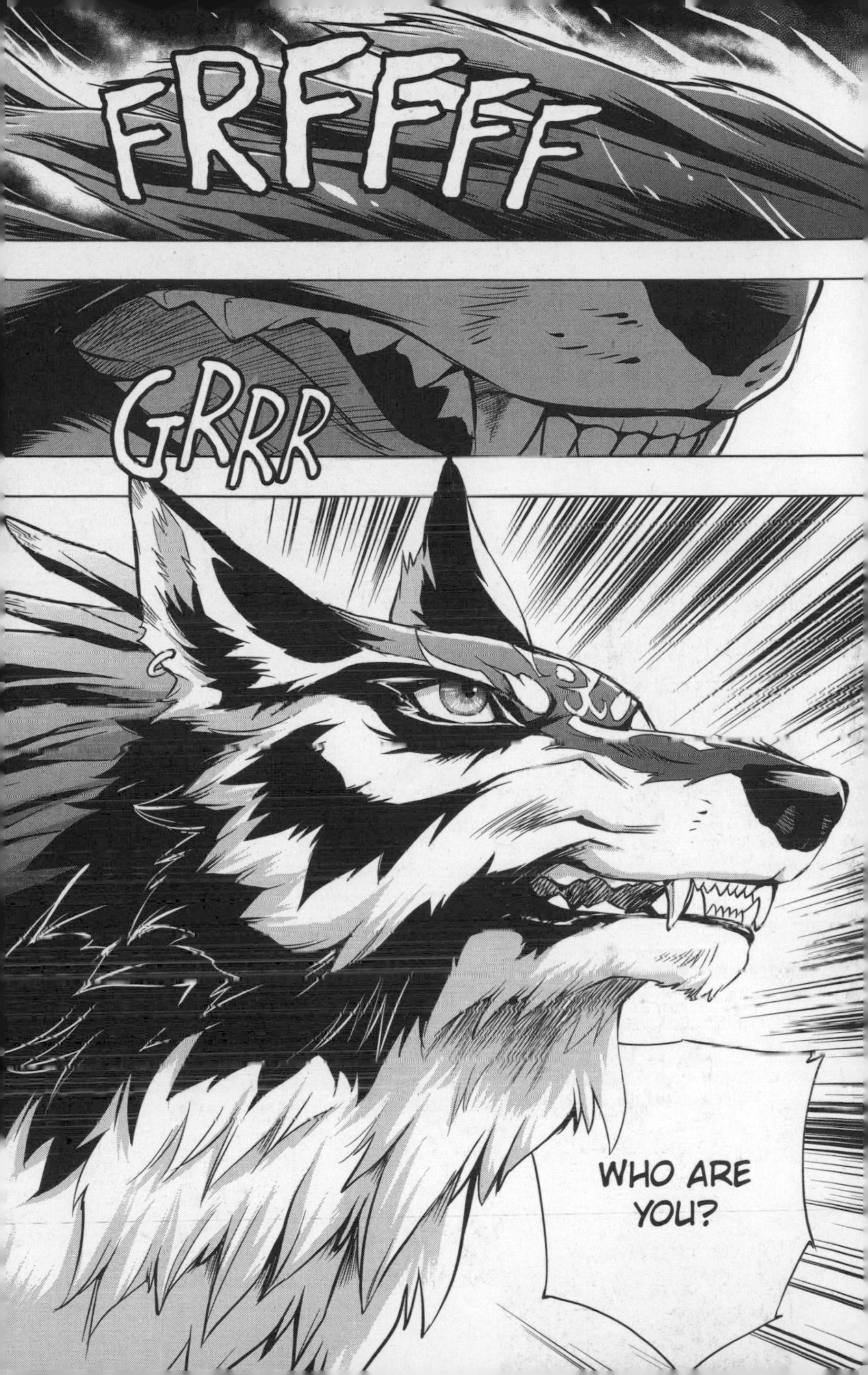
FRFFFF
GRRR
WHO ARE YOU?

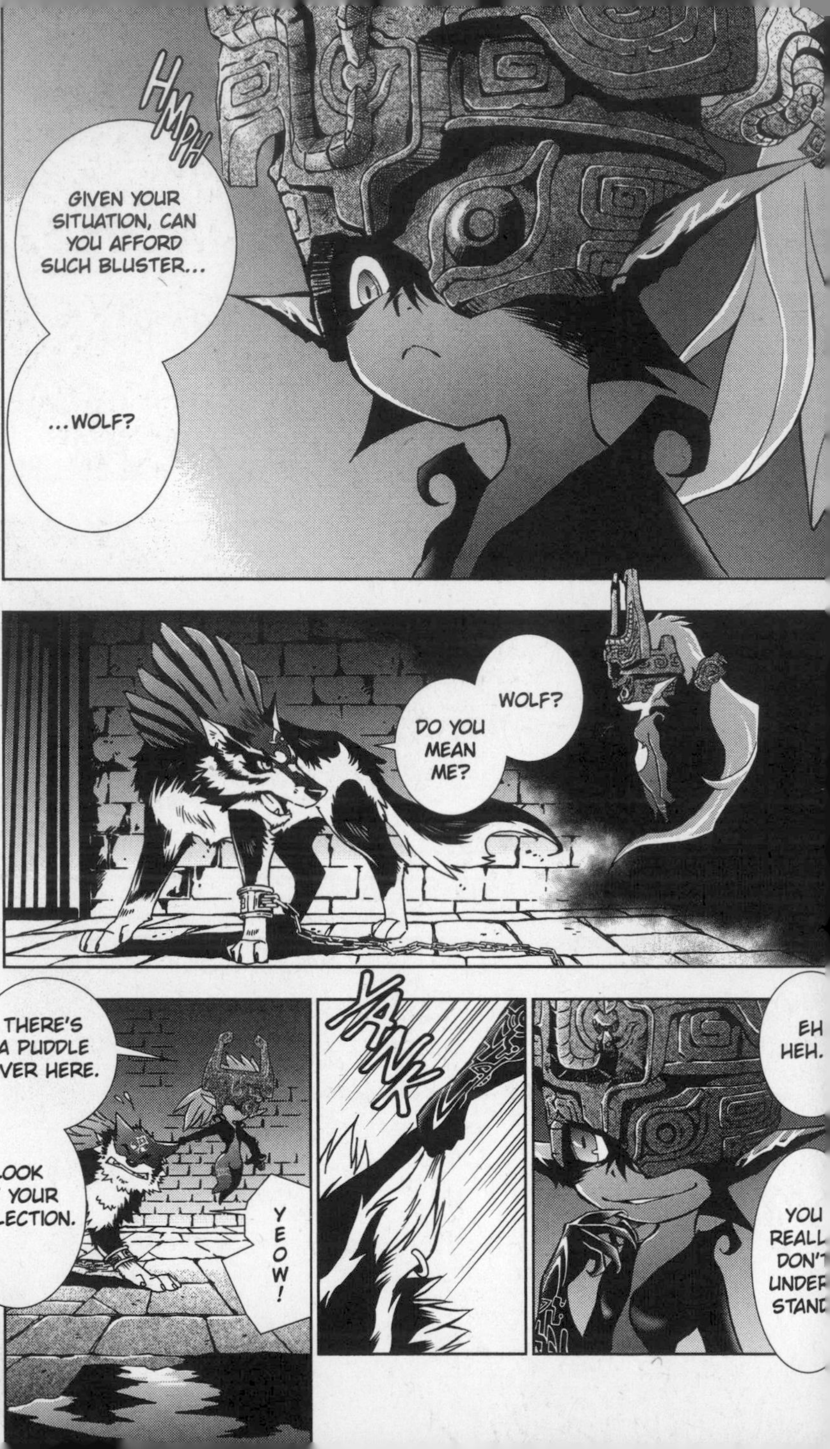
HMPH
GIVEN YOUR SITUATION, CAN YOU AFFORD SUCH BLUSTER...
...WOLF?
WOLF?
DO YOU MEAN ME?
EH HEH.
YOU REALL DON'T UNDER STAND
YANK
THERE'S A PUDDLE OVER HERE.
YEOW!
LOOK AT YOUR REFLECTION.

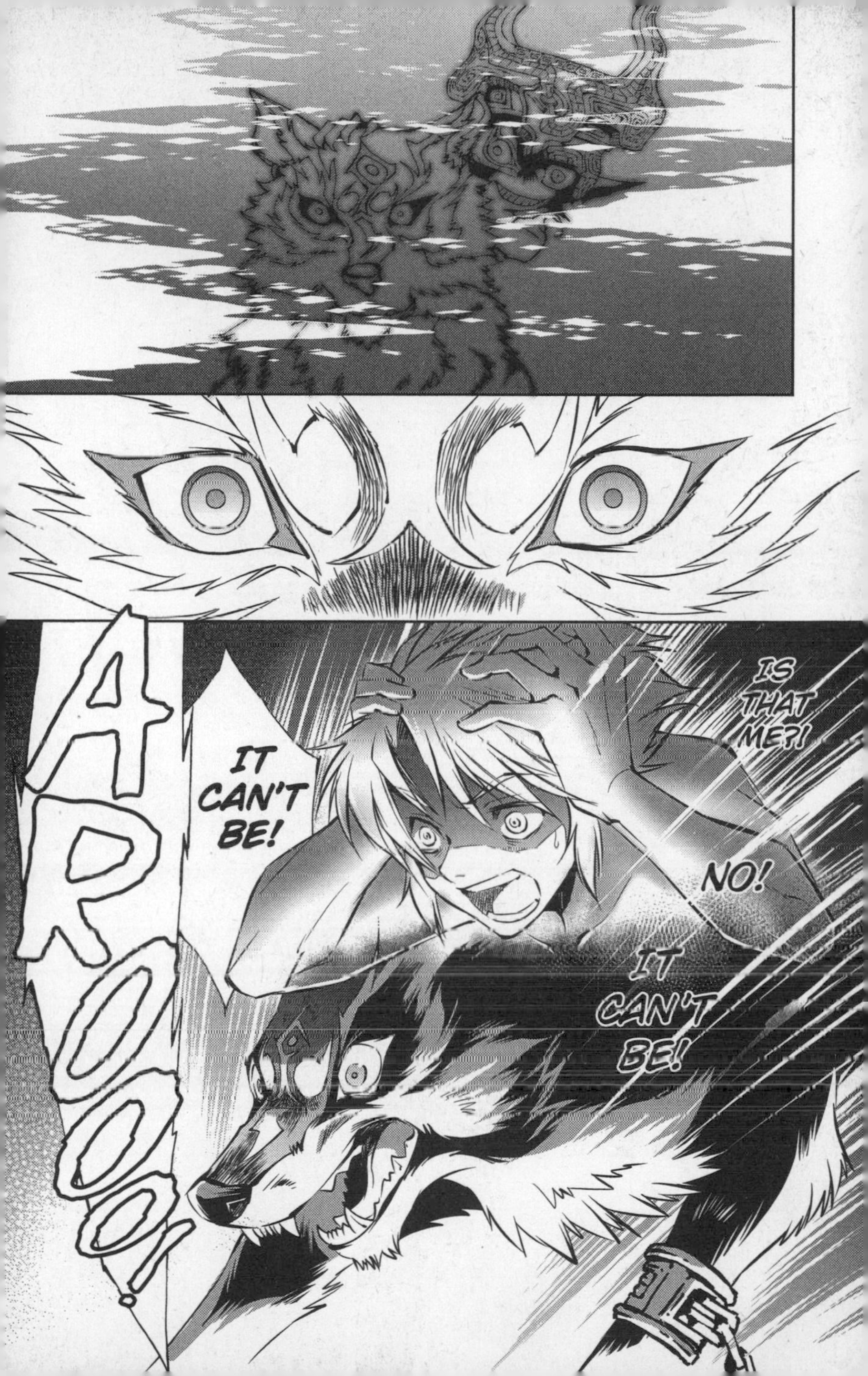
IS THAT ME?!
NO!
IT CAN'T BE!
IT CAN'T BE!
AROOOO!

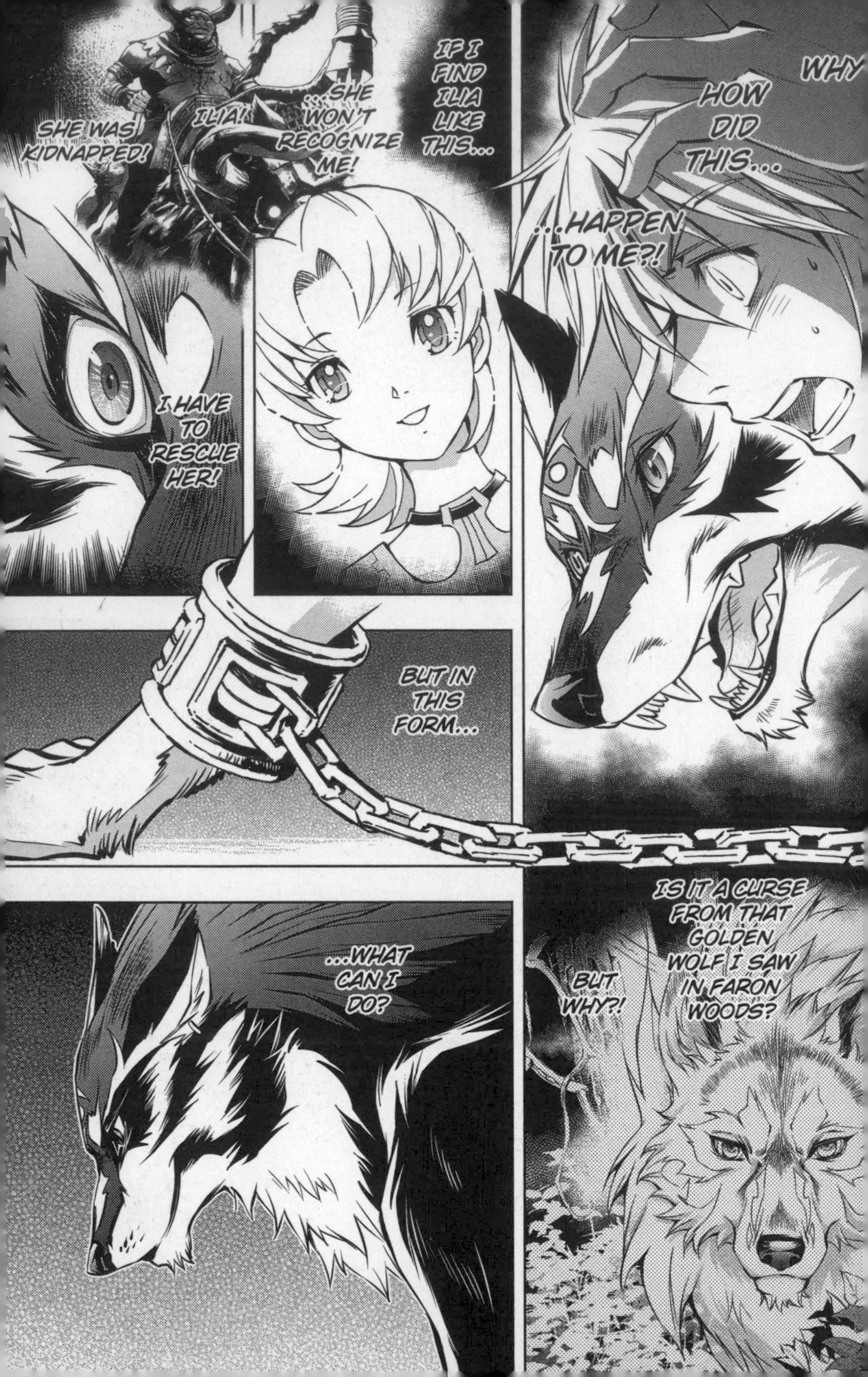
WHY
HOW DID THIS...
...HAPPEN TO ME?!
IF I FIND ILIA LIKE THIS...
...SHE WON'T RECOGNIZE ME!
ILIA!
SHE WAS KIDNAPPED!
I HAVE TO RESCUE HER!
BUT IN THIS FORM...
IS IT A CURSE FROM THAT GOLDEN WOLF I SAW IN FARON WOODS?
BUT WHY?!
...WHAT CAN I DO?

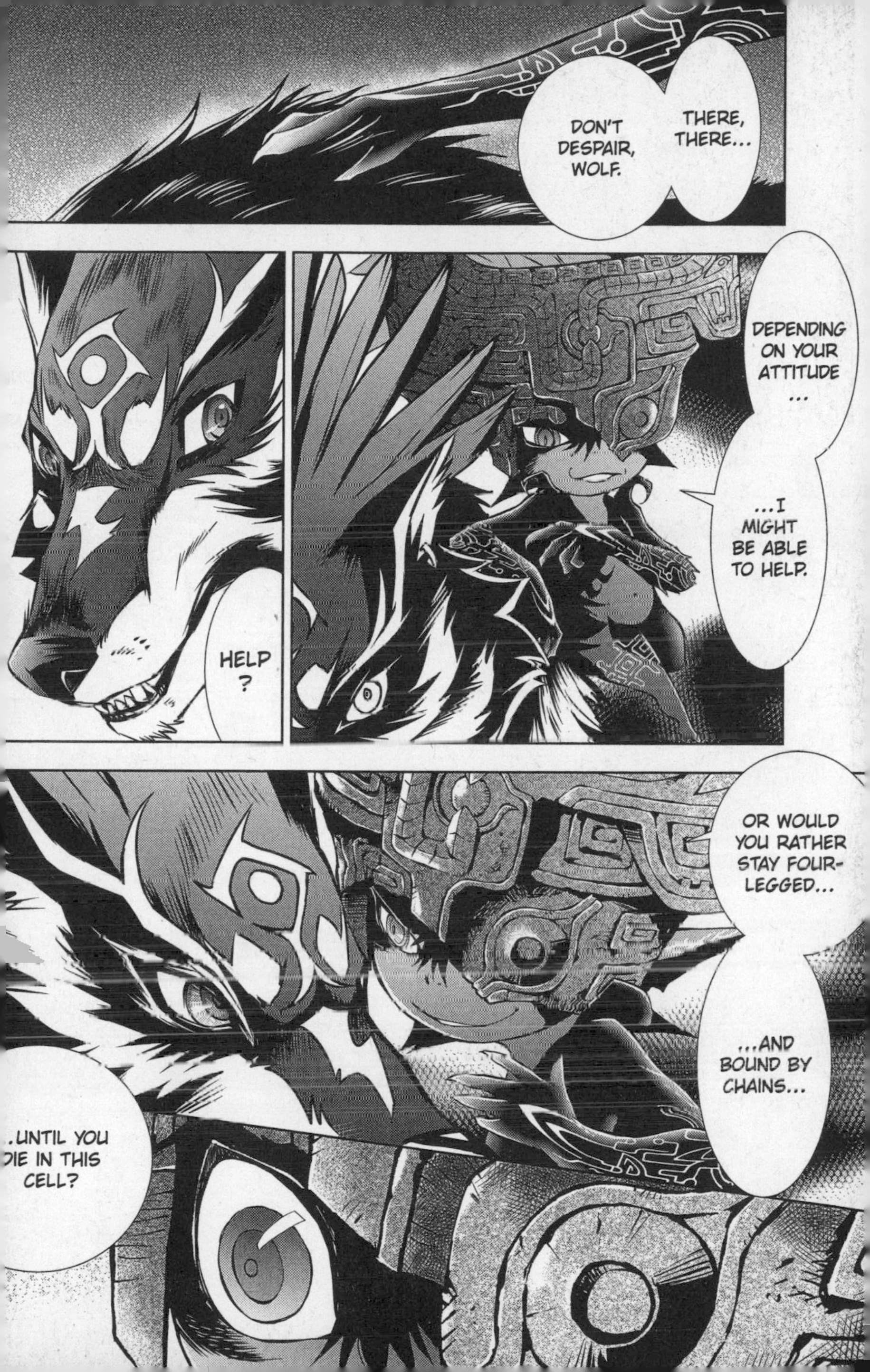
THERE, THERE...
DON'T DESPAIR, WOLF.
DEPENDING ON YOUR ATTITUDE ...
...I MIGHT BE ABLE TO HELP.
HELP ?
OR WOULD YOU RATHER STAY FOUR-LEGGED...
...AND BOUND BY CHAINS...
.UNTIL YOU DIE IN THIS CELL?

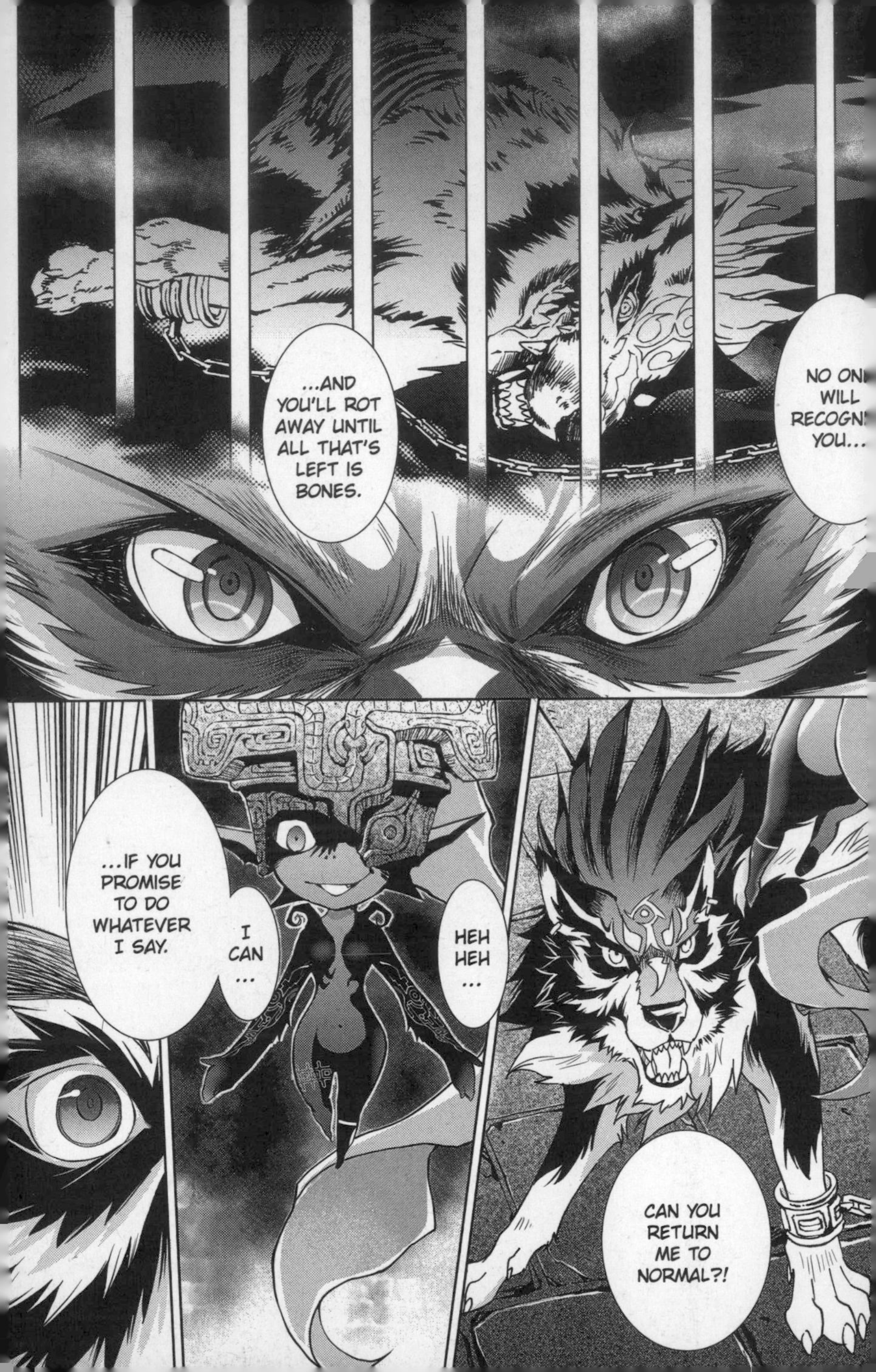
NO ON WILL RECOGN YOU...
...AND YOU'LL ROT AWAY UNTIL ALL THAT'S LEFT IS BONES.
CAN YOU RETURN ME TO NORMAL?!
HEH HEH ...
I CAN ...
...IF YOU PROMISE TO DO WHATEVER I SAY.

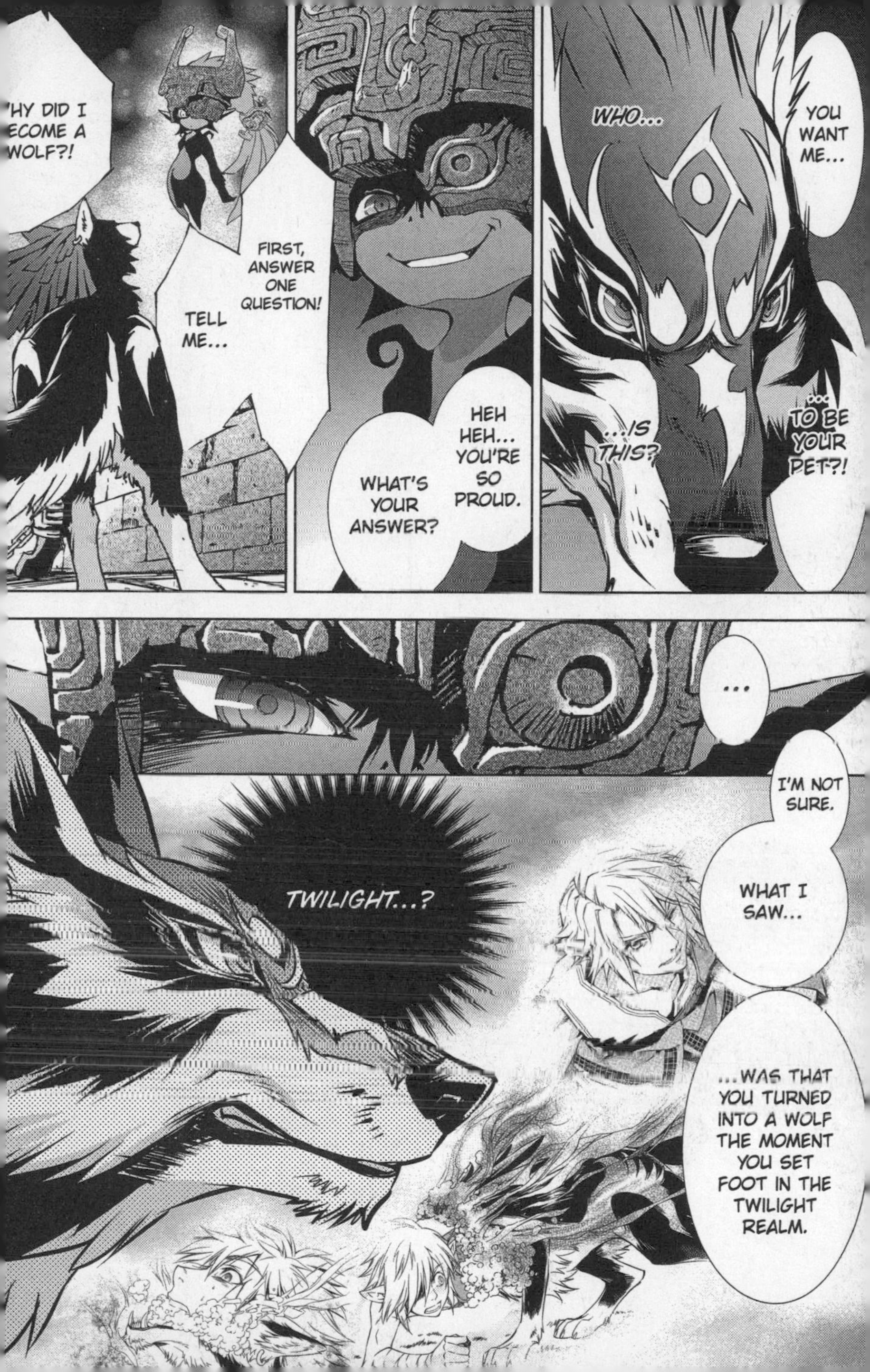
YOU WANT ME...
WHO...
...TO BE YOUR PET?!
...IS THIS?
HEH HEH... YOU'RE SO PROUD.
WHAT'S YOUR ANSWER?
'HY DID I ECOME A WOLF?!
FIRST, ANSWER ONE QUESTION!
TELL ME...
...
I'M NOT SURE.
WHAT I SAW...
...WAS THAT YOU TURNED INTO A WOLF THE MOMENT YOU SET FOOT IN THE TWILIGHT REALM.
TWILIGHT...?

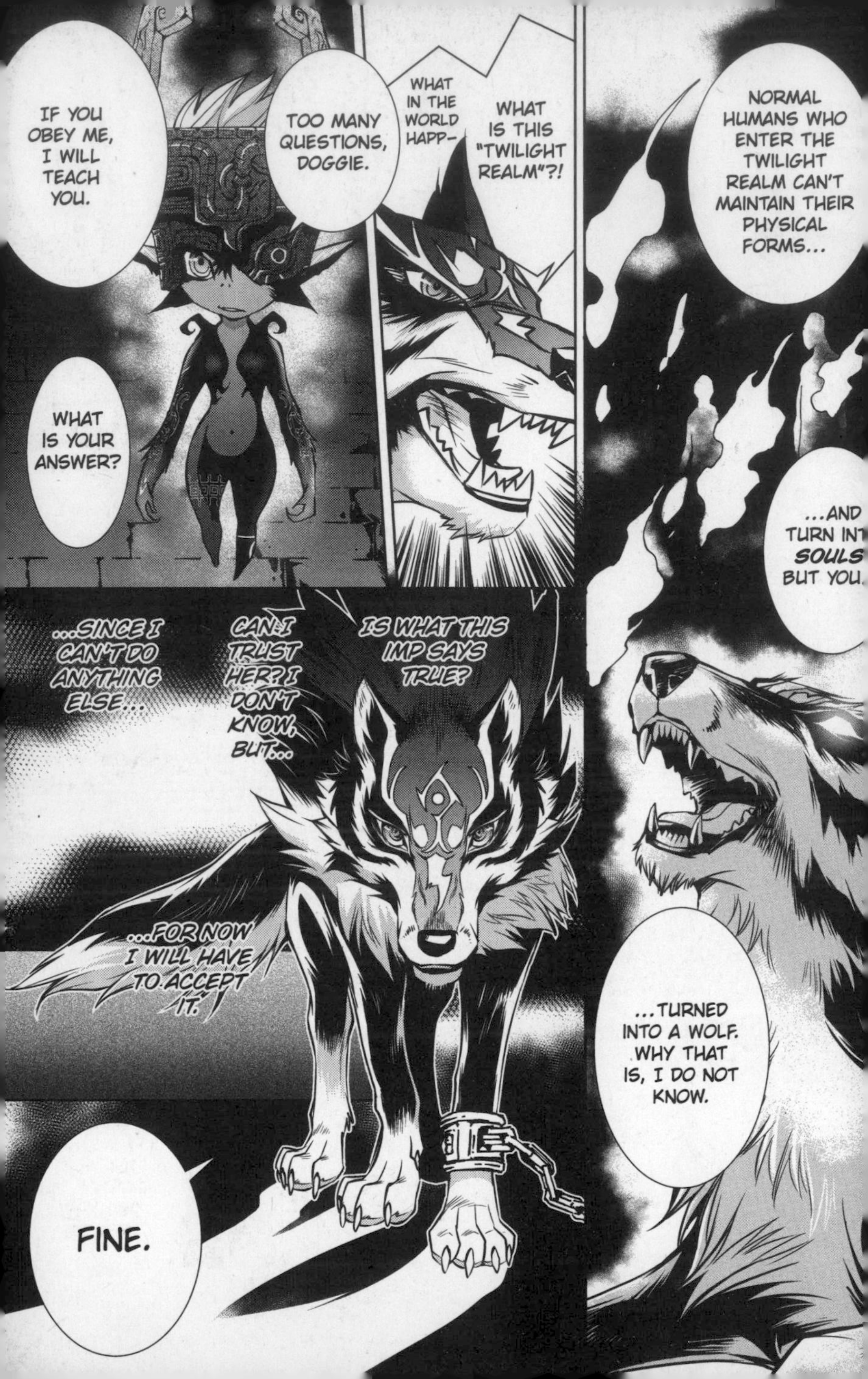
NORMAL HUMANS WHO ENTER THE TWILIGHT REALM CAN'T MAINTAIN THEIR PHYSICAL FORMS...
...AND TURN INT *SOULS* BUT YOU.
...TURNED INTO A WOLF. WHY THAT IS, I DO NOT KNOW.
WHAT IS THIS "TWILIGHT REALM"?!
WHAT IN THE WORLD HAPP-
TOO MANY QUESTIONS, DOGGIE.
IF YOU OBEY ME, I WILL TEACH YOU.
WHAT IS YOUR ANSWER?
IS WHAT THIS IMP SAYS TRUE?
CAN I TRUST HER? I DON'T KNOW, BUT...
...SINCE I CAN'T DO ANYTHING ELSE...
...FOR NOW I WILL HAVE TO ACCEPT IT.
FINE.

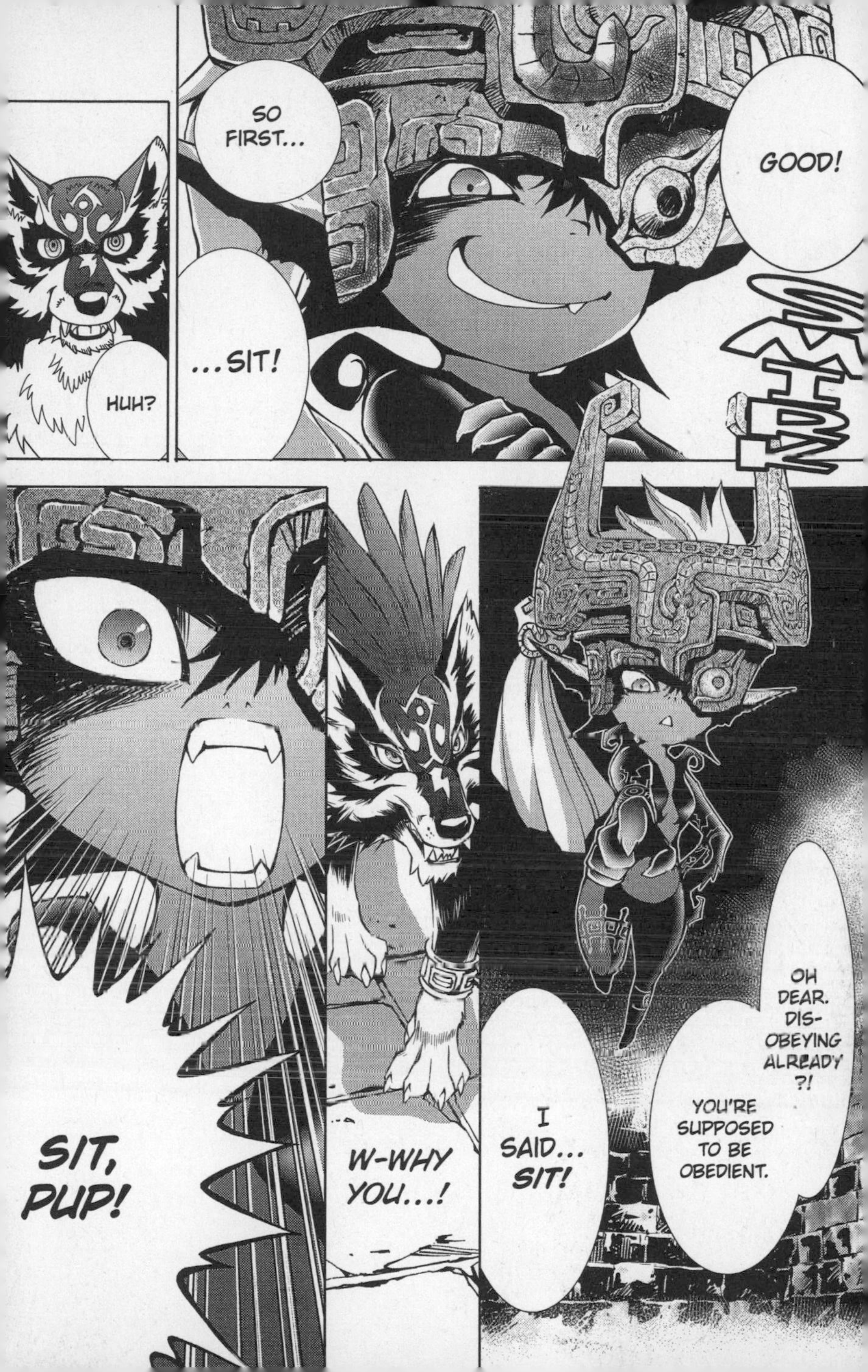
GOOD!
SO FIRST...
...SIT!
HUH?
OH DEAR. DIS-OBEYING ALREADY?!
YOU'RE SUPPOSED TO BE OBEDIENT.
I SAID... SIT!
W-WHY YOU...!
SIT, PUP!

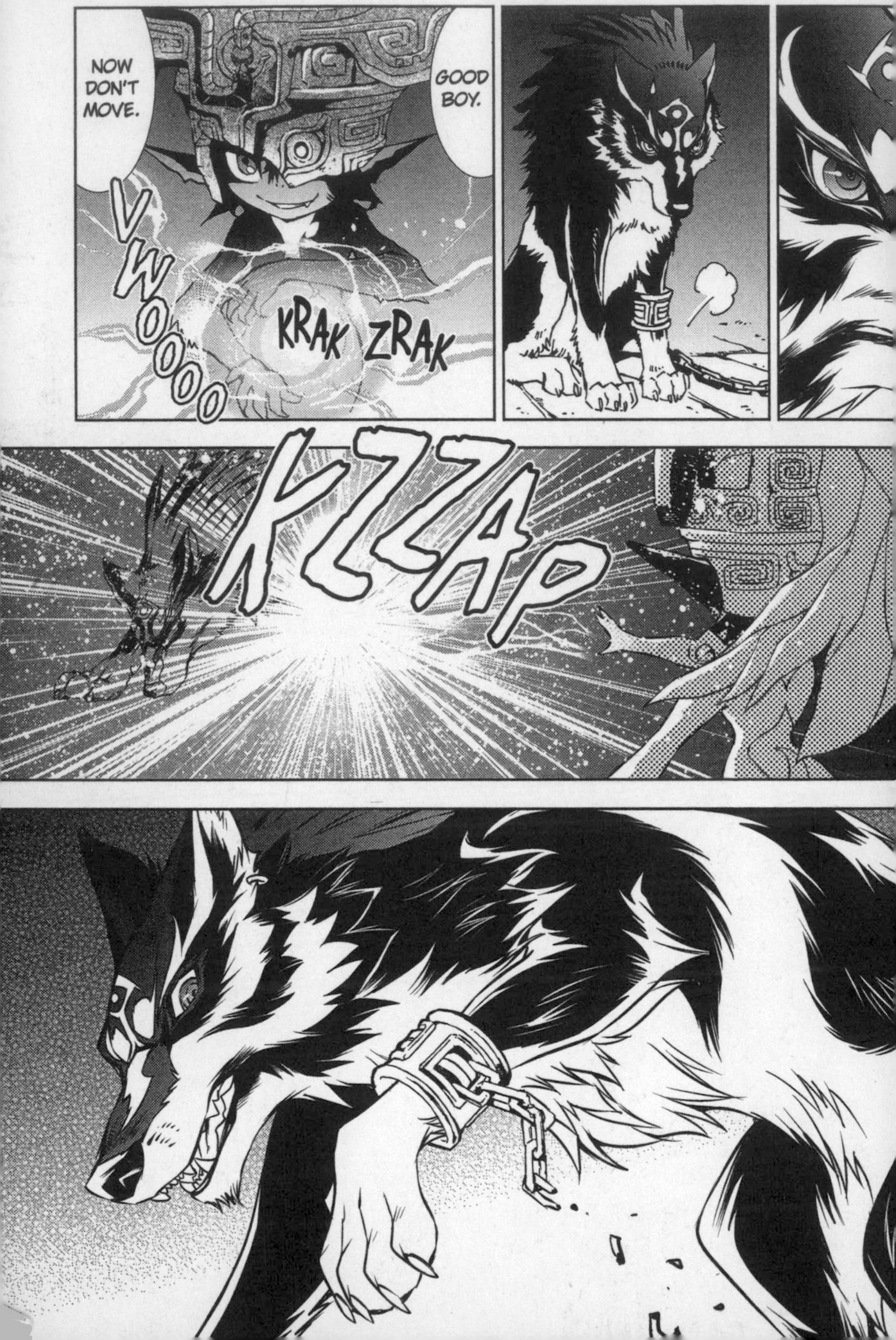
GOOD BOY.
NOW DON'T MOVE.
VWOOOO
KRAK ZRAK
KZZAP

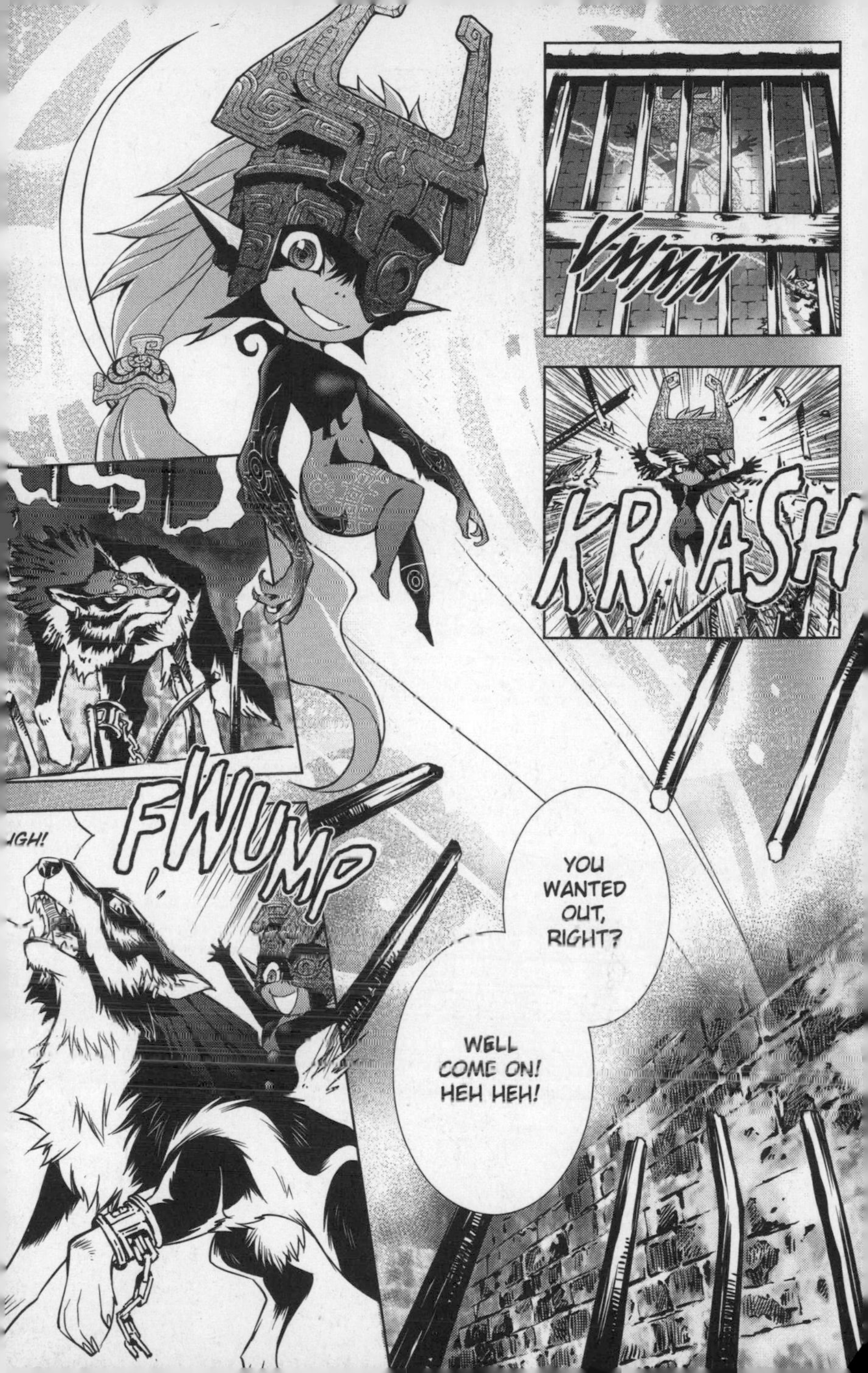

VMMM
KRASH
YOU WANTED OUT, RIGHT?
WELL COME ON! HEH HEH!
FWUMP
UGH!

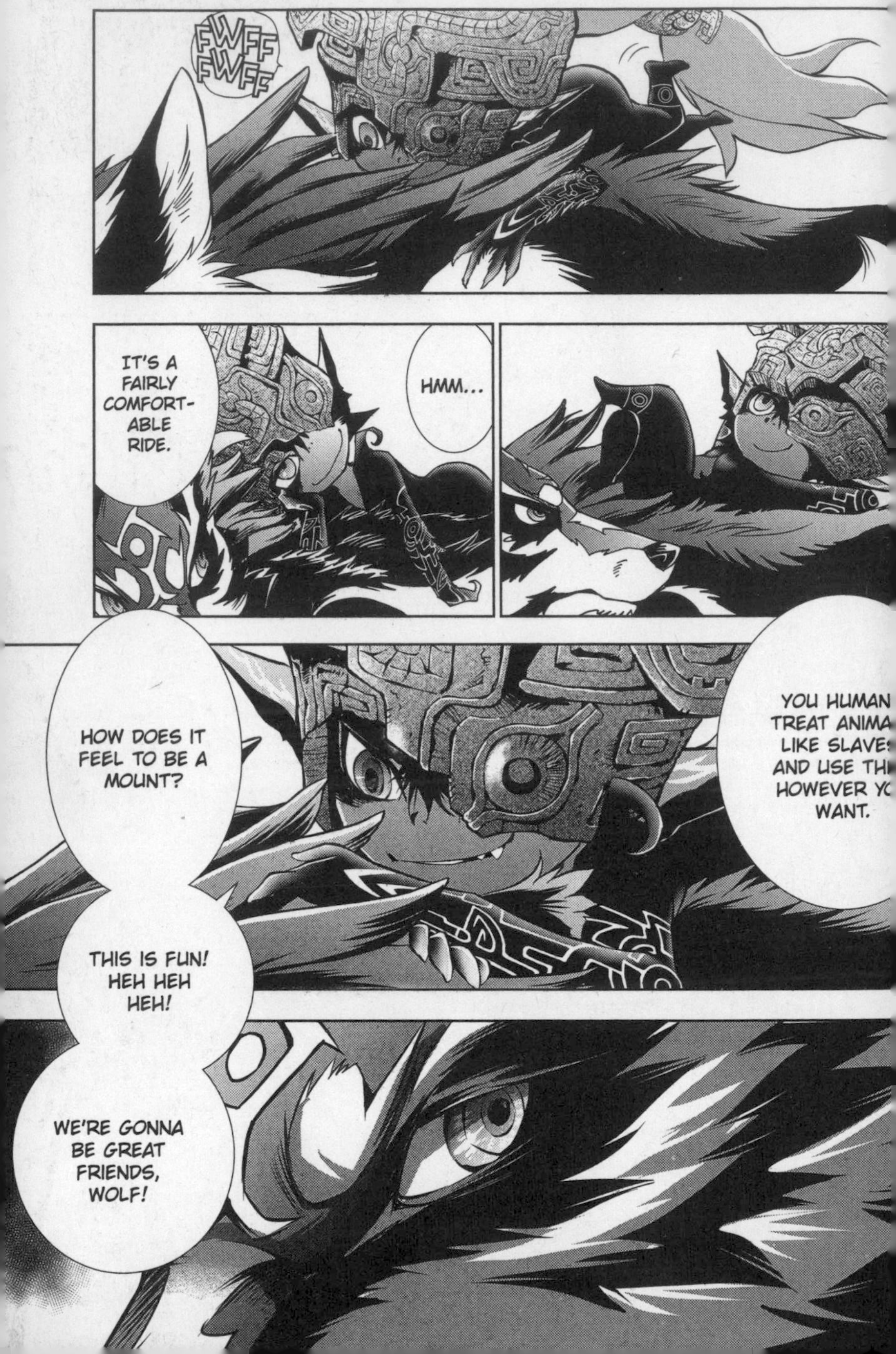
FWFF FWFF
HMM...
IT'S A FAIRLY COMFORT-ABLE RIDE.
YOU HUMAN TREAT ANIMA LIKE SLAVE AND USE TH HOWEVER YO WANT.
HOW DOES IT FEEL TO BE A MOUNT?
THIS IS FUN! HEH HEH HEH!
WE'RE GONNA BE GREAT FRIENDS, WOLF!

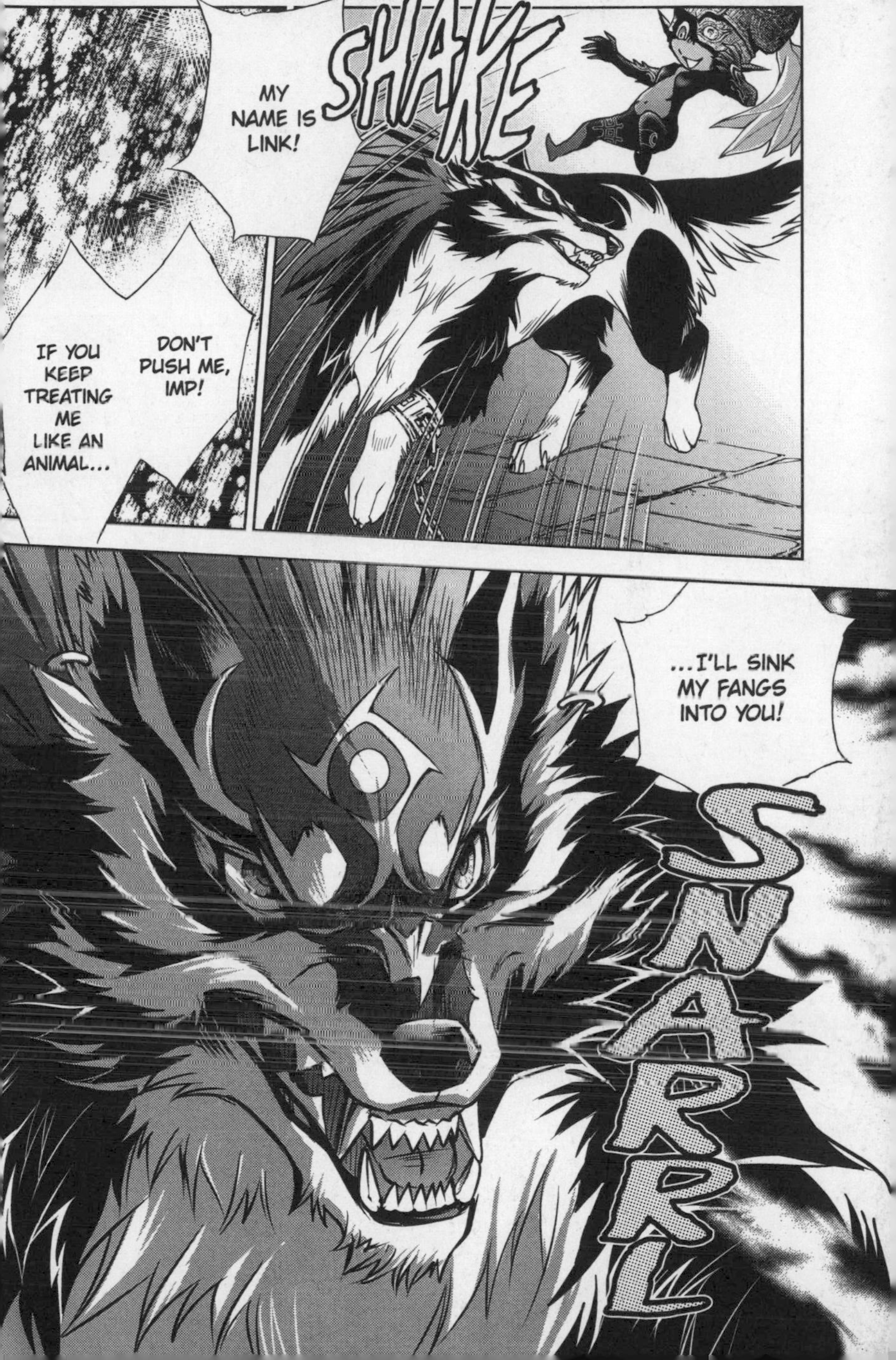
SHAKE
MY NAME IS LINK!
DON'T PUSH ME, IMP!
IF YOU KEEP TREATING ME LIKE AN ANIMAL...
...I'LL SINK MY FANGS INTO YOU!
SNARL

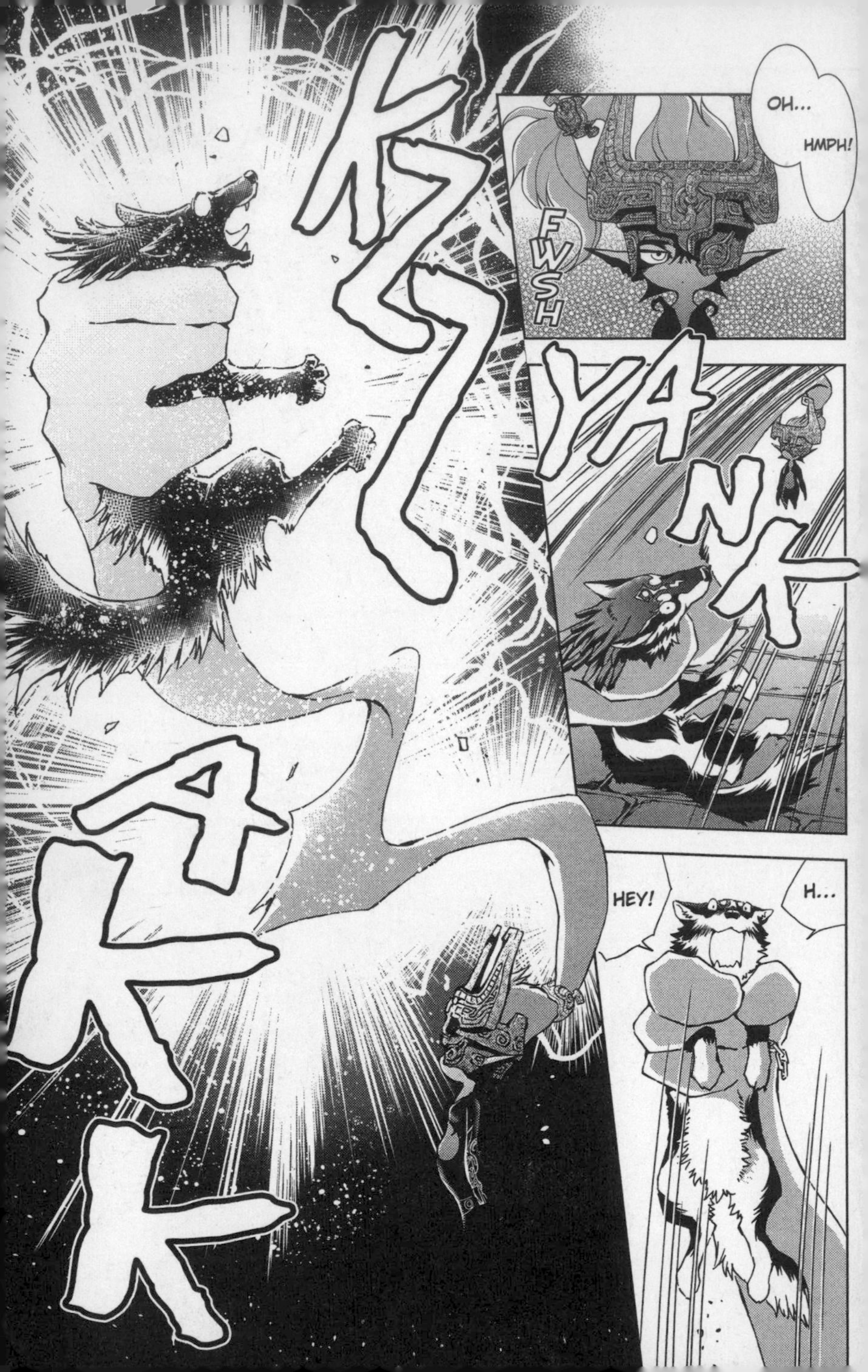
OH...
HMPH!
FWSH
YANK
H...
HEY!

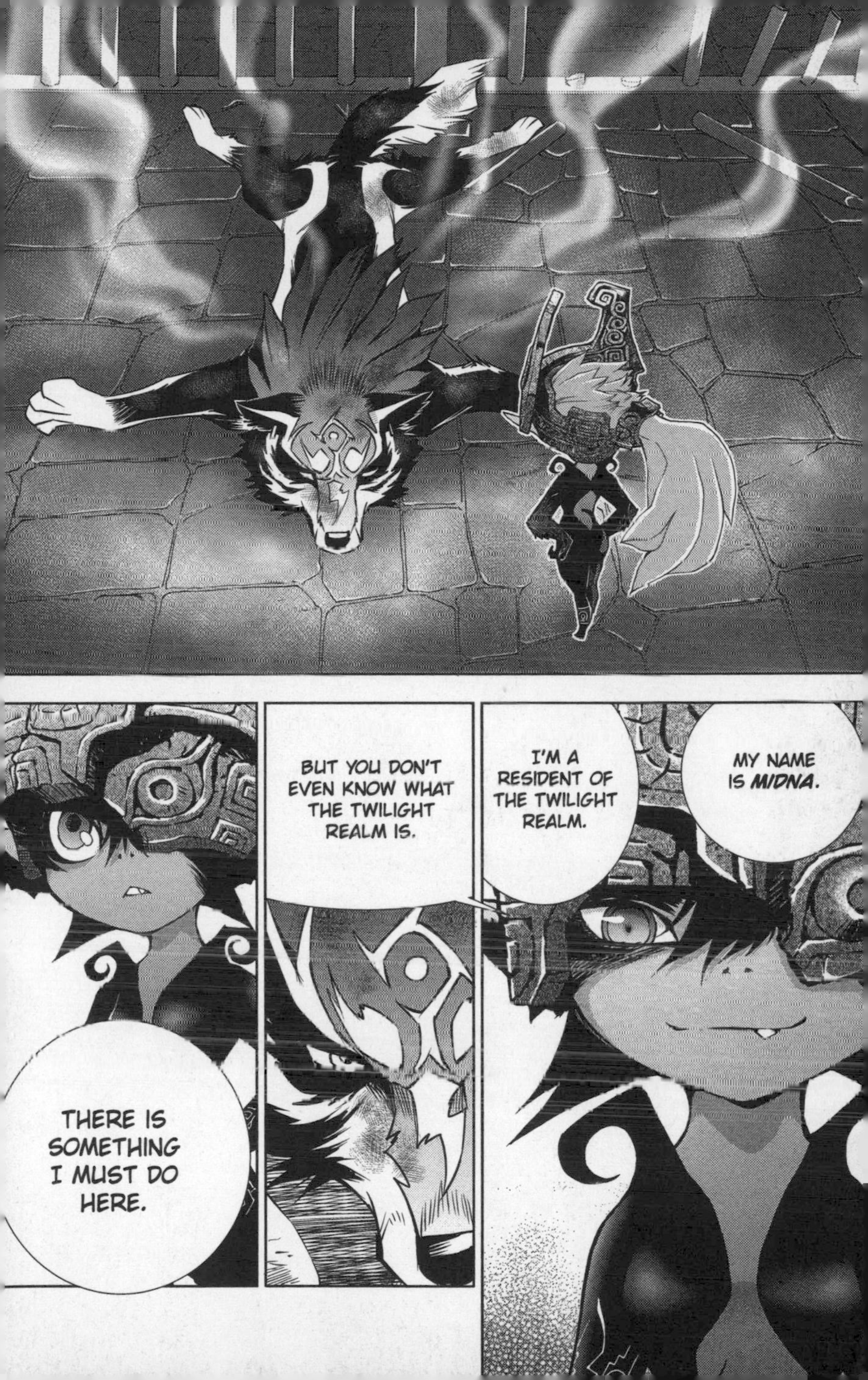
MY NAME IS *MIDNA*.
I'M A RESIDENT OF THE TWILIGHT REALM.
BUT YOU DON'T EVEN KNOW WHAT THE TWILIGHT REALM IS.
THERE IS SOMETHING I MUST DO HERE.

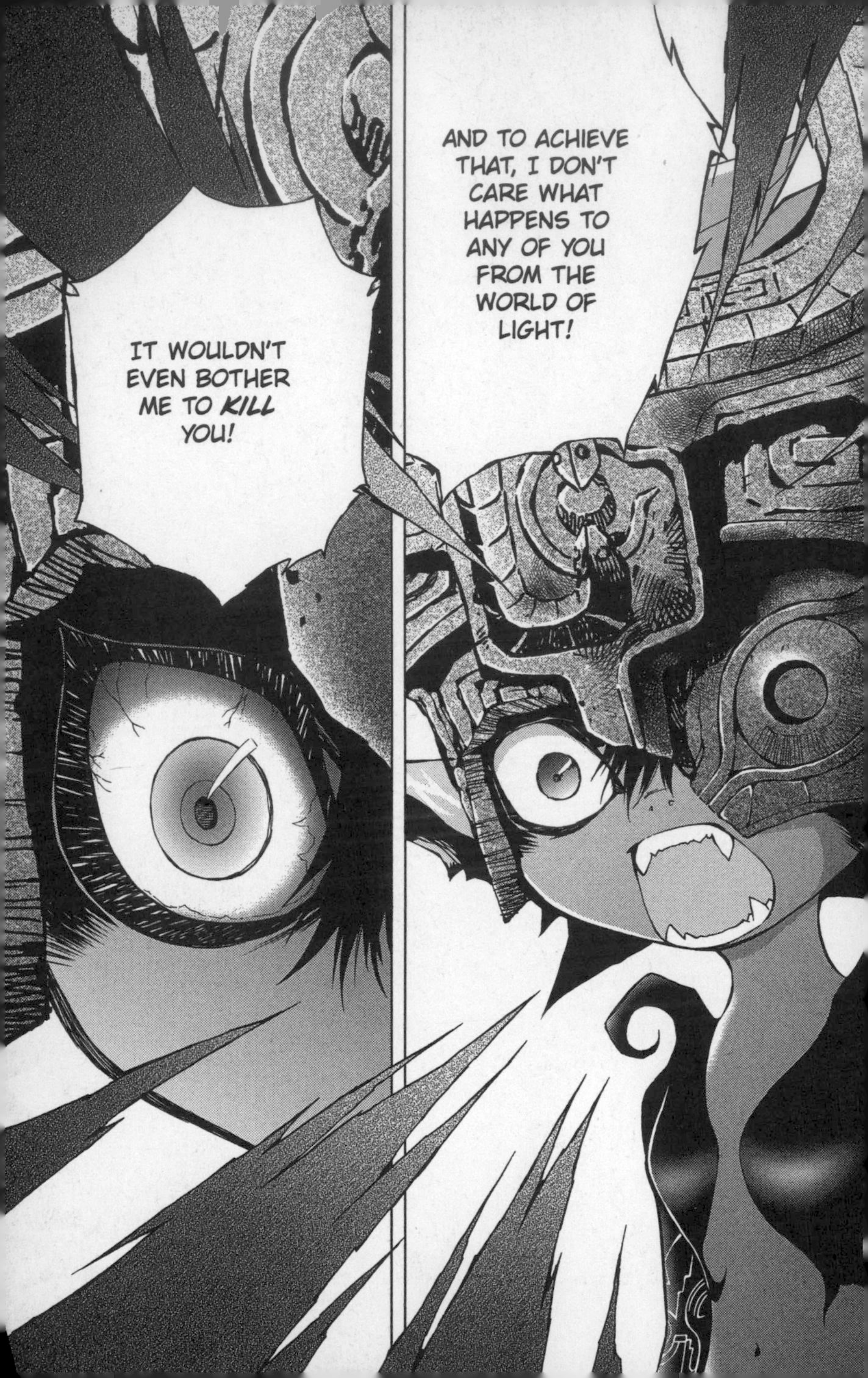
AND TO ACHIEVE THAT, I DON'T CARE WHAT HAPPENS TO ANY OF YOU FROM THE WORLD OF LIGHT!
IT WOULDN'T EVEN BOTHER ME TO *KILL* YOU!

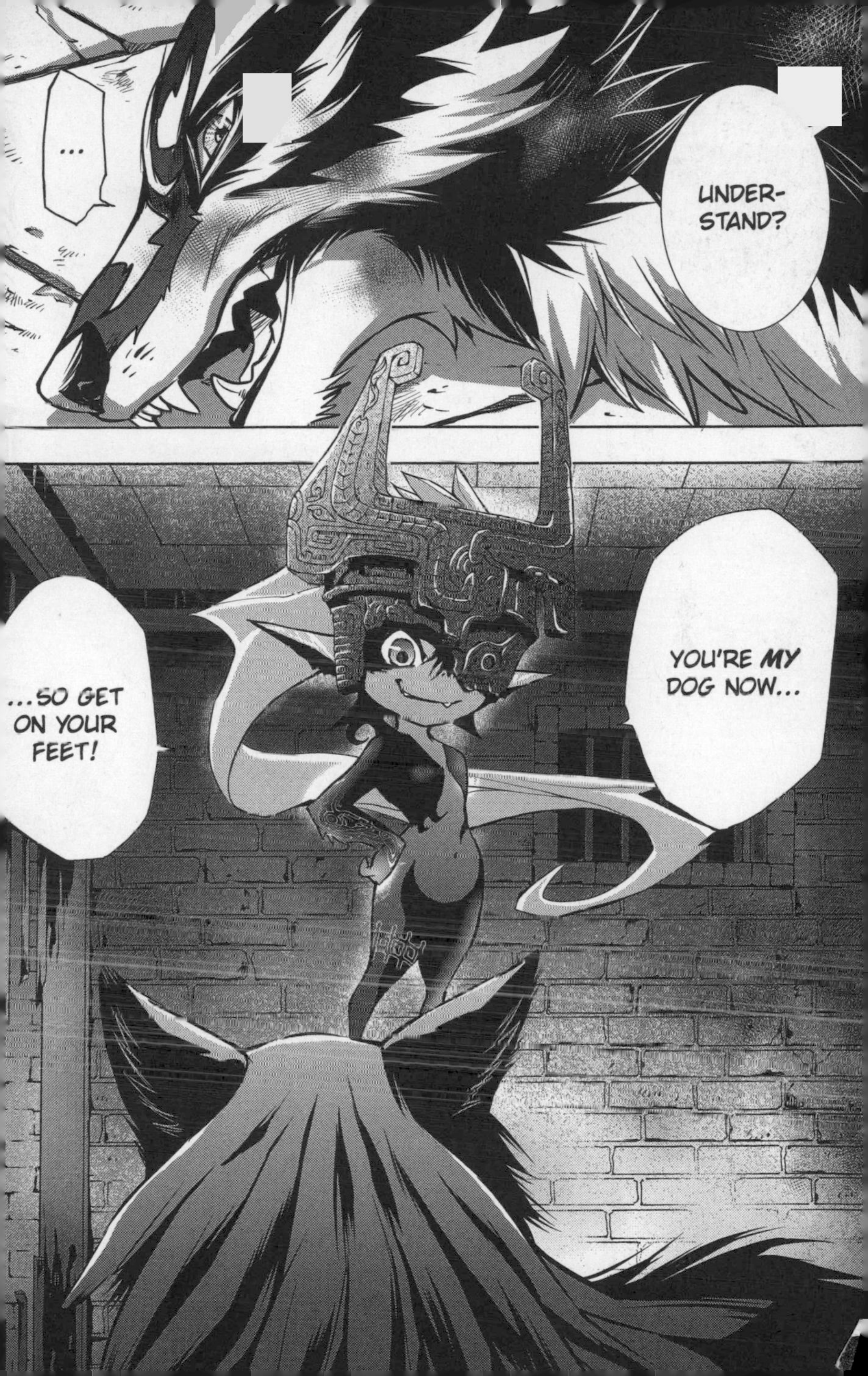
UNDER-STAND?
...
YOU'RE *MY* DOG NOW...
...SO GET ON YOUR FEET!

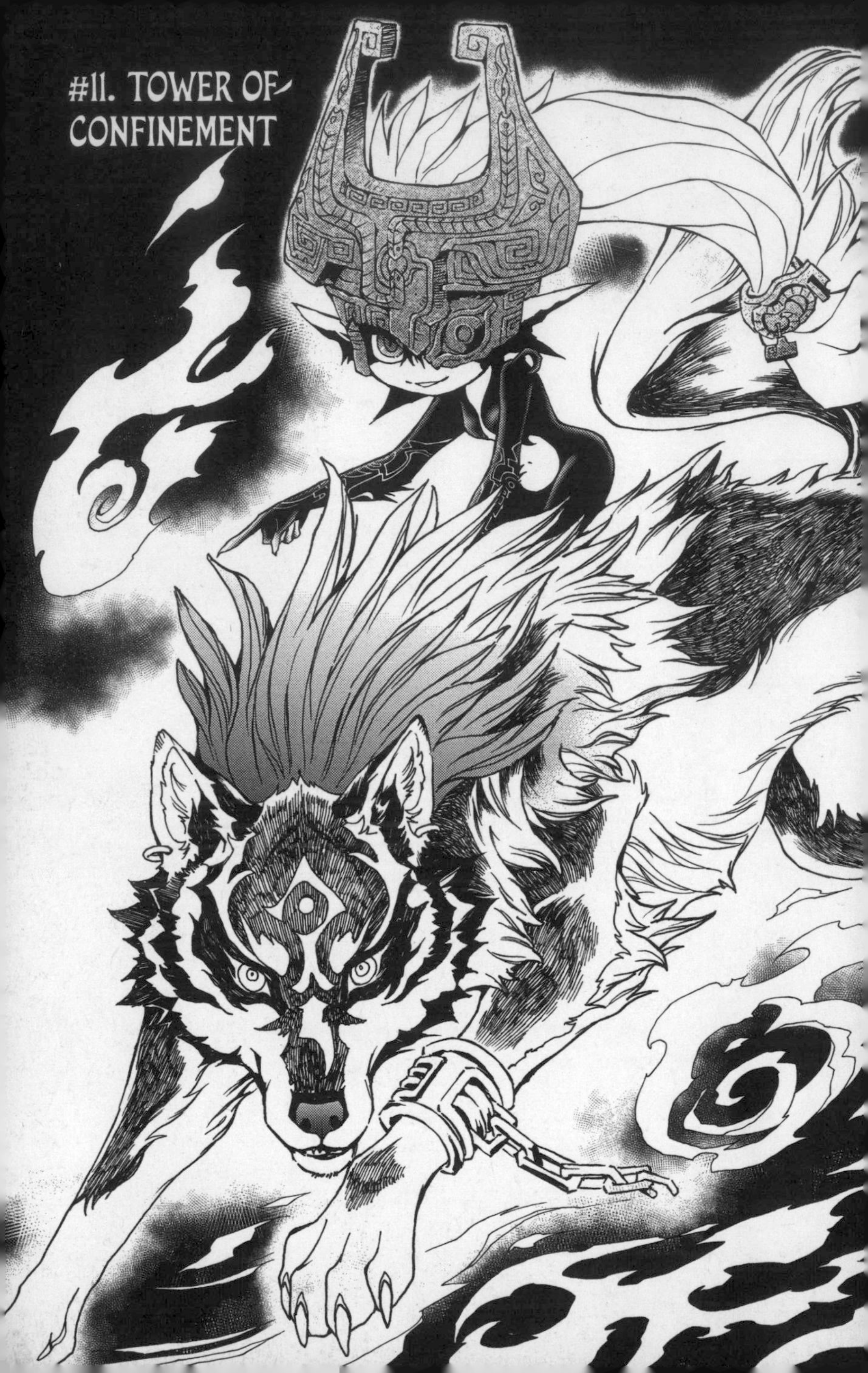
#11. TOWER OF CONFINEMENT

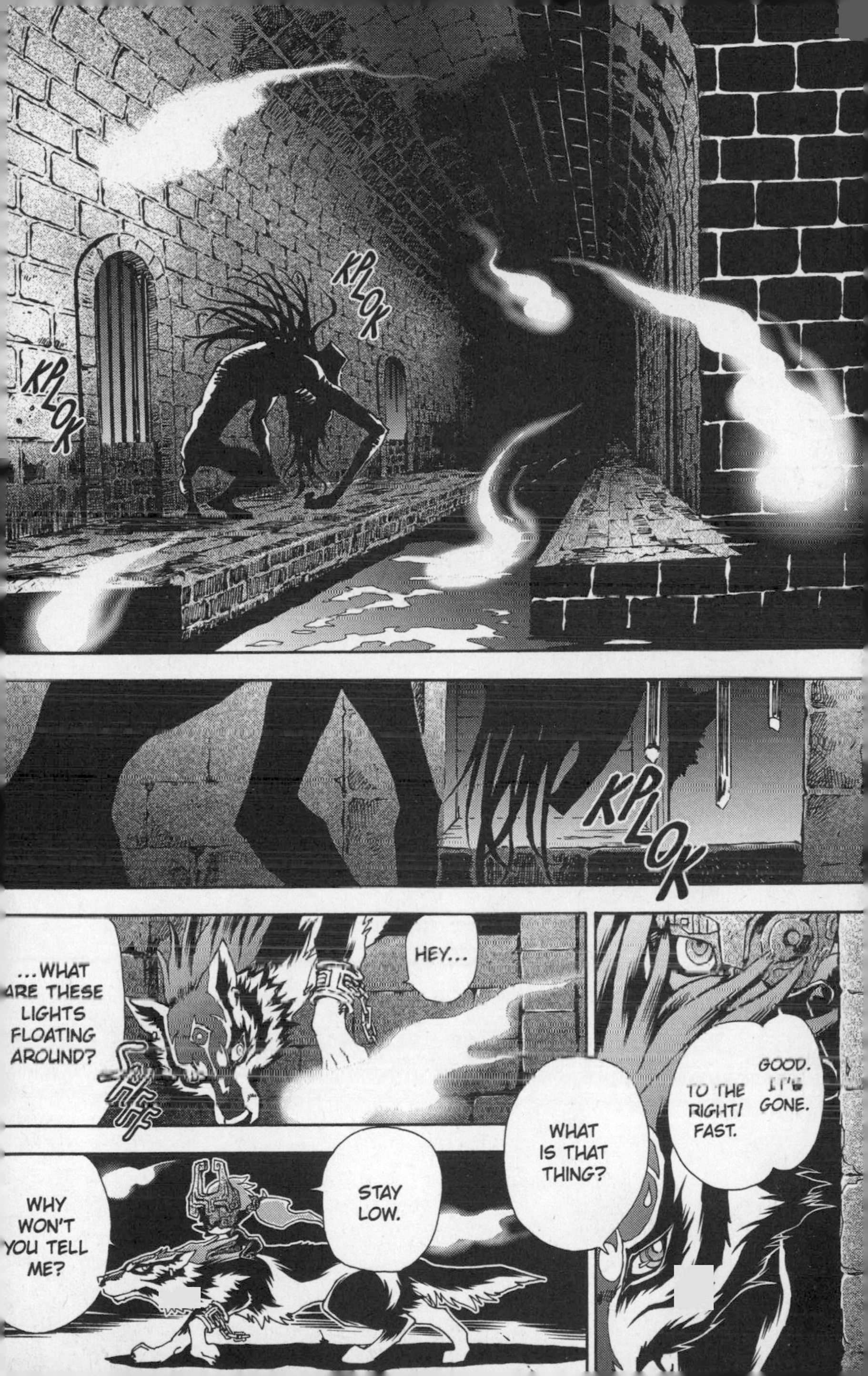
KPLOK
KPLOK
KPLOK
GOOD. IT'S GONE.
TO THE RIGHT! FAST.
HEY...
...WHAT ARE THESE LIGHTS FLOATING AROUND?
WHAT IS THAT THING?
STAY LOW.
WHY WON'T YOU TELL ME?

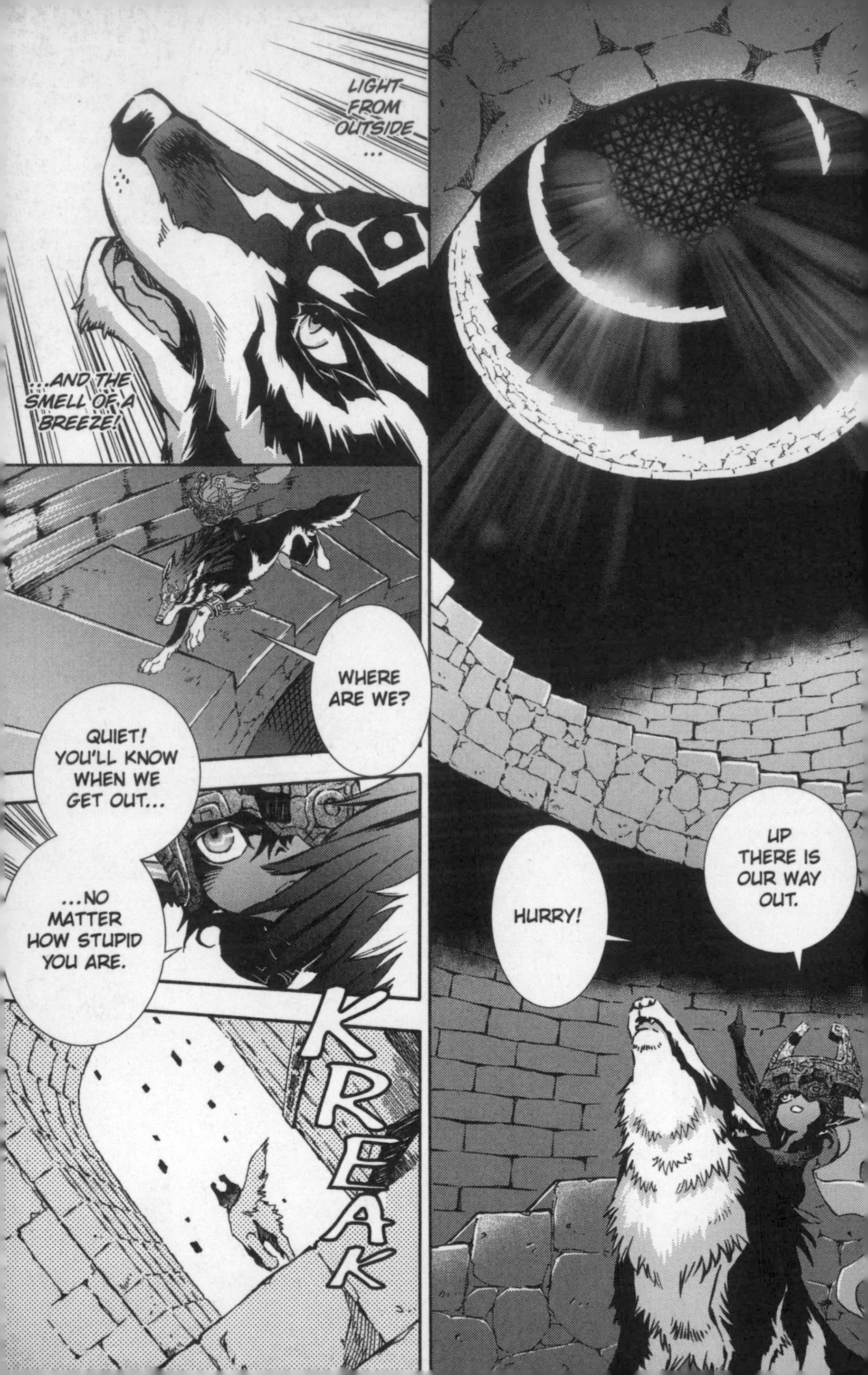
UP THERE IS OUR WAY OUT.
HURRY!
LIGHT FROM OUTSIDE...
...AND THE SMELL OF A BREEZE!
WHERE ARE WE?
QUIET! YOU'LL KNOW WHEN WE GET OUT...
...NO MATTER HOW STUPID YOU ARE.
KREAK

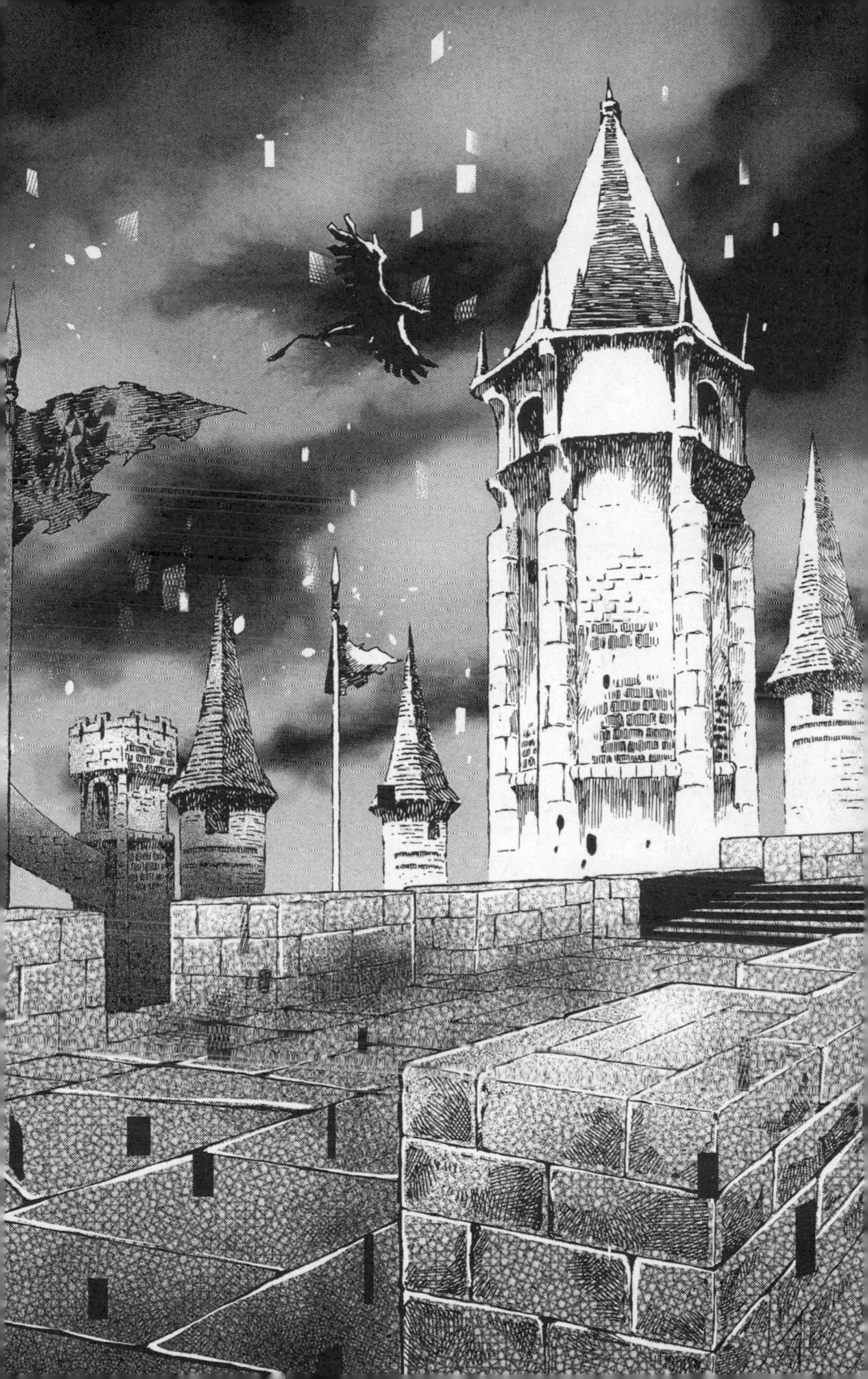

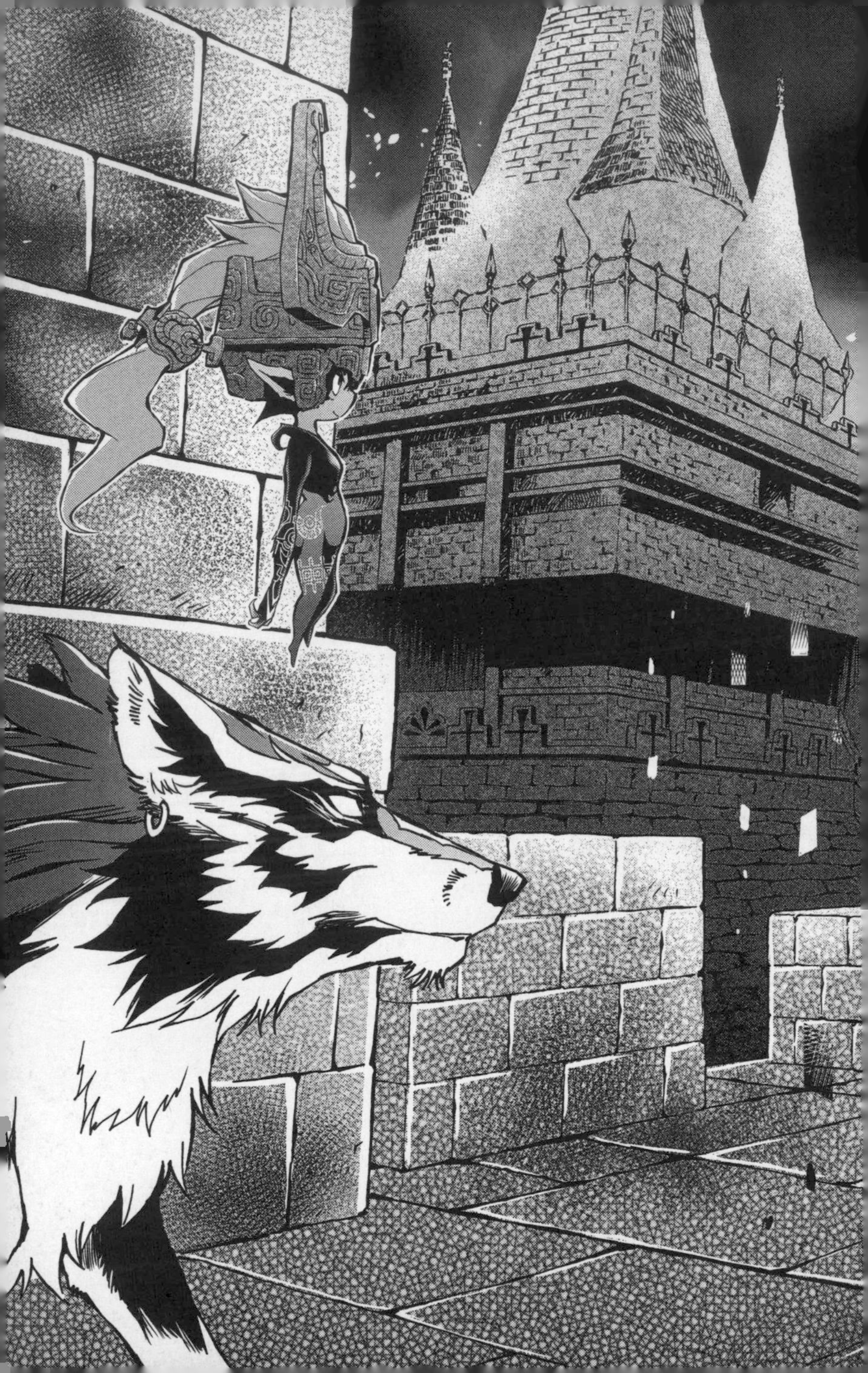

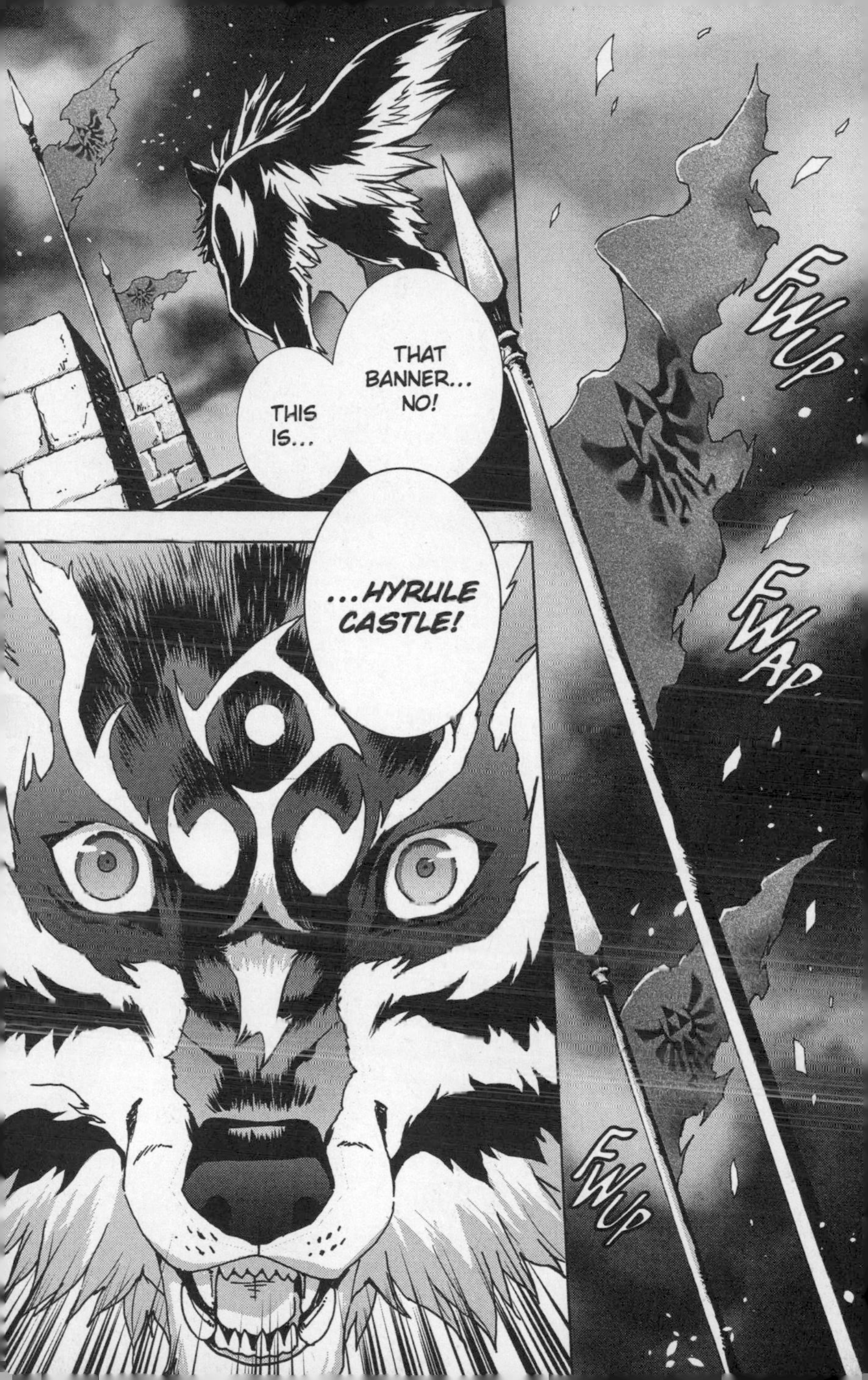
FWUP
FWAP
FWUP
THAT BANNER... NO!
THIS IS...
...HYRULE CASTLE!

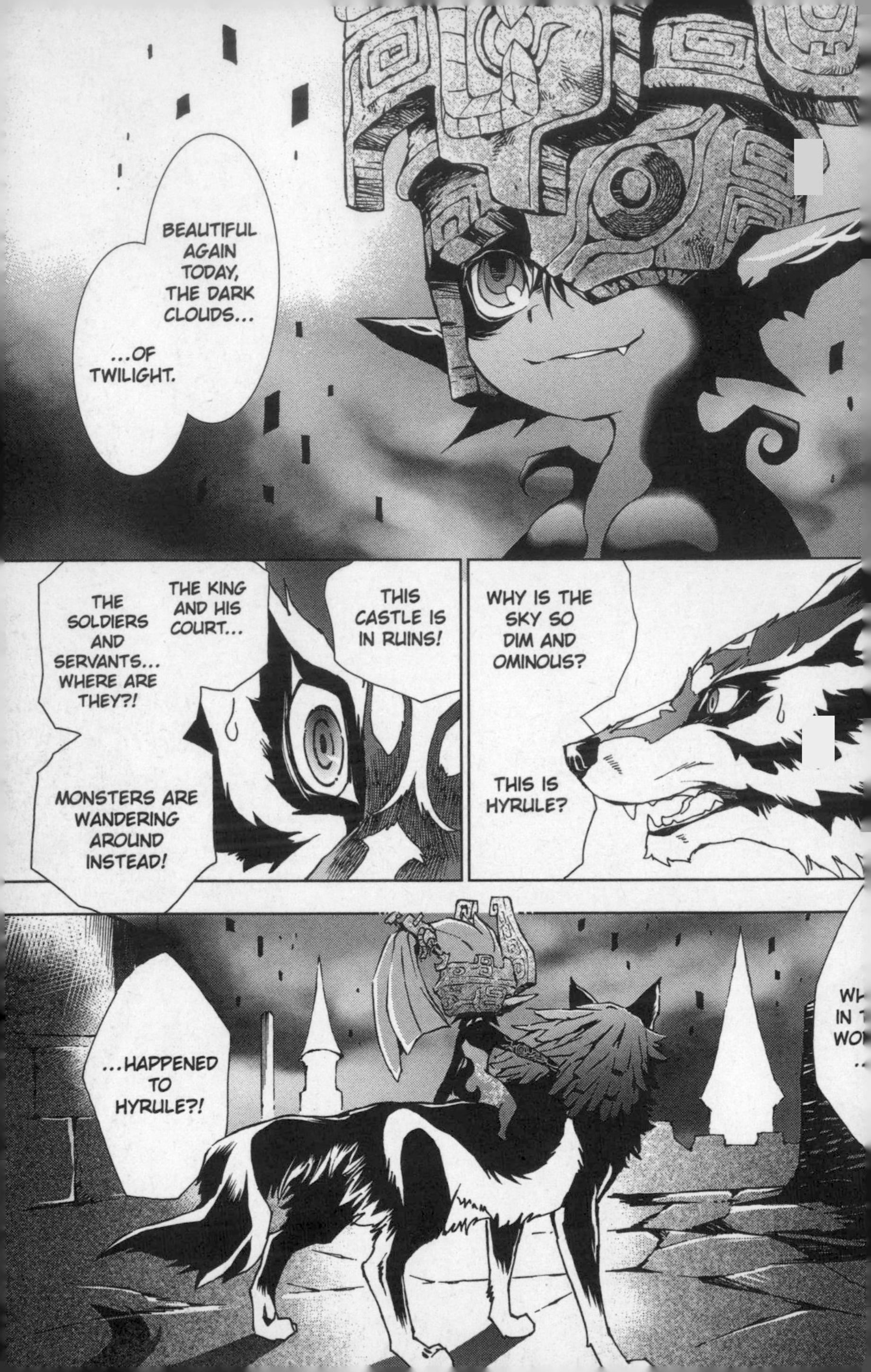
BEAUTIFUL AGAIN TODAY, THE DARK CLOUDS...
...OF TWILIGHT.
WHY IS THE SKY SO DIM AND OMINOUS?
THIS IS HYRULE?
THIS CASTLE IS IN RUINS!
THE KING AND HIS COURT...
THE SOLDIERS AND SERVANTS... WHERE ARE THEY?!
MONSTERS ARE WANDERING AROUND INSTEAD!
...HAPPENED TO HYRULE?!

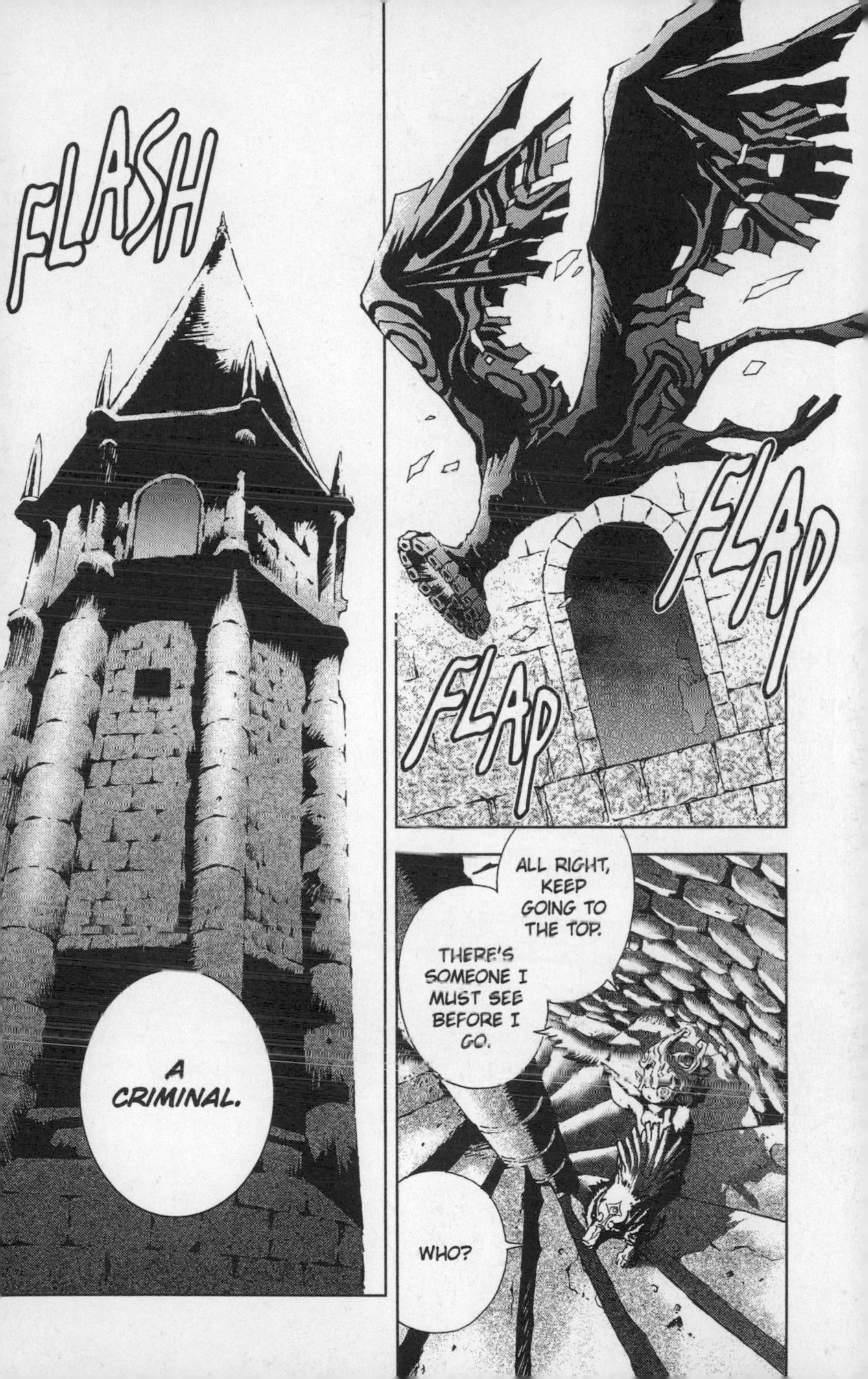
FLAP
FLAP
ALL RIGHT, KEEP GOING TO THE TOP.
THERE'S SOMEONE I MUST SEE BEFORE I GO.
WHO?
FLASH
A CRIMINAL.

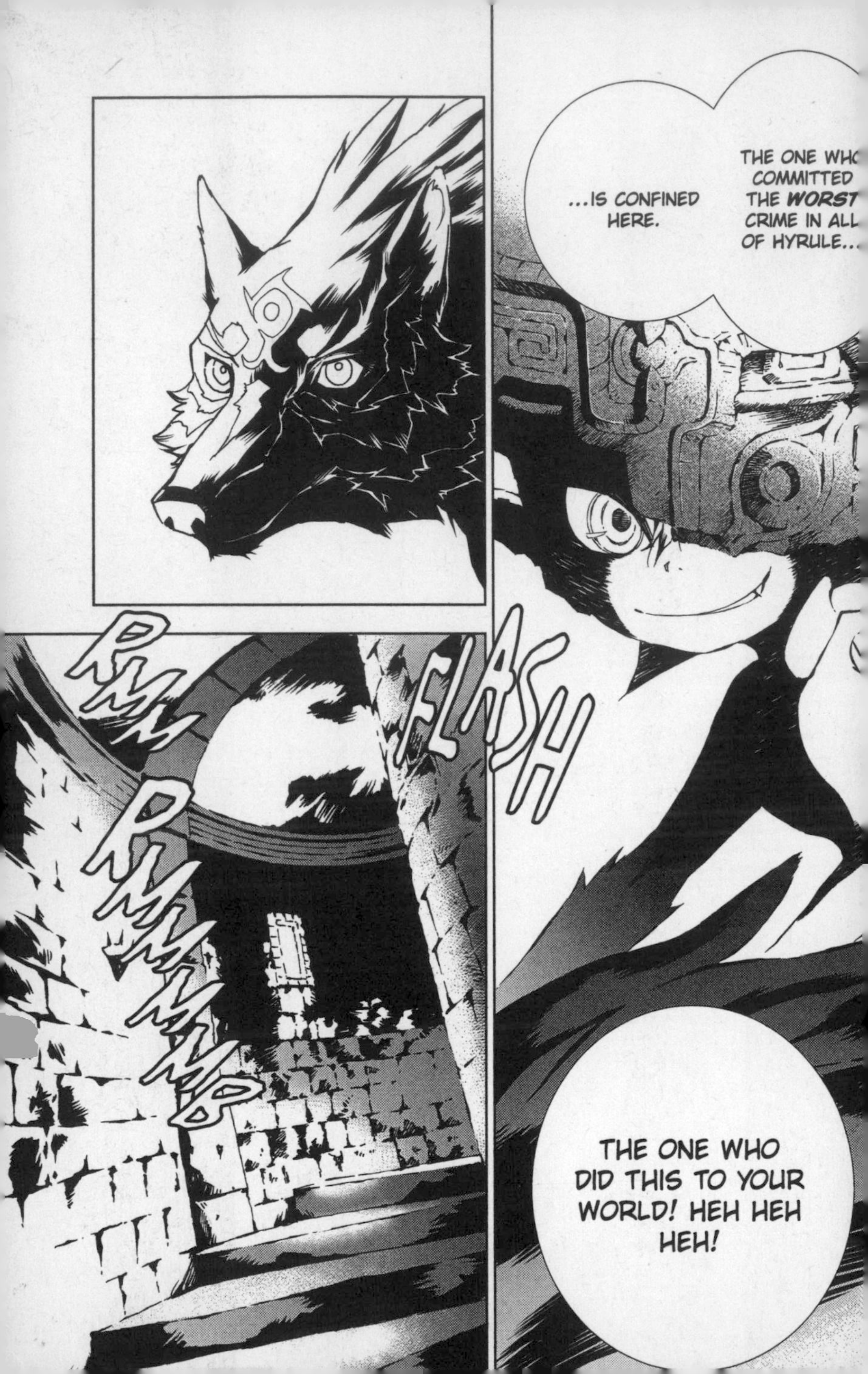
THE ONE WHO COMMITTED THE **WORST** CRIME IN ALL OF HYRULE...
...IS CONFINED HERE.
THE ONE WHO DID THIS TO YOUR WORLD! HEH HEH HEH!
FLASH
RMMM RMMMMMB

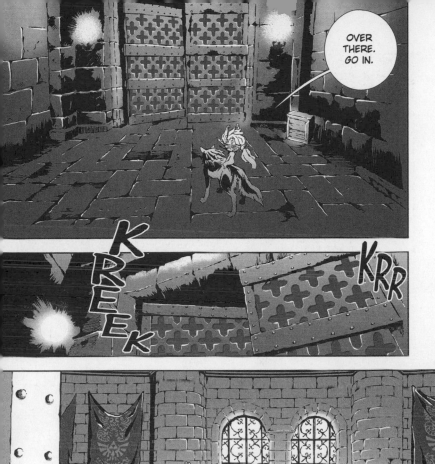

OVER THERE. GO IN.

KREEK

KRR

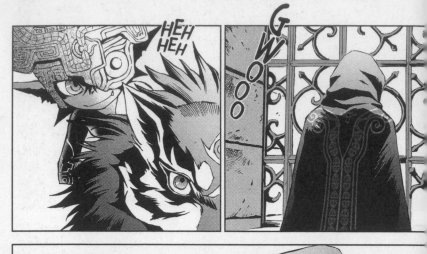

HEH HEH

G WOOO OO

WHp

GRRR

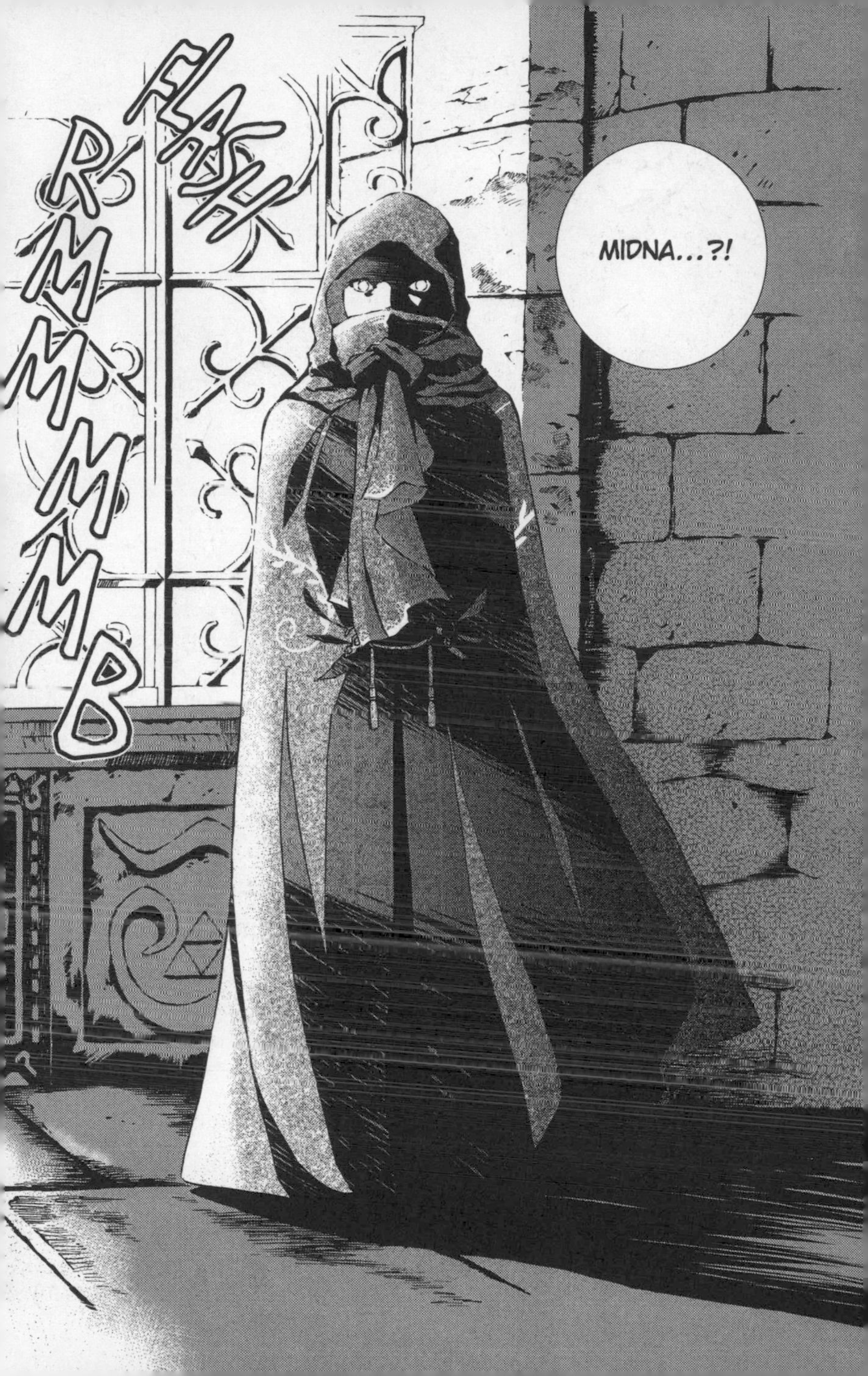
MIDNA...?!
FLASH
RMMMMB

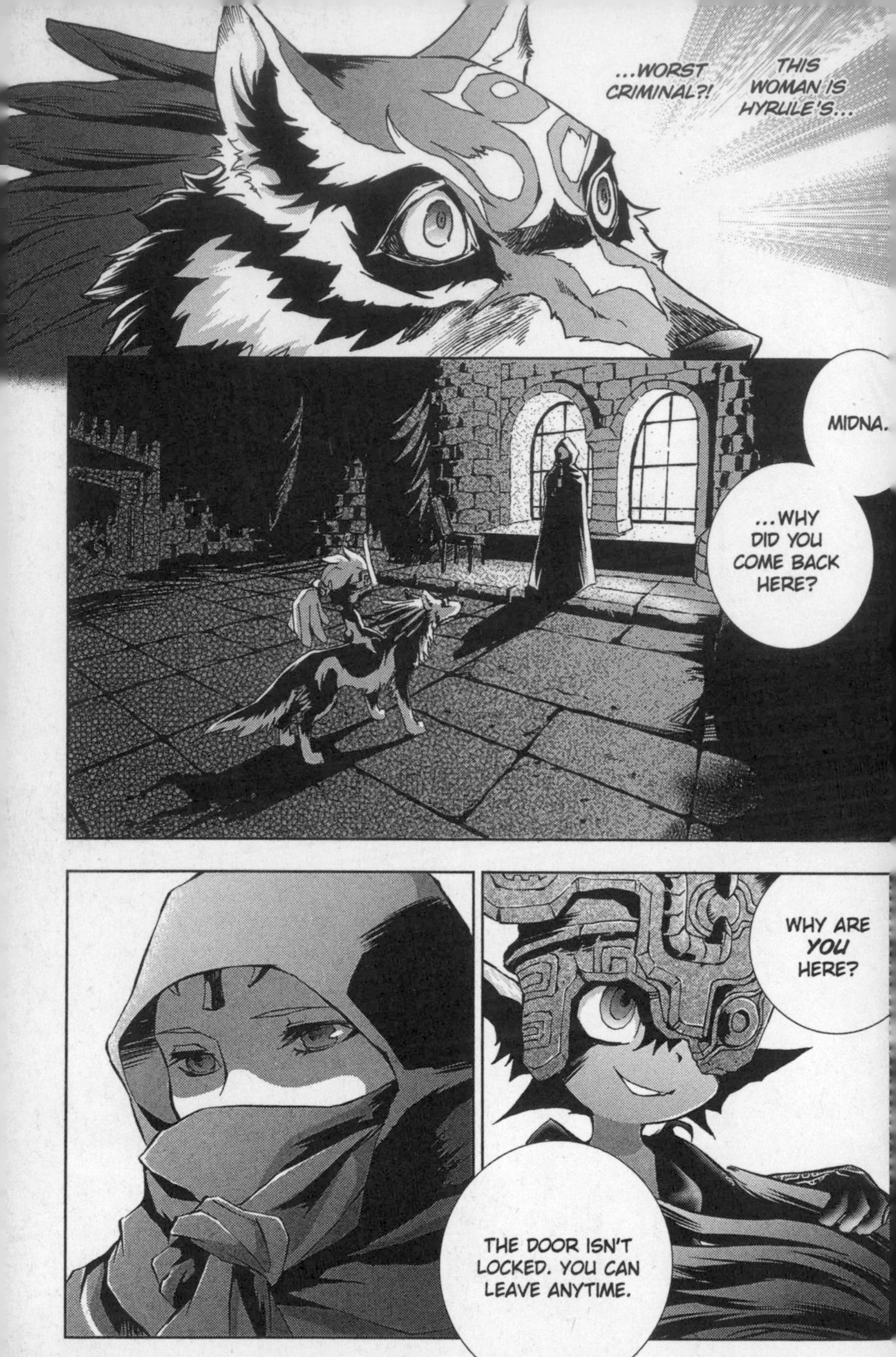
THIS WOMAN IS HYRULE'S...
...WORST CRIMINAL?!
MIDNA.
...WHY DID YOU COME BACK HERE?
WHY ARE *YOU* HERE?
THE DOOR ISN'T LOCKED. YOU CAN LEAVE ANYTIME.

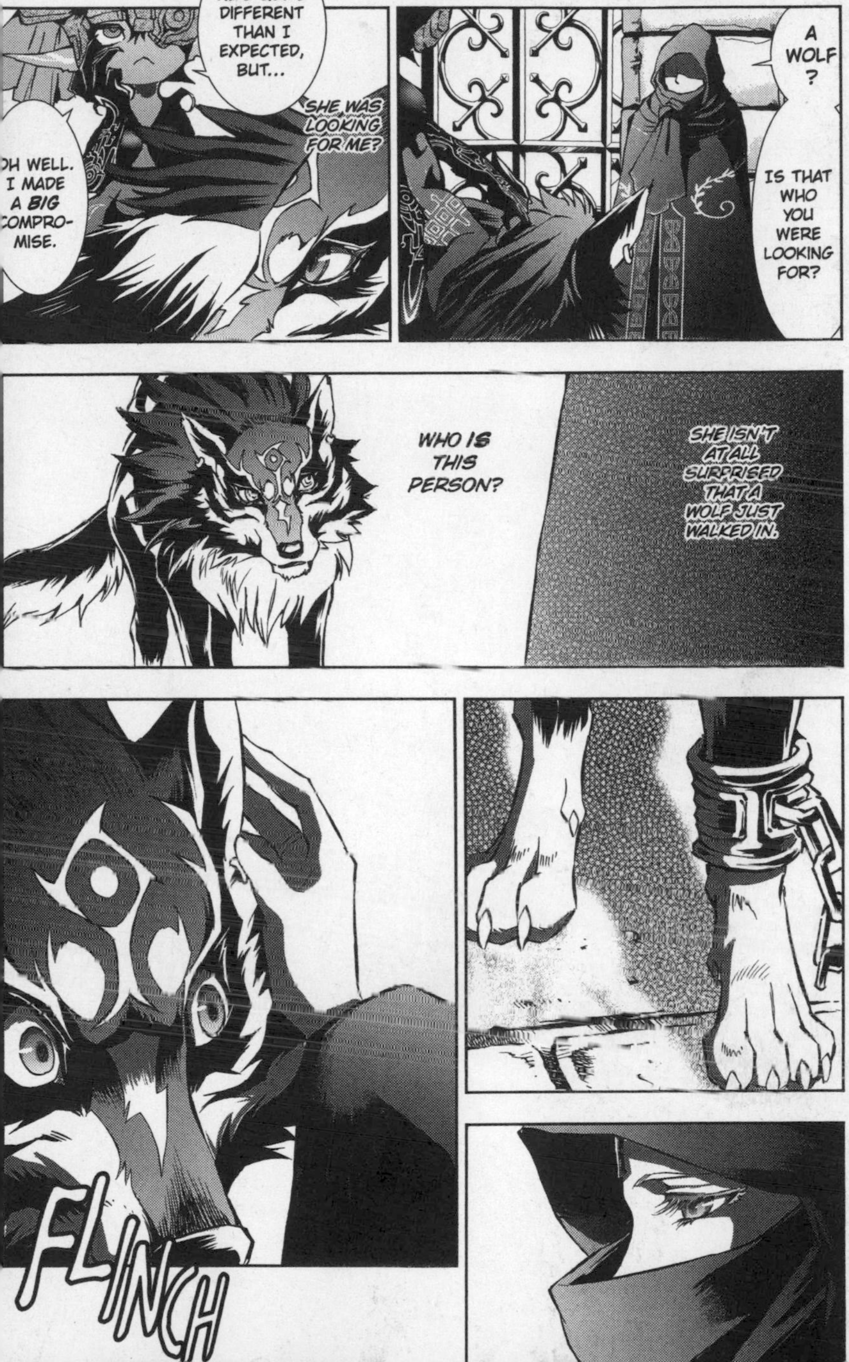
A WOLF?
IS THAT WHO YOU WERE LOOKING FOR?
HE'S QUITE DIFFERENT THAN I EXPECTED, BUT...
SHE WAS LOOKING FOR ME?
OH WELL. I MADE A *BIG* COMPROMISE.
SHE ISN'T AT ALL SURPRISED THAT A WOLF JUST WALKED IN.
WHO *IS* THIS PERSON?
FLINCH

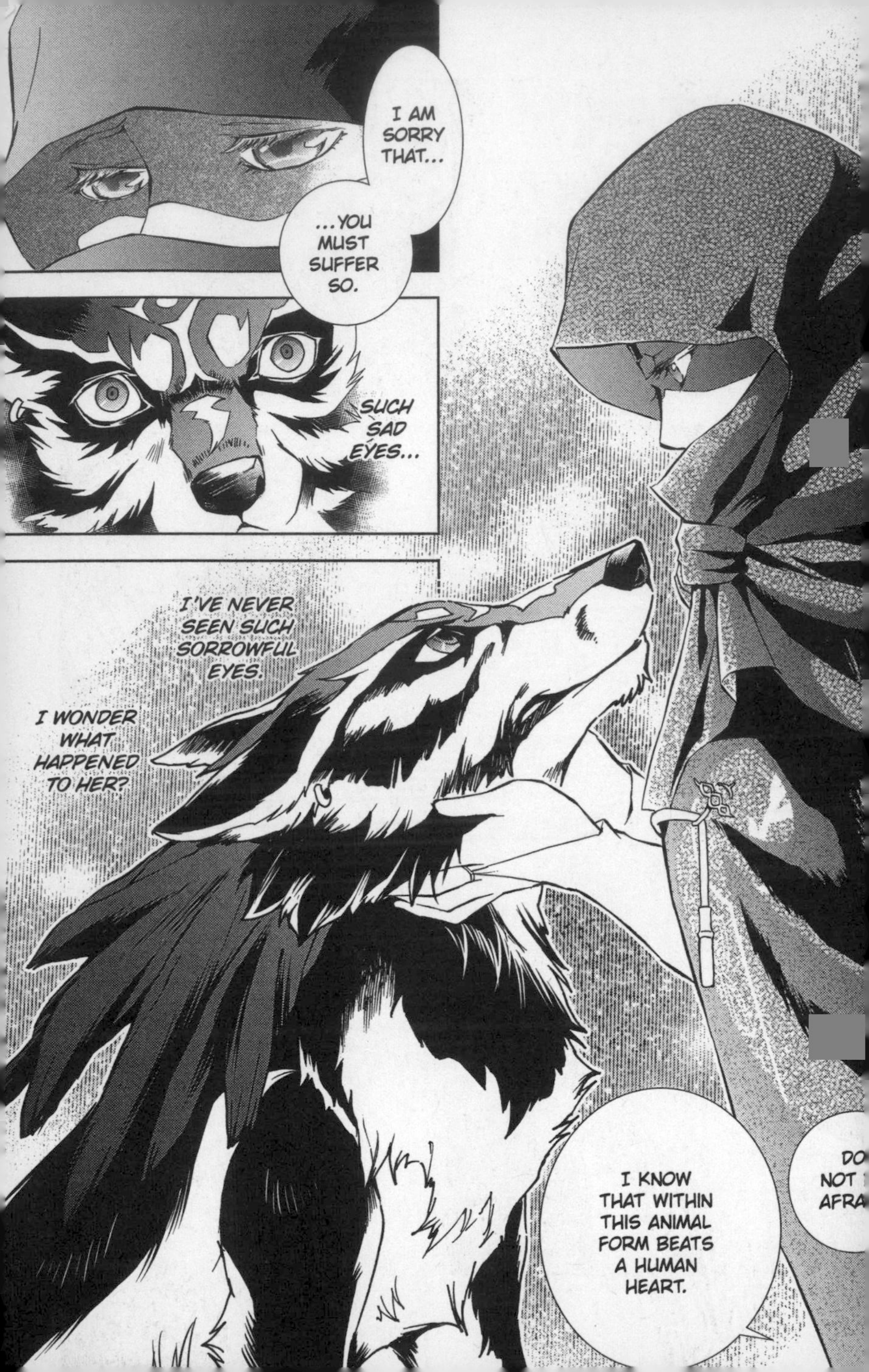
I AM SORRY THAT...
...YOU MUST SUFFER SO.
SUCH SAD EYES...
I'VE NEVER SEEN SUCH SORROWFUL EYES.
I WONDER WHAT HAPPENED TO HER?
DO NOT AFRA
I KNOW THAT WITHIN THIS ANIMAL FORM BEATS A HUMAN HEART.

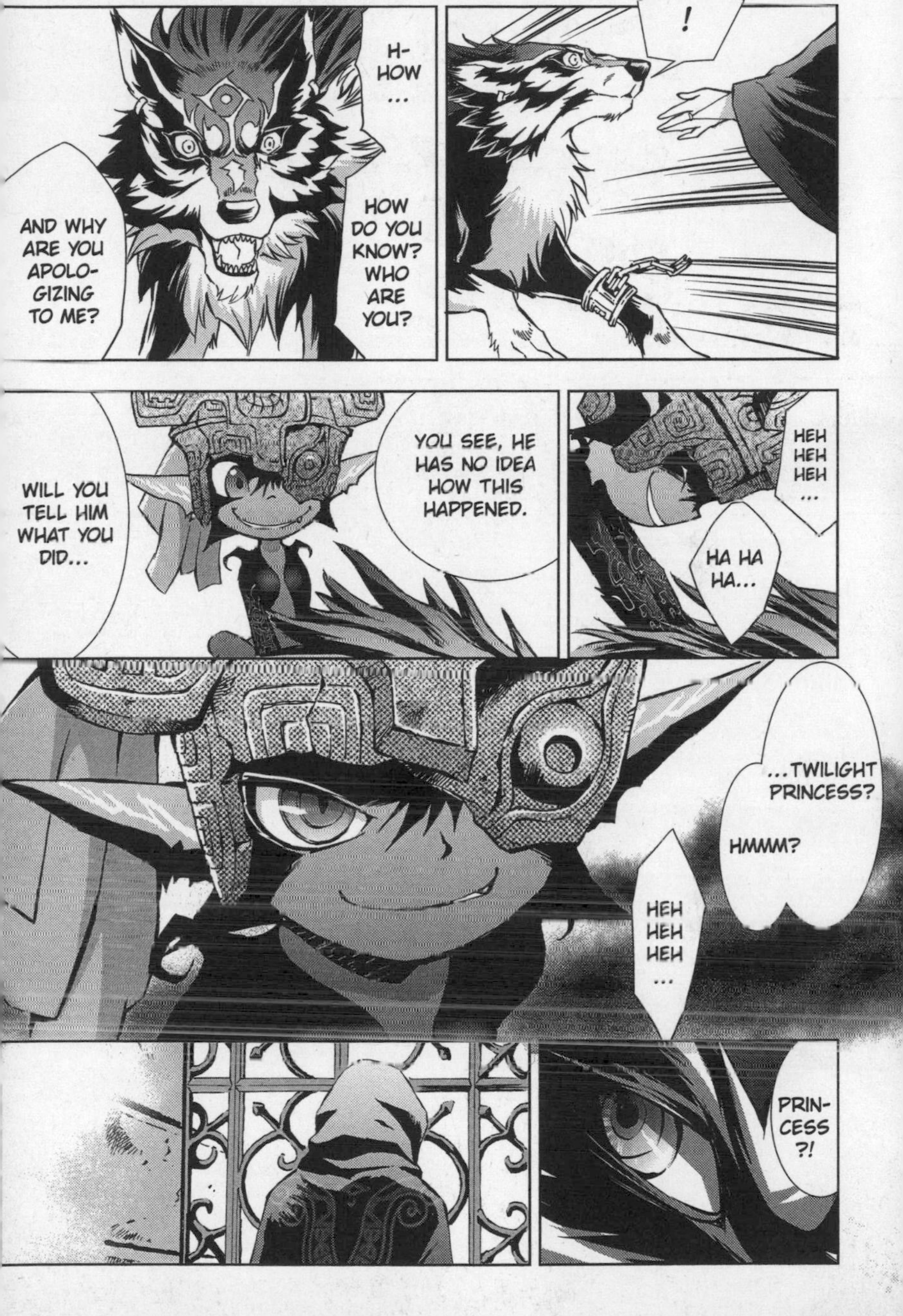
!
H- HOW ...
HOW DO YOU KNOW? WHO ARE YOU?
AND WHY ARE YOU APOLO- GIZING TO ME?
HEH HEH HEH ...
HA HA HA...
YOU SEE, HE HAS NO IDEA HOW THIS HAPPENED.
WILL YOU TELL HIM WHAT YOU DID...
...TWILIGHT PRINCESS?
HMMM?
HEH HEH HEH ...
PRIN- CESS ?!

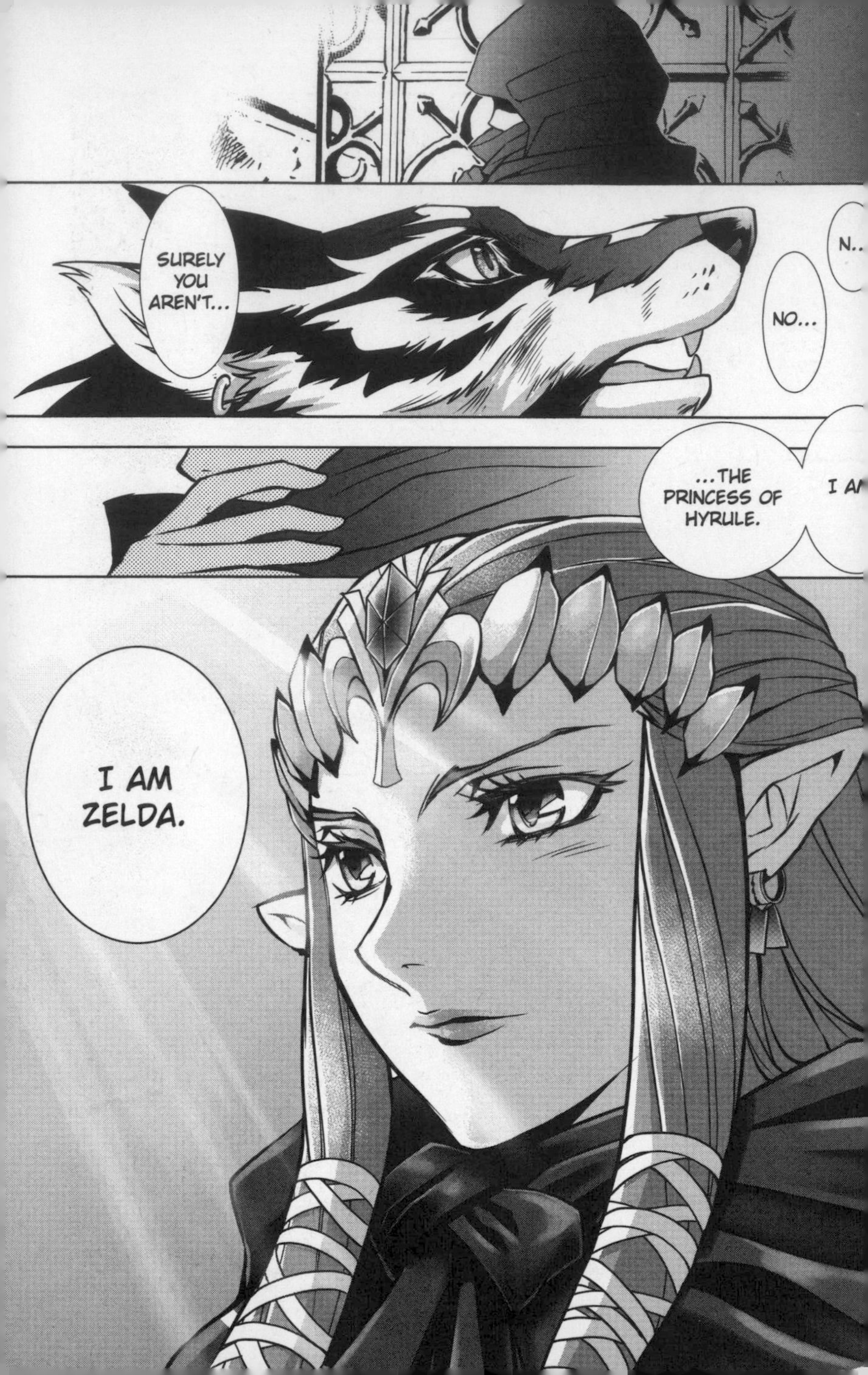
N...
NO...
SURELY YOU AREN'T...
I A
...THE PRINCESS OF HYRULE.
I AM ZELDA.

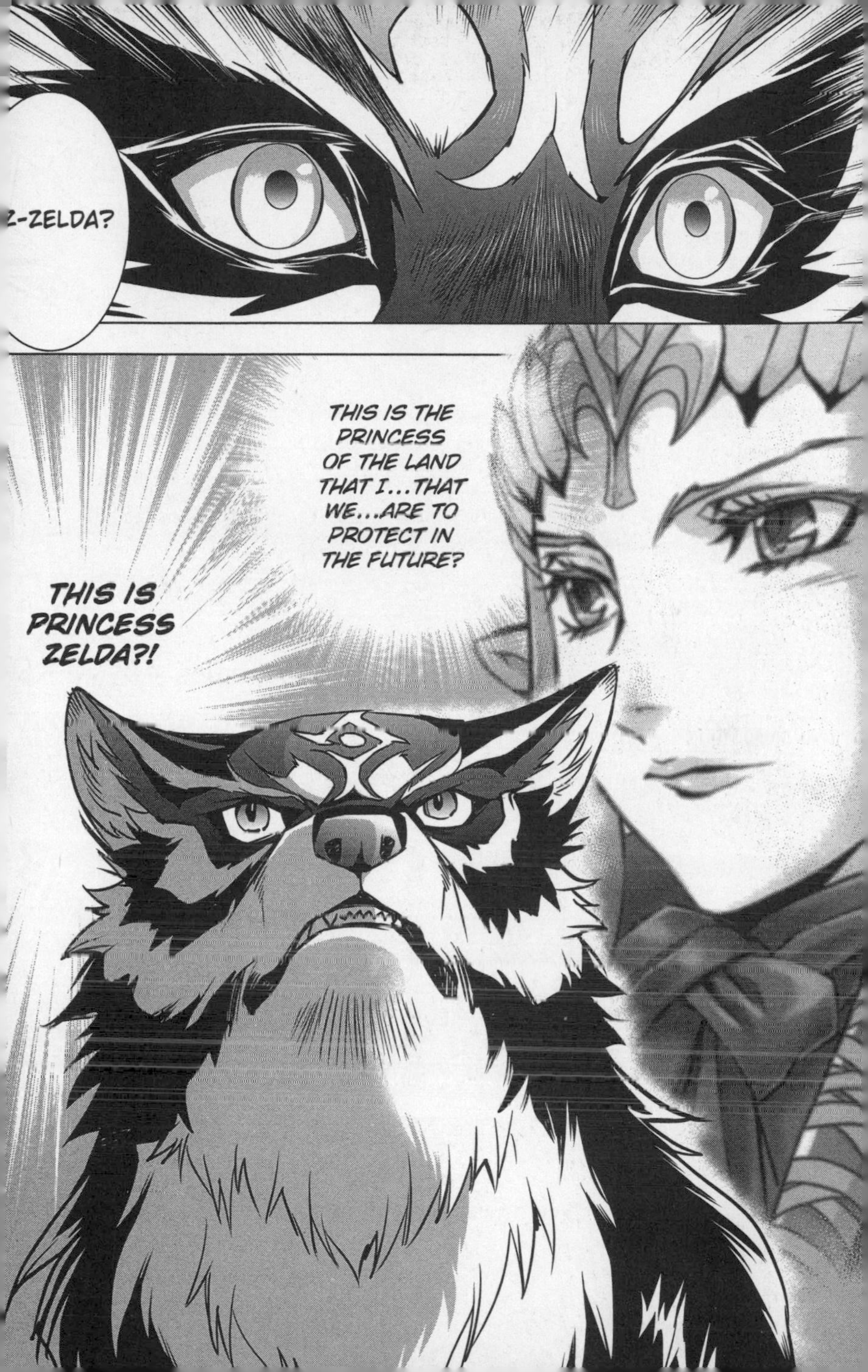
Z-ZELDA?
THIS IS THE PRINCESS OF THE LAND THAT I...THAT WE...ARE TO PROTECT IN THE FUTURE?
THIS IS PRINCESS ZELDA?!

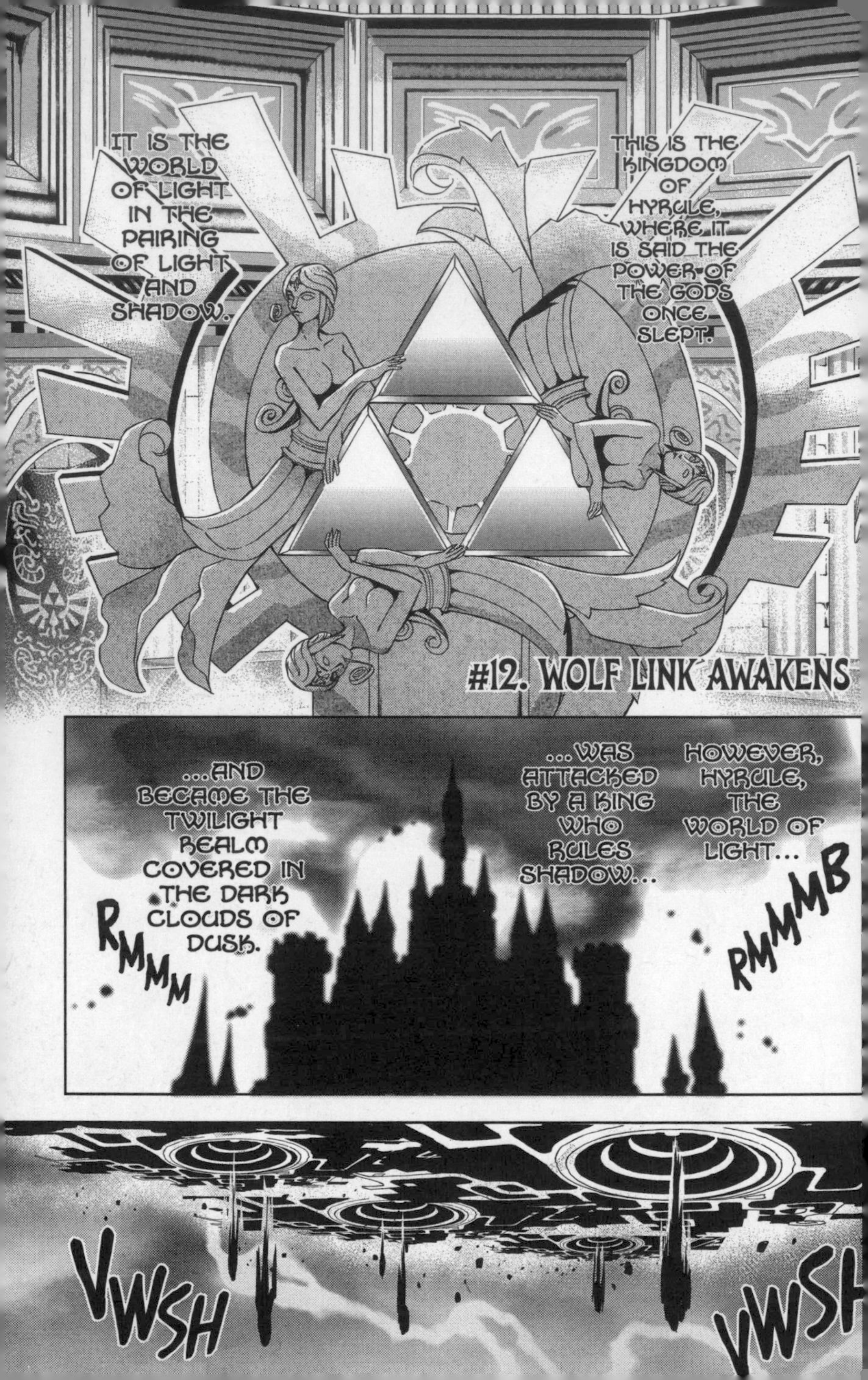
THIS IS THE KINGDOM OF HYRULE, WHERE IT IS SAID THE POWER OF THE GODS ONCE SLEPT.
IT IS THE WORLD OF LIGHT IN THE PAIRING OF LIGHT AND SHADOW.
#12. WOLF LINK AWAKENS
HOWEVER, HYRULE, THE WORLD OF LIGHT...
...WAS ATTACKED BY A KING WHO RULES SHADOW...
...AND BECAME THE TWILIGHT REALM COVERED IN THE DARK CLOUDS OF DUSK.
RMMMB
RMMM
VWSH
VWSH

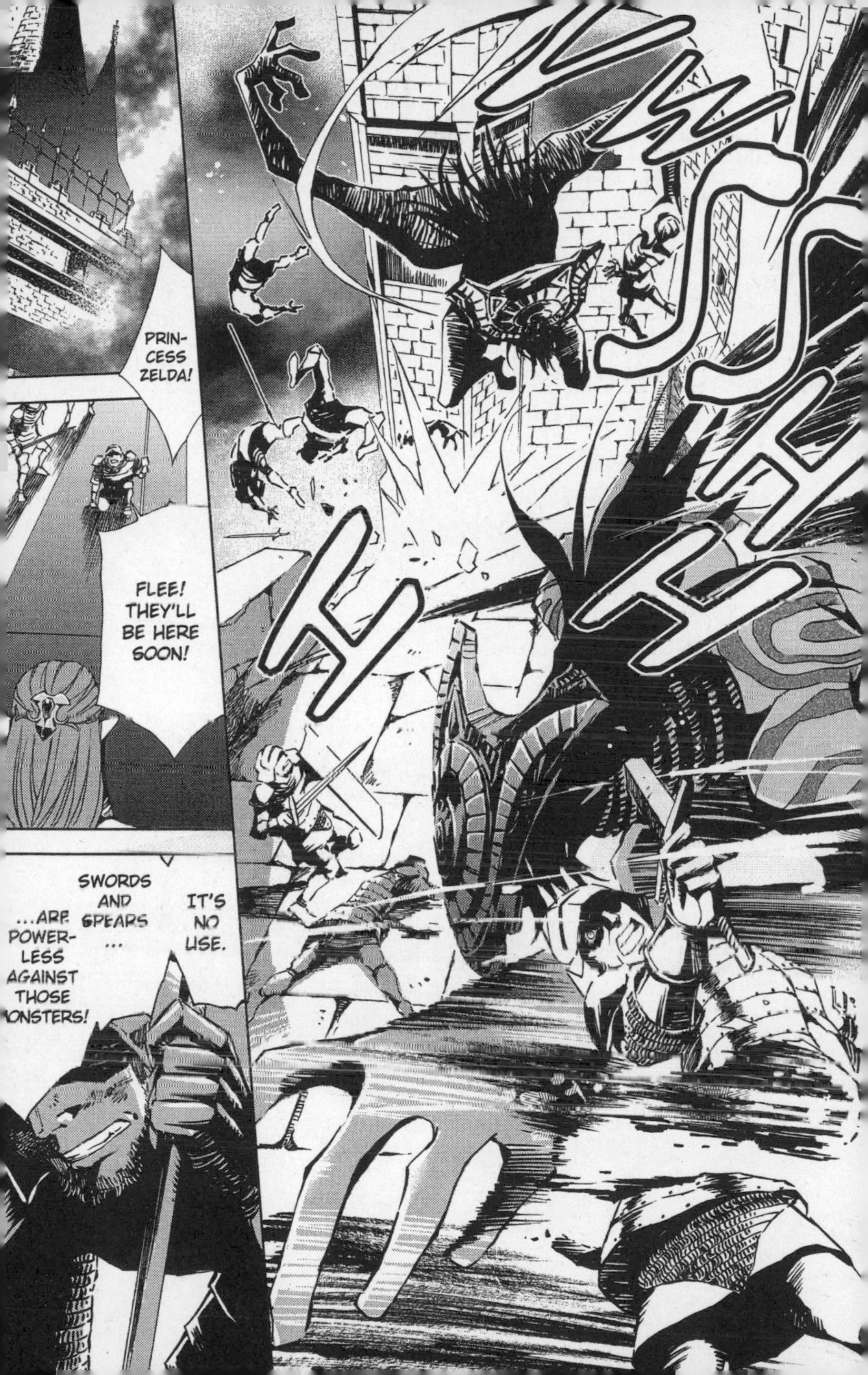
PRIN-CESS ZELDA!
FLEE! THEY'LL BE HERE SOON!
IT'S NO USE.
SWORDS AND SPEARS...
...ARE POWER-LESS AGAINST THOSE MONSTERS!

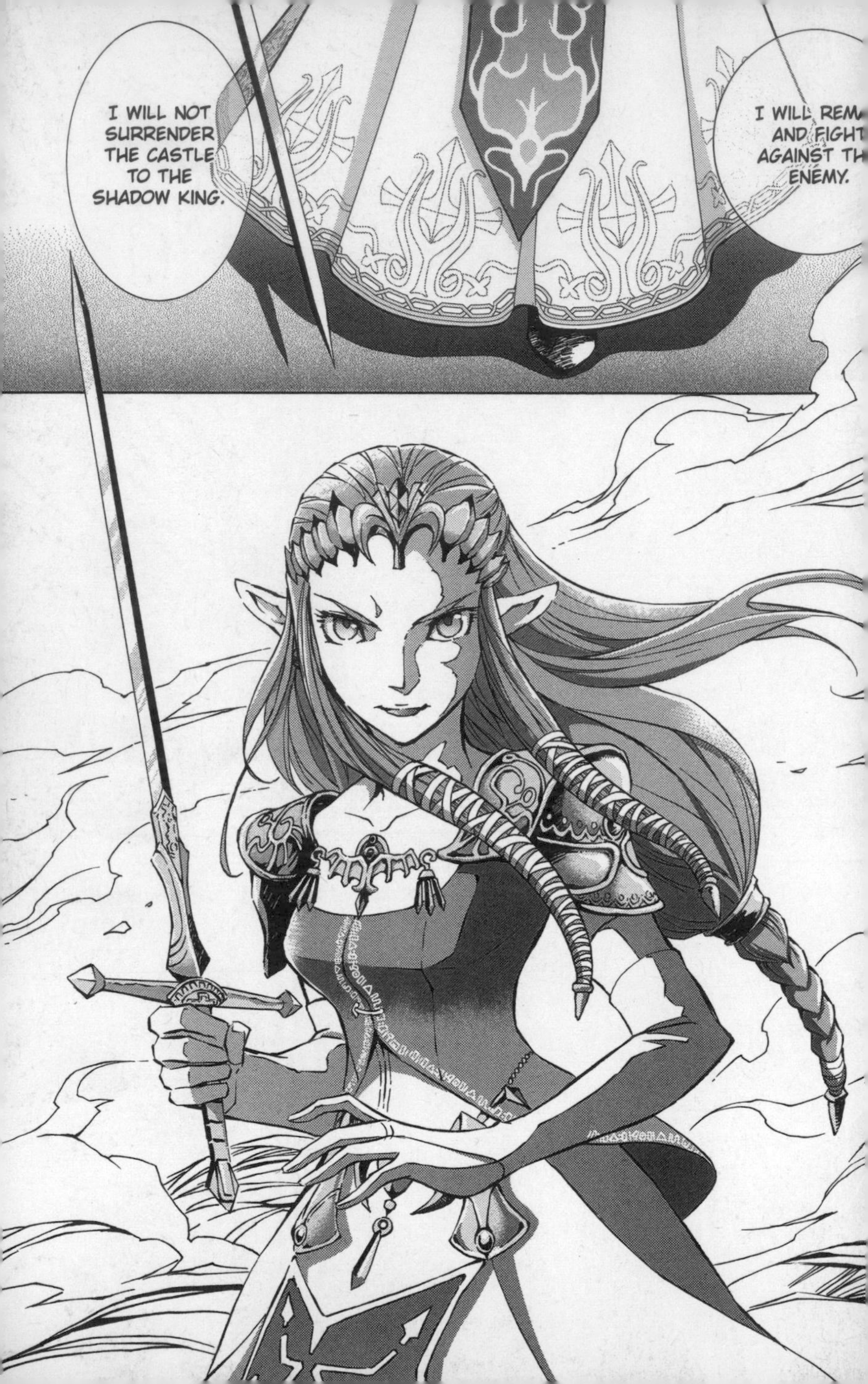
I WILL REM AND FIGHT AGAINST TH ENEMY.
I WILL NOT SURRENDER THE CASTLE TO THE SHADOW KING.

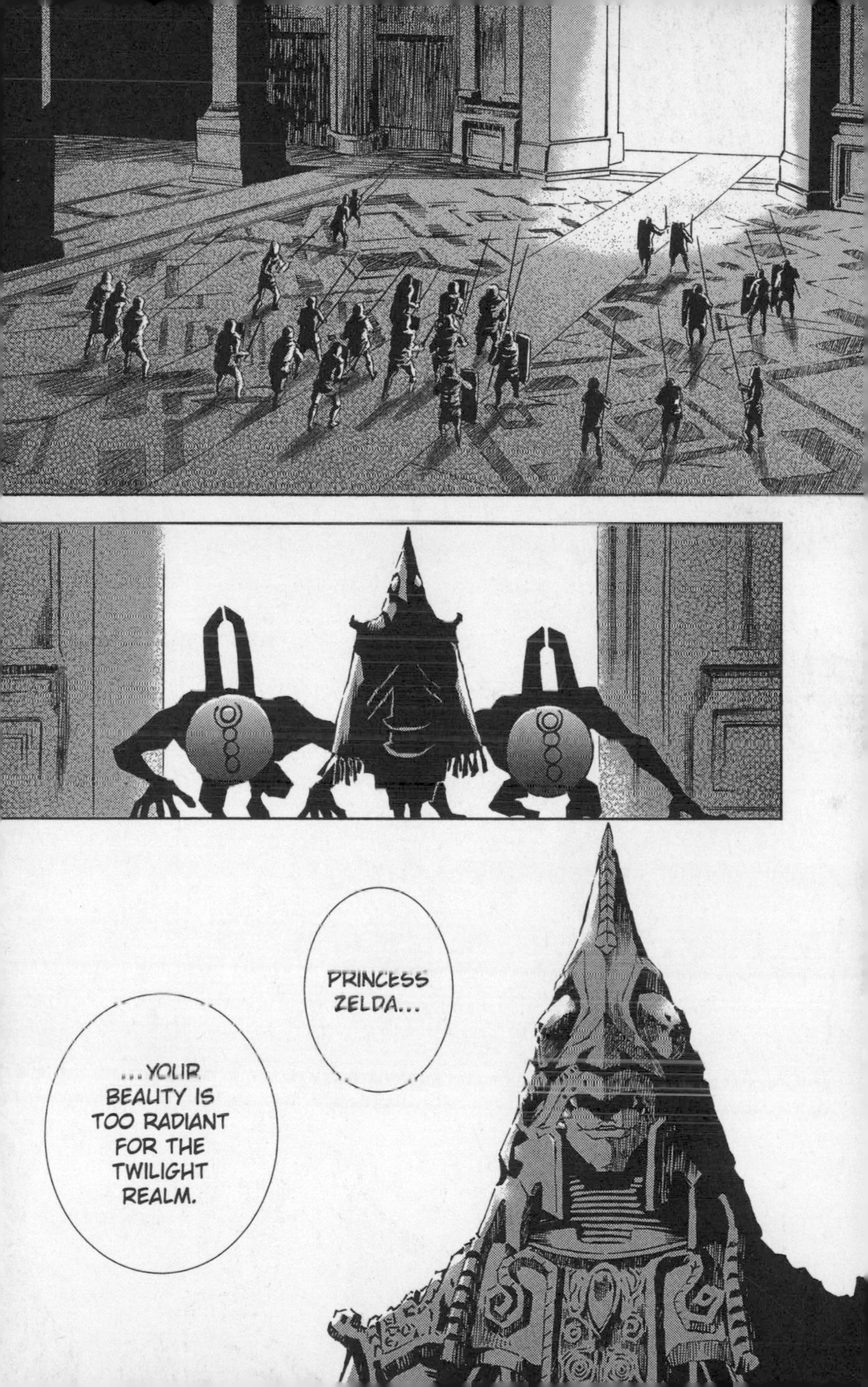
PRINCESS ZELDA...
...YOUR BEAUTY IS TOO RADIANT FOR THE TWILIGHT REALM.

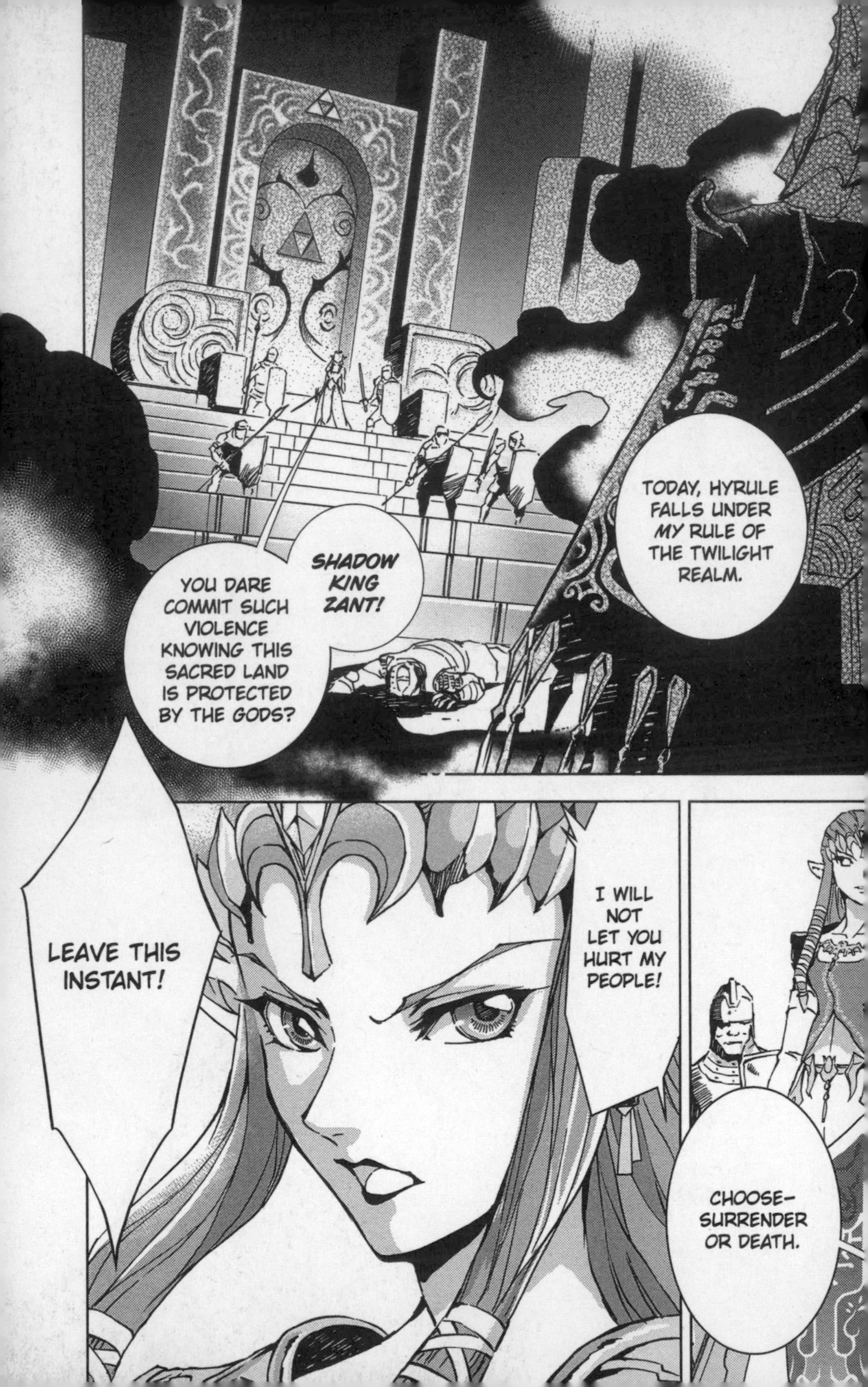
TODAY, HYRULE FALLS UNDER MY RULE OF THE TWILIGHT REALM.
SHADOW KING ZANT!
YOU DARE COMMIT SUCH VIOLENCE KNOWING THIS SACRED LAND IS PROTECTED BY THE GODS?
CHOOSE-SURRENDER OR DEATH.
I WILL NOT LET YOU HURT MY PEOPLE!
LEAVE THIS INSTANT!

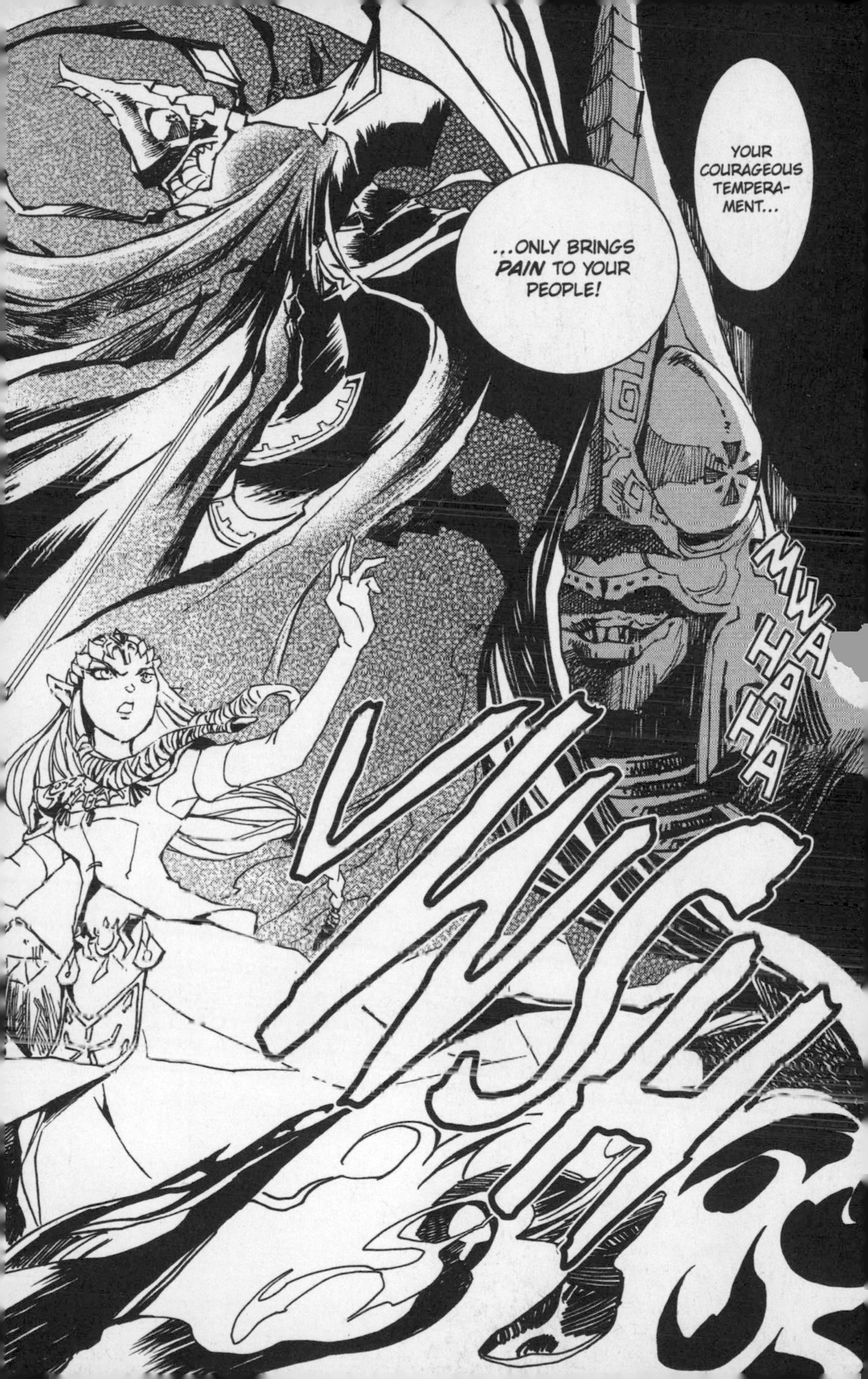
YOUR COURAGEOUS TEMPERA-MENT...
...ONLY BRINGS **PAIN** TO YOUR PEOPLE!
MWAHAHAHA

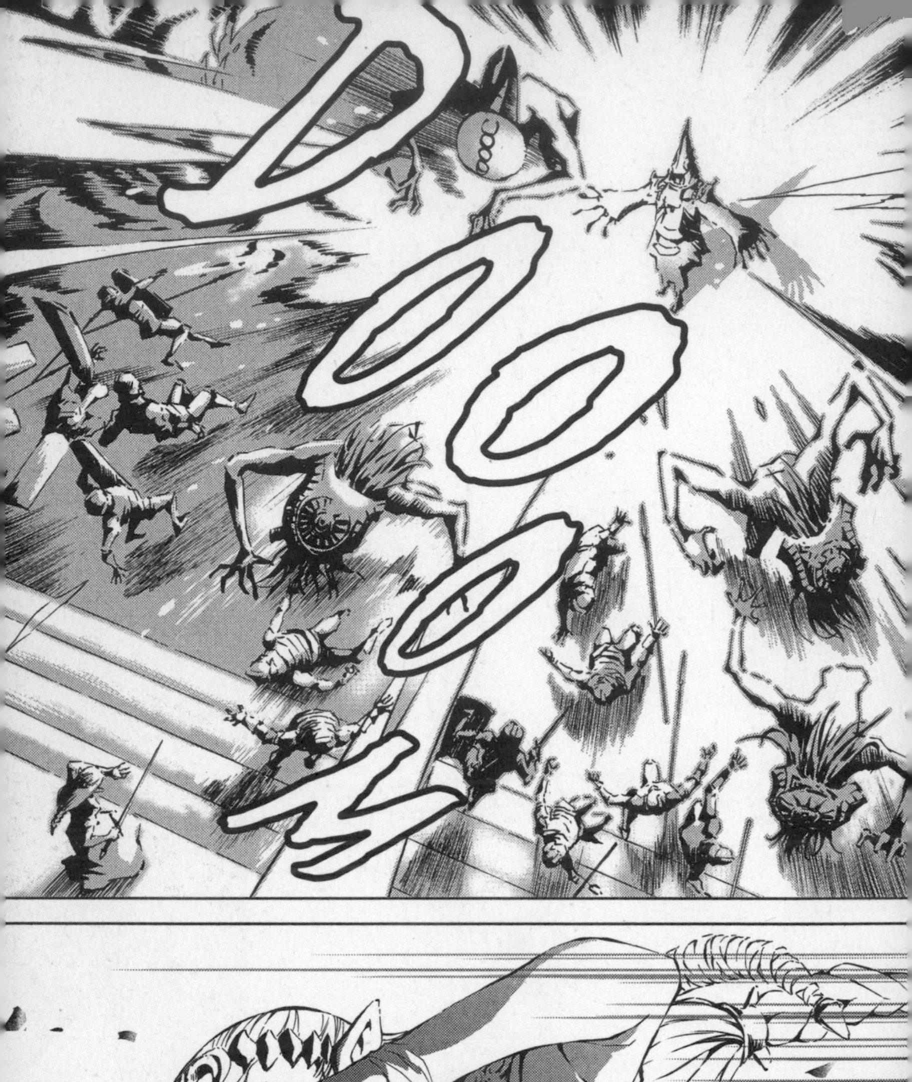
DOOOM
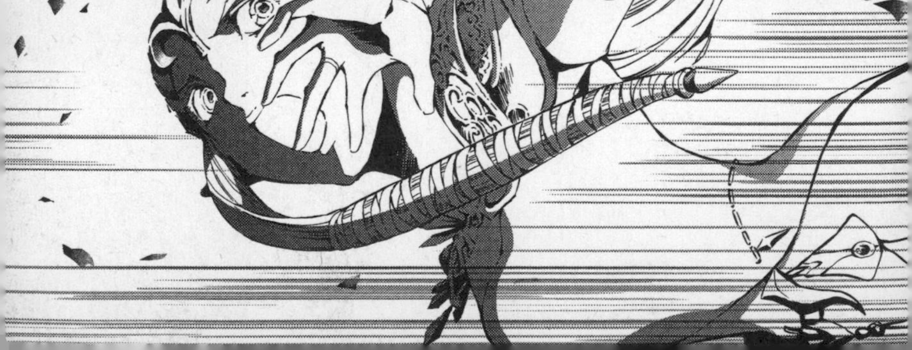

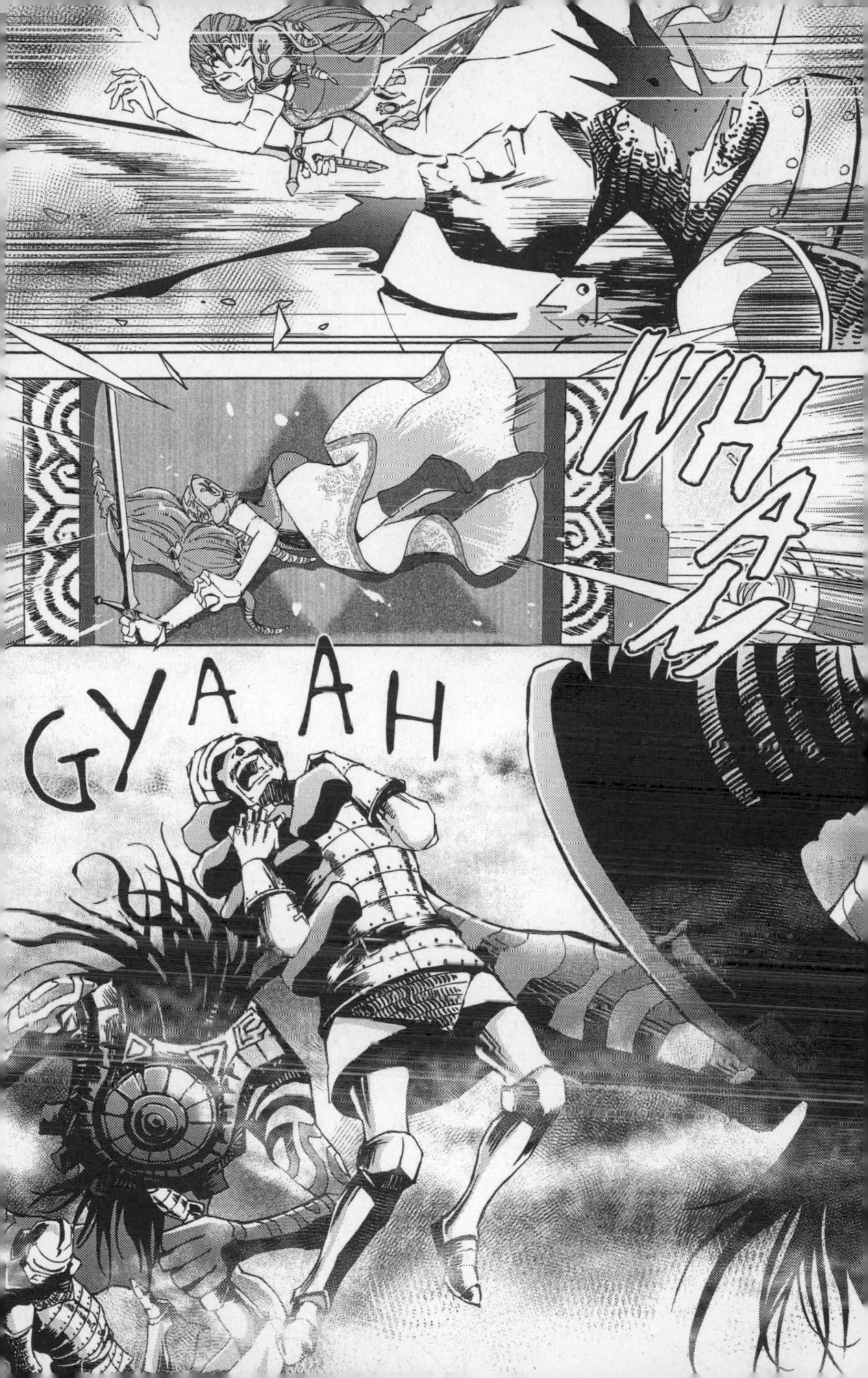
WHAM
GYAAH

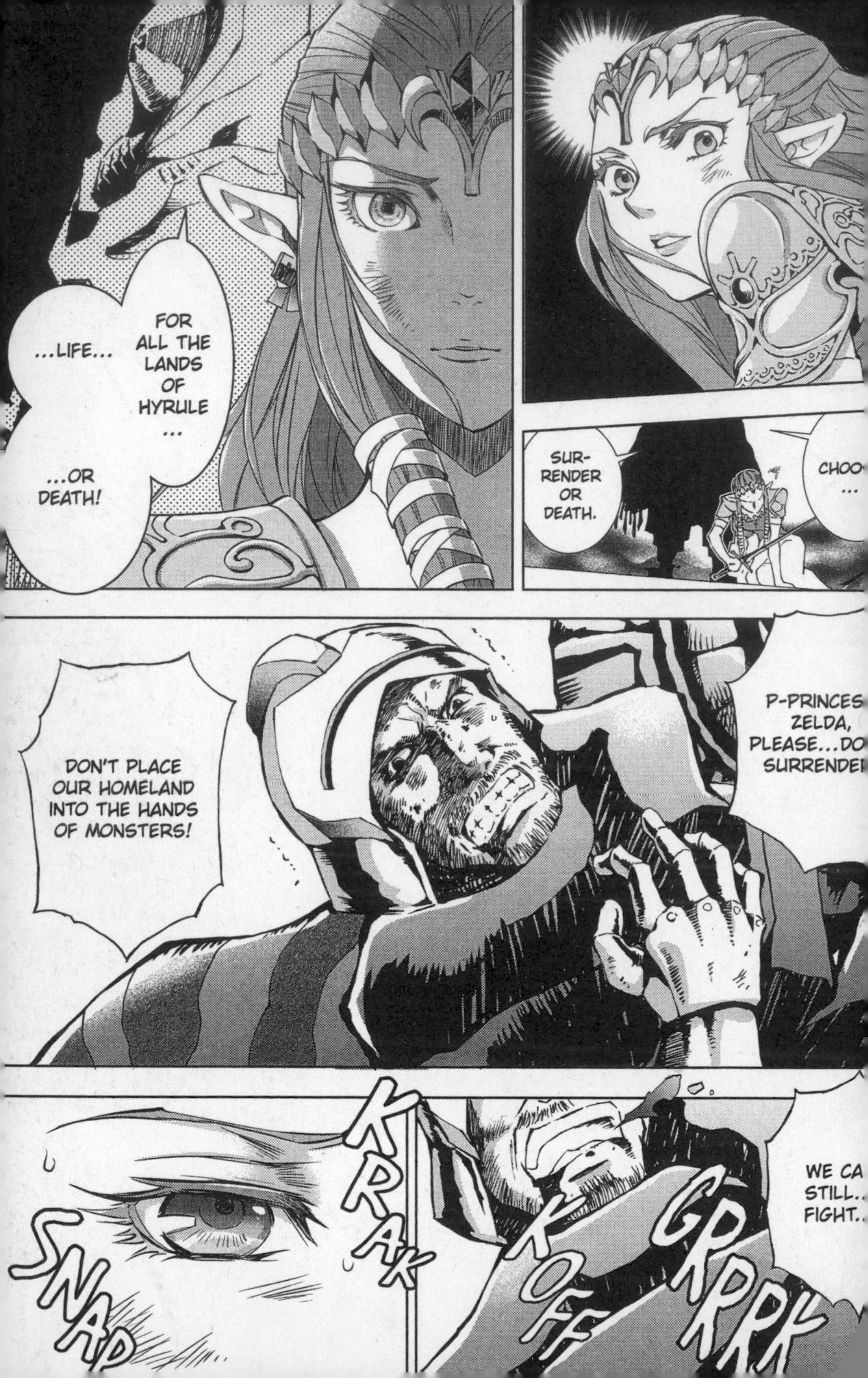
CHOO- ...
SUR-RENDER OR DEATH.
FOR ALL THE LANDS OF HYRULE ...
...LIFE...
...OR DEATH!
P-PRINCES ZELDA, PLEASE...DO SURRENDE
DON'T PLACE OUR HOMELAND INTO THE HANDS OF MONSTERS!
WE CA STILL... FIGHT...
GRRRK
KOFF
KRAK
SNAP

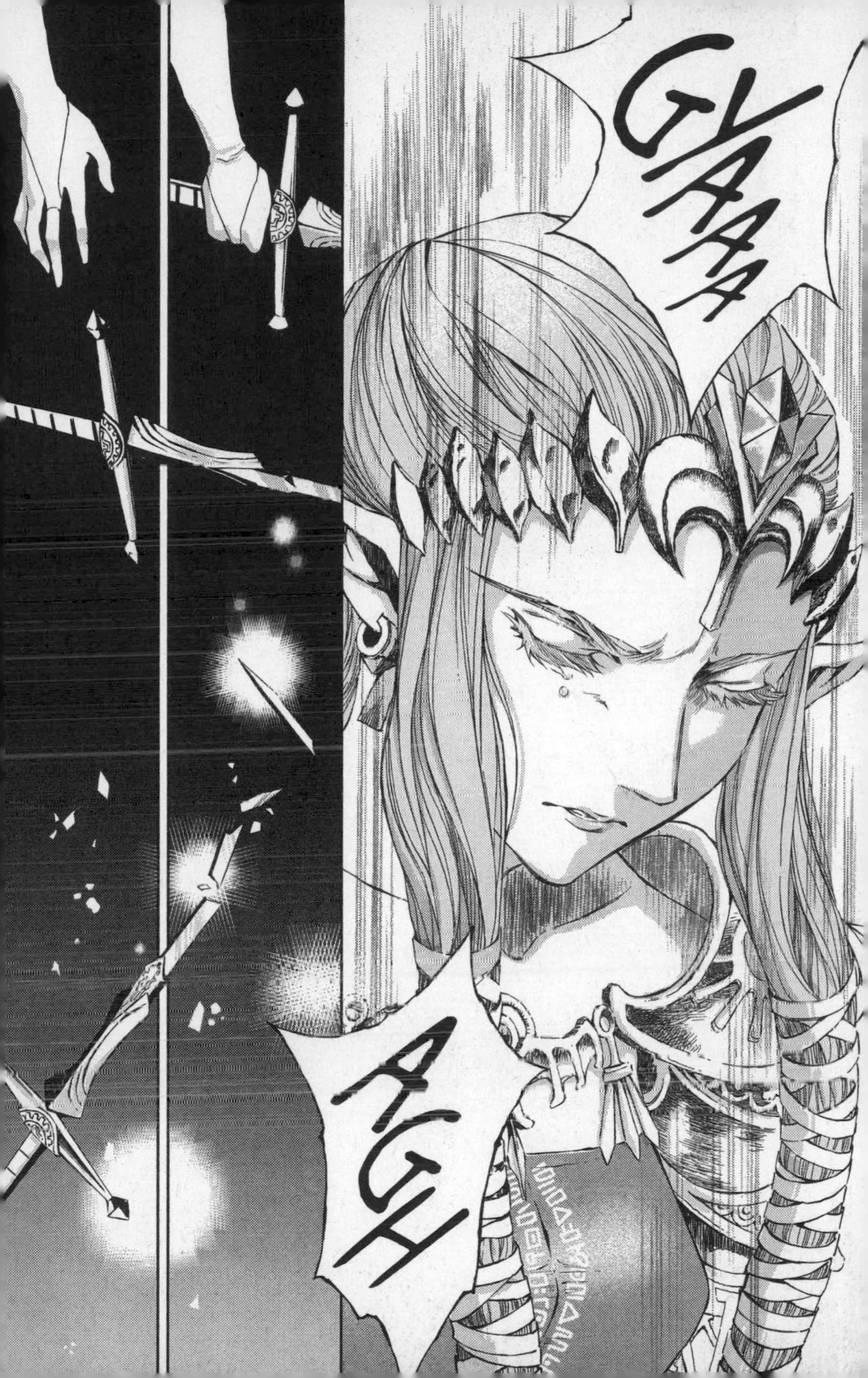
GYAAA
AGH

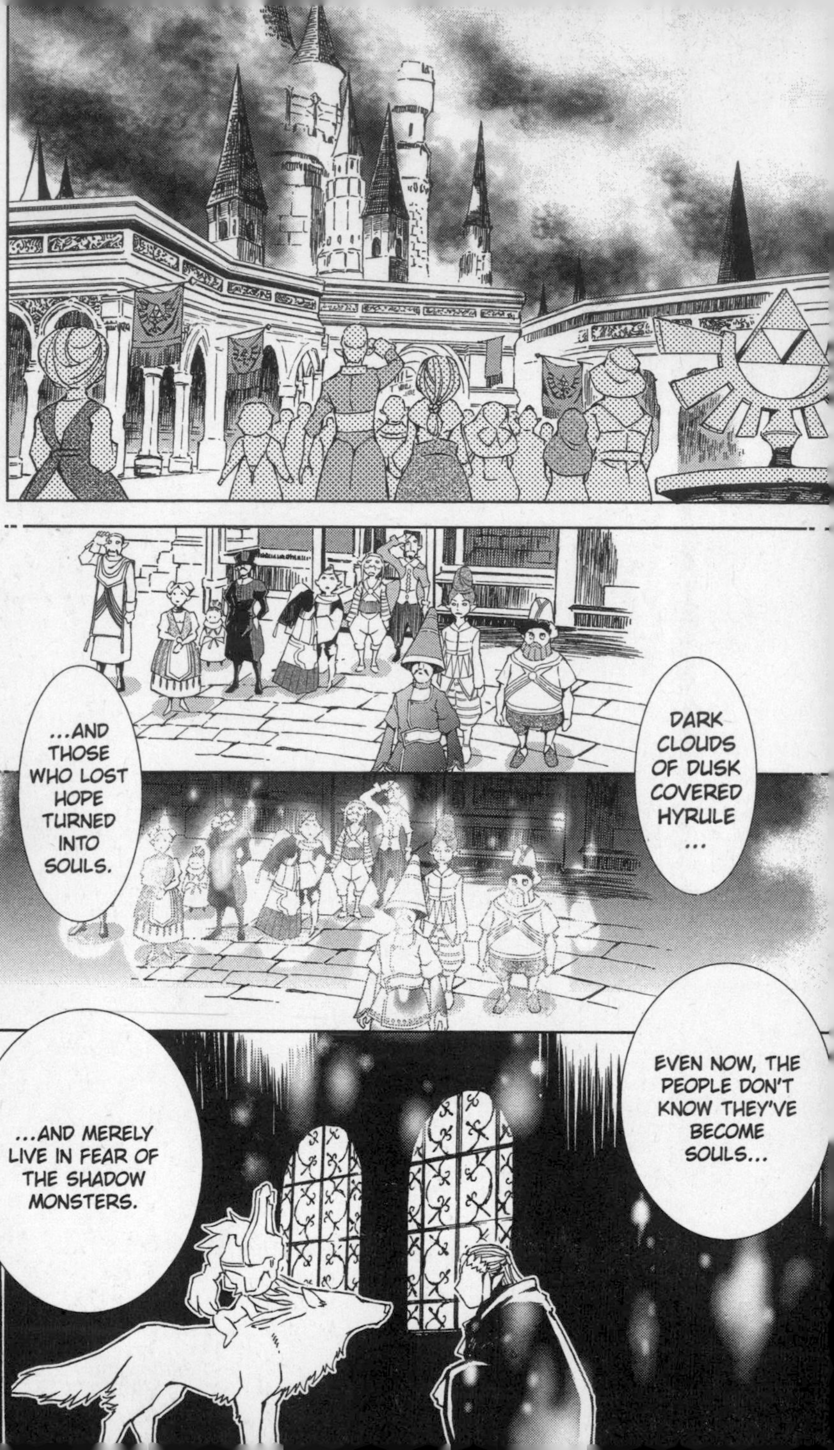
DARK CLOUDS OF DUSK COVERED HYRULE...
...AND THOSE WHO LOST HOPE TURNED INTO SOULS.
EVEN NOW, THE PEOPLE DON'T KNOW THEY'VE BECOME SOULS...
...AND MERELY LIVE IN FEAR OF THE SHADOW MONSTERS.

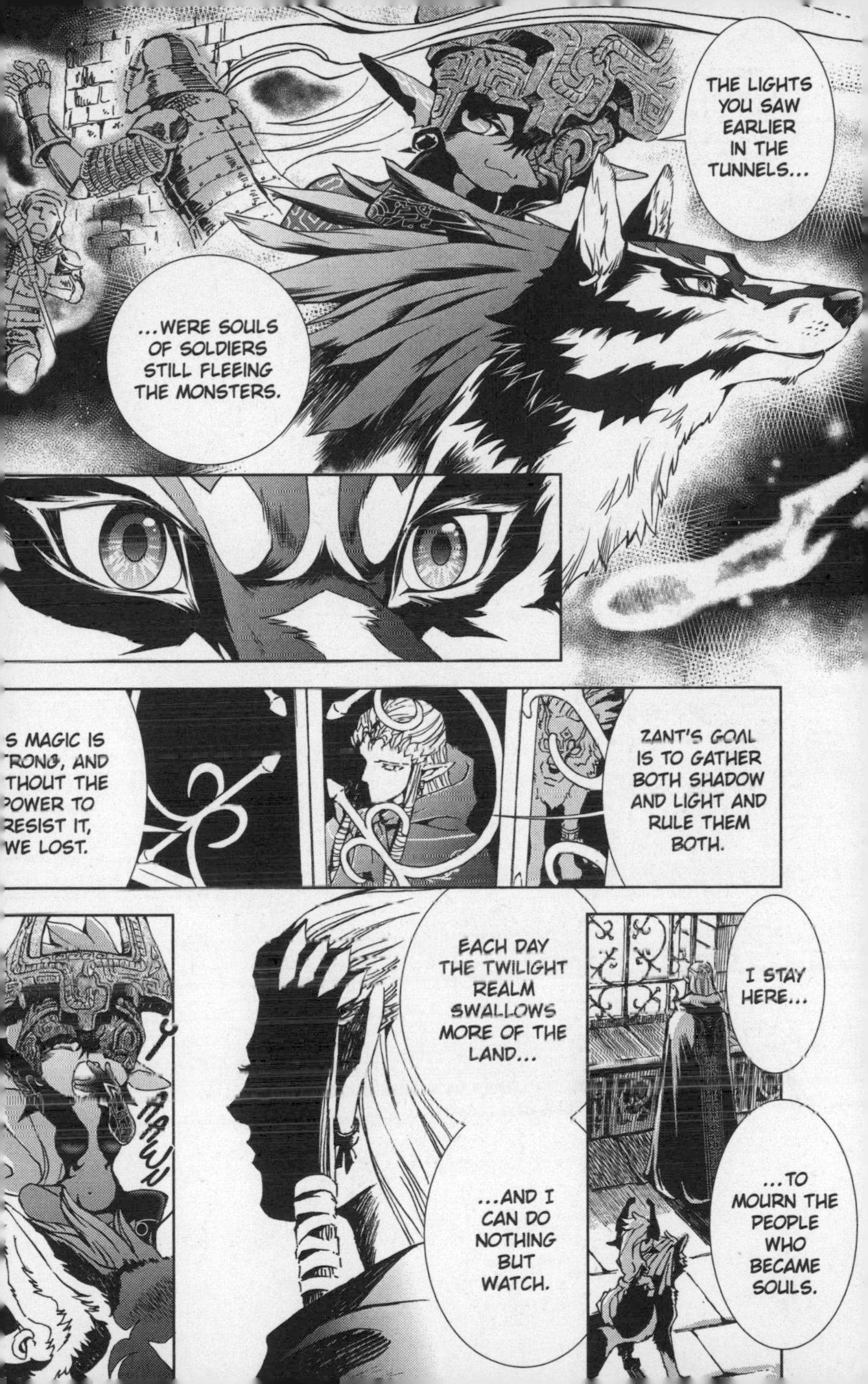
THE LIGHTS YOU SAW EARLIER IN THE TUNNELS...
...WERE SOULS OF SOLDIERS STILL FLEEING THE MONSTERS.
ZANT'S GOAL IS TO GATHER BOTH SHADOW AND LIGHT AND RULE THEM BOTH.
S MAGIC IS TRONG, AND THOUT THE POWER TO RESIST IT, WE LOST.
I STAY HERE...
...TO MOURN THE PEOPLE WHO BECAME SOULS.
EACH DAY THE TWILIGHT REALM SWALLOWS MORE OF THE LAND...
...AND I CAN DO NOTHING BUT WATCH.

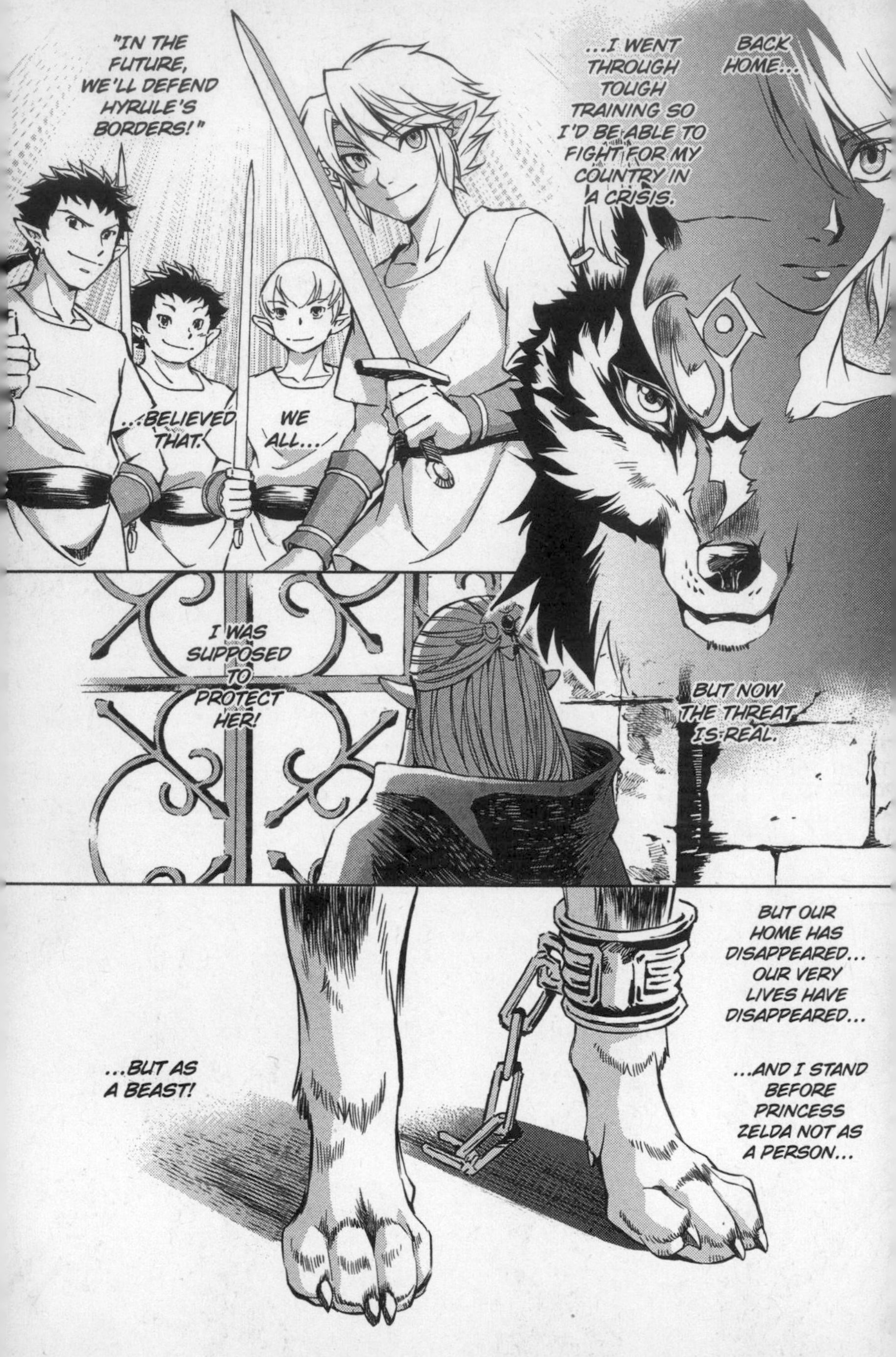
BACK HOME...
...I WENT THROUGH TOUGH TRAINING SO I'D BE ABLE TO FIGHT FOR MY COUNTRY IN A CRISIS.
"IN THE FUTURE, WE'LL DEFEND HYRULE'S BORDERS!"
WE ALL...
...BELIEVED THAT.
BUT NOW THE THREAT IS REAL.
I WAS SUPPOSED TO PROTECT HER!
BUT OUR HOME HAS DISAPPEARED... OUR VERY LIVES HAVE DISAPPEARED...
...AND I STAND BEFORE PRINCESS ZELDA NOT AS A PERSON...
...BUT AS A BEAST!

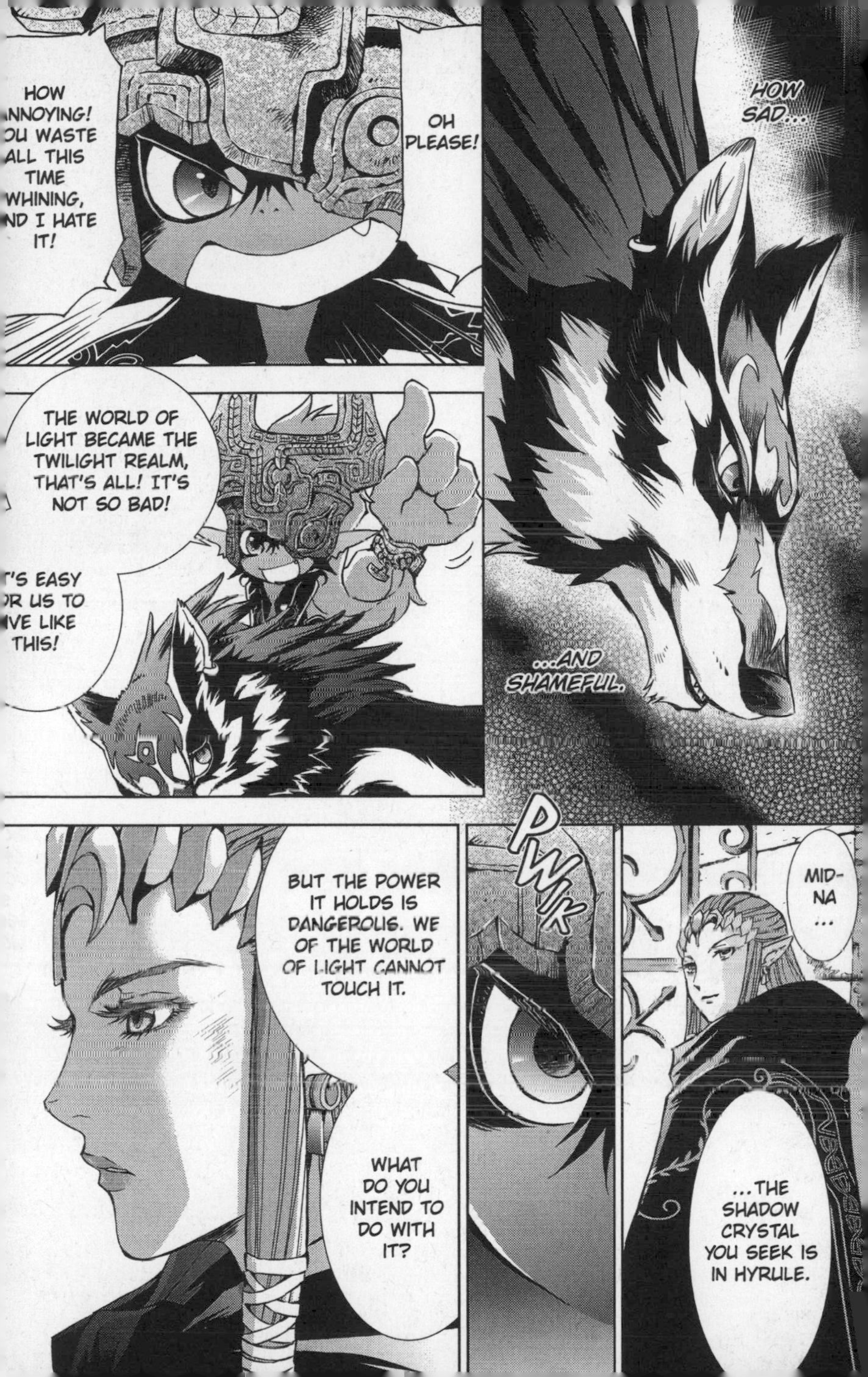
HOW SAD...
...AND SHAMEFUL.
OH PLEASE!
HOW NNOYING! OU WASTE ALL THIS TIME WHINING, ND I HATE IT!
THE WORLD OF LIGHT BECAME THE TWILIGHT REALM, THAT'S ALL! IT'S NOT SO BAD!
'S EASY R US TO VE LIKE THIS!
MID-NA ...
...THE SHADOW CRYSTAL YOU SEEK IS IN HYRULE.
PWIK
BUT THE POWER IT HOLDS IS DANGEROUS. WE OF THE WORLD OF LIGHT CANNOT TOUCH IT.
WHAT DO YOU INTEND TO DO WITH IT?

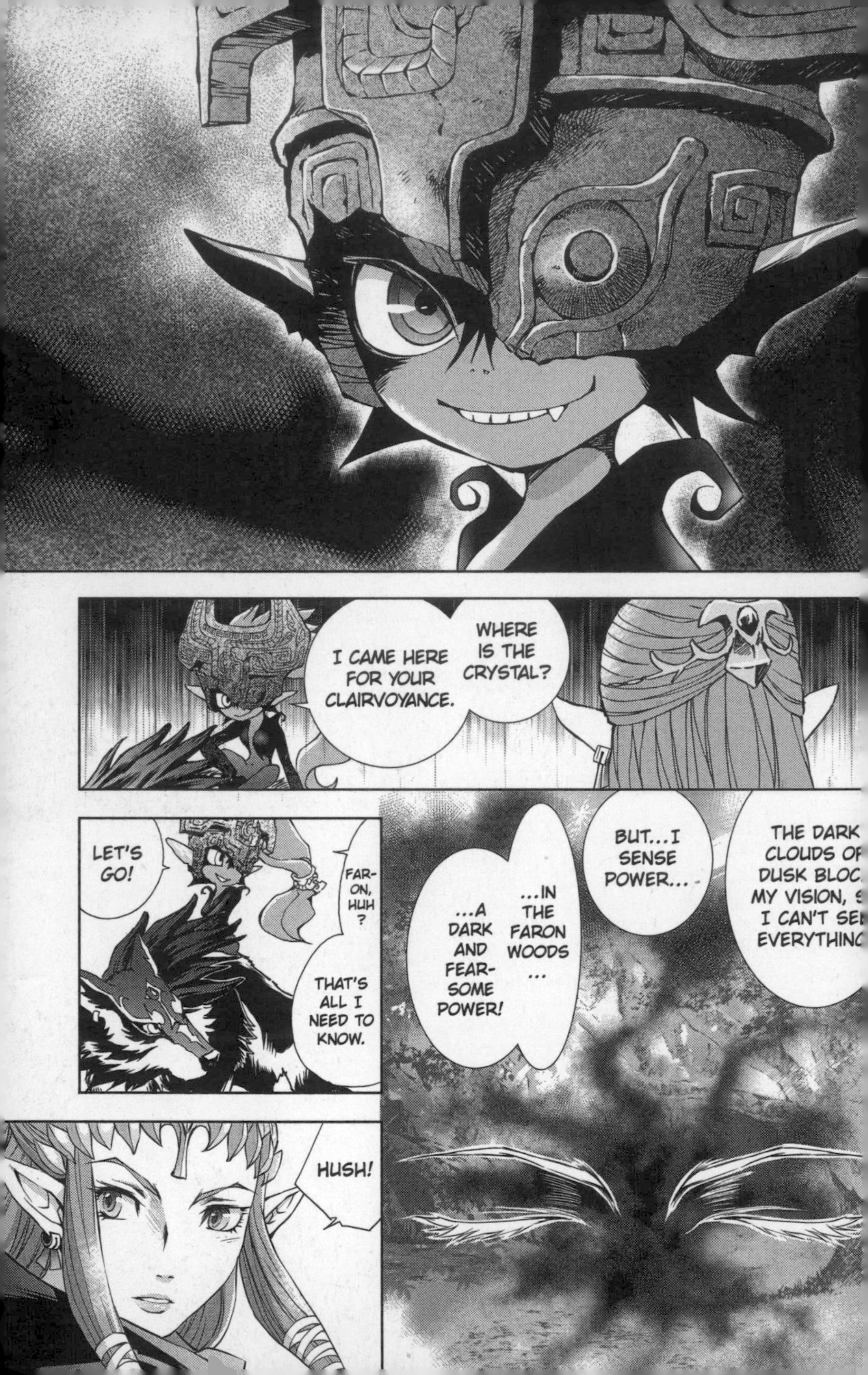
WHERE IS THE CRYSTAL?
I CAME HERE FOR YOUR CLAIRVOYANCE.
THE DARK CLOUDS OF DUSK BLOC MY VISION, I CAN'T SE EVERYTHIN
BUT...I SENSE POWER...
...IN THE FARON WOODS...
...A DARK AND FEAR-SOME POWER!
FAR-ON, HUH?
THAT'S ALL I NEED TO KNOW.
LET'S GO!
HUSH!

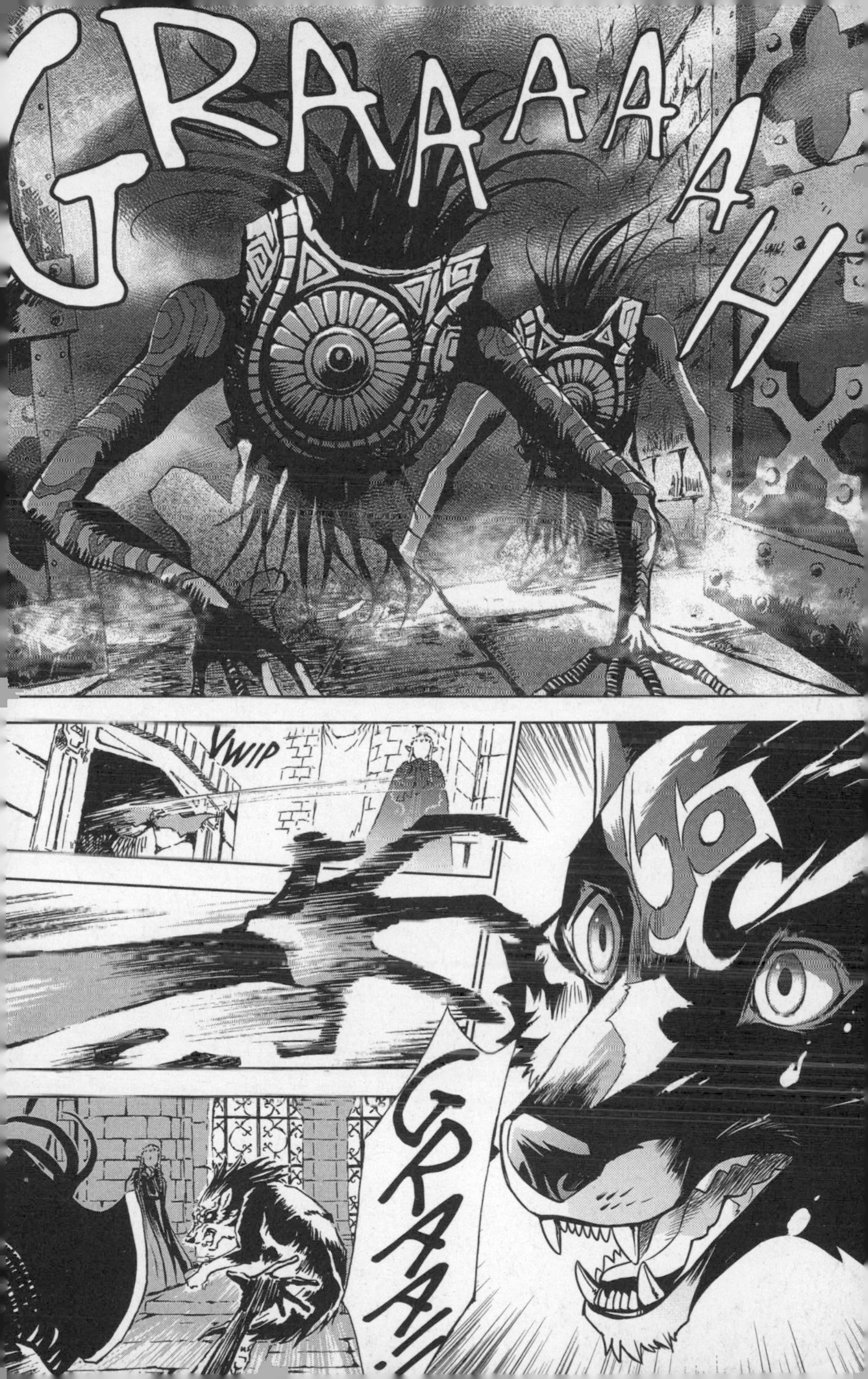
GRAAAAAH
VWIP
GRAA!!

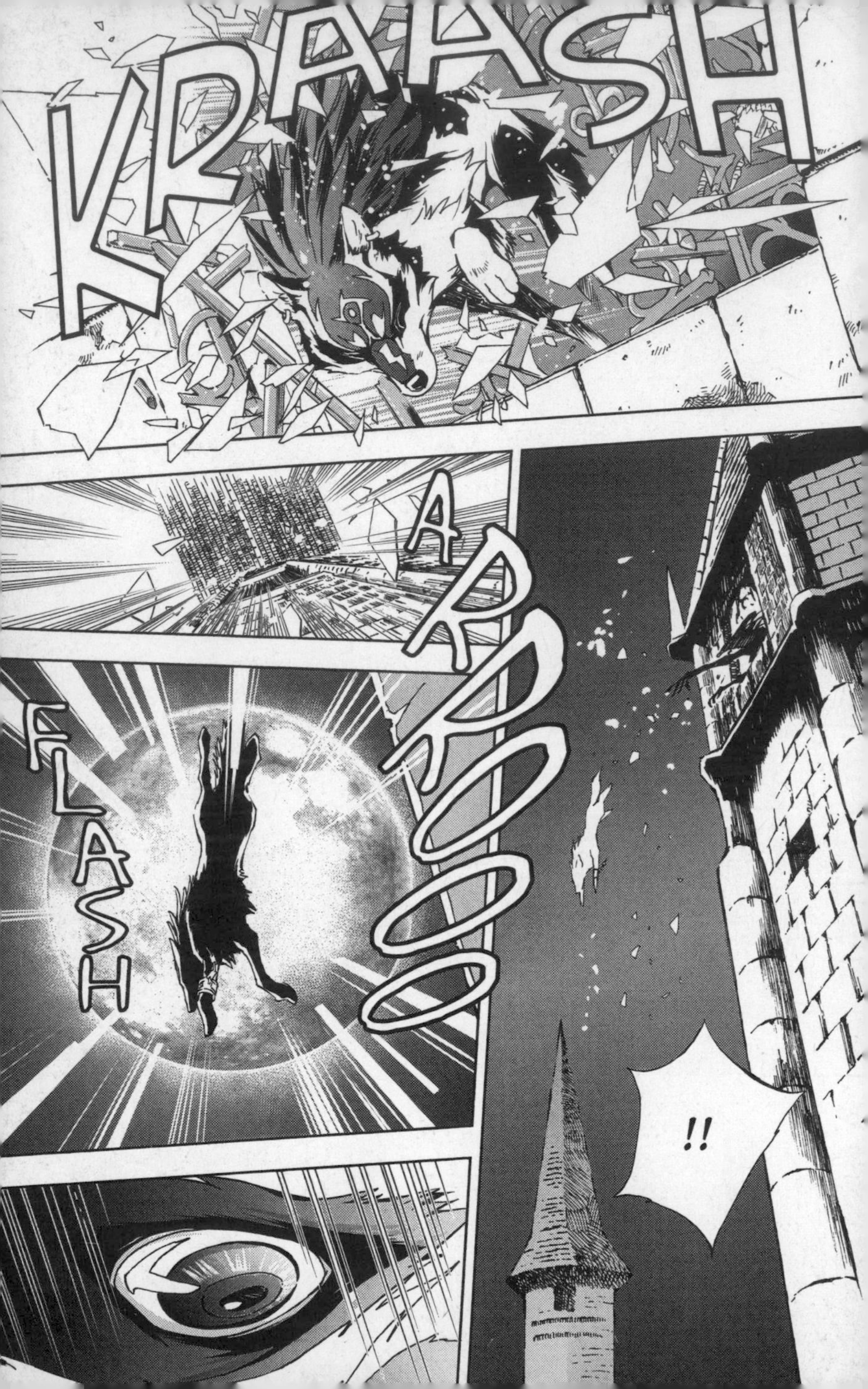
KRASH
ARROOOO
!!
FLASH

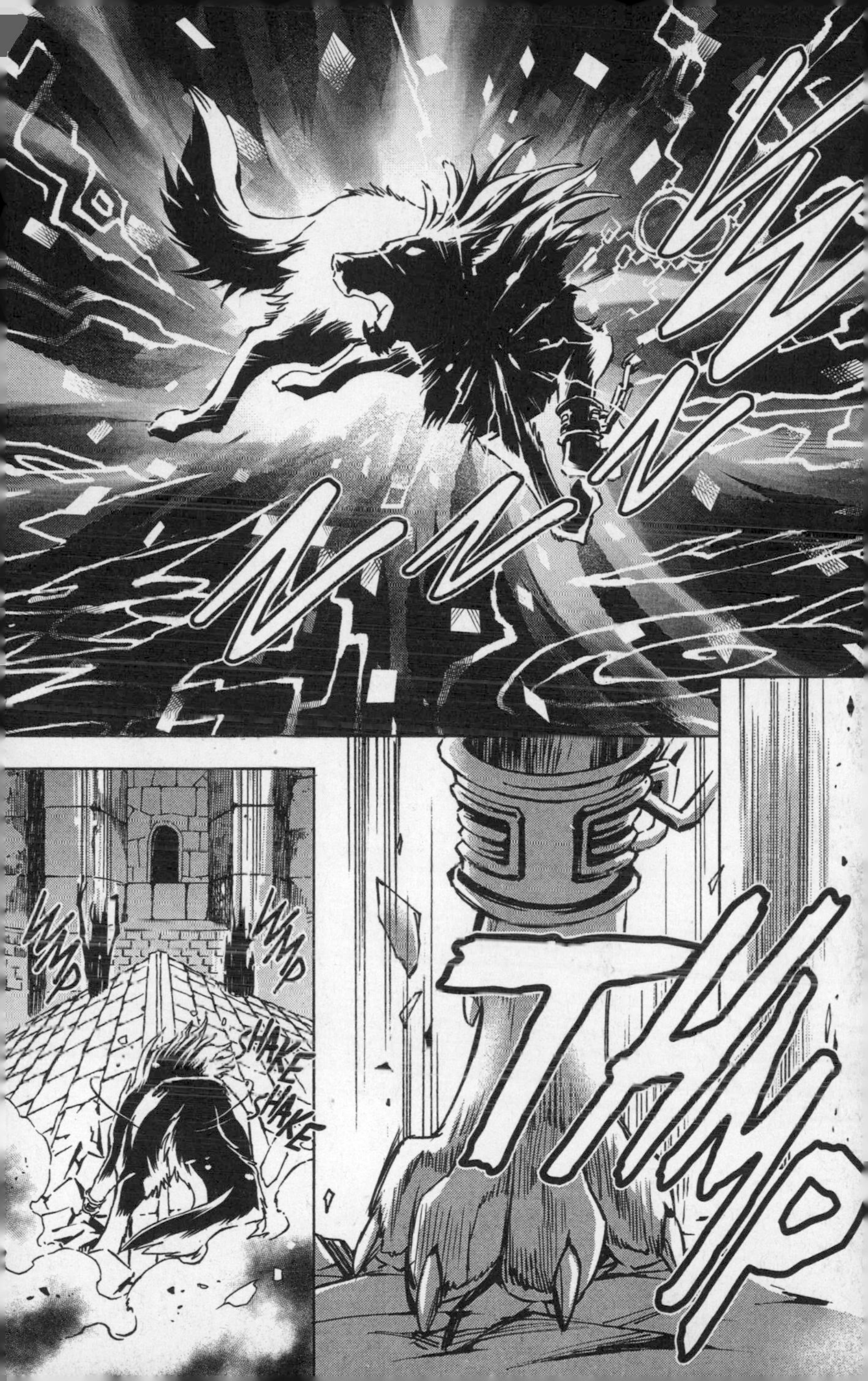
THMP
WMMP
WMMP
SHAKE
SHAKE

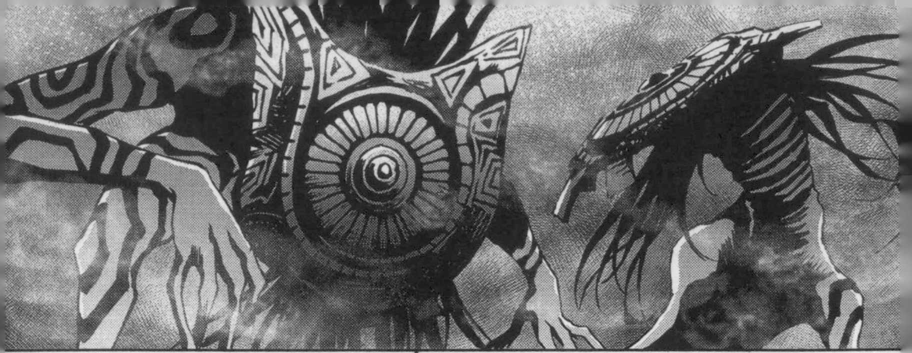
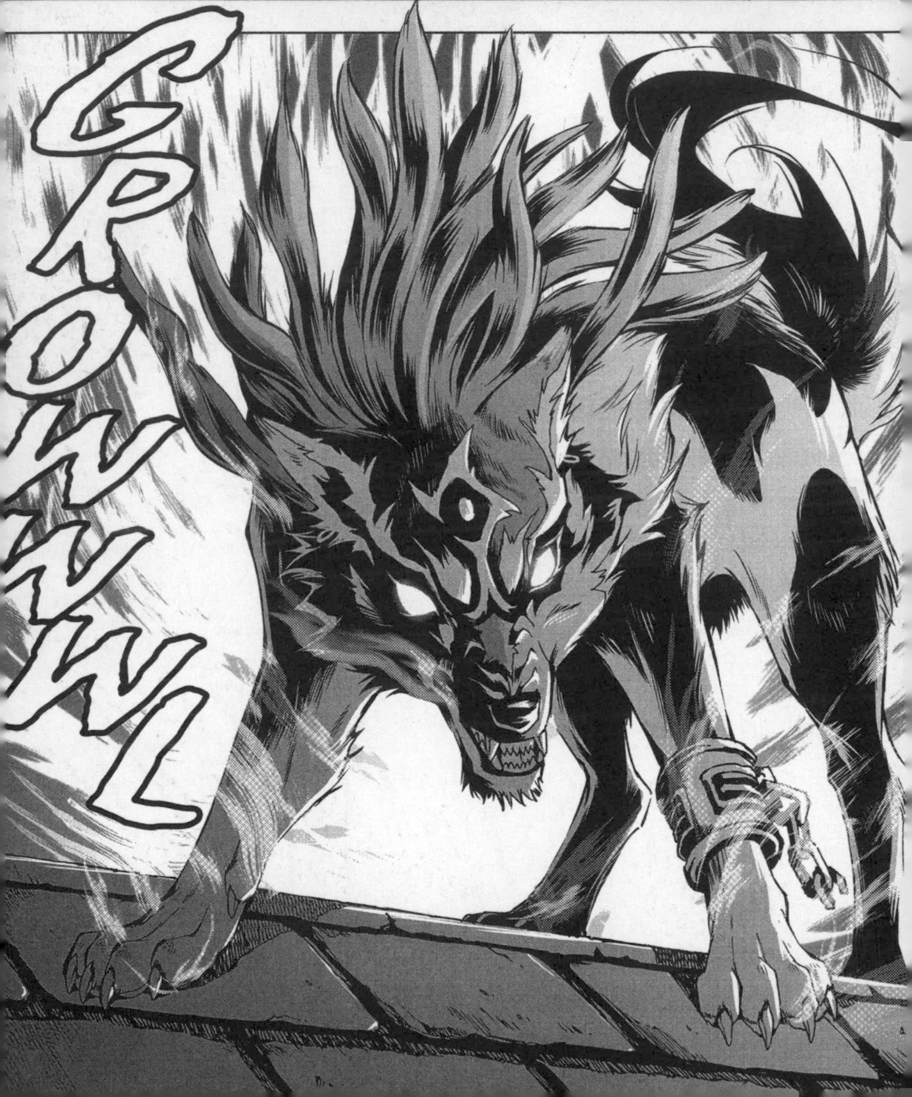
GROWWWL

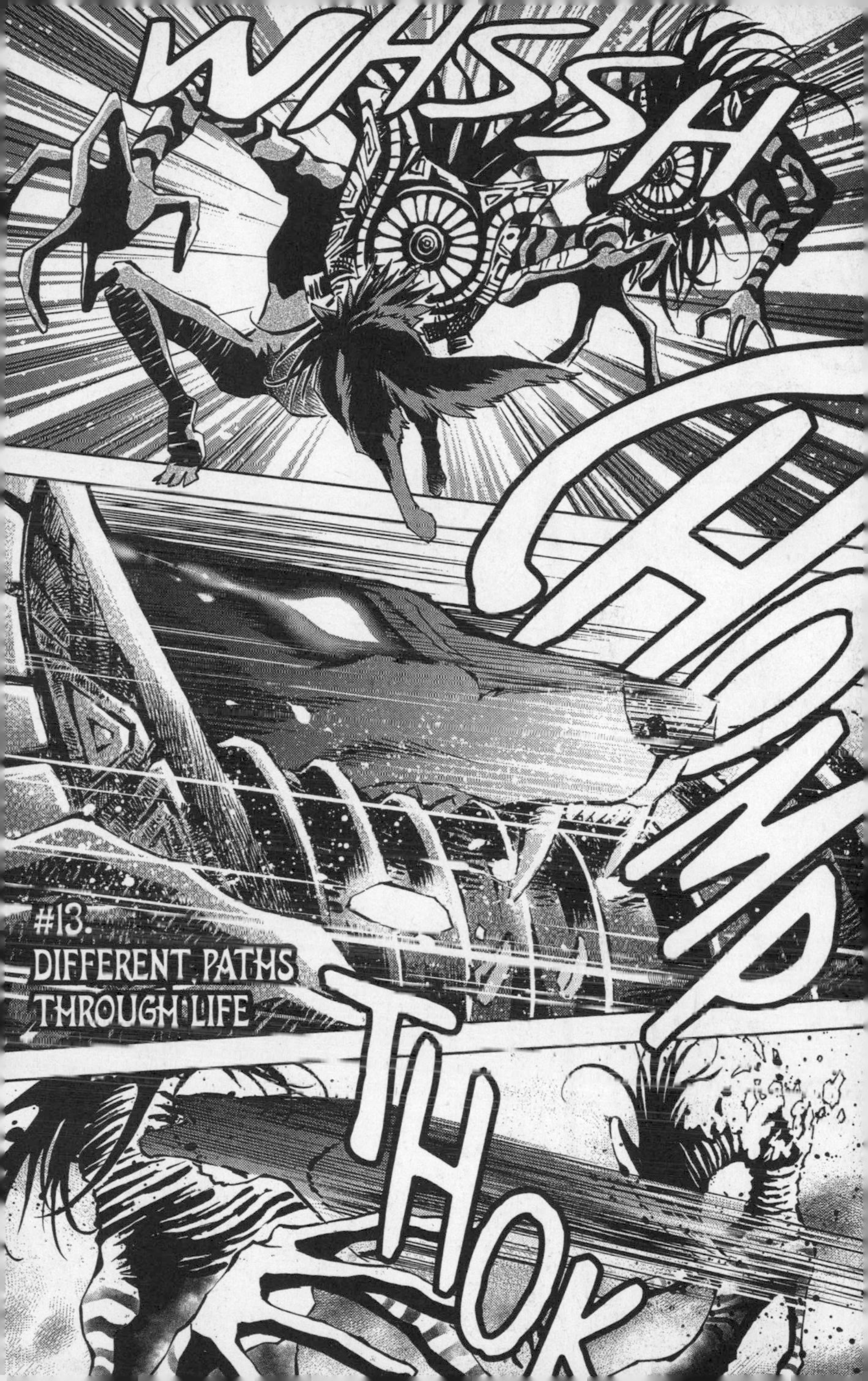
WHSSH
CHOMP
#13.
DIFFERENT PATHS THROUGH LIFE
THOK

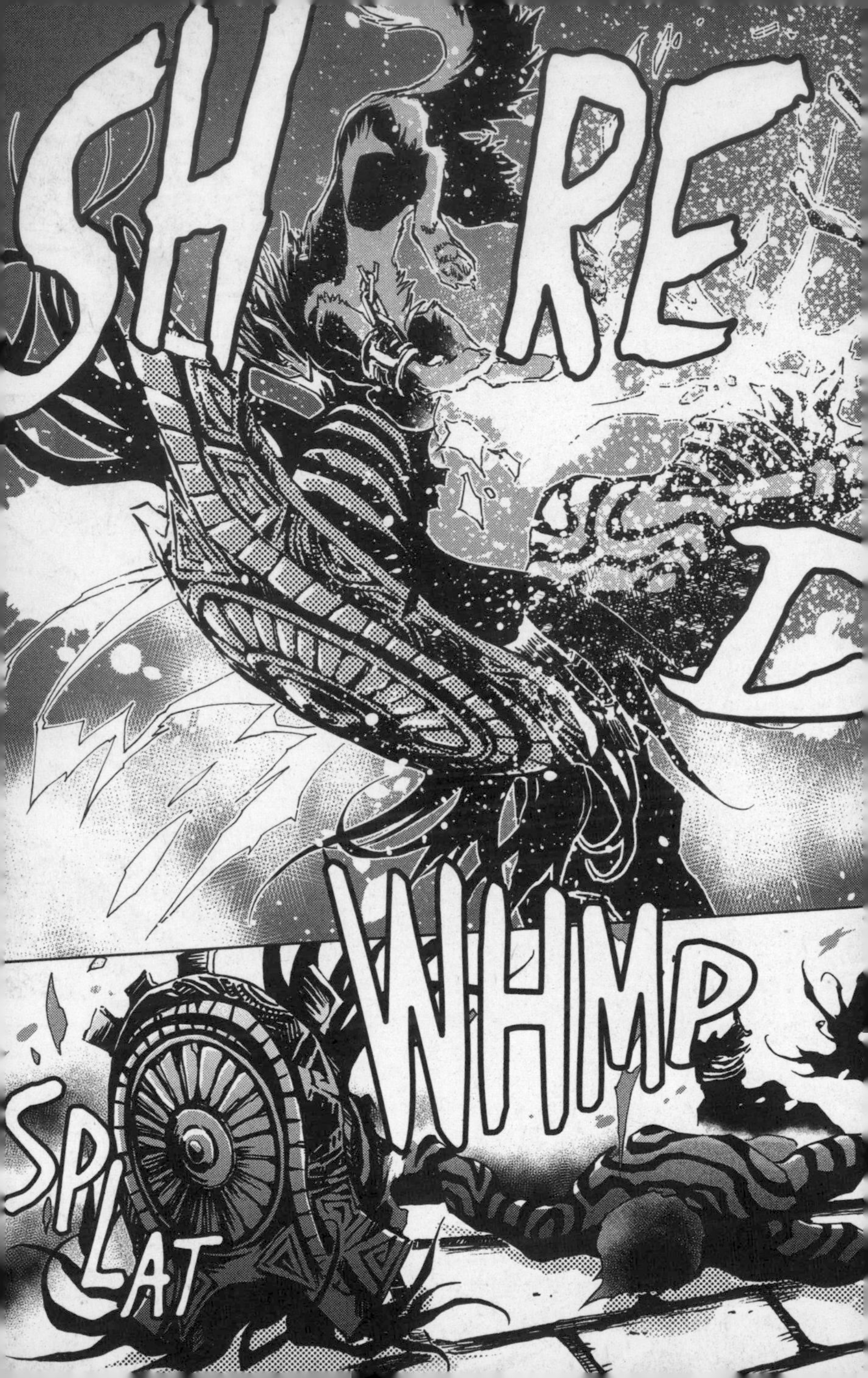
SHRED
WHMP
SPLAT

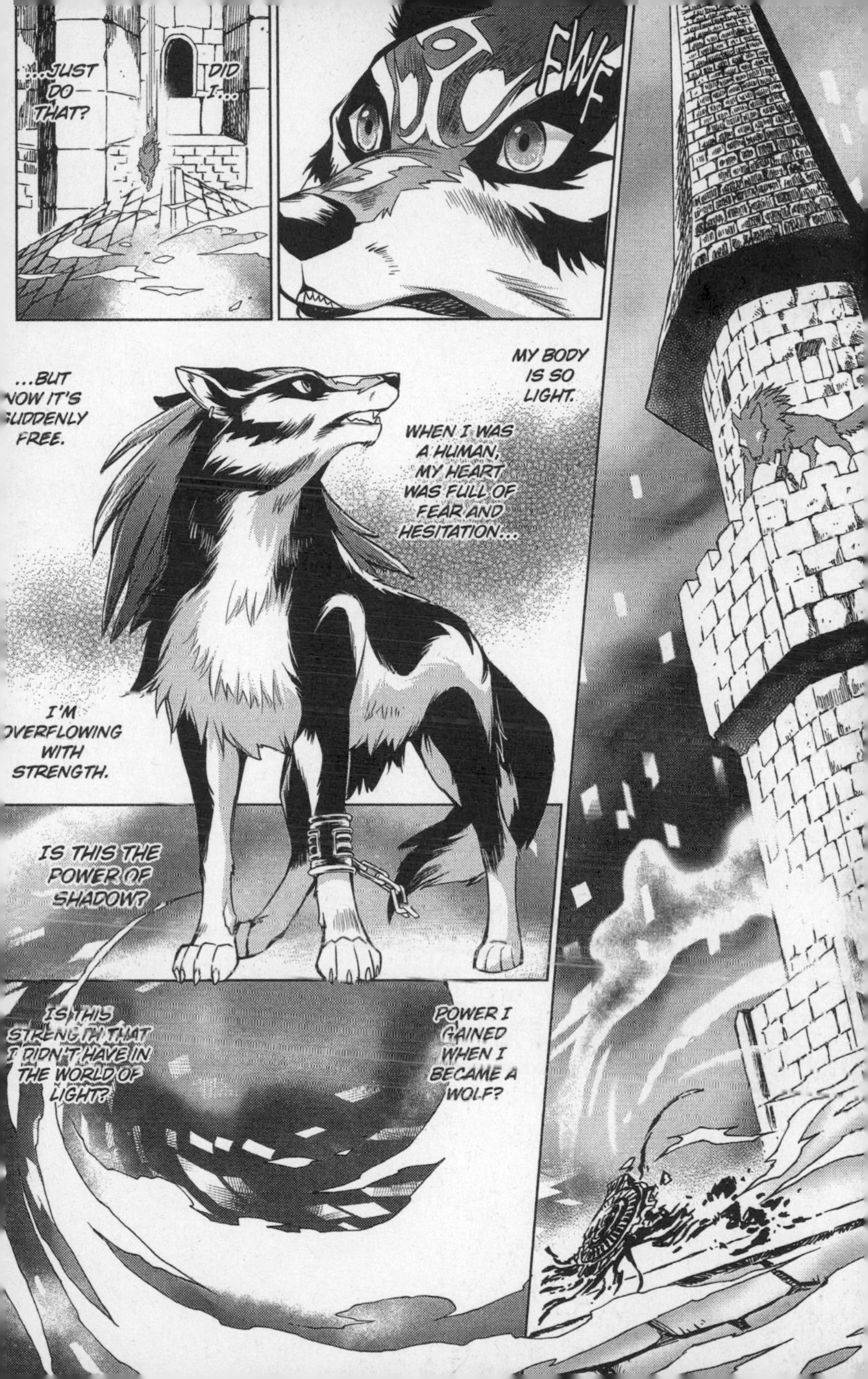
FWF
DID I...
...JUST DO— THAT?
MY BODY IS SO LIGHT.
WHEN I WAS A HUMAN, MY HEART WAS FULL OF FEAR AND HESITATION...
...BUT NOW IT'S SUDDENLY FREE.
I'M OVERFLOWING WITH STRENGTH.
IS THIS THE POWER OF SHADOW?
POWER I GAINED WHEN I BECAME A WOLF?
IS THIS STRENGTH THAT I DIDN'T HAVE IN THE WORLD OF LIGHT?

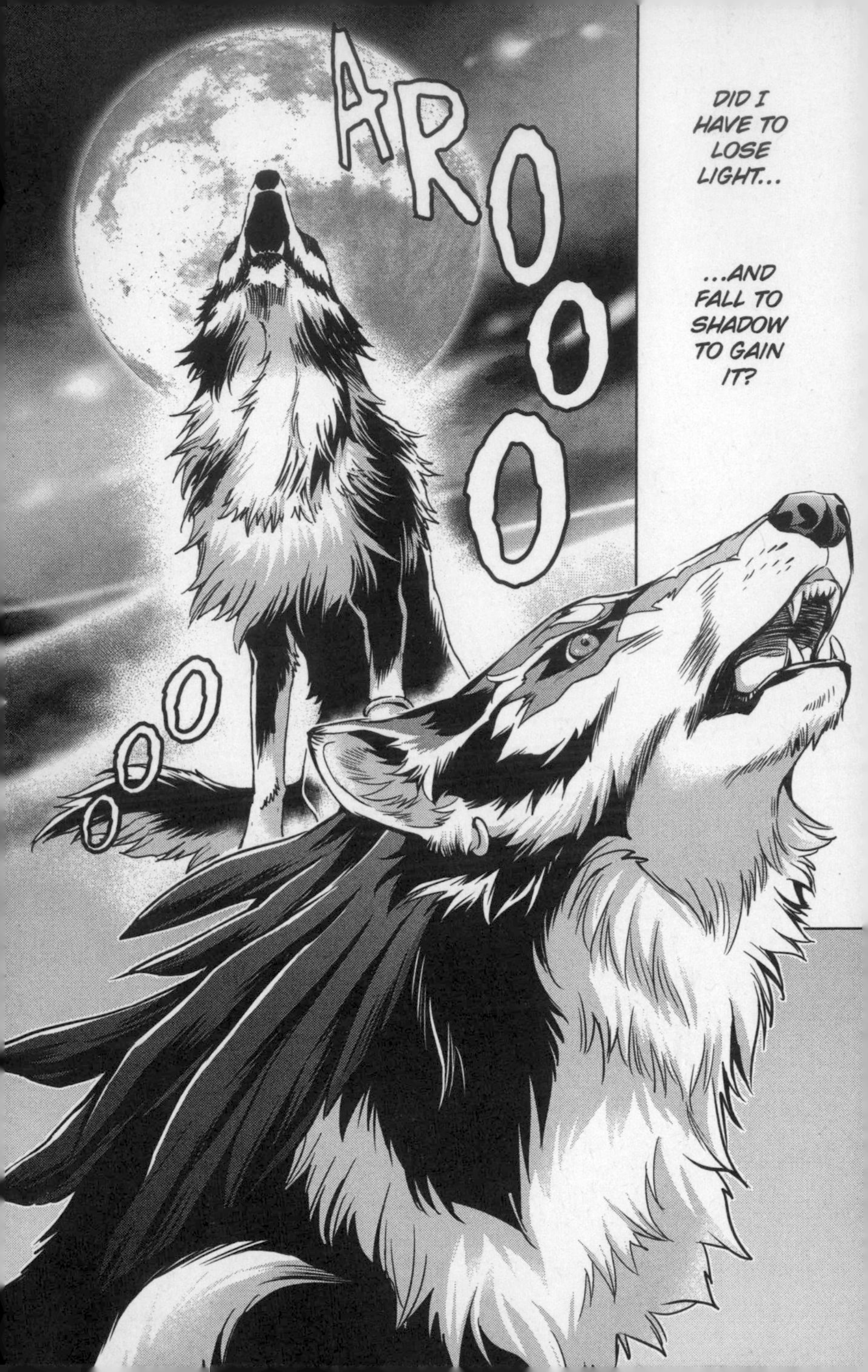
DID I HAVE TO LOSE LIGHT...
...AND FALL TO SHADOW TO GAIN IT?
AROOOOOOO

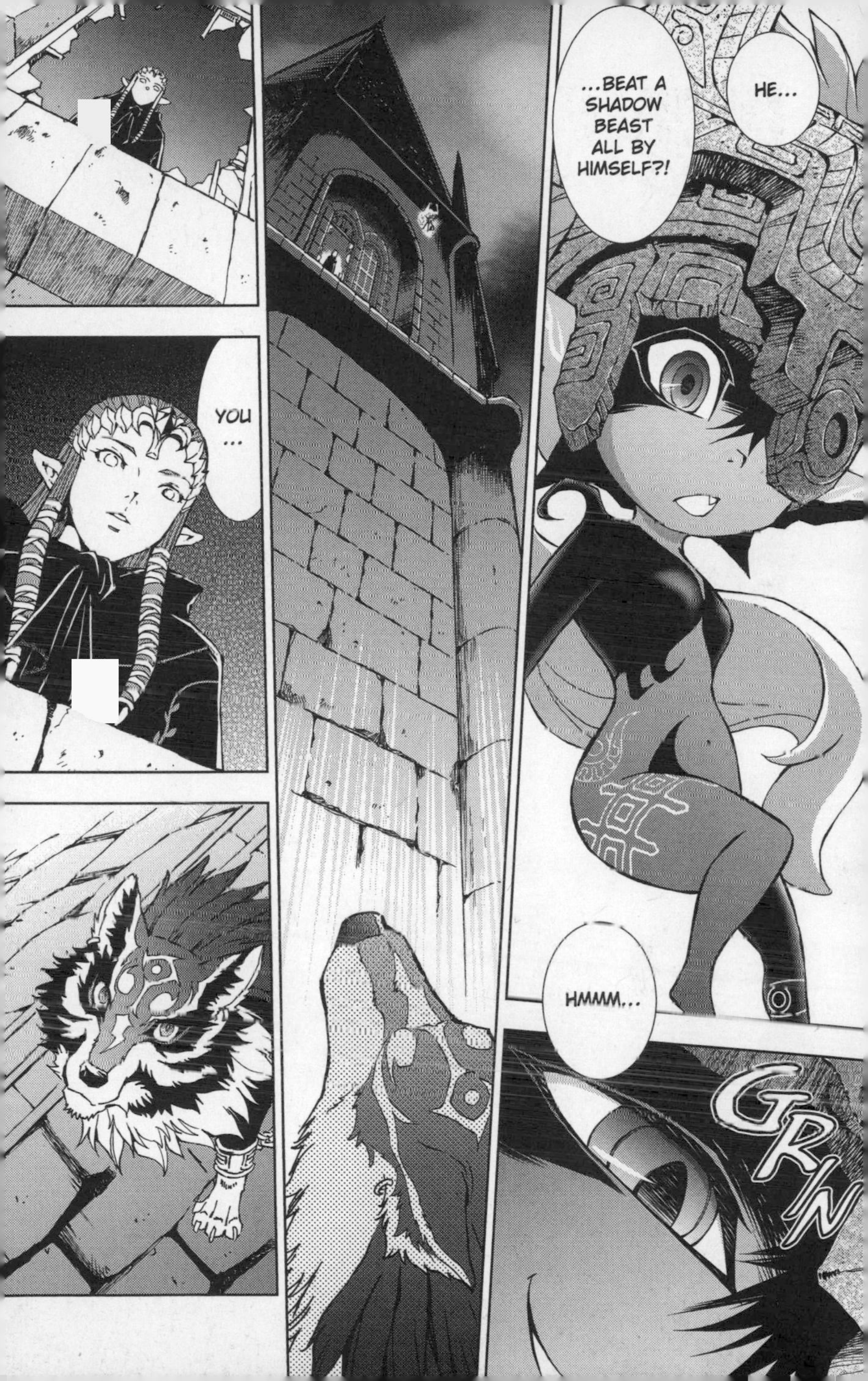
HE...
...BEAT A SHADOW BEAST ALL BY HIMSELF?!
HMMM...
GRN
YOU ...

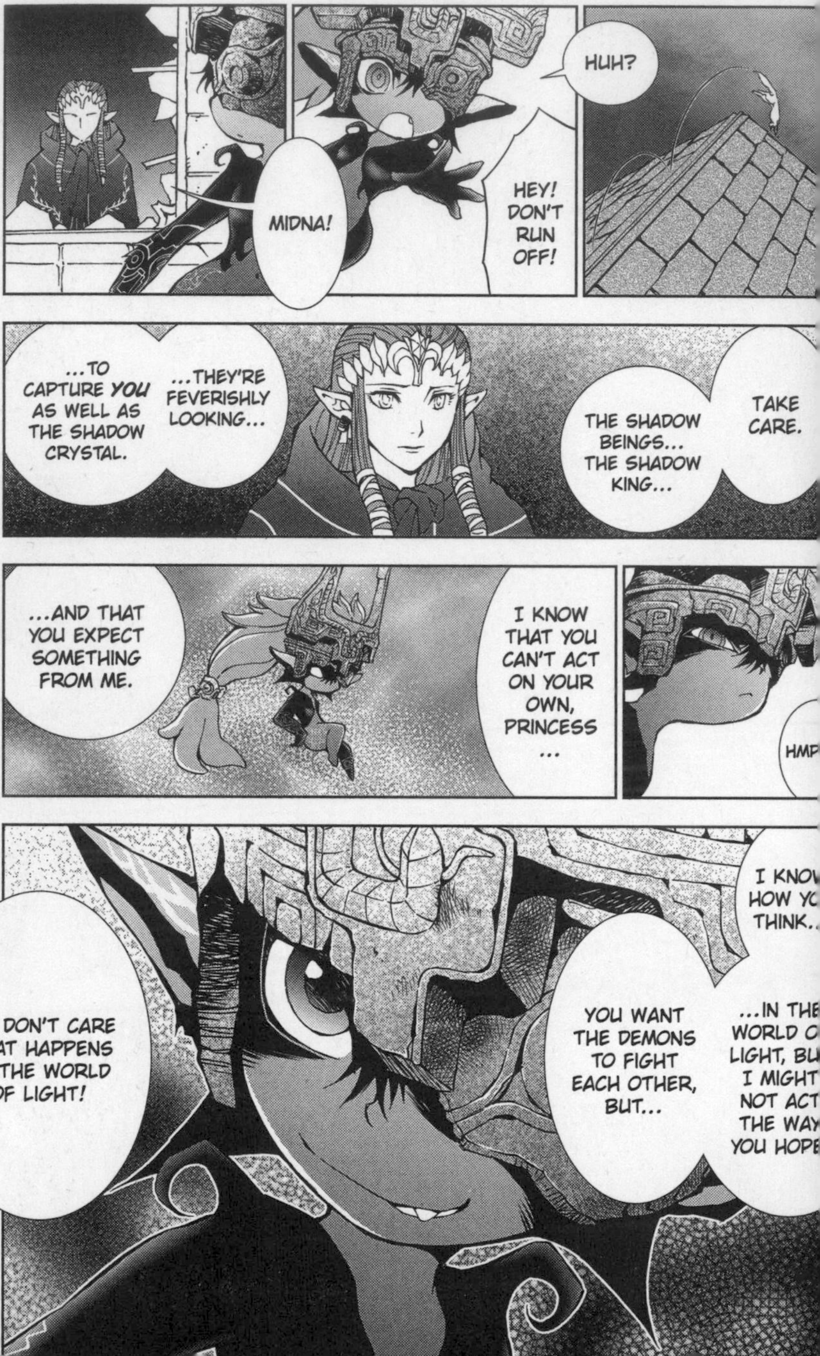
HUH?
HEY! DON'T RUN OFF!
MIDNA!
TAKE CARE.
THE SHADOW BEINGS... THE SHADOW KING...
...THEY'RE FEVERISHLY LOOKING...
...TO CAPTURE *YOU* AS WELL AS THE SHADOW CRYSTAL.
HMP
I KNOW THAT YOU CAN'T ACT ON YOUR OWN, PRINCESS ...
...AND THAT YOU EXPECT SOMETHING FROM ME.
I KNOW HOW YO THINK..
...IN THE WORLD O LIGHT, BU I MIGHT NOT ACT THE WAY YOU HOPE
YOU WANT THE DEMONS TO FIGHT EACH OTHER, BUT...
...I DON'T CARE WHAT HAPPENS TO THE WORLD OF LIGHT!

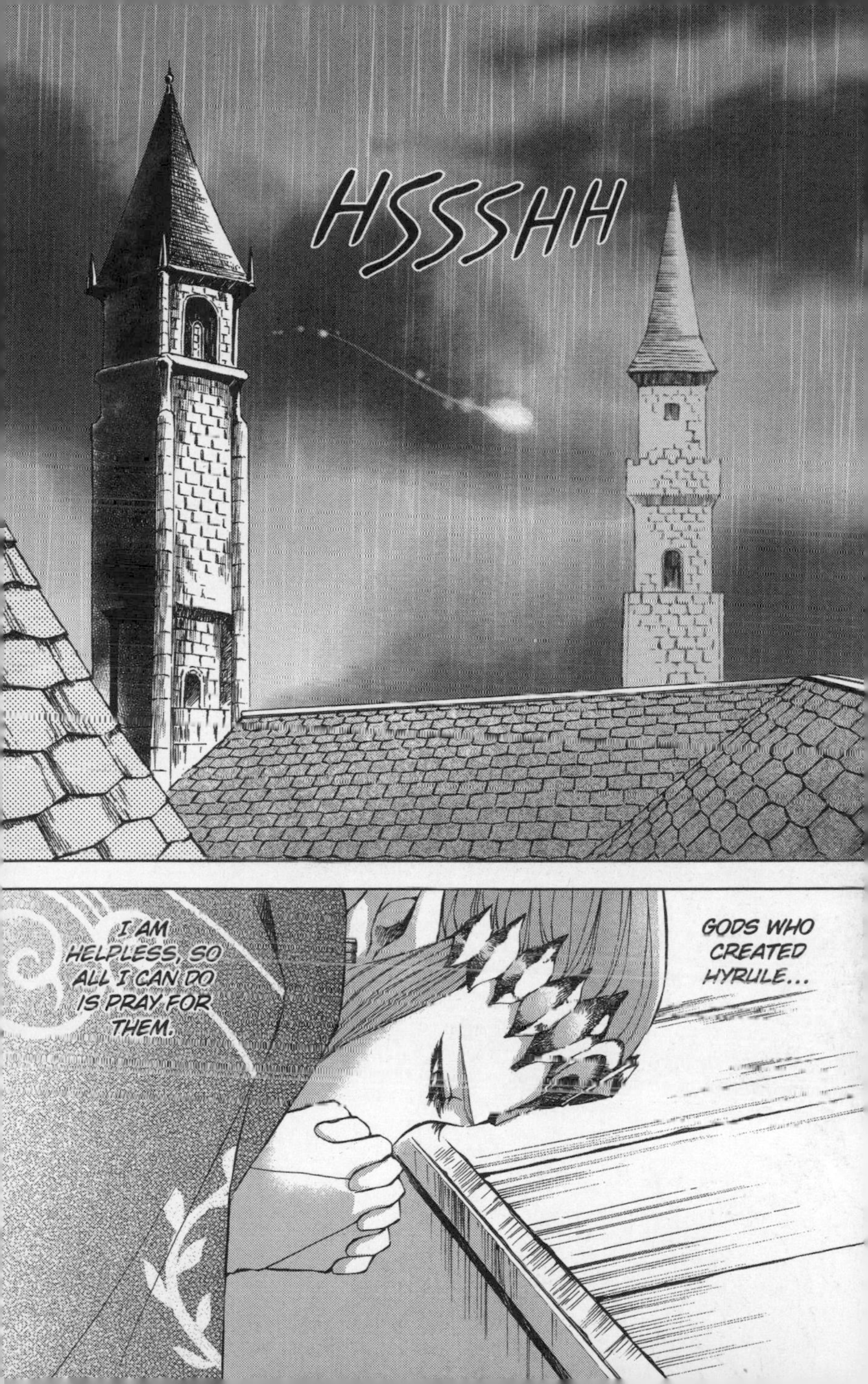
HSSSHH
GODS WHO CREATED HYRULE...
I AM HELPLESS, SO ALL I CAN DO IS PRAY FOR THEM.

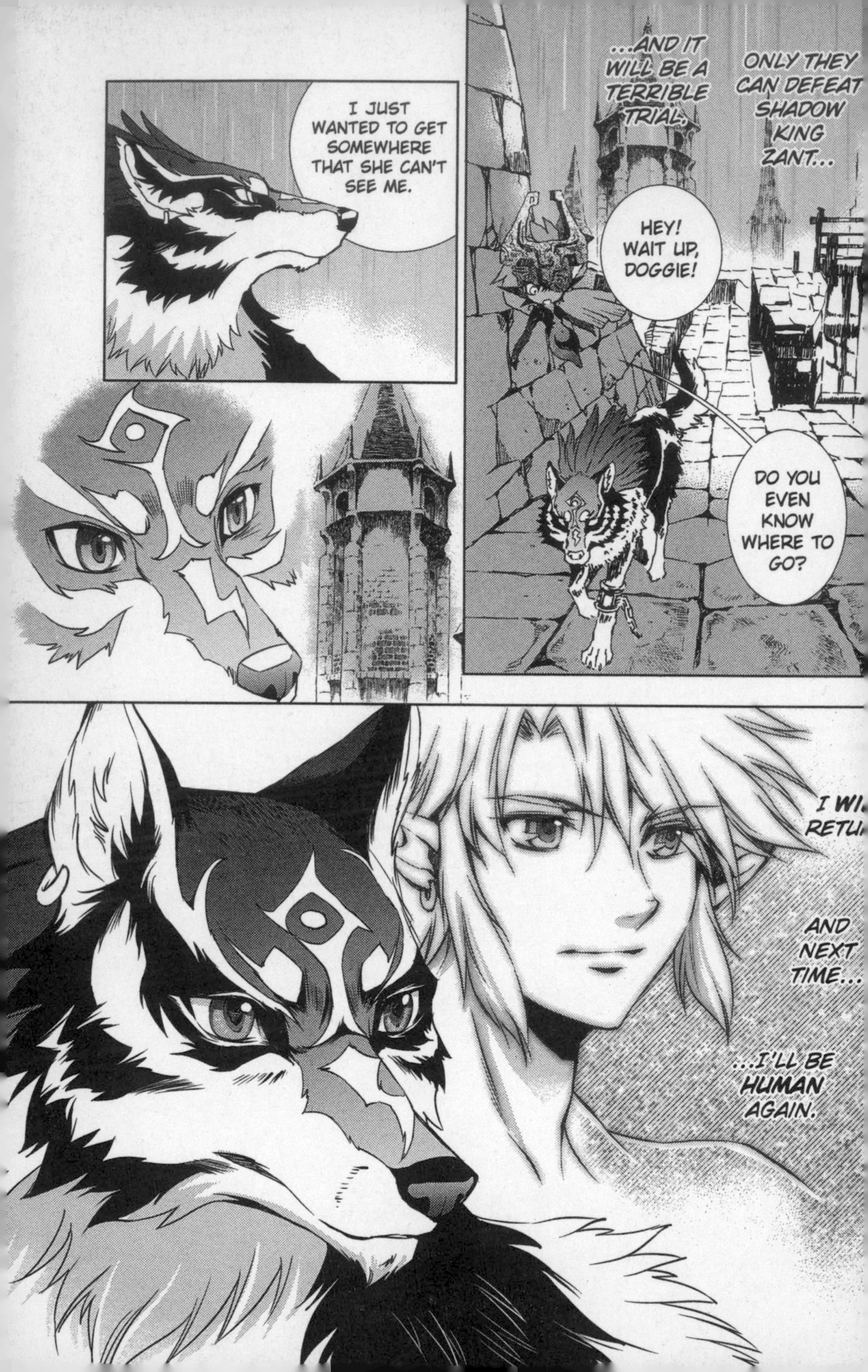
ONLY THEY CAN DEFEAT SHADOW KING ZANT...
...AND IT WILL BE A TERRIBLE TRIAL.
HEY! WAIT UP, DOGGIE!
DO YOU EVEN KNOW WHERE TO GO?
I JUST WANTED TO GET SOMEWHERE THAT SHE CAN'T SEE ME.
I WI RETU
AND NEXT TIME...
...I'LL BE HUMAN AGAIN.

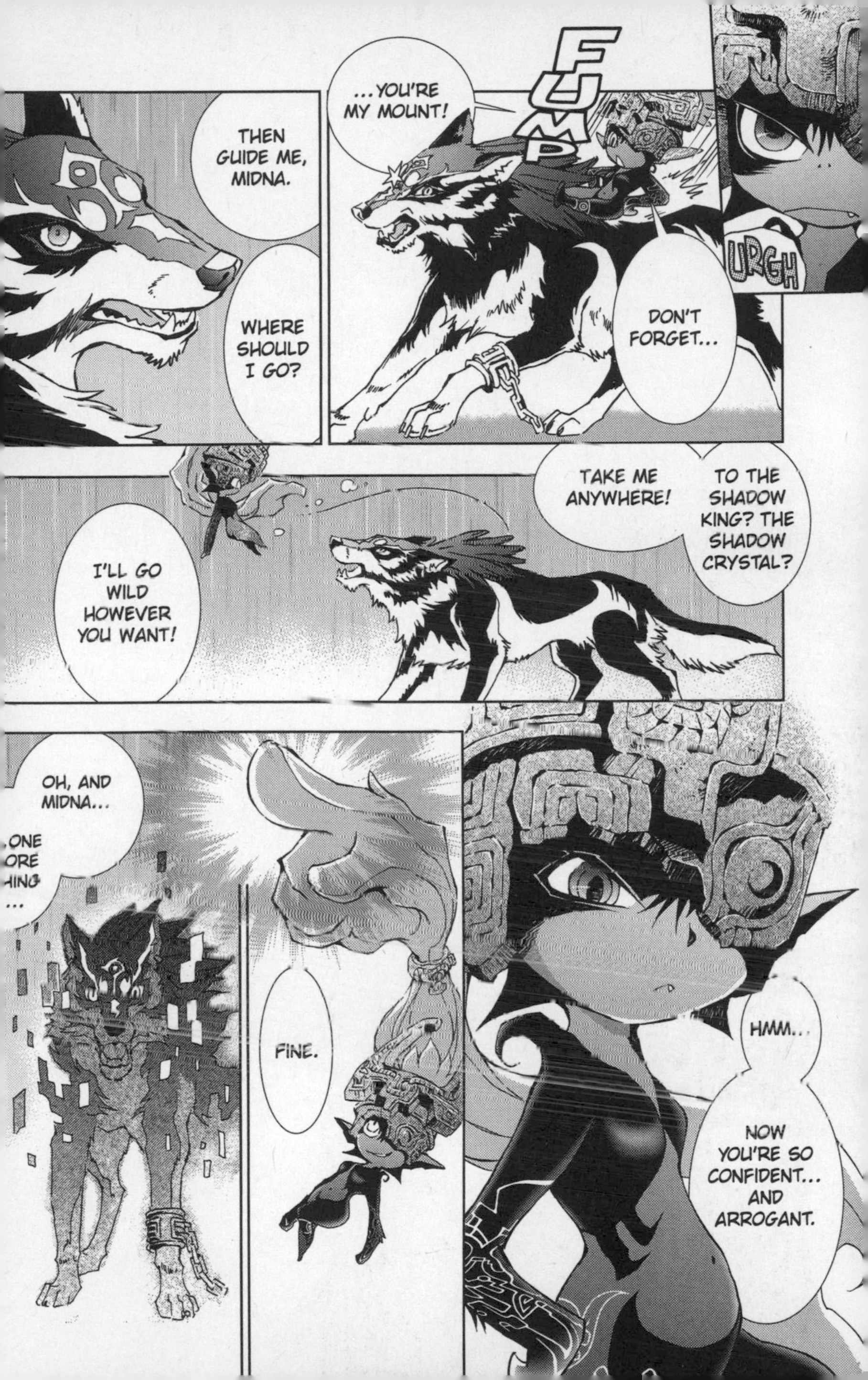
URGH
FUMP
DON'T FORGET...
...YOU'RE MY MOUNT!
THEN GUIDE ME, MIDNA.
WHERE SHOULD I GO?
TO THE SHADOW KING? THE SHADOW CRYSTAL?
TAKE ME ANYWHERE!
I'LL GO WILD HOWEVER YOU WANT!
HMM...
NOW YOU'RE SO CONFIDENT... AND ARROGANT.
FINE.
OH, AND MIDNA...

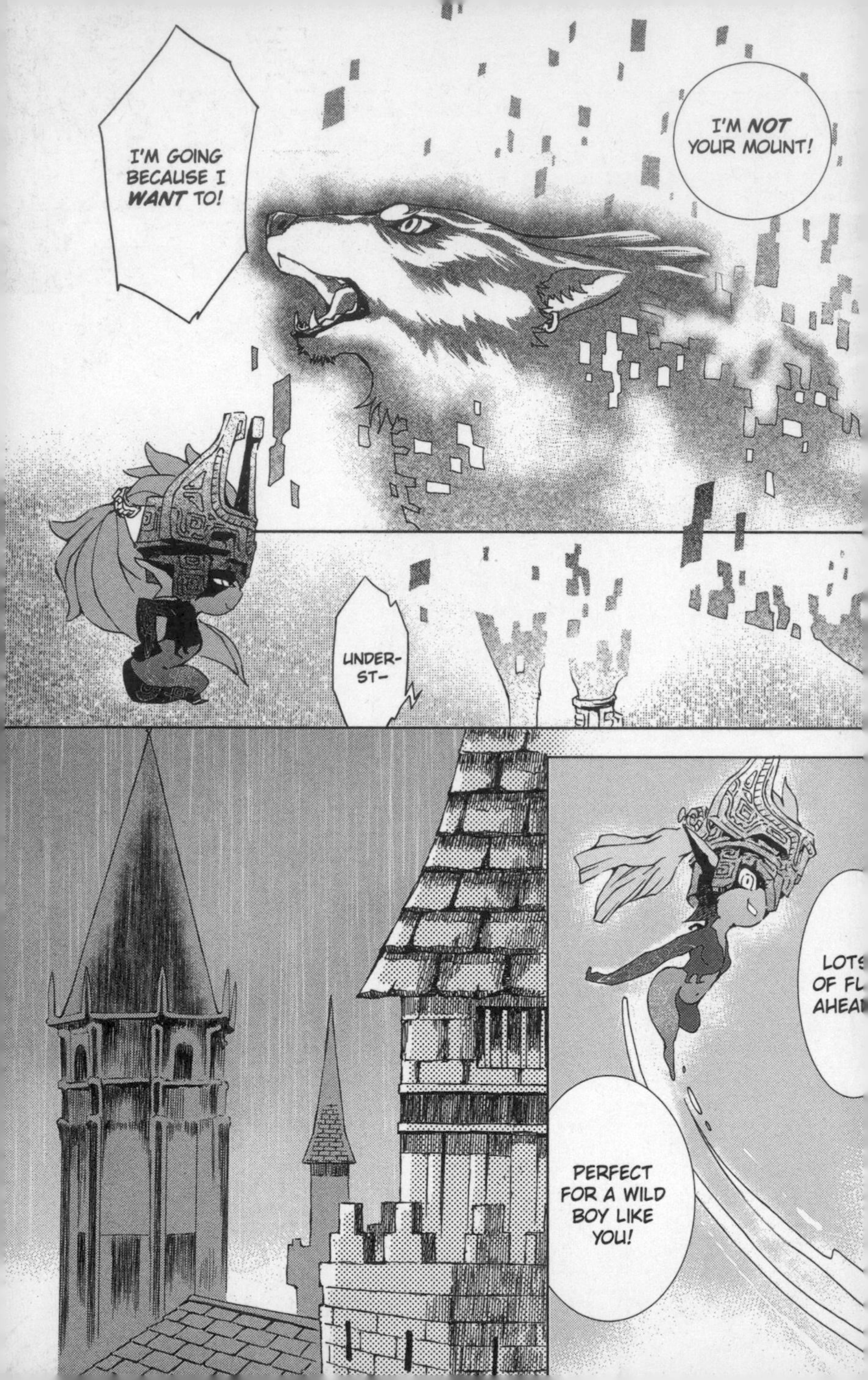
I'M NOT YOUR MOUNT!
I'M GOING BECAUSE I WANT TO!
UNDER-ST-
LOTS OF FL AHEA
PERFECT FOR A WILD BOY LIKE YOU!

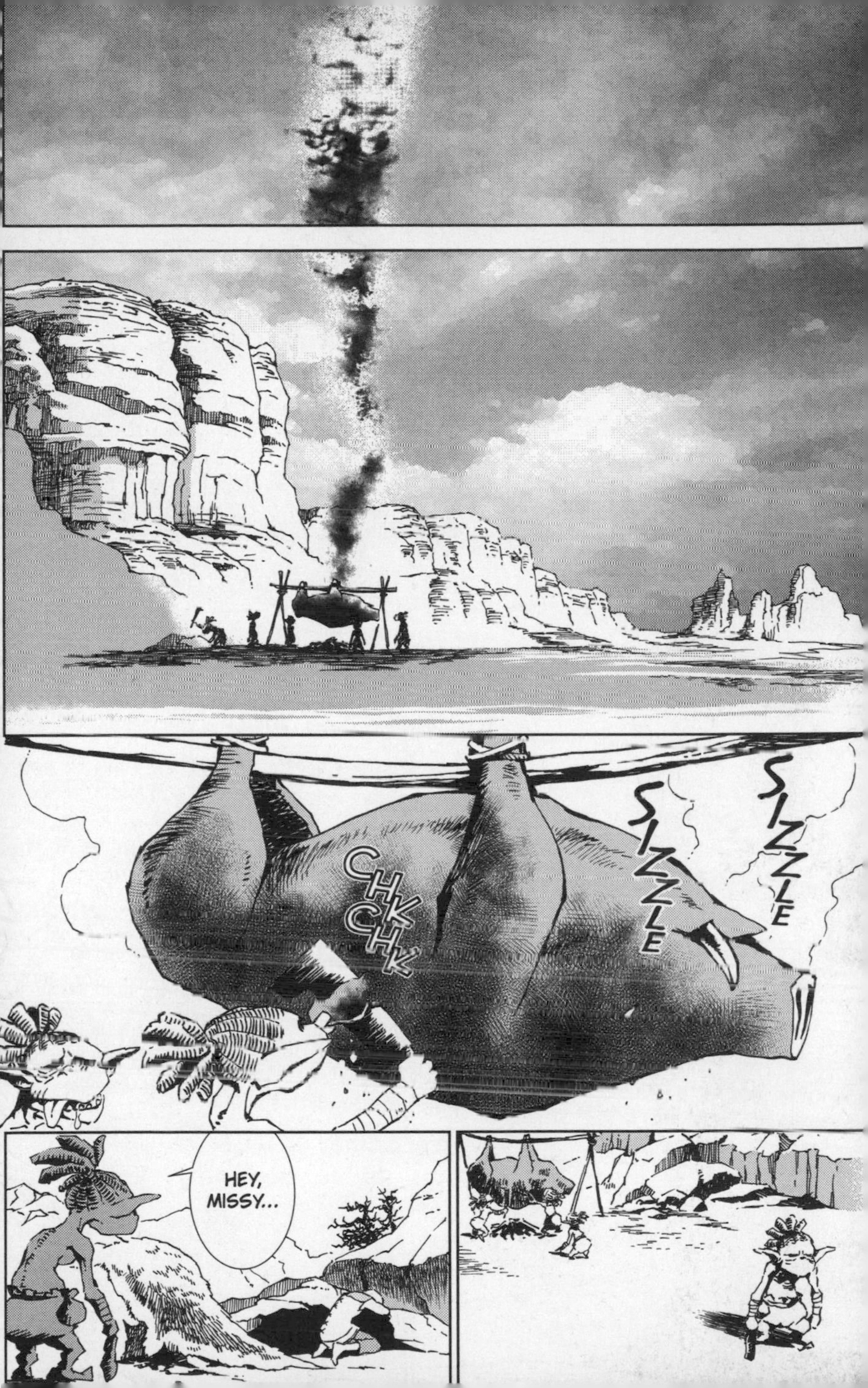
SIZZLE
SIZZLE
CHK CHK
HEY, MISSY...

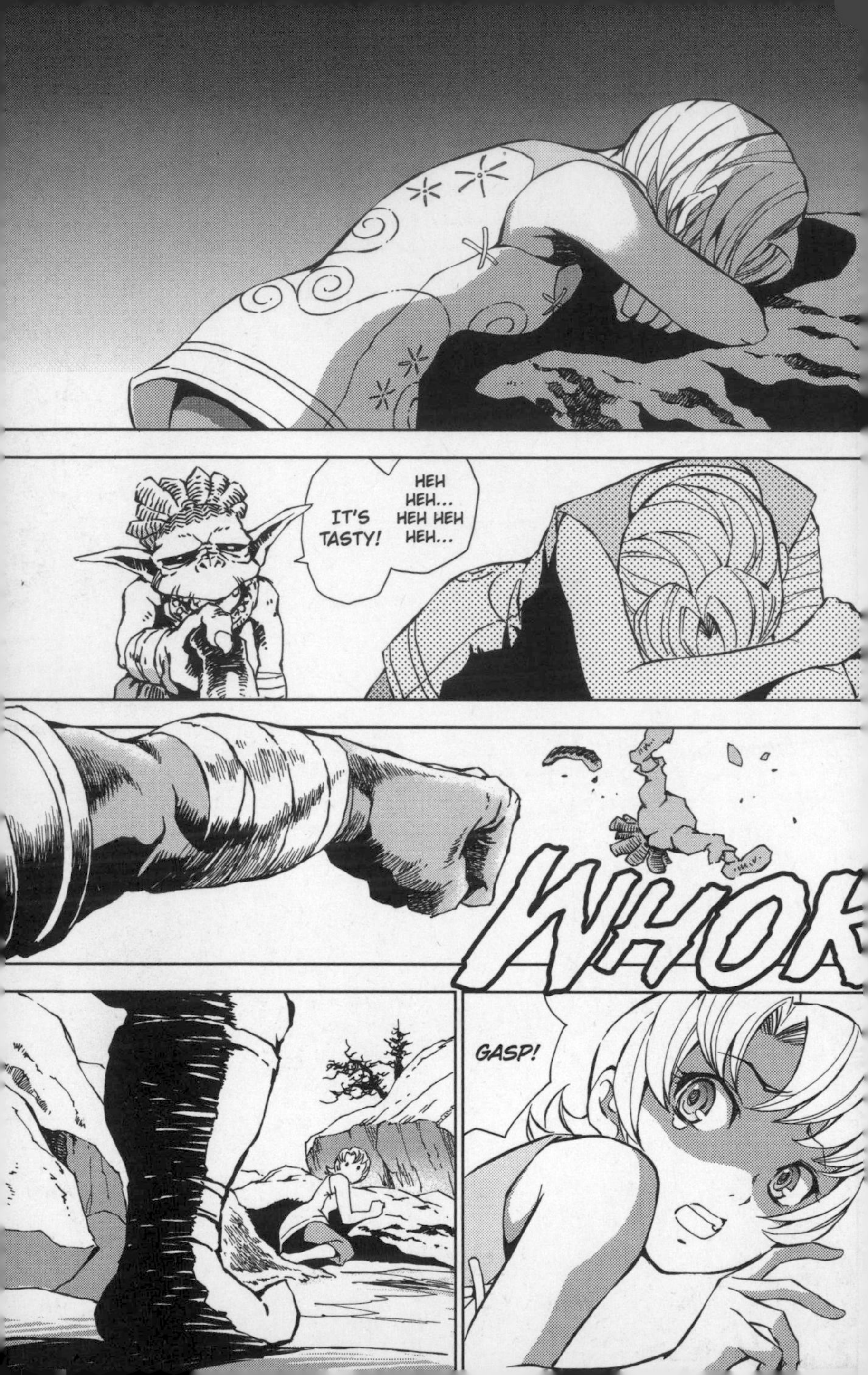
HEH HEH... HEH HEH HEH...
IT'S TASTY!
WHOK
GASP!

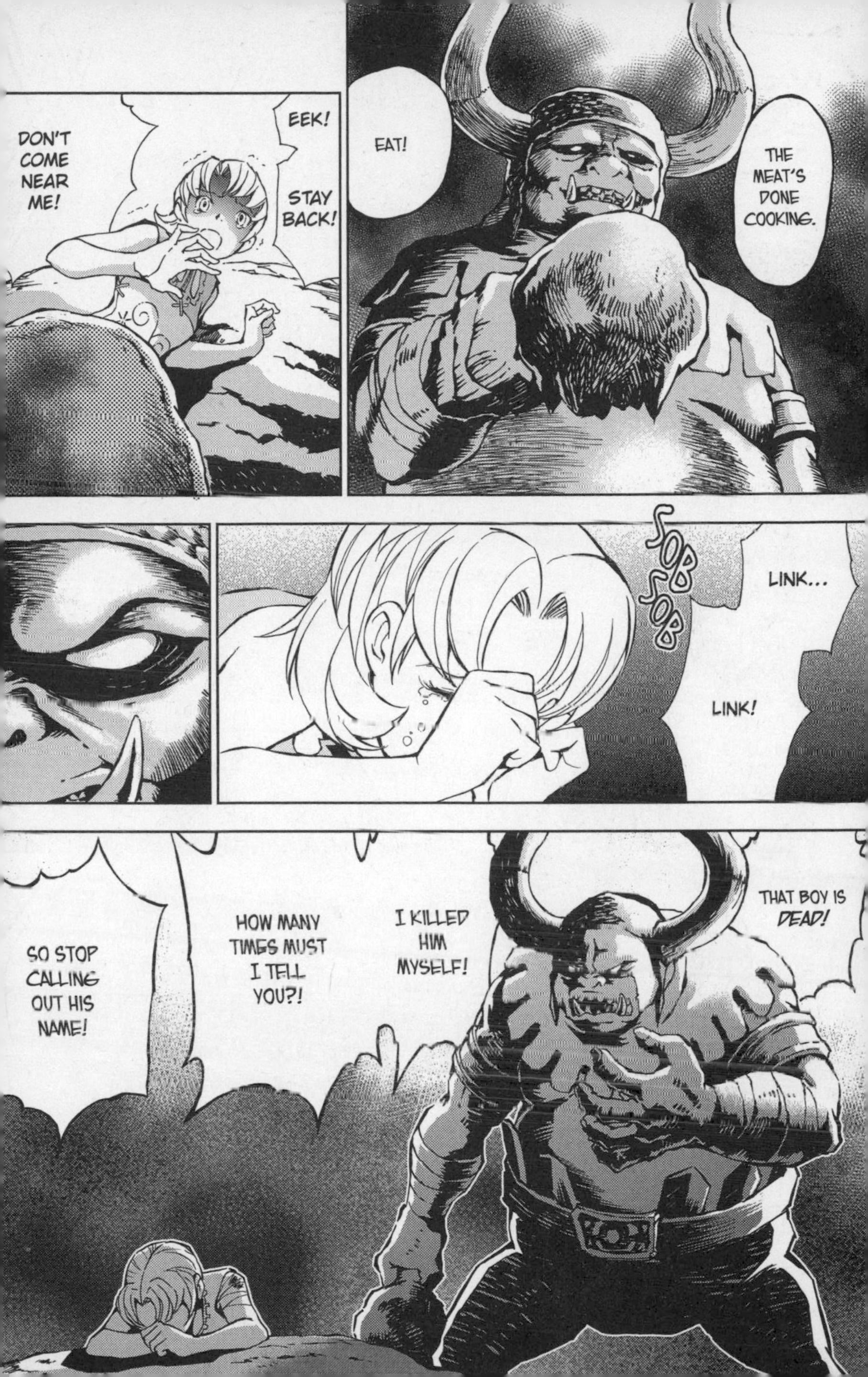
THE MEAT'S DONE COOKING.
EAT!
EEK!
STAY BACK!
DON'T COME NEAR ME!
LINK...
SOB SOB
LINK!
THAT BOY IS *DEAD!*
I KILLED HIM MYSELF!
HOW MANY TIMES MUST I TELL YOU?!
SO STOP CALLING OUT HIS NAME!

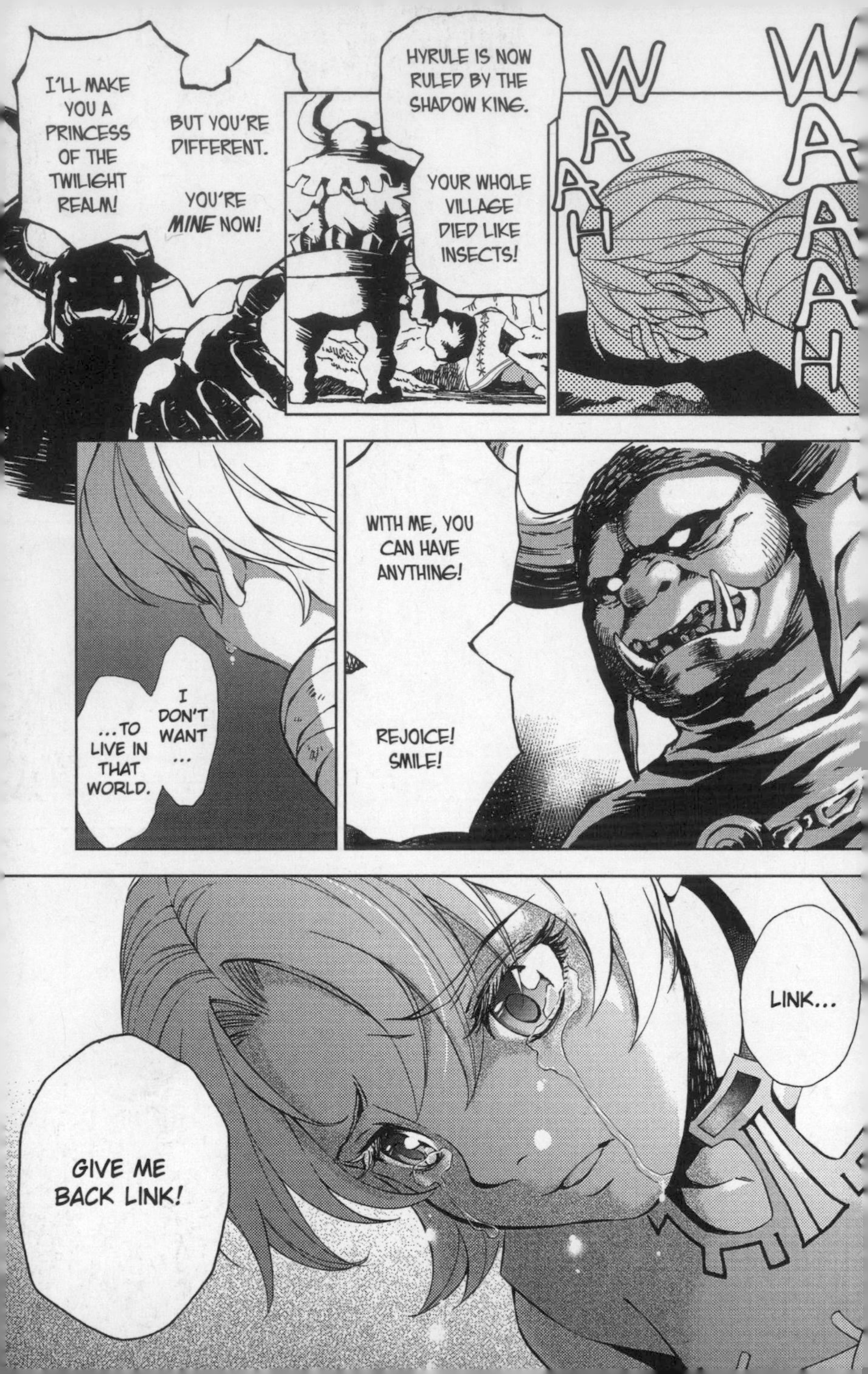
WAAAAH
WAAH
HYRULE IS NOW RULED BY THE SHADOW KING.
YOUR WHOLE VILLAGE DIED LIKE INSECTS!
BUT YOU'RE DIFFERENT.
YOU'RE *MINE* NOW!
I'LL MAKE YOU A PRINCESS OF THE TWILIGHT REALM!
WITH ME, YOU CAN HAVE ANYTHING!
REJOICE! SMILE!
I DON'T WANT...
...TO LIVE IN THAT WORLD.
LINK...
GIVE ME BACK LINK!

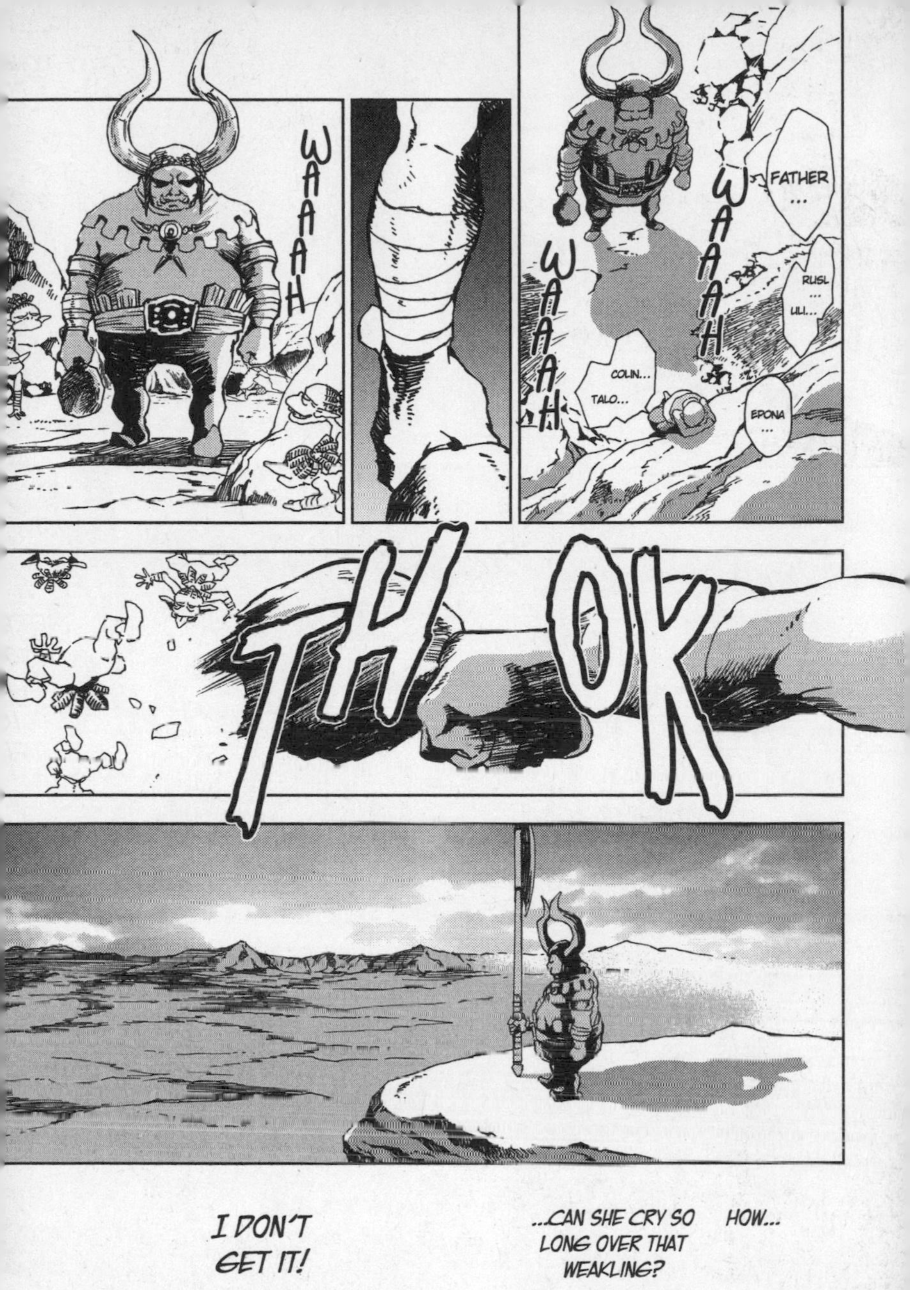
FATHER...
RUSL... ULI...
WAAAAH
COLIN... TALO...
EPONA...
WAAAAH
WAAAH
TH OK
HOW...
...CAN SHE CRY SO LONG OVER THAT WEAKLING?
I DON'T GET IT!

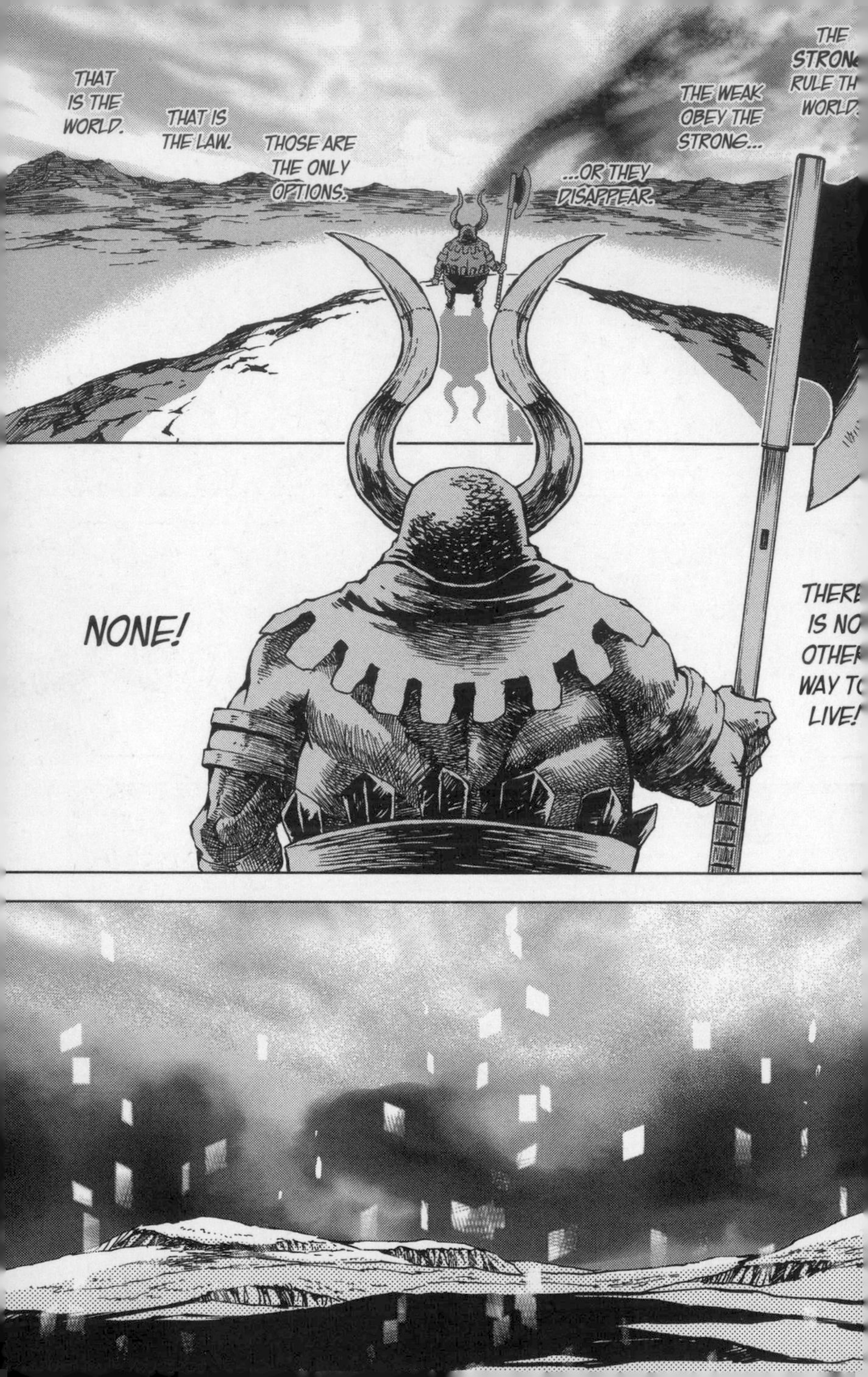
THE STRONG RULE TH WORLD.
THE WEAK OBEY THE STRONG...
...OR THEY DISAPPEAR.
THOSE ARE THE ONLY OPTIONS.
THAT IS THE LAW.
THAT IS THE WORLD.
THERE IS NO OTHER WAY TO LIVE!
NONE!

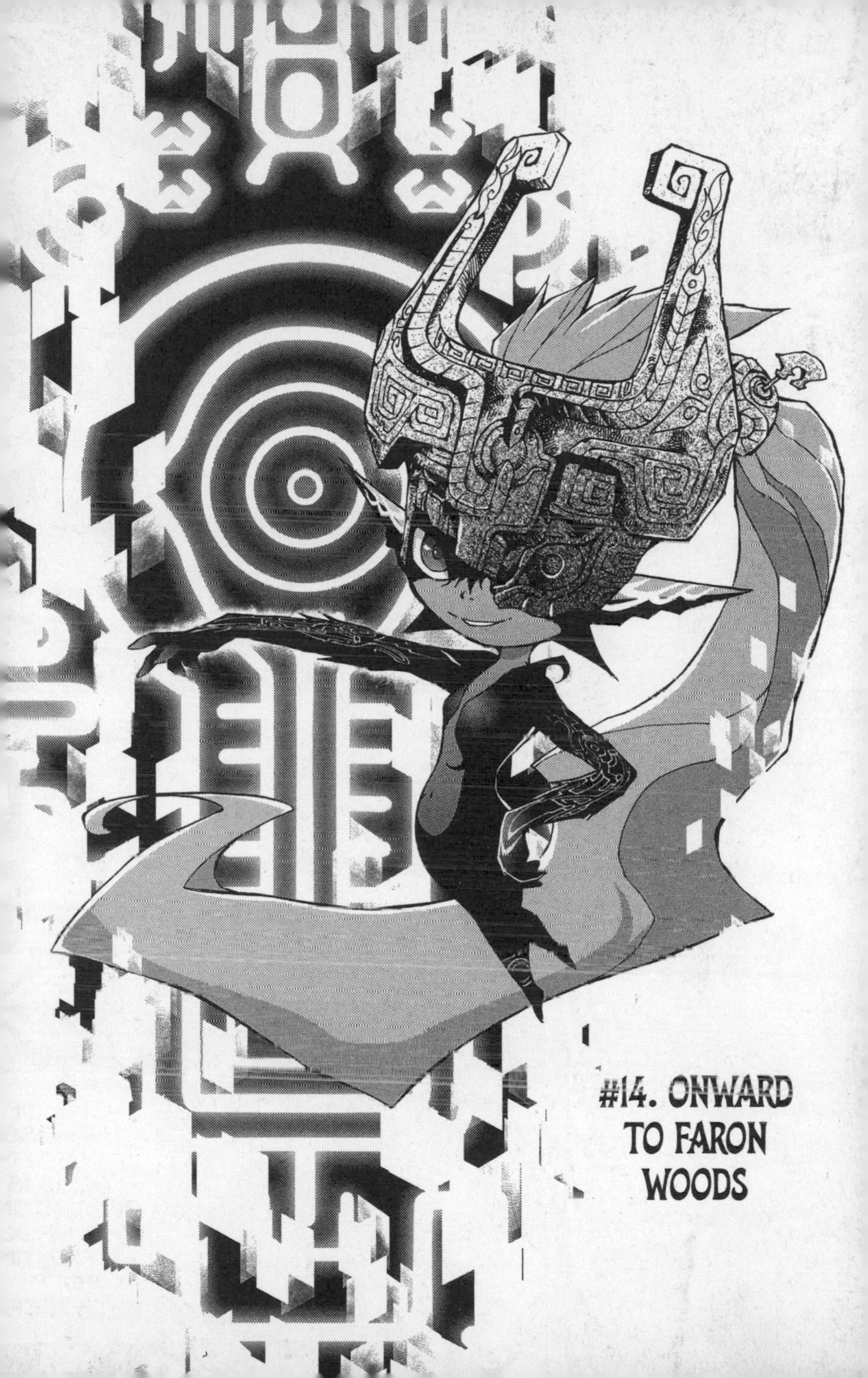

#14. ONWARD TO FARON WOODS

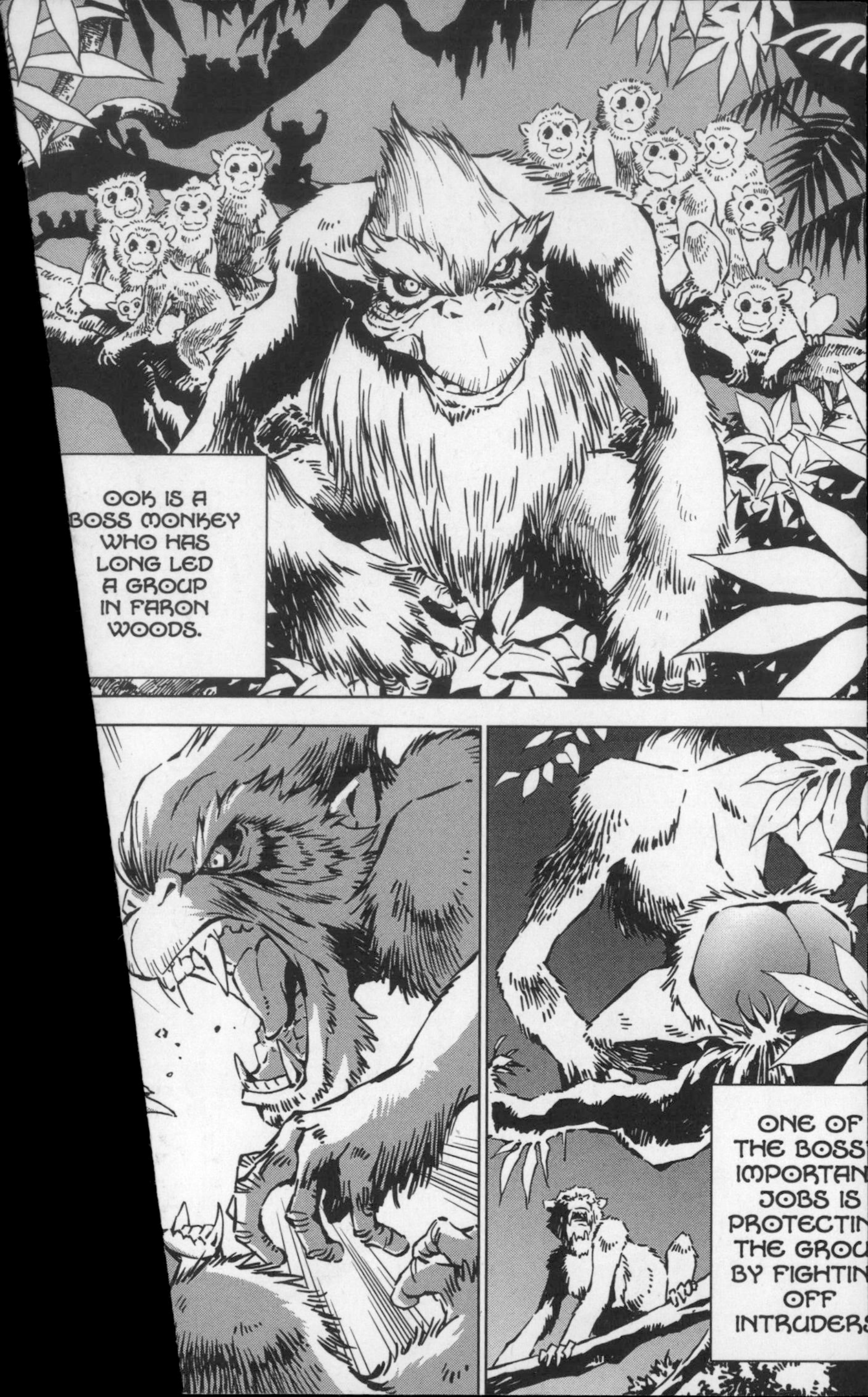
OOK IS A BOSS MONKEY WHO HAS LONG LED A GROUP IN FARON WOODS.
ONE OF THE BOSS' IMPORTAN JOBS IS PROTECTIN THE GROU BY FIGHTIN OFF INTRUDERS

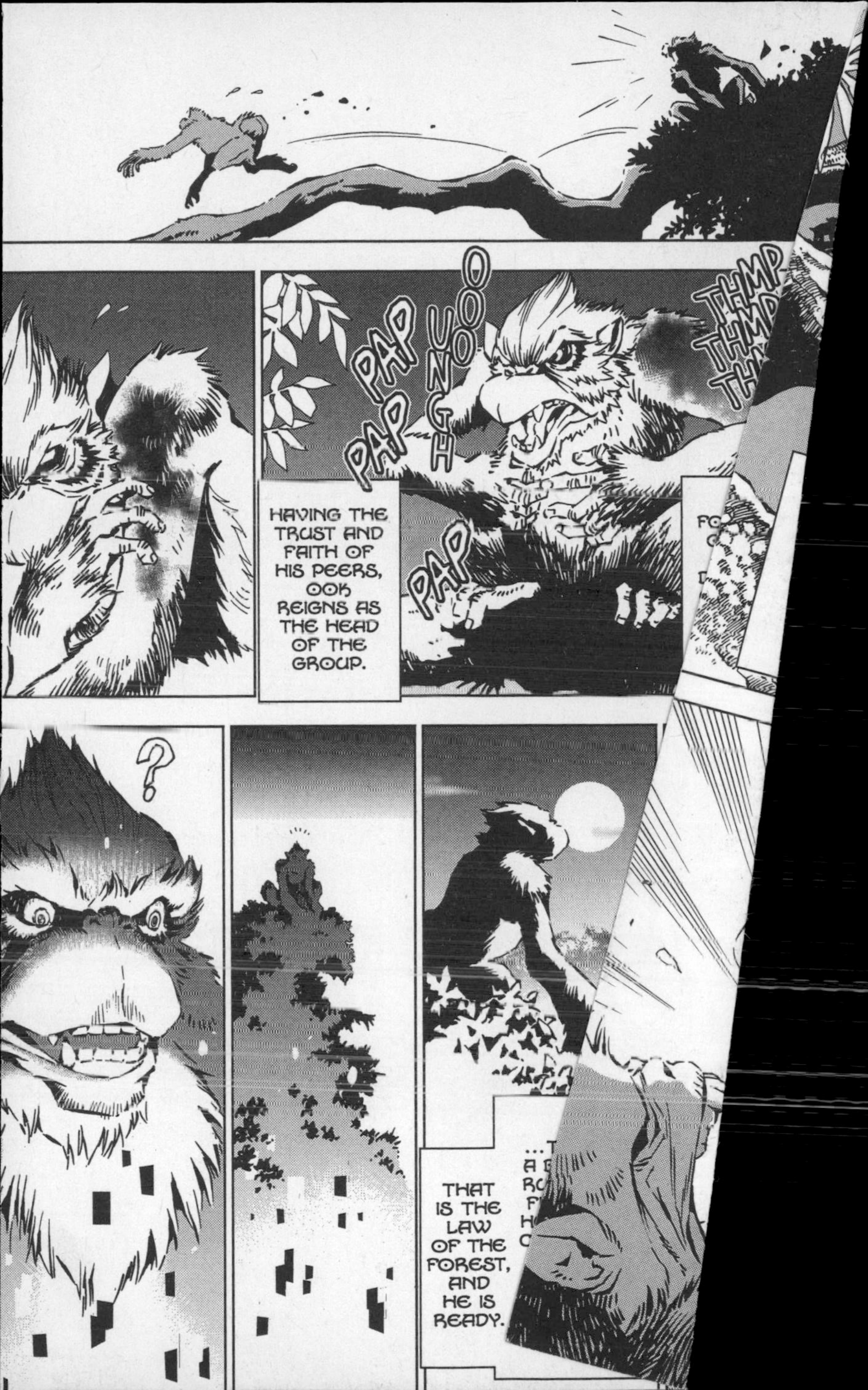
OOOO
UNGH
PAP PAP
PAP
HAVING THE TRUST AND FAITH OF HIS PEERS, OOK REIGNS AS THE HEAD OF THE GROUP.
THAT IS THE LAW OF THE FOREST, AND HE IS READY.
?

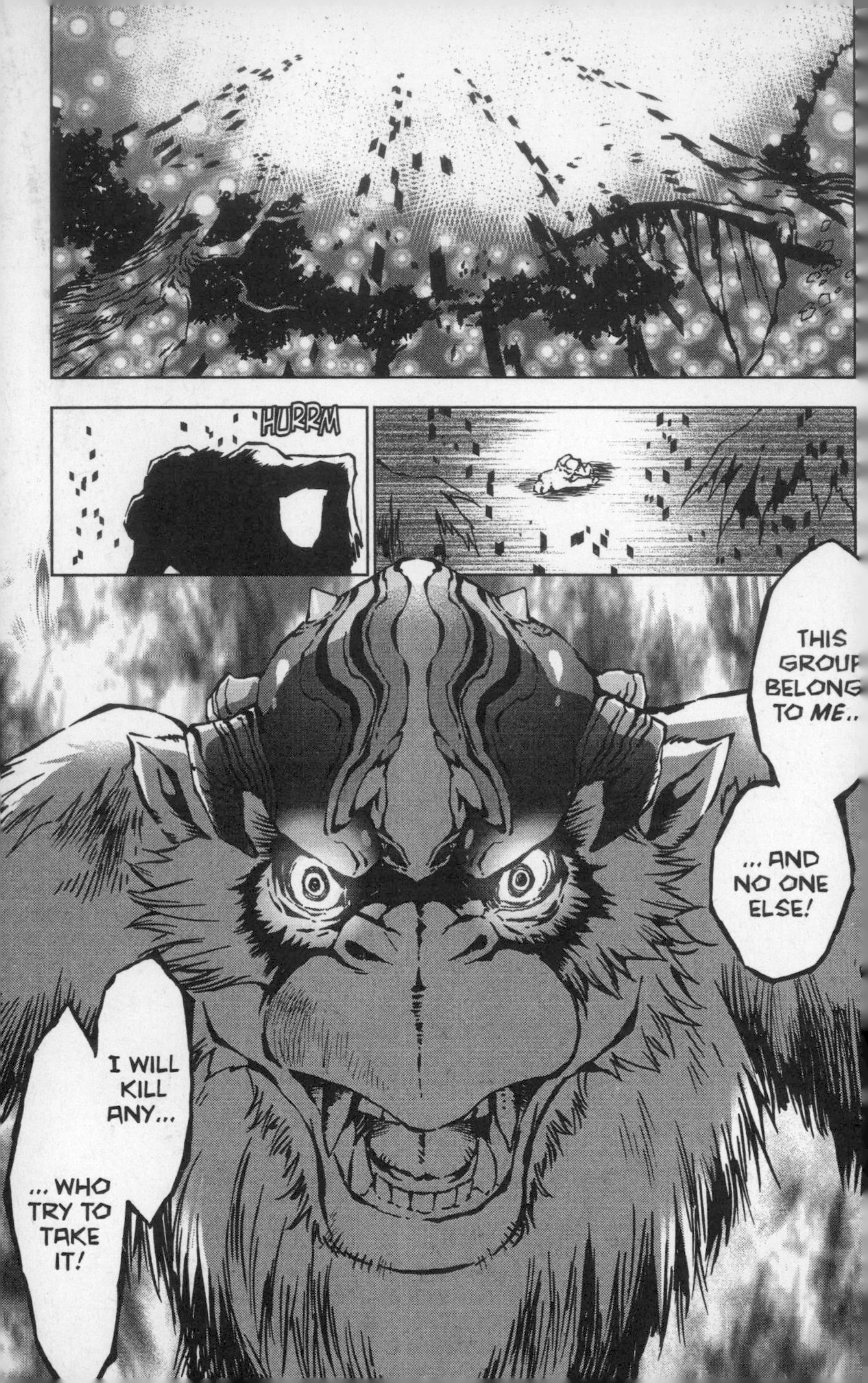
HURRM
THIS GROUP BELONG TO ME..
...AND NO ONE ELSE!
I WILL KILL ANY...
...WHO TRY TO TAKE IT!

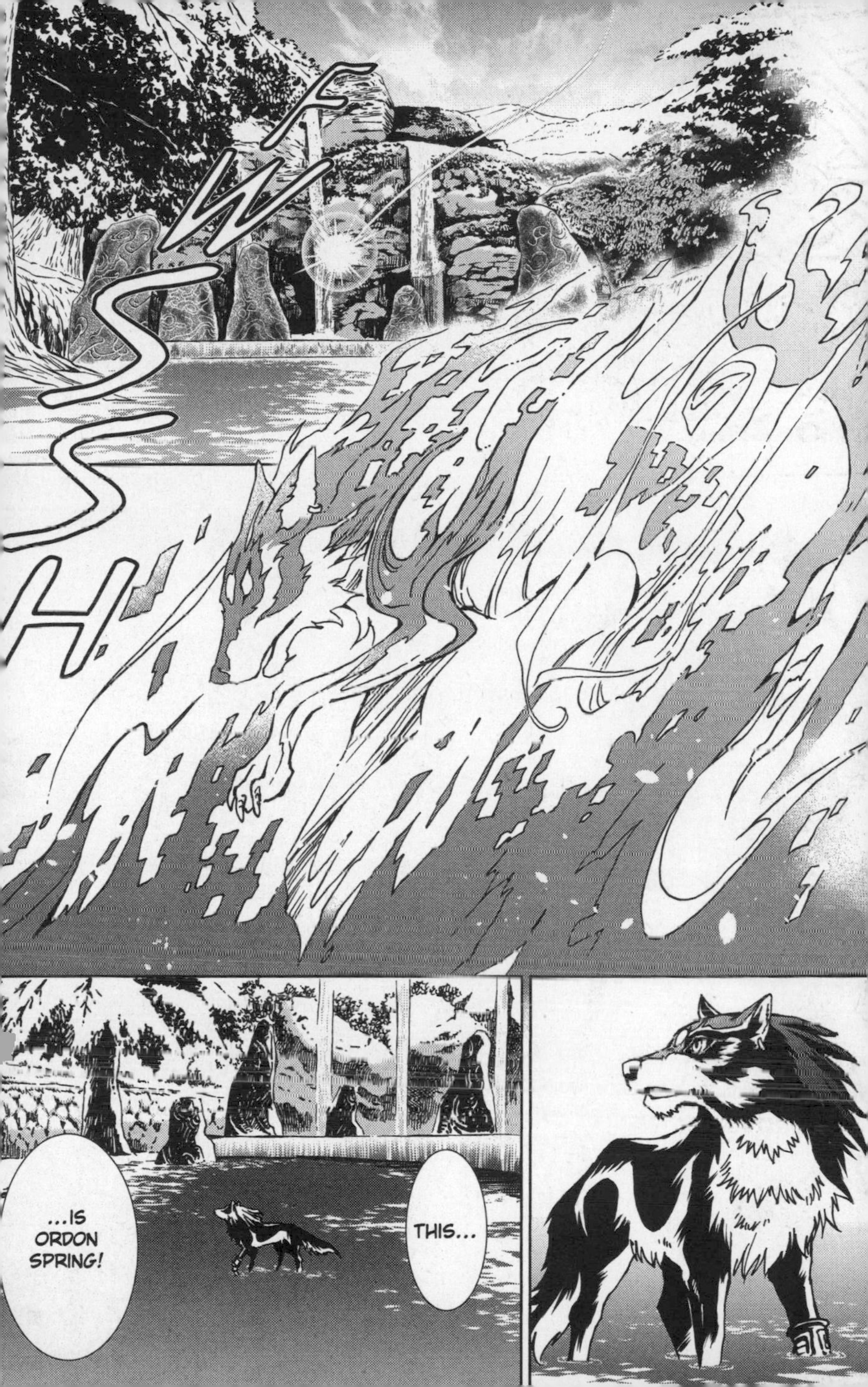
FWSSH
THIS...
...IS ORDON SPRING!

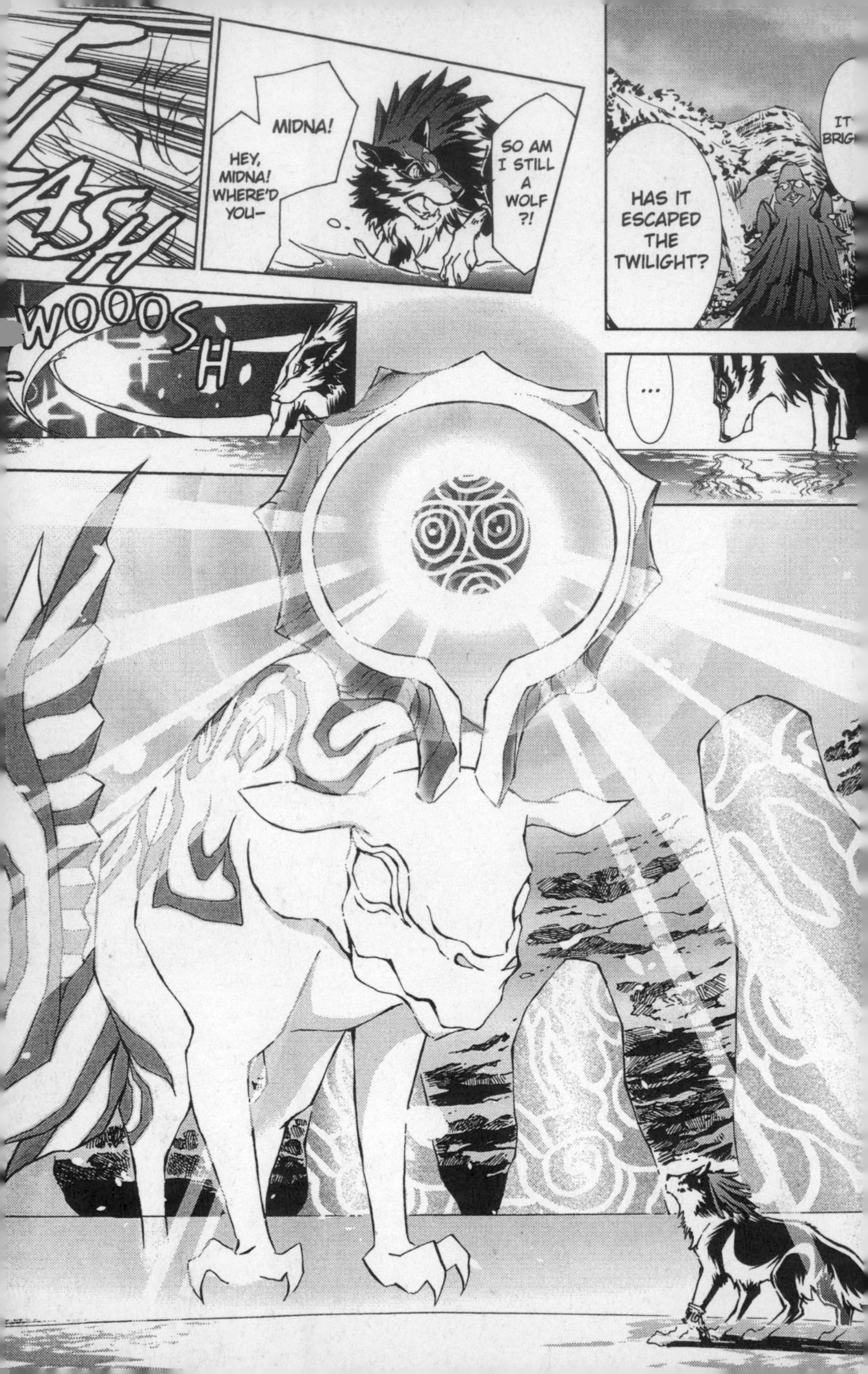
IT BRIG
HAS IT ESCAPED THE TWILIGHT?
SO AM I STILL A WOLF?!
MIDNA!
HEY, MIDNA! WHERE'D YOU-
F ASH
...
WOOOSH

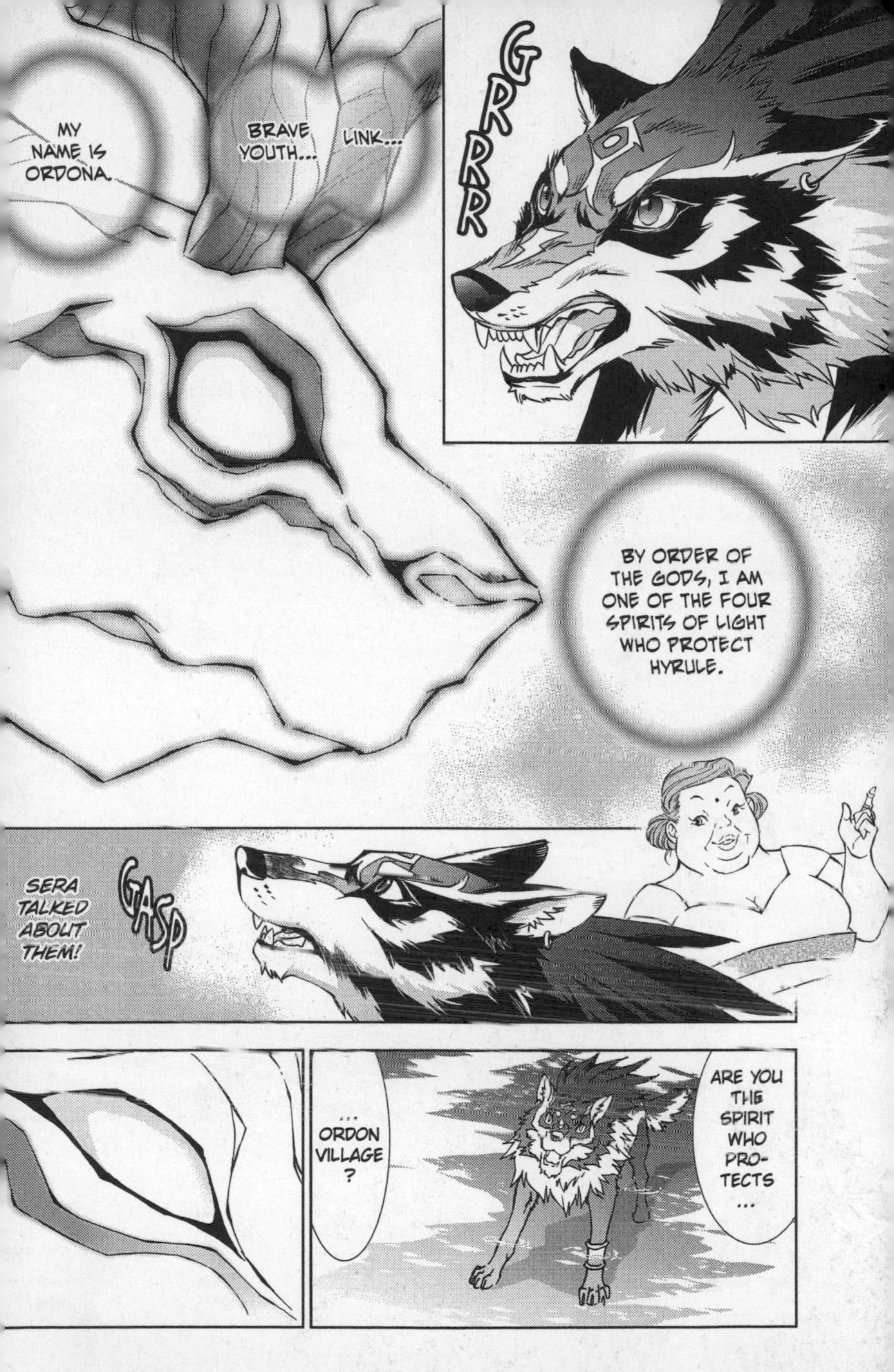
GRRRR
LINK...
BRAVE YOUTH...
MY NAME IS ORDONA.
BY ORDER OF THE GODS, I AM ONE OF THE FOUR SPIRITS OF LIGHT WHO PROTECT HYRULE.
GASP
SERA TALKED ABOUT THEM!
ARE YOU THE SPIRIT WHO PRO-TECTS...
...ORDON VILLAGE?

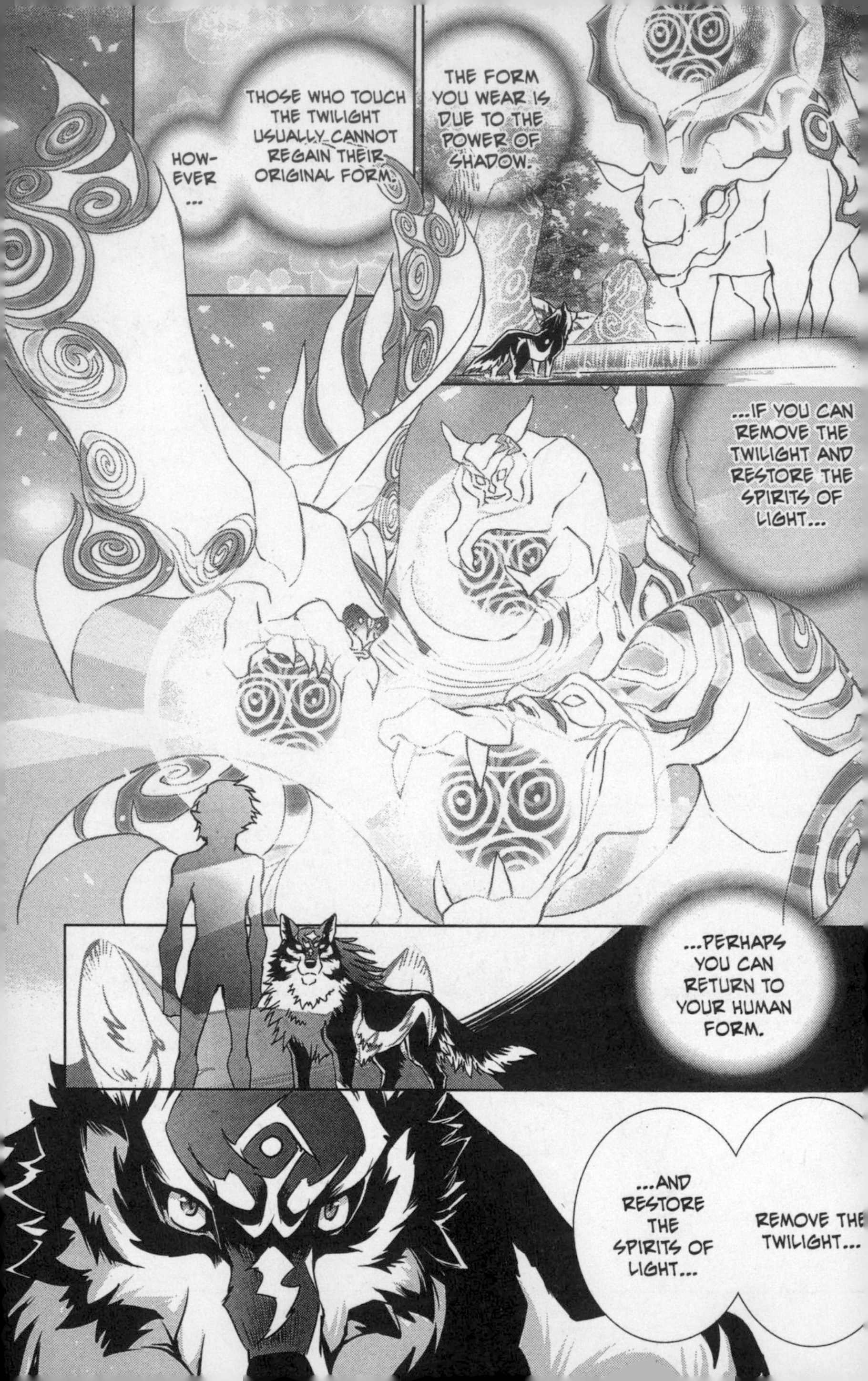
THE FORM YOU WEAR IS DUE TO THE POWER OF SHADOW.
THOSE WHO TOUCH THE TWILIGHT USUALLY CANNOT REGAIN THEIR ORIGINAL FORM.
HOW-EVER...
...IF YOU CAN REMOVE THE TWILIGHT AND RESTORE THE SPIRITS OF LIGHT...
...PERHAPS YOU CAN RETURN TO YOUR HUMAN FORM.
REMOVE THE TWILIGHT...
...AND RESTORE THE SPIRITS OF LIGHT...

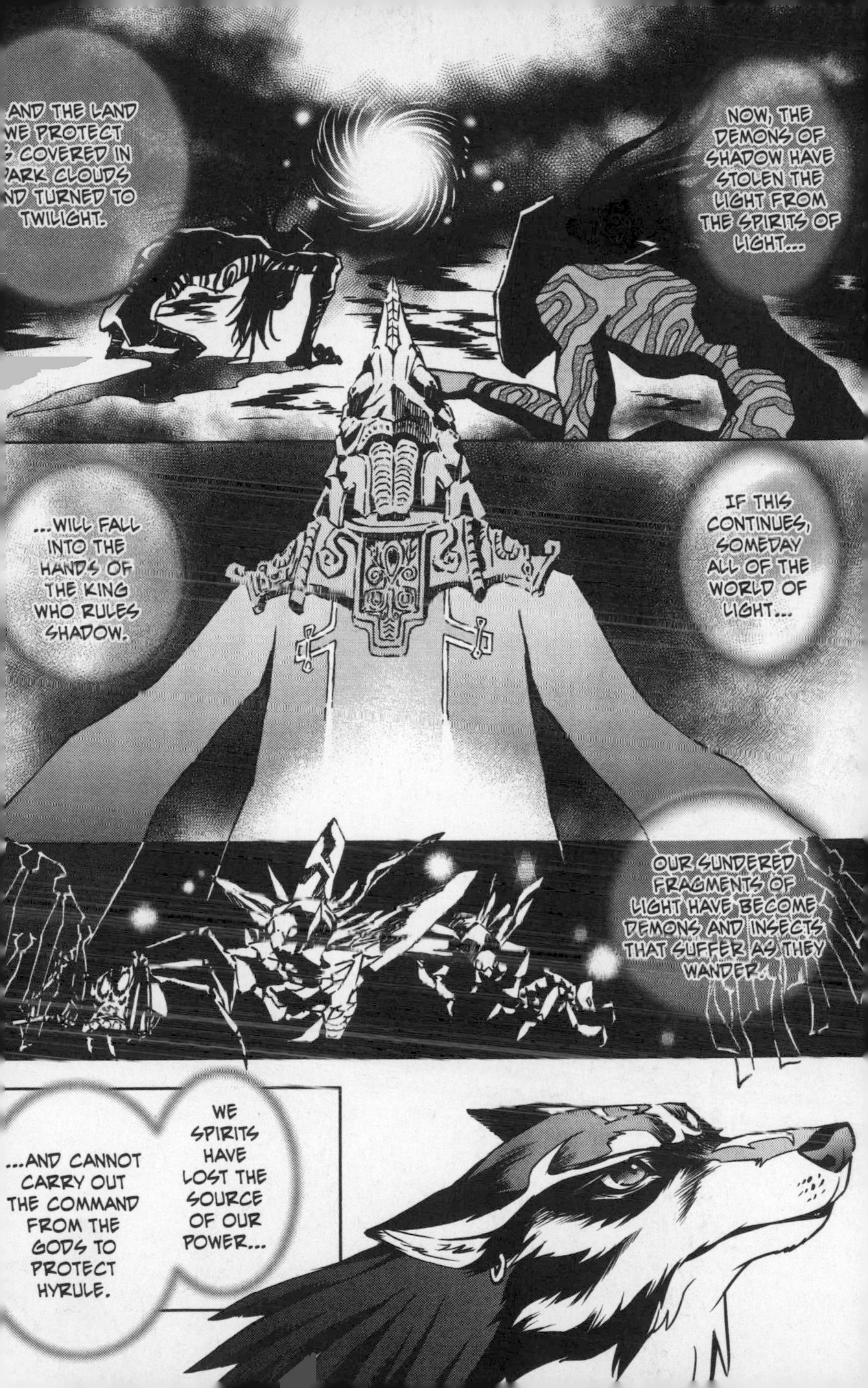
NOW, THE DEMONS OF SHADOW HAVE STOLEN THE LIGHT FROM THE SPIRITS OF LIGHT...
...AND THE LAND WE PROTECT S COVERED IN ARK CLOUDS ND TURNED TO TWILIGHT.
IF THIS CONTINUES, SOMEDAY ALL OF THE WORLD OF LIGHT...
...WILL FALL INTO THE HANDS OF THE KING WHO RULES SHADOW.
OUR SUNDERED FRAGMENTS OF LIGHT HAVE BECOME DEMONS AND INSECTS THAT SUFFER AS THEY WANDER.
WE SPIRITS HAVE LOST THE SOURCE OF OUR POWER...
...AND CANNOT CARRY OUT THE COMMAND FROM THE GODS TO PROTECT HYRULE.

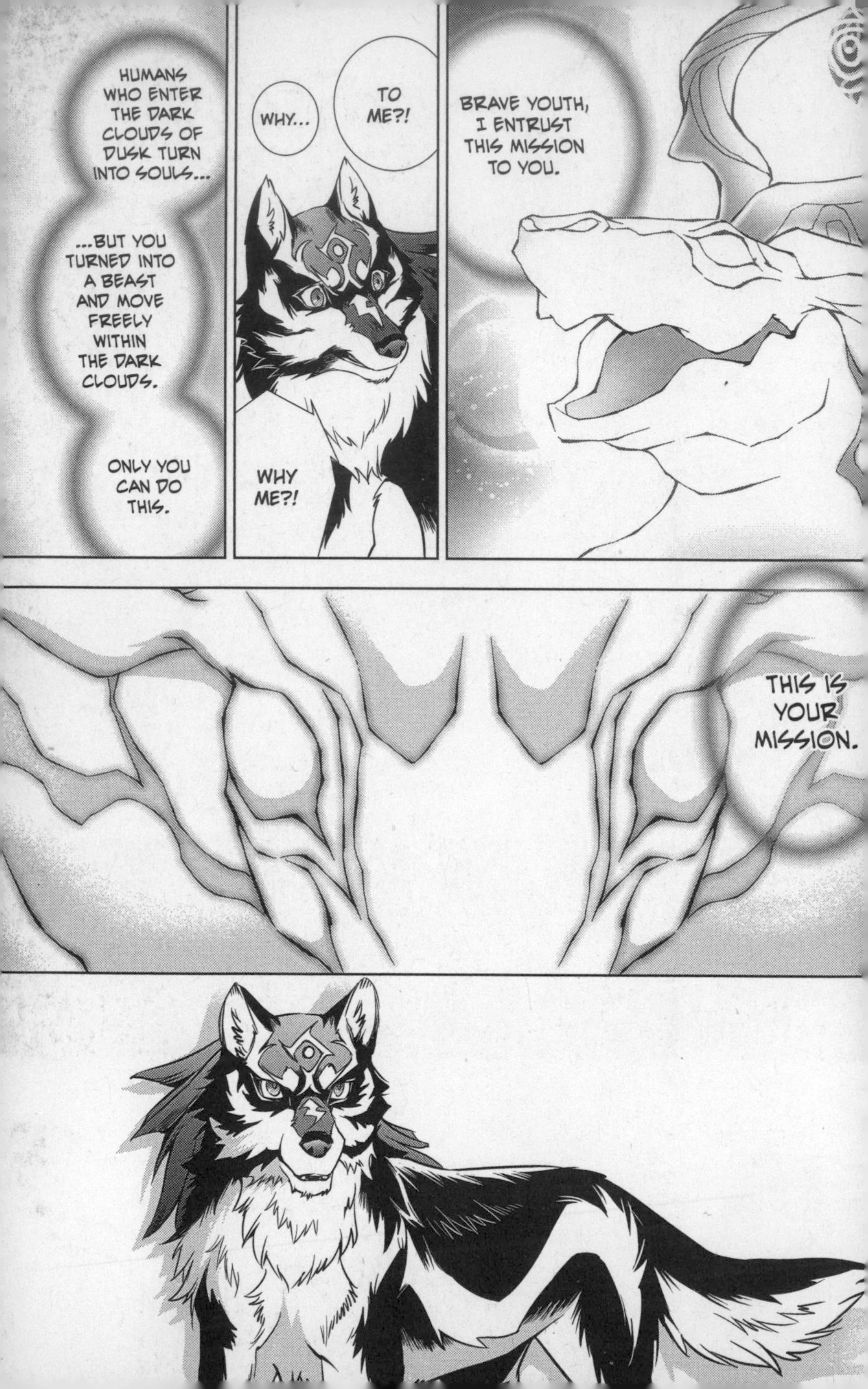
BRAVE YOUTH, I ENTRUST THIS MISSION TO YOU.
TO ME?!
WHY...
WHY ME?!
HUMANS WHO ENTER THE DARK CLOUDS OF DUSK TURN INTO SOULS...
...BUT YOU TURNED INTO A BEAST AND MOVE FREELY WITHIN THE DARK CLOUDS.
ONLY YOU CAN DO THIS.
THIS IS YOUR MISSION.

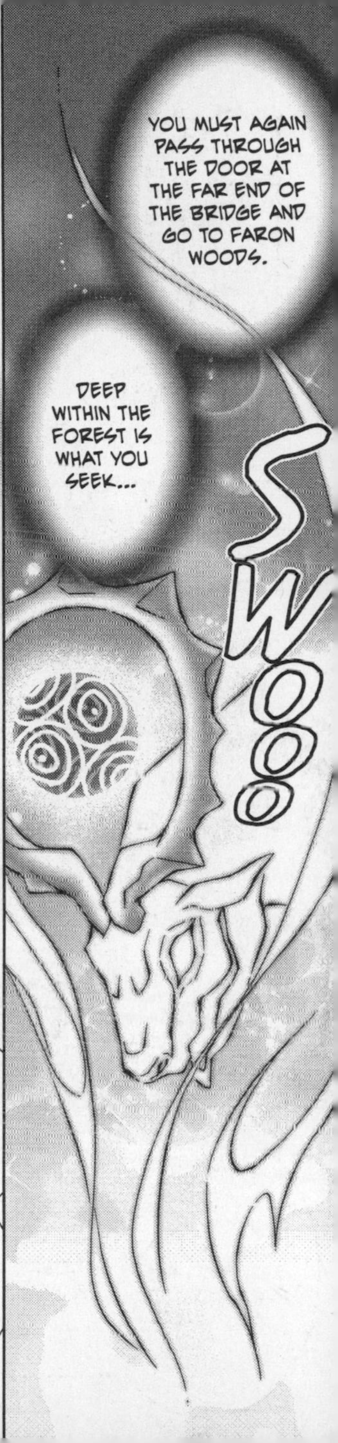
YOU MUST AGAIN PASS THROUGH THE DOOR AT THE FAR END OF THE BRIDGE AND GO TO FARON WOODS.
DEEP WITHIN THE FOREST IS WHAT YOU SEEK...
SWOOO
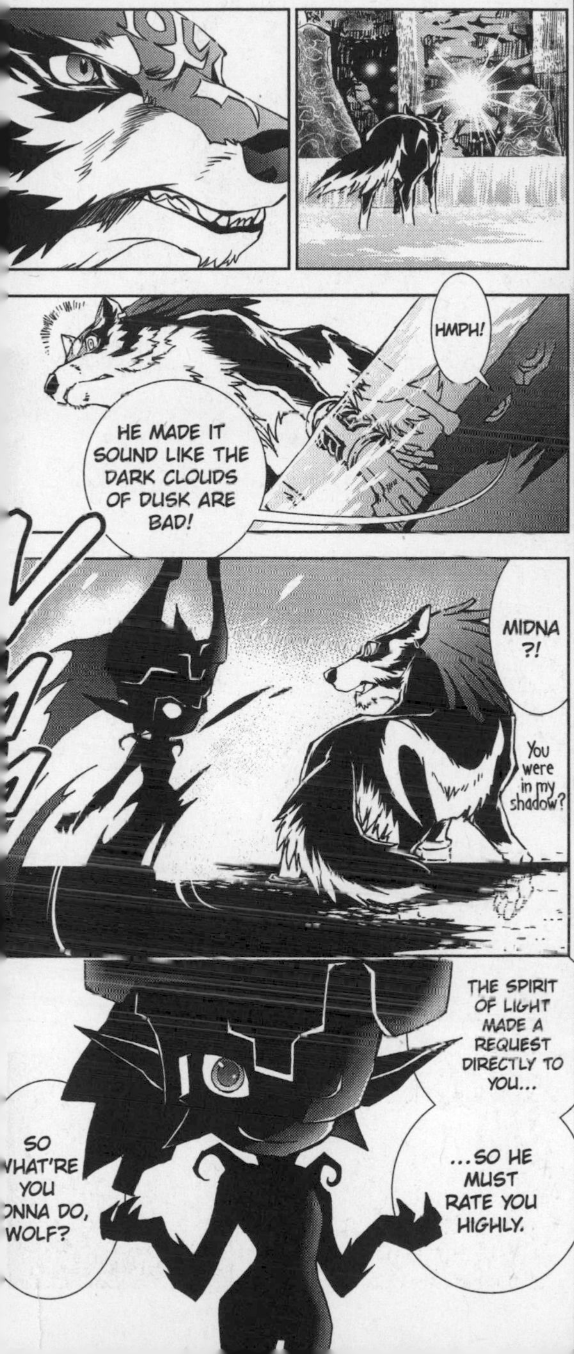
HMPH!
HE MADE IT SOUND LIKE THE DARK CLOUDS OF DUSK ARE BAD!
MIDNA ?!
You were in my shadow?
THE SPIRIT OF LIGHT MADE A REQUEST DIRECTLY TO YOU...
...SO HE MUST RATE YOU HIGHLY.
SO WHAT'RE YOU ONNA DO, WOLF?

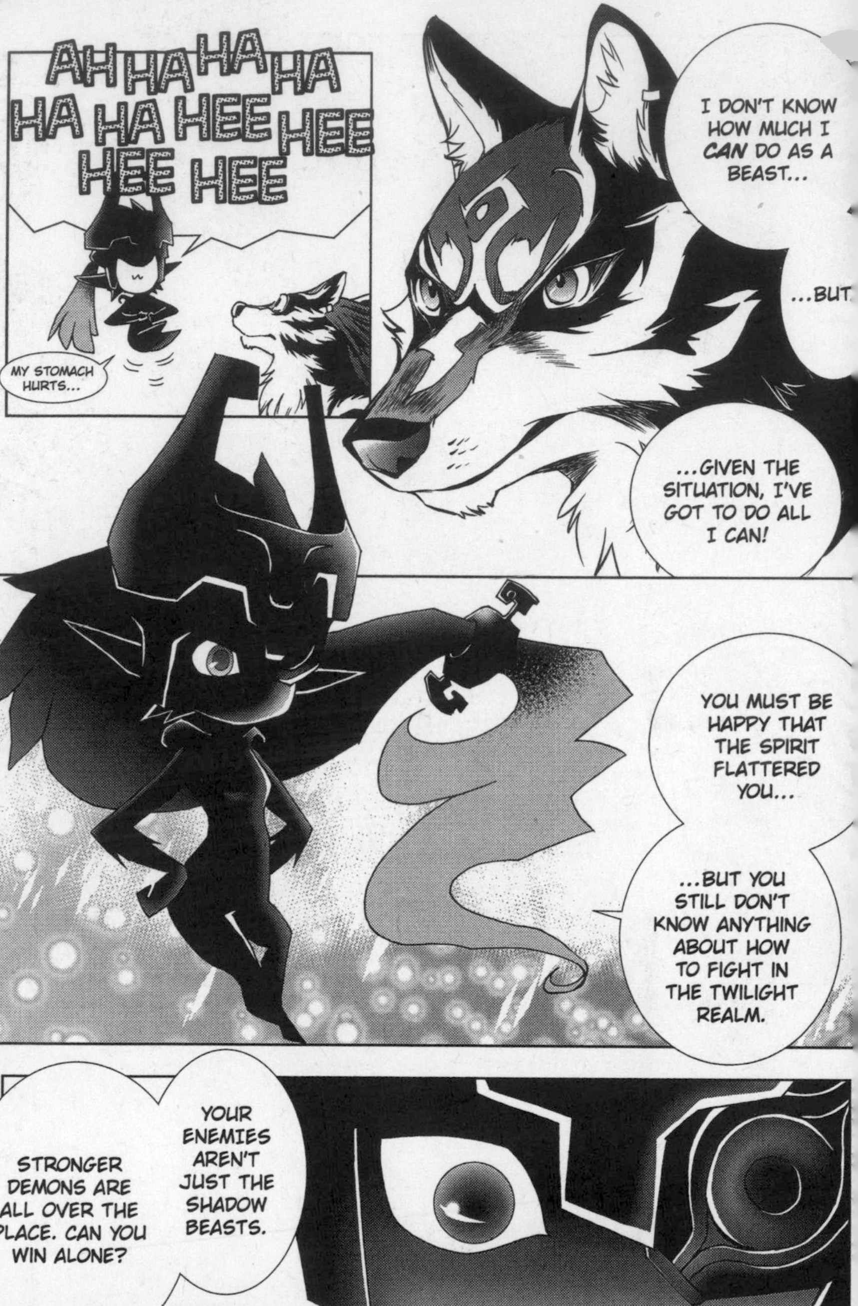
I DON'T KNOW HOW MUCH I CAN DO AS A BEAST...
...BUT
...GIVEN THE SITUATION, I'VE GOT TO DO ALL I CAN!
AH HA HA HA HA HA HA HEE HEE HEE HEE HEE
MY STOMACH HURTS...
YOU MUST BE HAPPY THAT THE SPIRIT FLATTERED YOU...
...BUT YOU STILL DON'T KNOW ANYTHING ABOUT HOW TO FIGHT IN THE TWILIGHT REALM.
YOUR ENEMIES AREN'T JUST THE SHADOW BEASTS.
STRONGER DEMONS ARE ALL OVER THE PLACE. CAN YOU WIN ALONE?

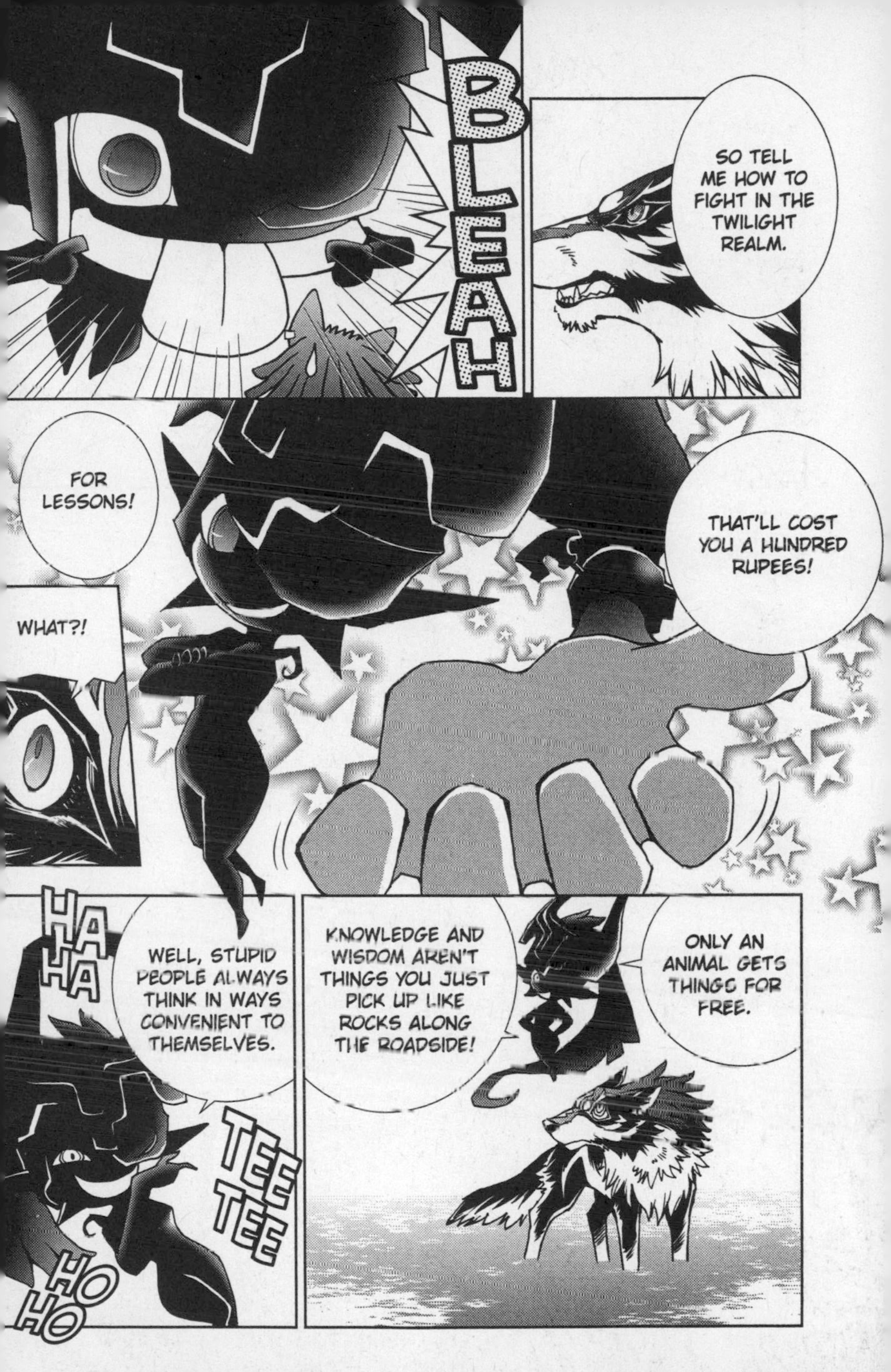
SO TELL ME HOW TO FIGHT IN THE TWILIGHT REALM.
BLEAAH
THAT'LL COST YOU A HUNDRED RUPEES!
FOR LESSONS!
WHAT?!
ONLY AN ANIMAL GETS THINGS FOR FREE.
KNOWLEDGE AND WISDOM AREN'T THINGS YOU JUST PICK UP LIKE ROCKS ALONG THE ROADSIDE!
HA HA HA
WELL, STUPID PEOPLE ALWAYS THINK IN WAYS CONVENIENT TO THEMSELVES.
TEE TEE
HO HO

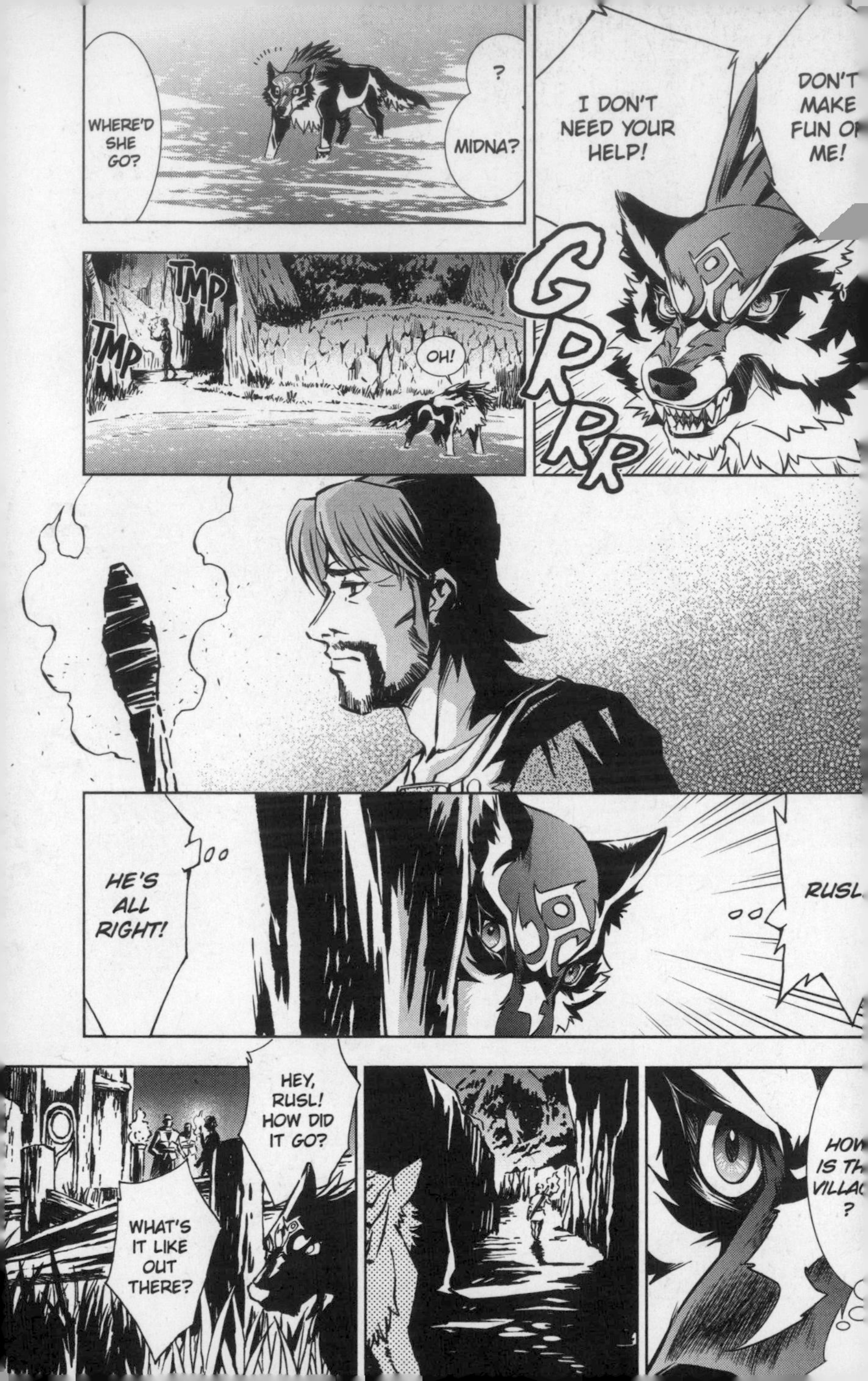
DON'T MAKE FUN O ME!
I DON'T NEED YOUR HELP!
GRRR
?
MIDNA?
WHERE'D SHE GO?
TMP
TMP
OH!
RUSL
HE'S ALL RIGHT!
HOW IS TH VILLA ?
HEY, RUSL! HOW DID IT GO?
WHAT'S IT LIKE OUT THERE?

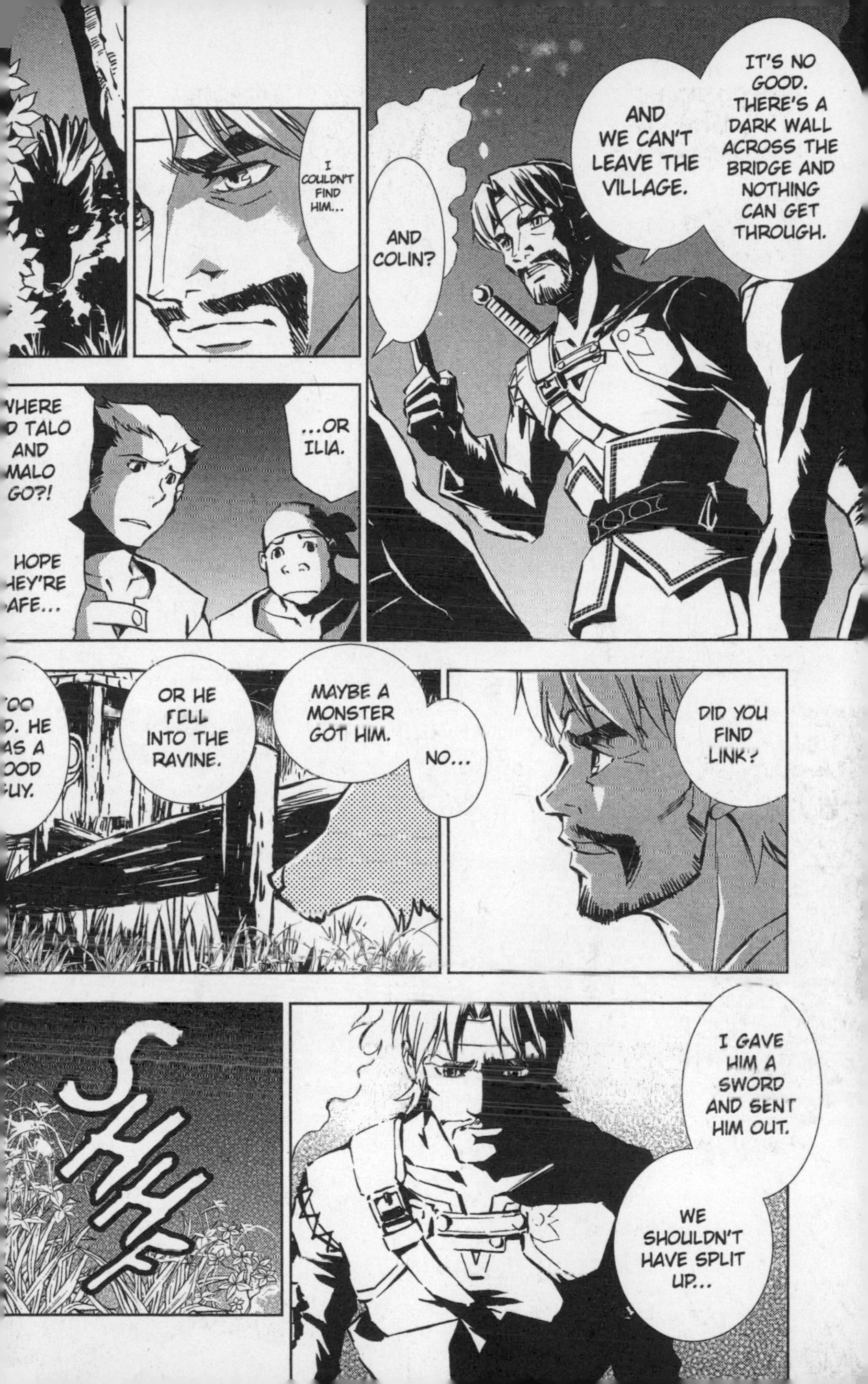

IT'S NO GOOD. THERE'S A DARK WALL ACROSS THE BRIDGE AND NOTHING CAN GET THROUGH.
AND WE CAN'T LEAVE THE VILLAGE.
AND COLIN?
I COULDN'T FIND HIM...
...OR ILIA.
VHERE D TALO AND MALO GO?!
HOPE HEY'RE AFE...
DID YOU FIND LINK?
NO...
MAYBE A MONSTER GOT HIM.
OR HE FELL INTO THE RAVINE.
TOO D. HE AS A OOD UY.
I GAVE HIM A SWORD AND SENT HIM OUT.
WE SHOULDN'T HAVE SPLIT UP...
SHHH

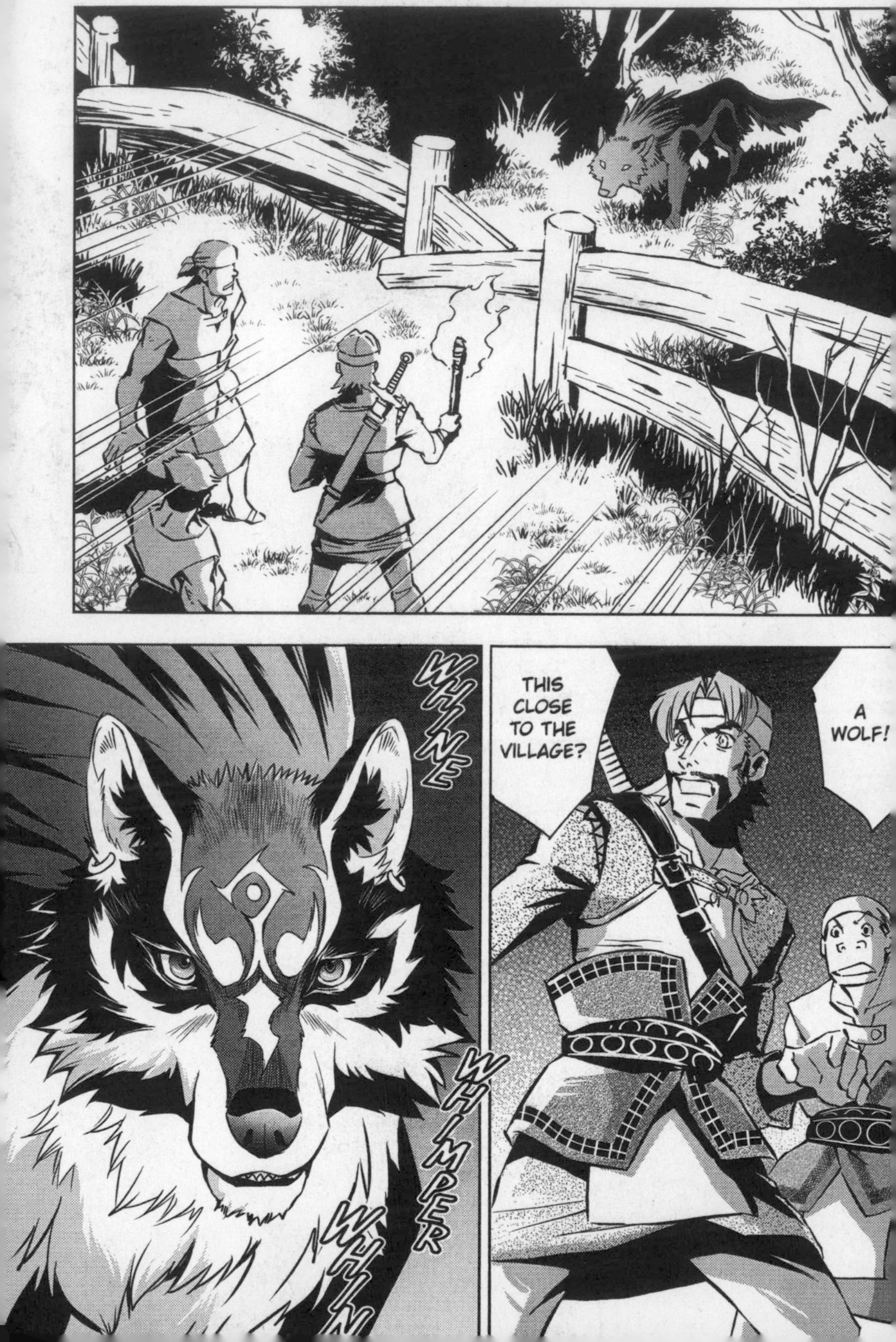
A WOLF!
THIS CLOSE TO THE VILLAGE?
WHINE
WHIMPER
WHIN

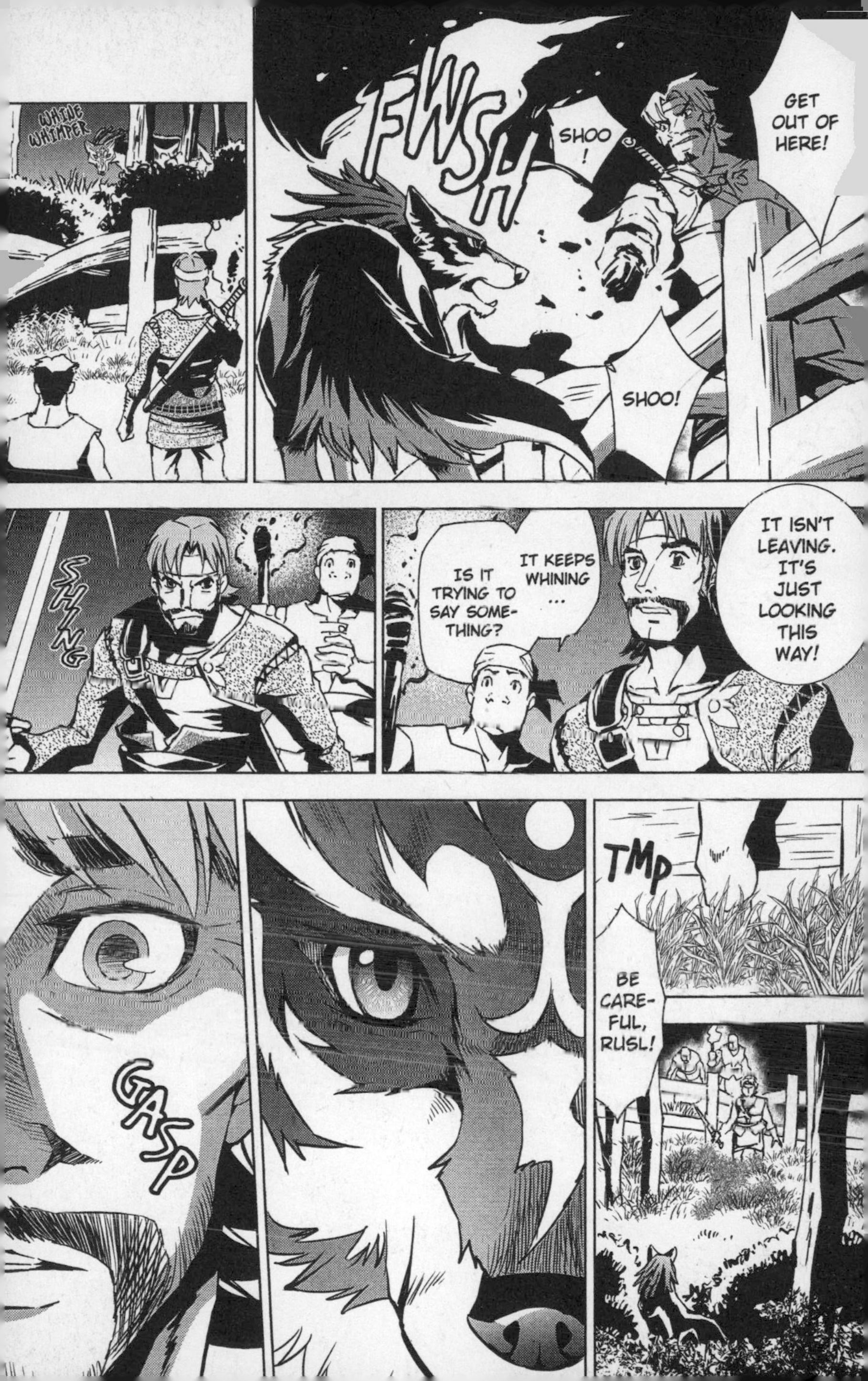
GET OUT OF HERE!
SHOO!
FWSH
SHOO!
WHINE WHIMPER
IT ISN'T LEAVING. IT'S JUST LOOKING THIS WAY!
IT KEEPS WHINING ...
IS IT TRYING TO SAY SOME-THING?
SHING
TMP
BE CARE-FUL, RUSL!
GASP

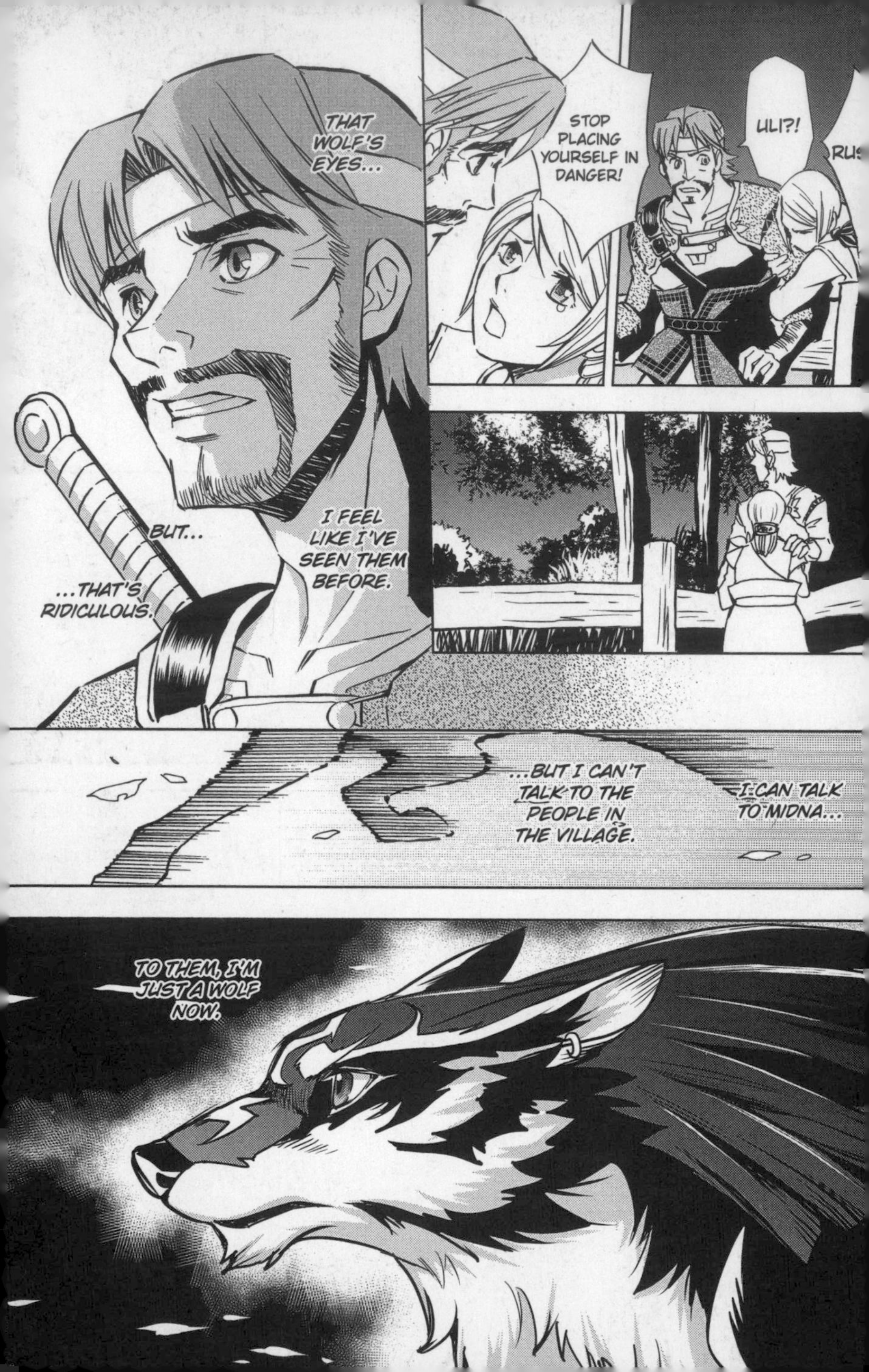
ULI?!
STOP PLACING YOURSELF IN DANGER!
THAT WOLF'S EYES...
I FEEL LIKE I'VE SEEN THEM BEFORE.
BUT...
...THAT'S RIDICULOUS.
I CAN TALK TO MIDNA...
...BUT I CAN'T TALK TO THE PEOPLE IN THE VILLAGE.
TO THEM, I'M JUST A WOLF NOW.

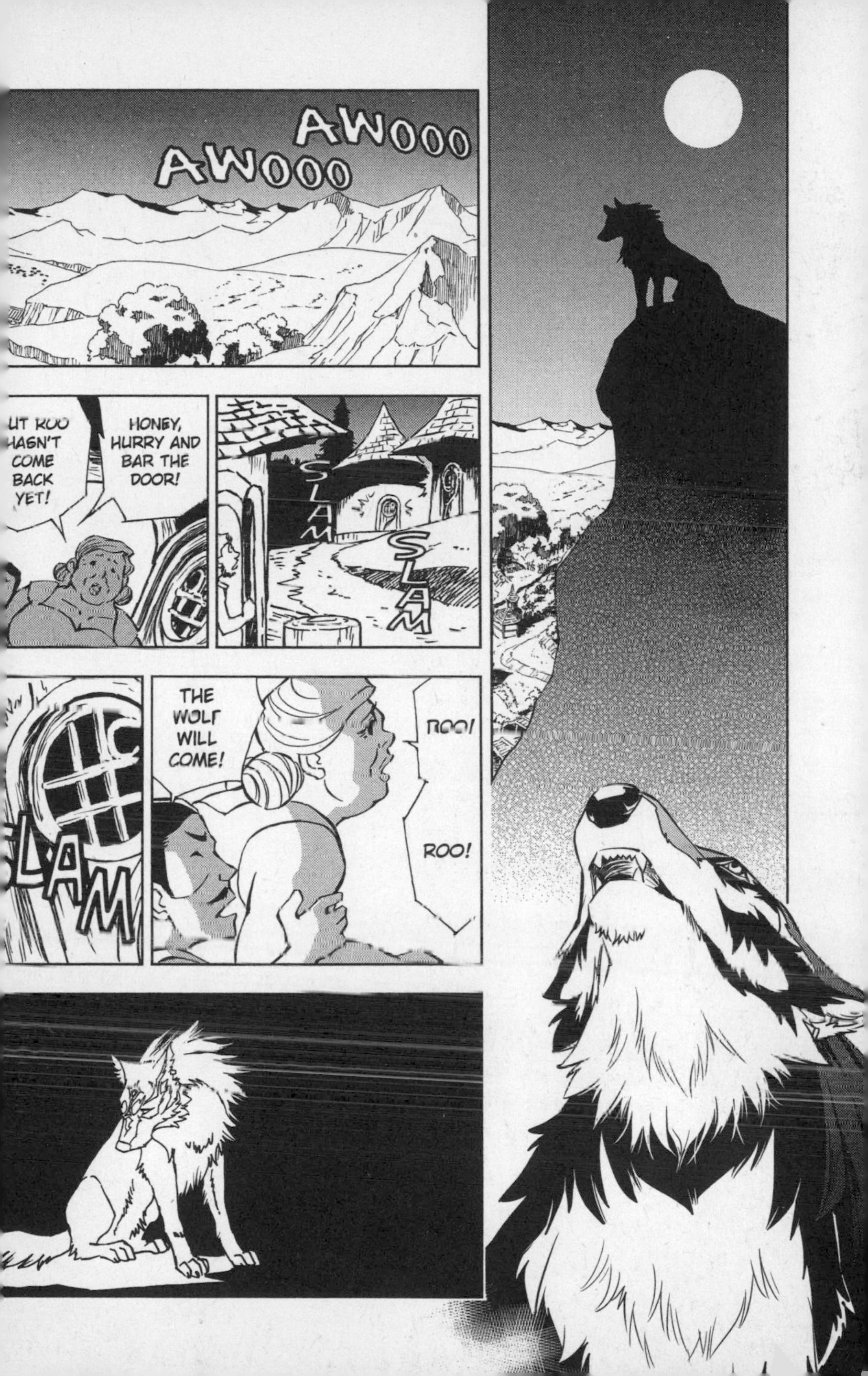
AWOOO
AWOOO
SLAM
SLAM
SLAM
HONEY, HURRY AND BAR THE DOOR!
UT ROO HASN'T COME BACK YET!
ROO!
ROO!
THE WOLF WILL COME!
SLAM

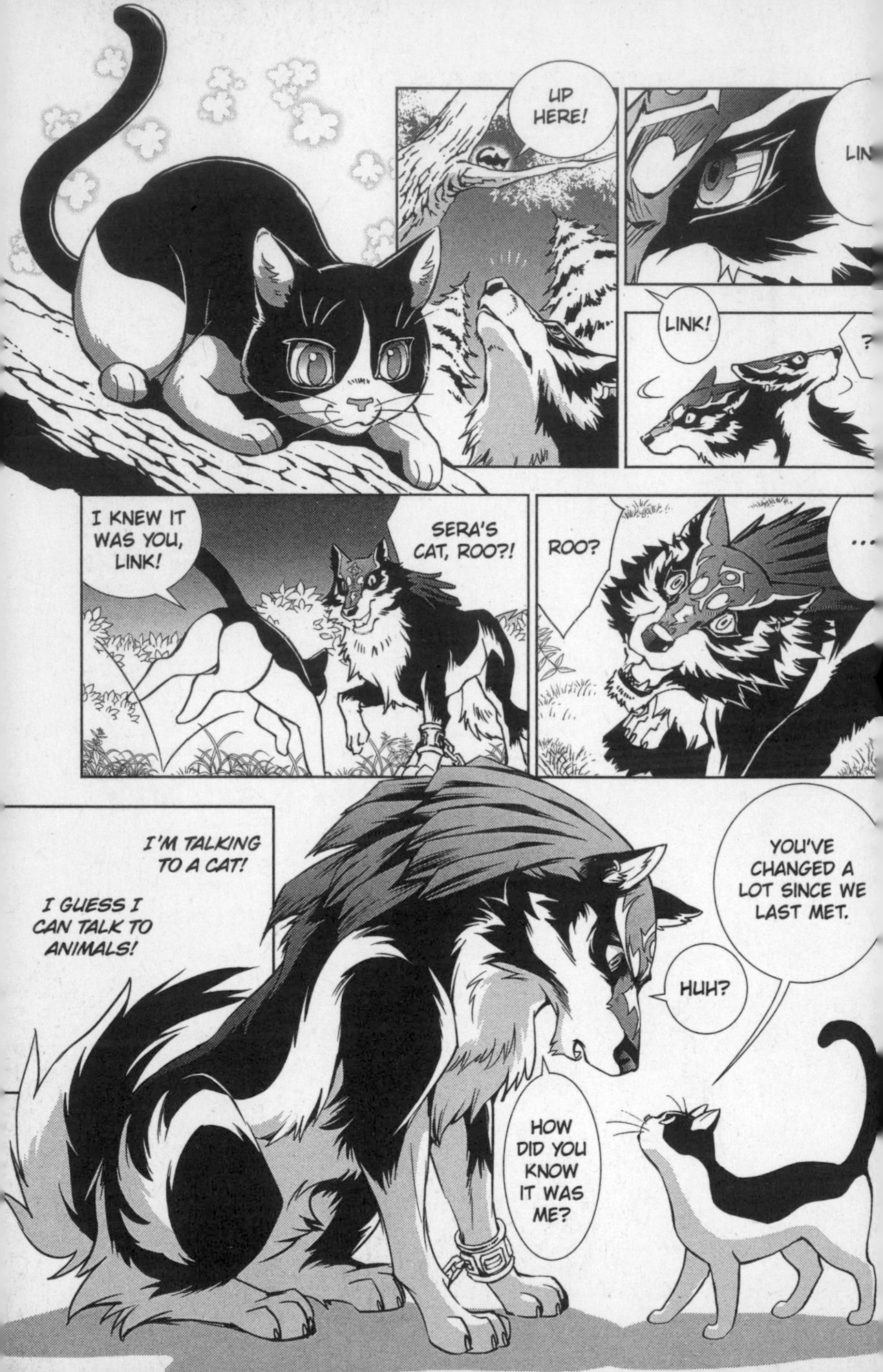

LIN
LINK!
?
UP HERE!
...
ROO?
SERA'S CAT, ROO?!
I KNEW IT WAS YOU, LINK!
YOU'VE CHANGED A LOT SINCE WE LAST MET.
HUH?
HOW DID YOU KNOW IT WAS ME?
I'M TALKING TO A CAT!
I GUESS I CAN TALK TO ANIMALS!

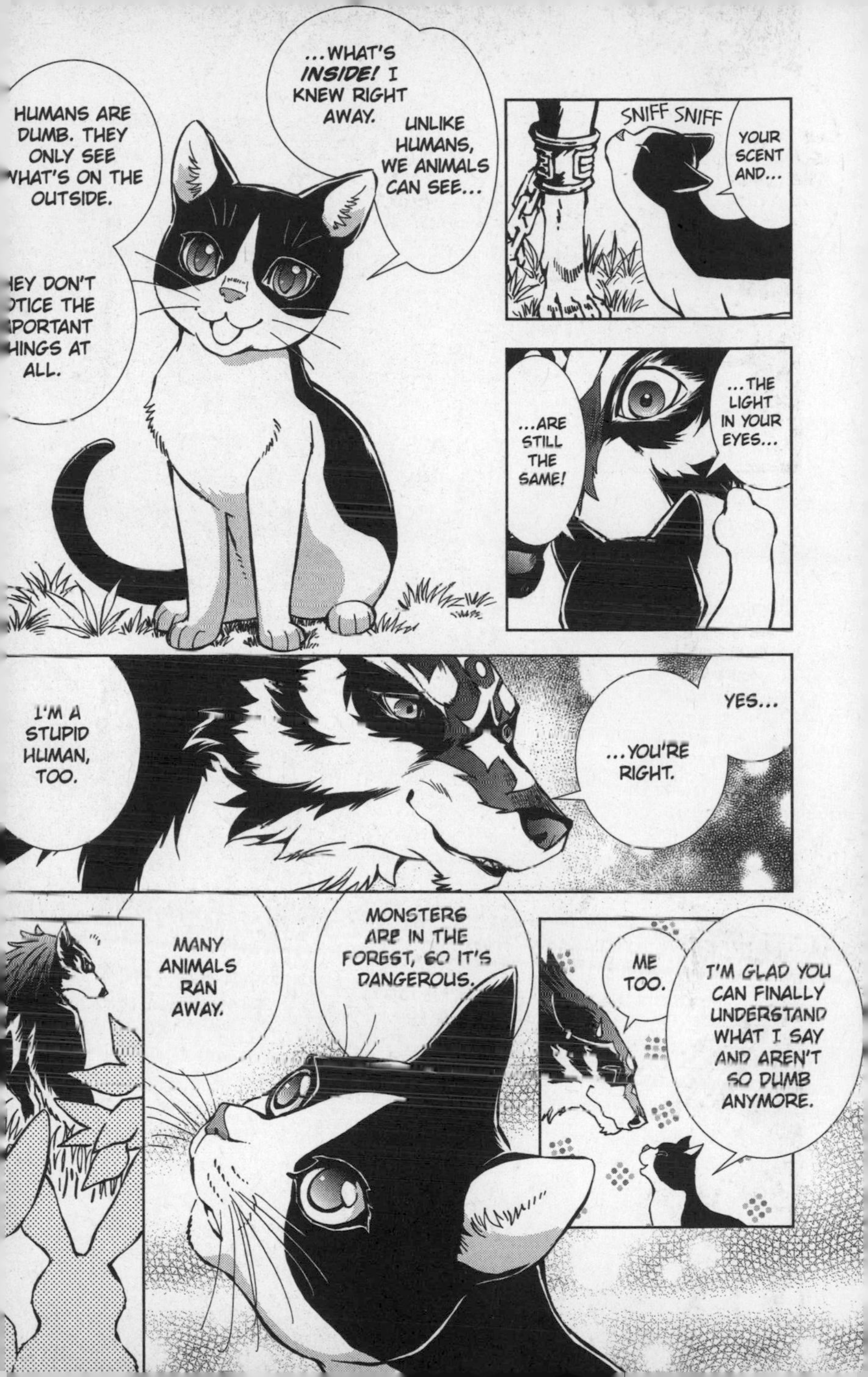
SNIFF SNIFF
YOUR SCENT AND...
...THE LIGHT IN YOUR EYES...
...ARE STILL THE SAME!
UNLIKE HUMANS, WE ANIMALS CAN SEE...
...WHAT'S *INSIDE!* I KNEW RIGHT AWAY.
HUMANS ARE DUMB. THEY ONLY SEE HAT'S ON THE OUTSIDE.
HEY DON'T OTICE THE PORTANT HINGS AT ALL.
YES...
...YOU'RE RIGHT.
I'M A STUPID HUMAN, TOO.
I'M GLAD YOU CAN FINALLY UNDERSTAND WHAT I SAY AND AREN'T SO DUMB ANYMORE.
ME TOO.
MONSTERS ARE IN THE FOREST, SO IT'S DANGEROUS.
MANY ANIMALS RAN AWAY.

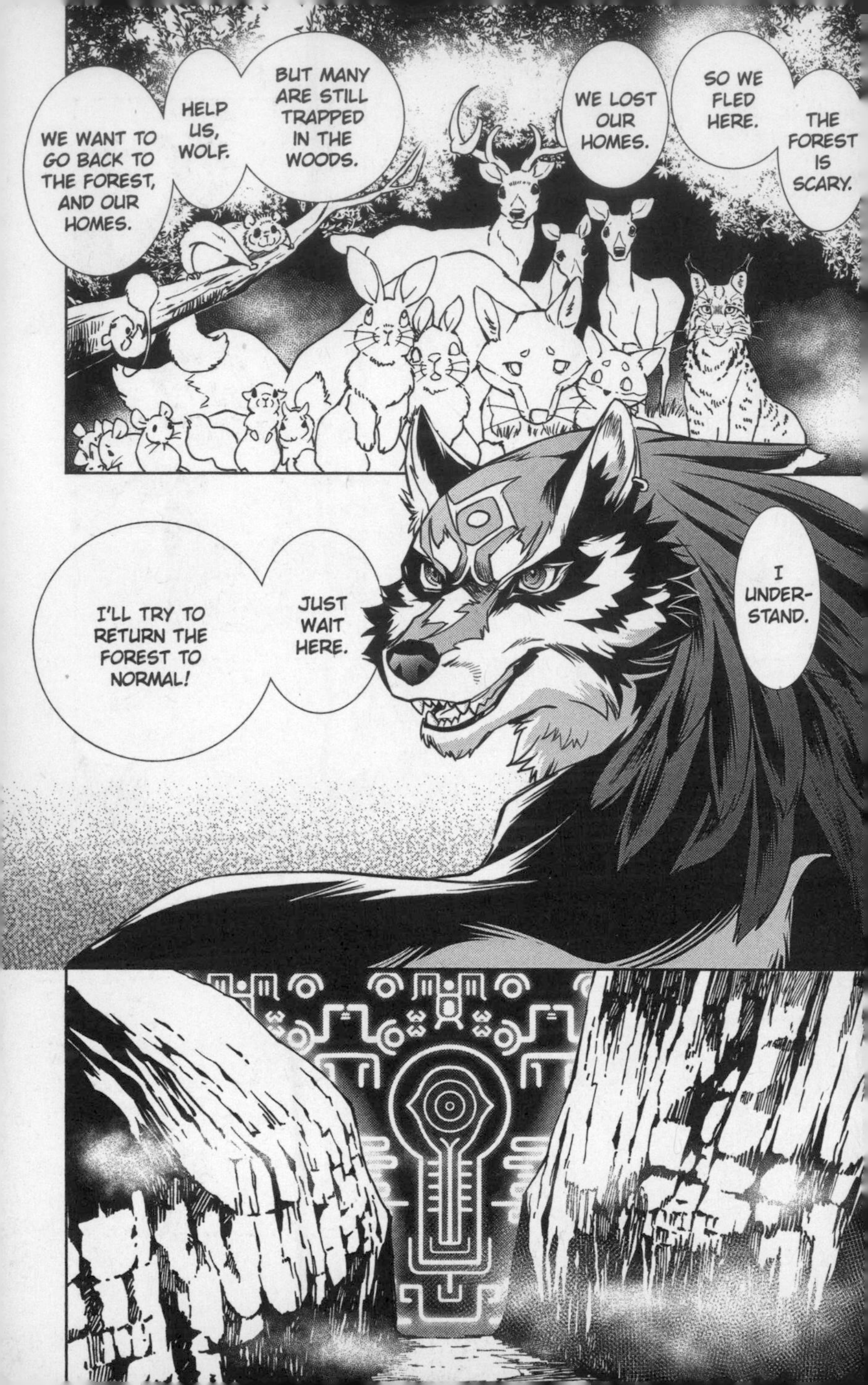
THE FOREST IS SCARY.
SO WE FLED HERE.
WE LOST OUR HOMES.
BUT MANY ARE STILL TRAPPED IN THE WOODS.
HELP US, WOLF.
WE WANT TO GO BACK TO THE FOREST, AND OUR HOMES.
I UNDER-STAND.
JUST WAIT HERE.
I'LL TRY TO RETURN THE FOREST TO NORMAL!

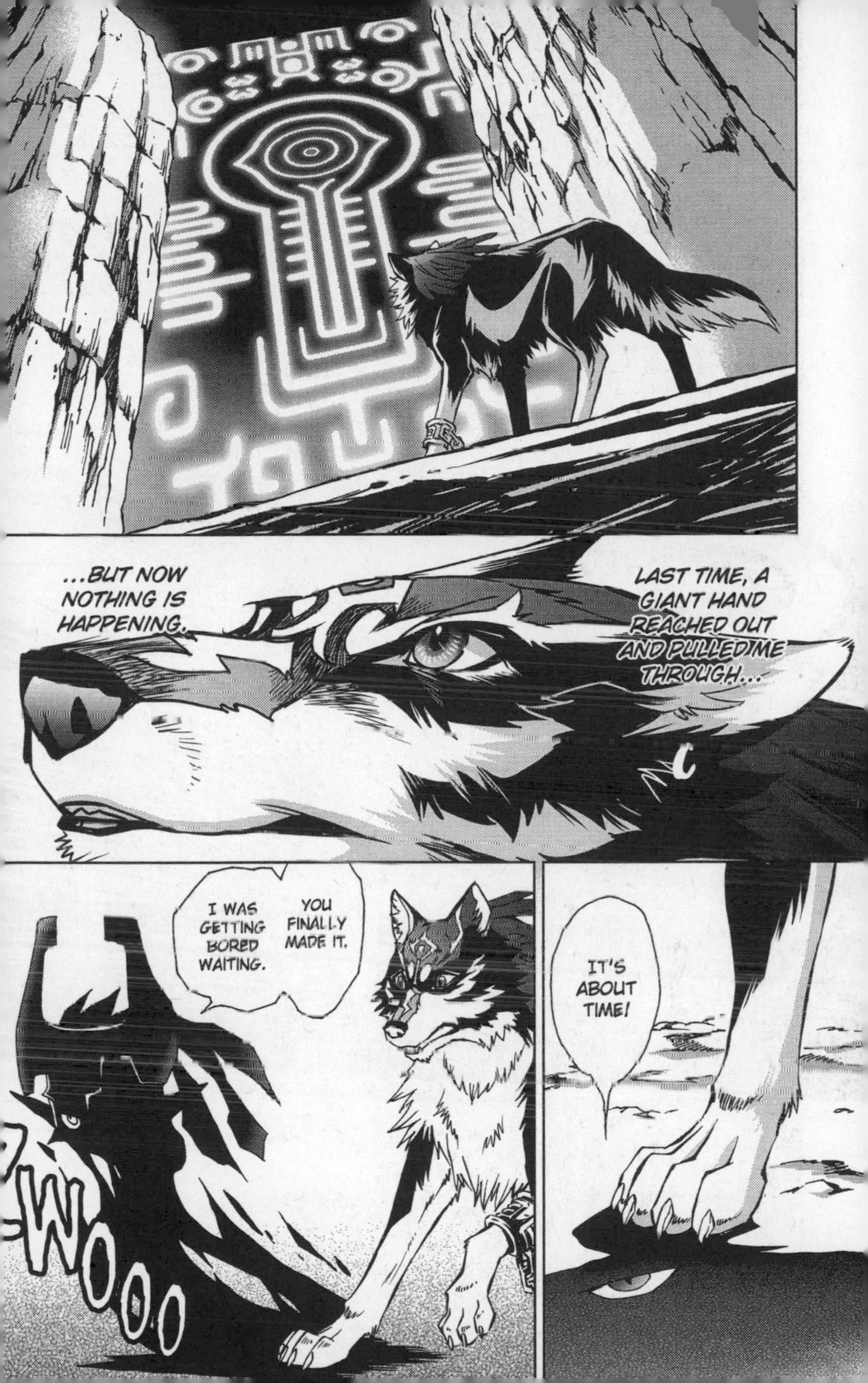
LAST TIME, A GIANT HAND REACHED OUT AND PULLED ME THROUGH...
...BUT NOW NOTHING IS HAPPENING.
IT'S ABOUT TIME!
YOU FINALLY MADE IT.
I WAS GETTING BORED WAITING.
WOOO

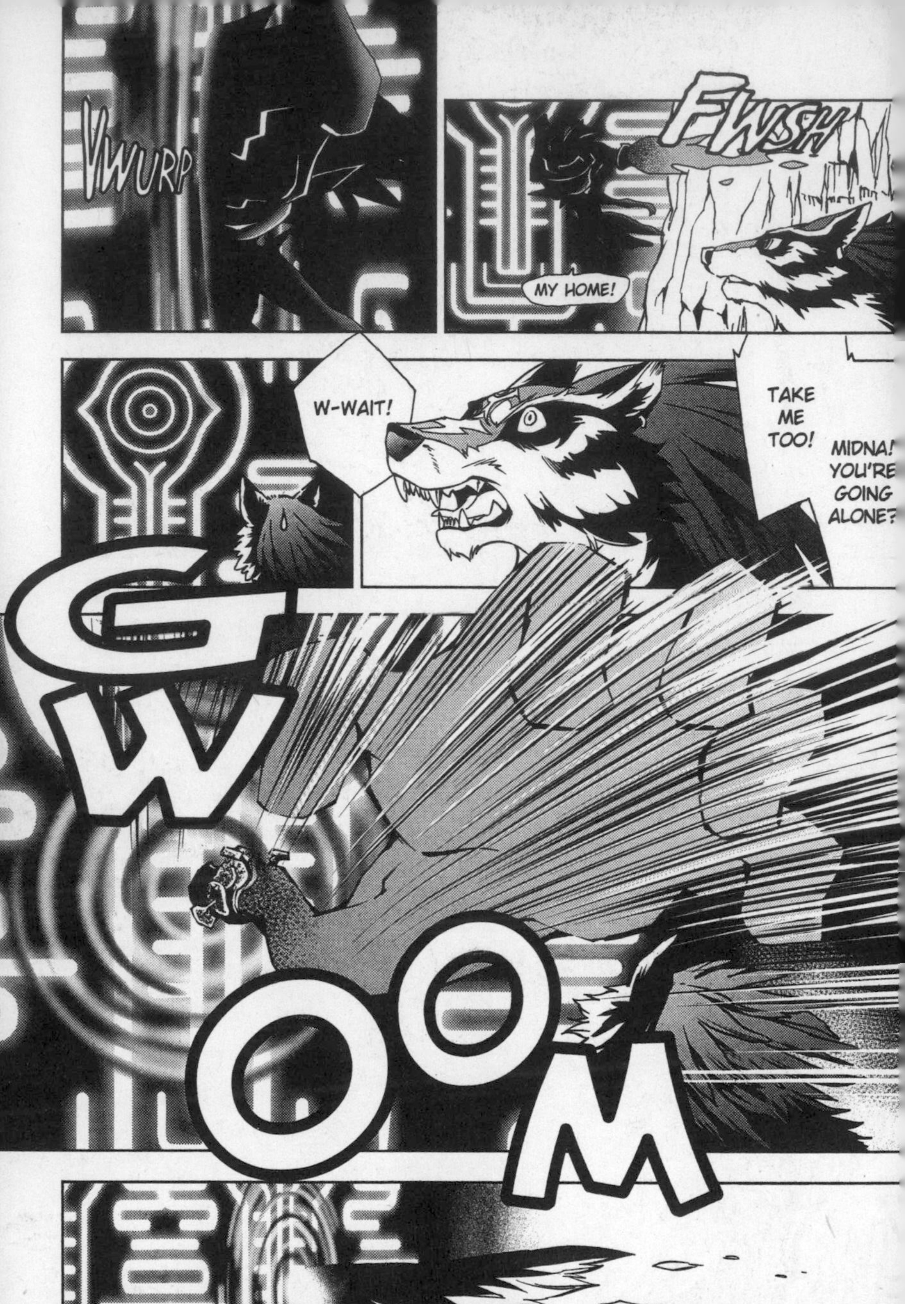
FWSH
MY HOME!
VWURP
MIDNA! YOU'RE GOING ALONE?
TAKE ME TOO!
W-WAIT!
GWOOOM

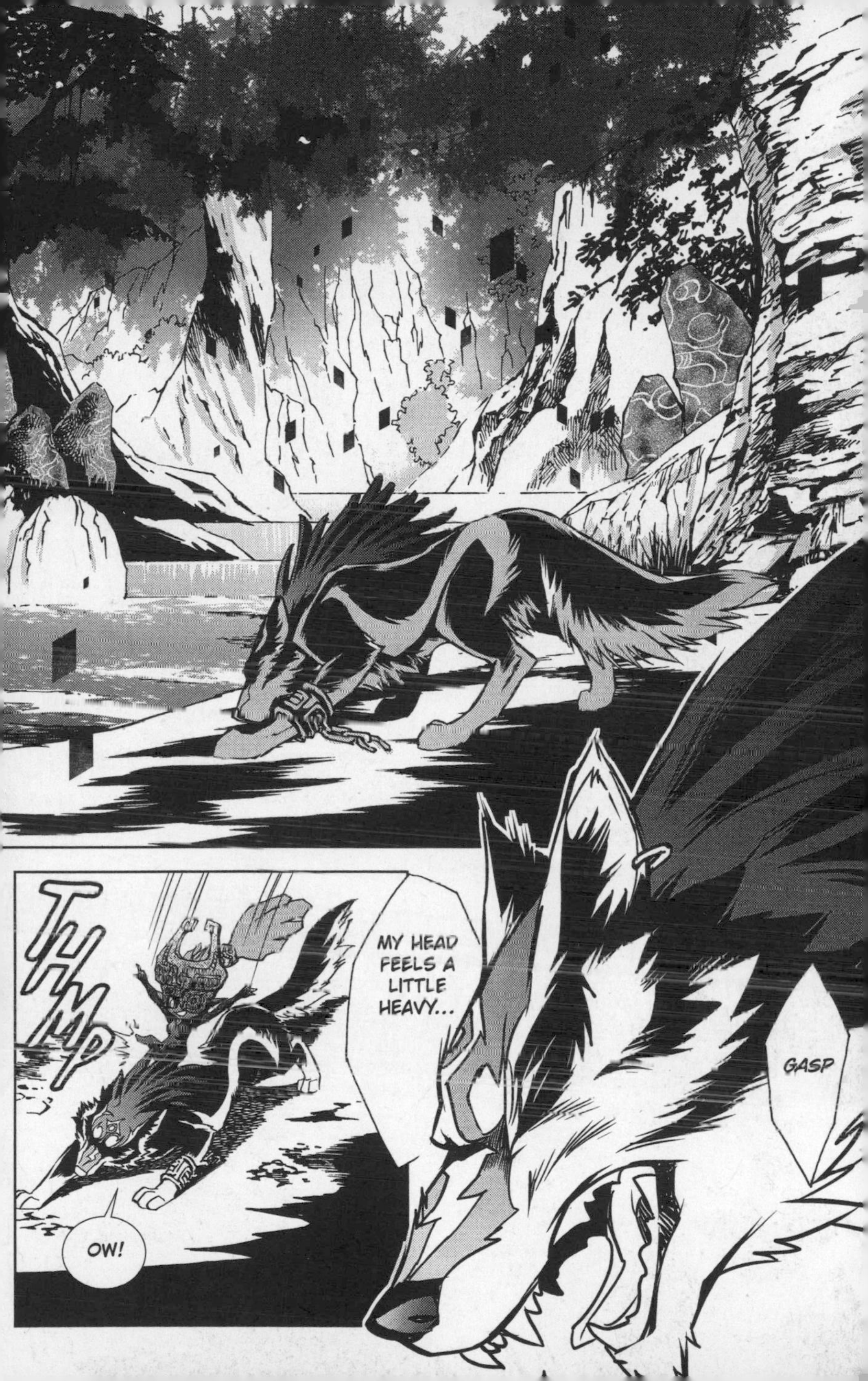
GASP
MY HEAD FEELS A LITTLE HEAVY...
THMP
OW!

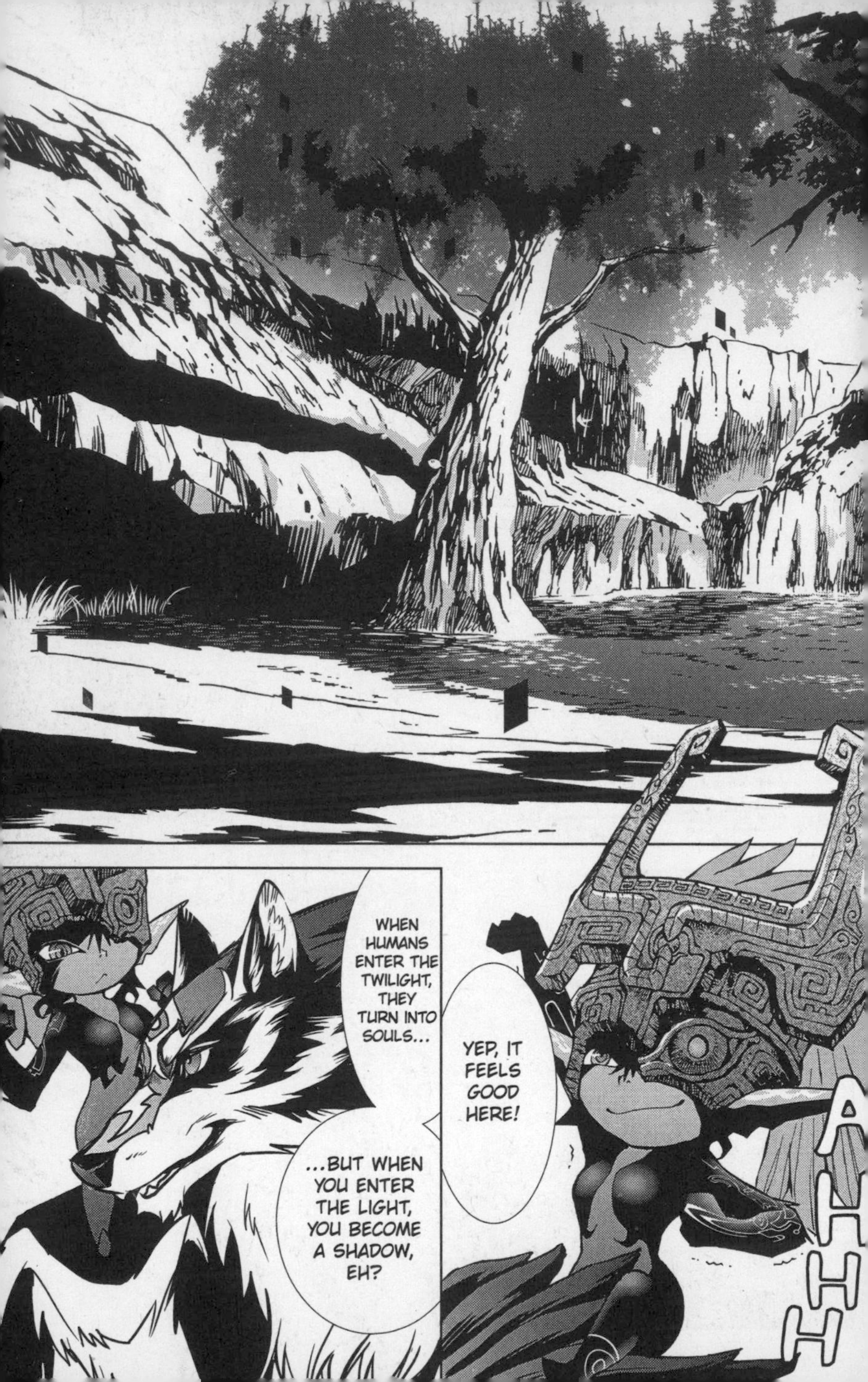
AHHHHH
YEP, IT FEELS GOOD HERE!
WHEN HUMANS ENTER THE TWILIGHT, THEY TURN INTO SOULS...
...BUT WHEN YOU ENTER THE LIGHT, YOU BECOME A SHADOW, EH?

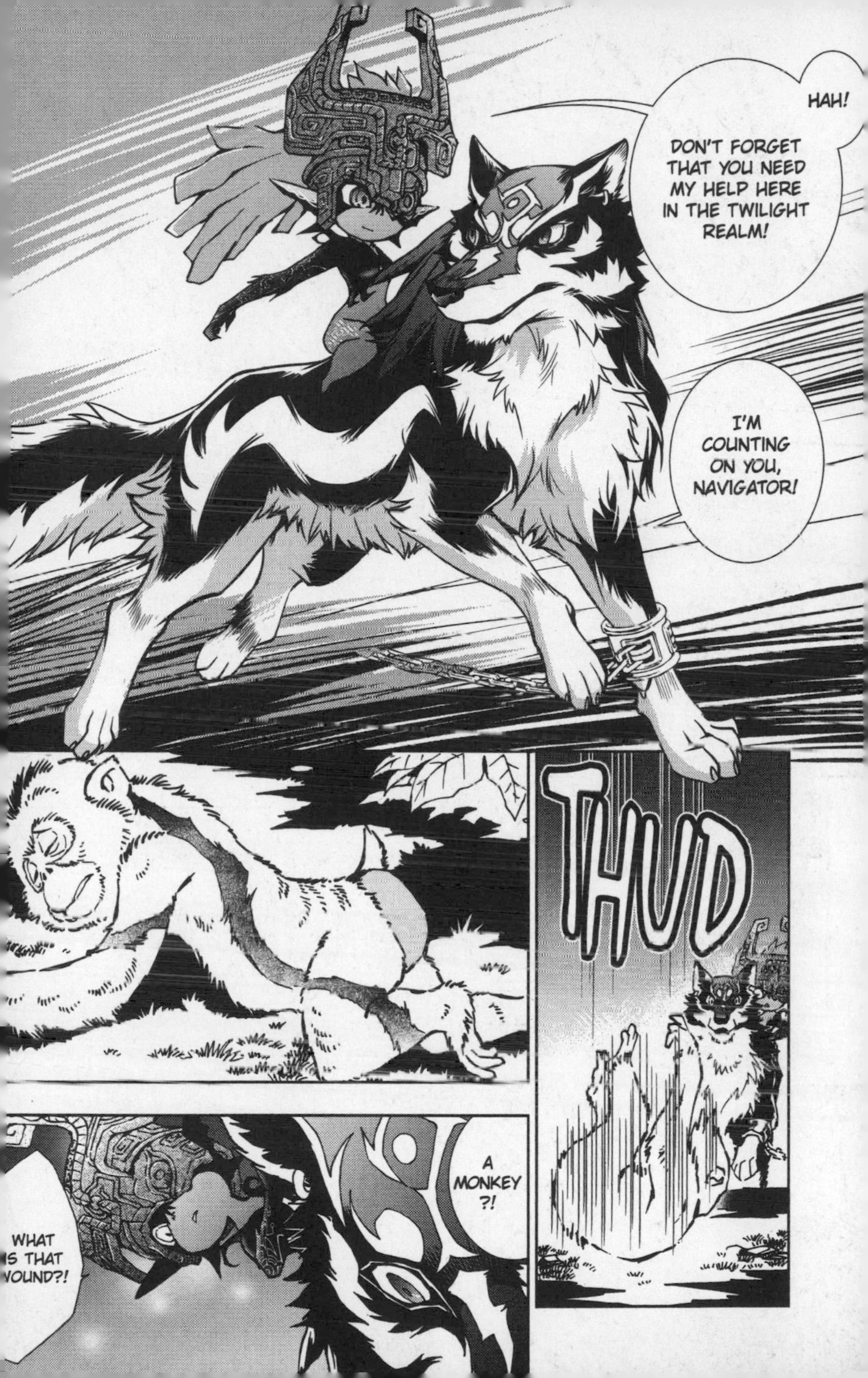

HAH!
DON'T FORGET THAT YOU NEED MY HELP HERE IN THE TWILIGHT REALM!
I'M COUNTING ON YOU, NAVIGATOR!
THUD
A MONKEY?!
WHAT IS THAT WOUND?!

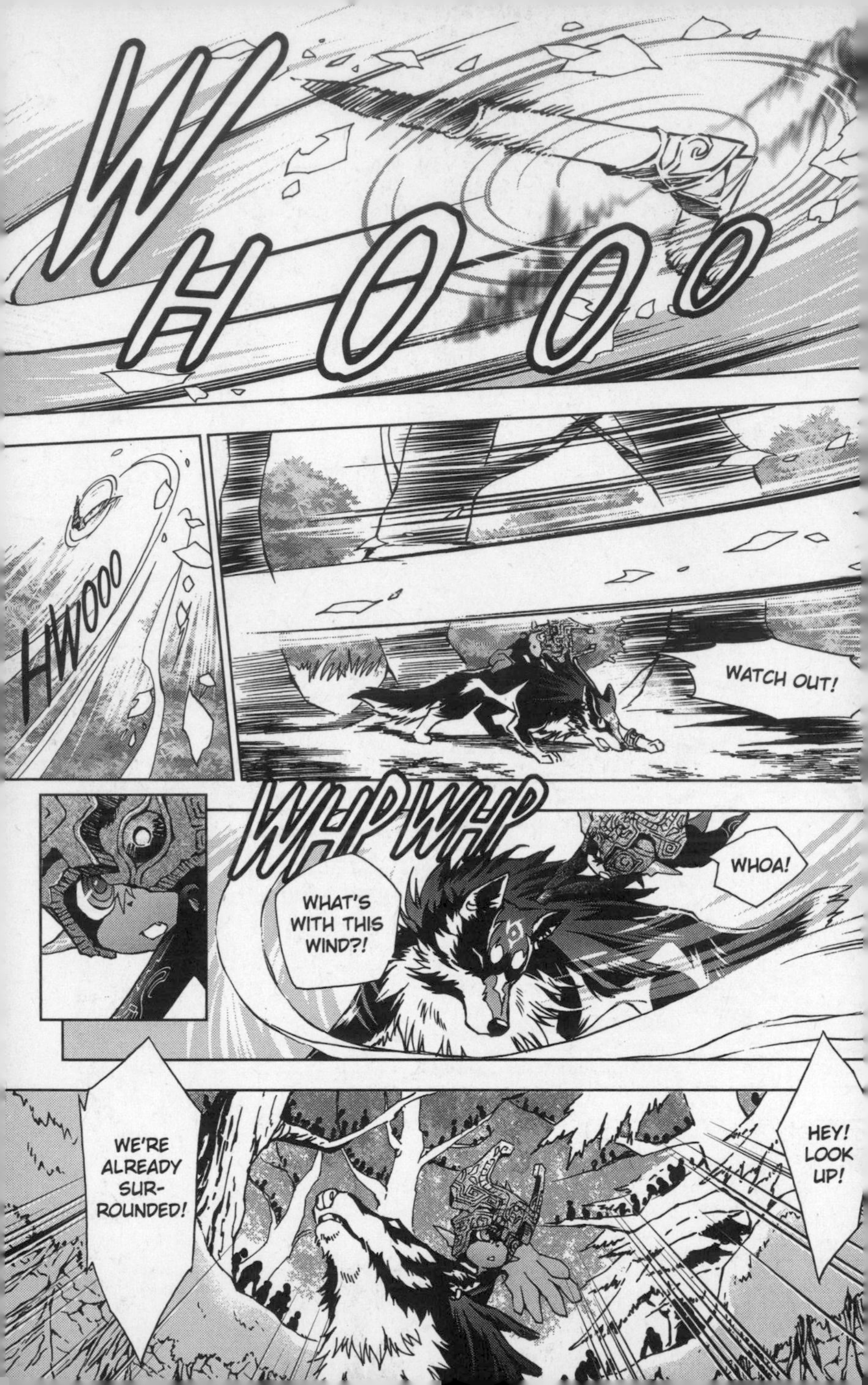
WHOOOO
WATCH OUT!
HWOOO
WHPWHP
WHOA!
WHAT'S WITH THIS WIND?!
HEY! LOOK UP!
WE'RE ALREADY SUR-ROUNDED!

HOO
EEEE
OO OO
EE

WHO
INTRUDES?

WHO
DARES?

HWOOOO

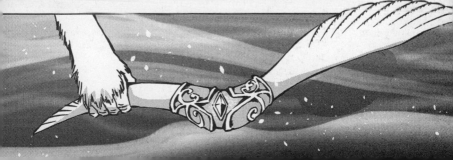

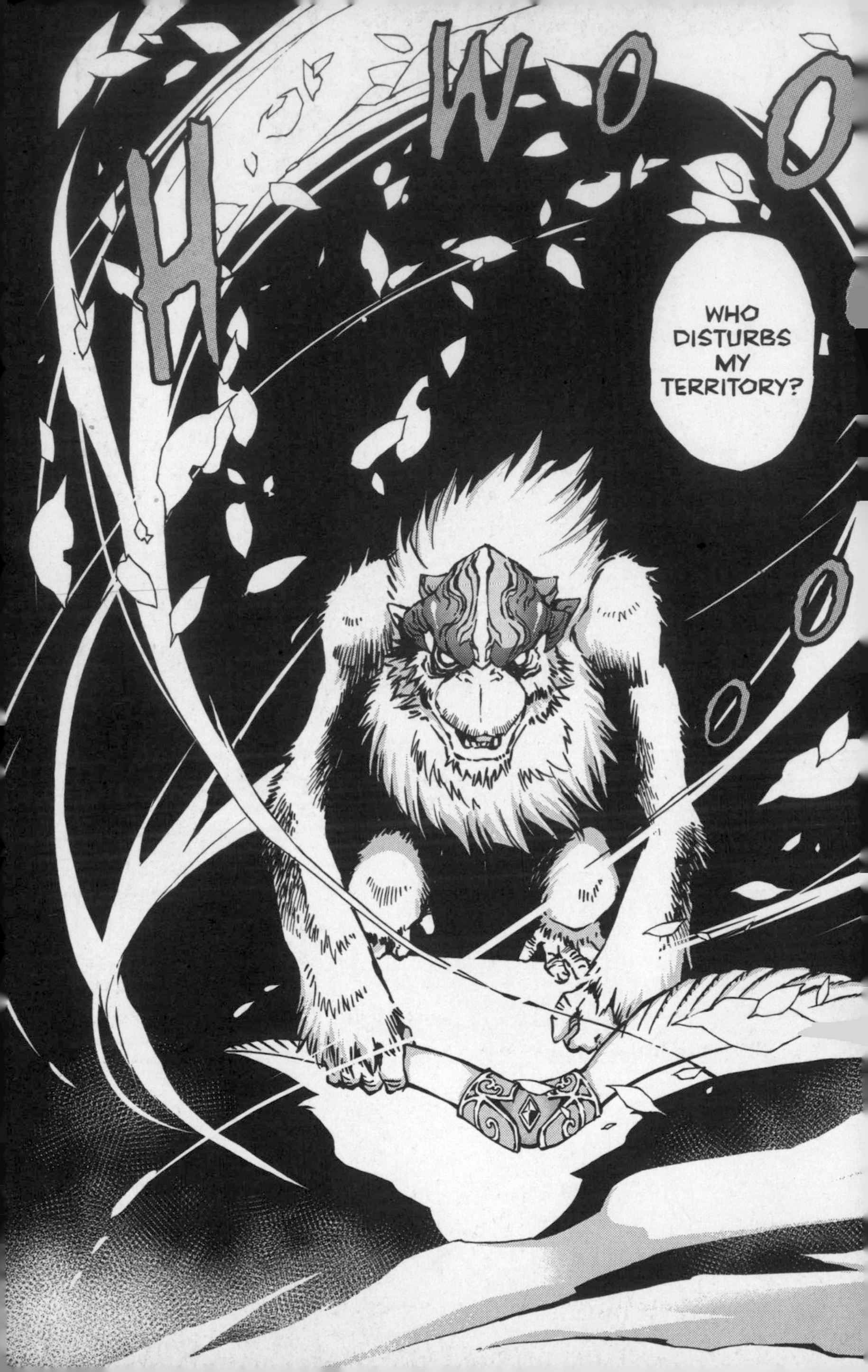
HWOO
WHO DISTURBS MY TERRITORY?
OOO

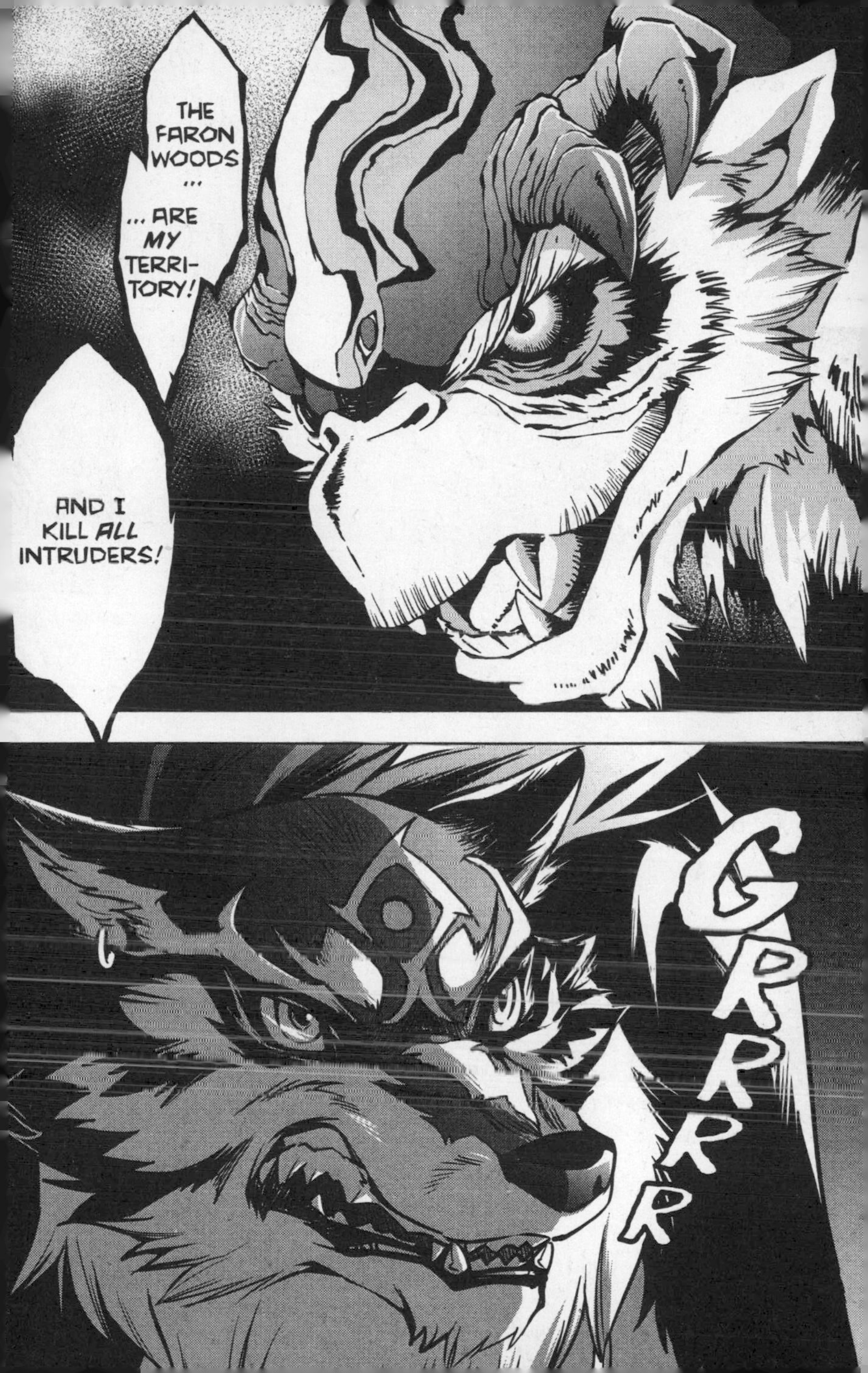
THE FARON WOODS ...
... ARE *MY* TERRITORY!
AND I KILL *ALL* INTRUDERS!
GRRRRR

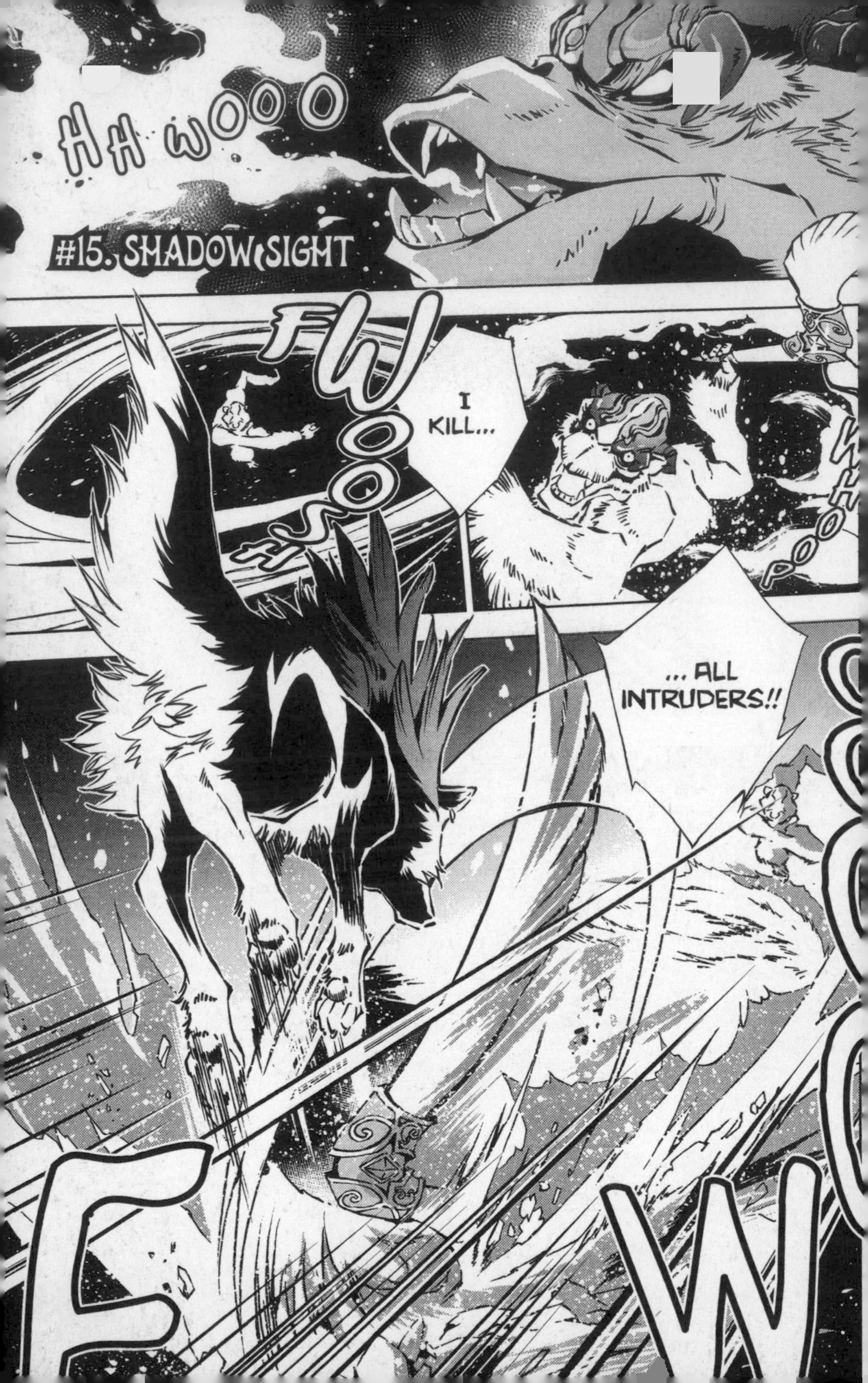
HH WOOO
#15. SHADOW SIGHT
WHOOP
I KILL...
FWOOSH
... ALL INTRUDERS!!

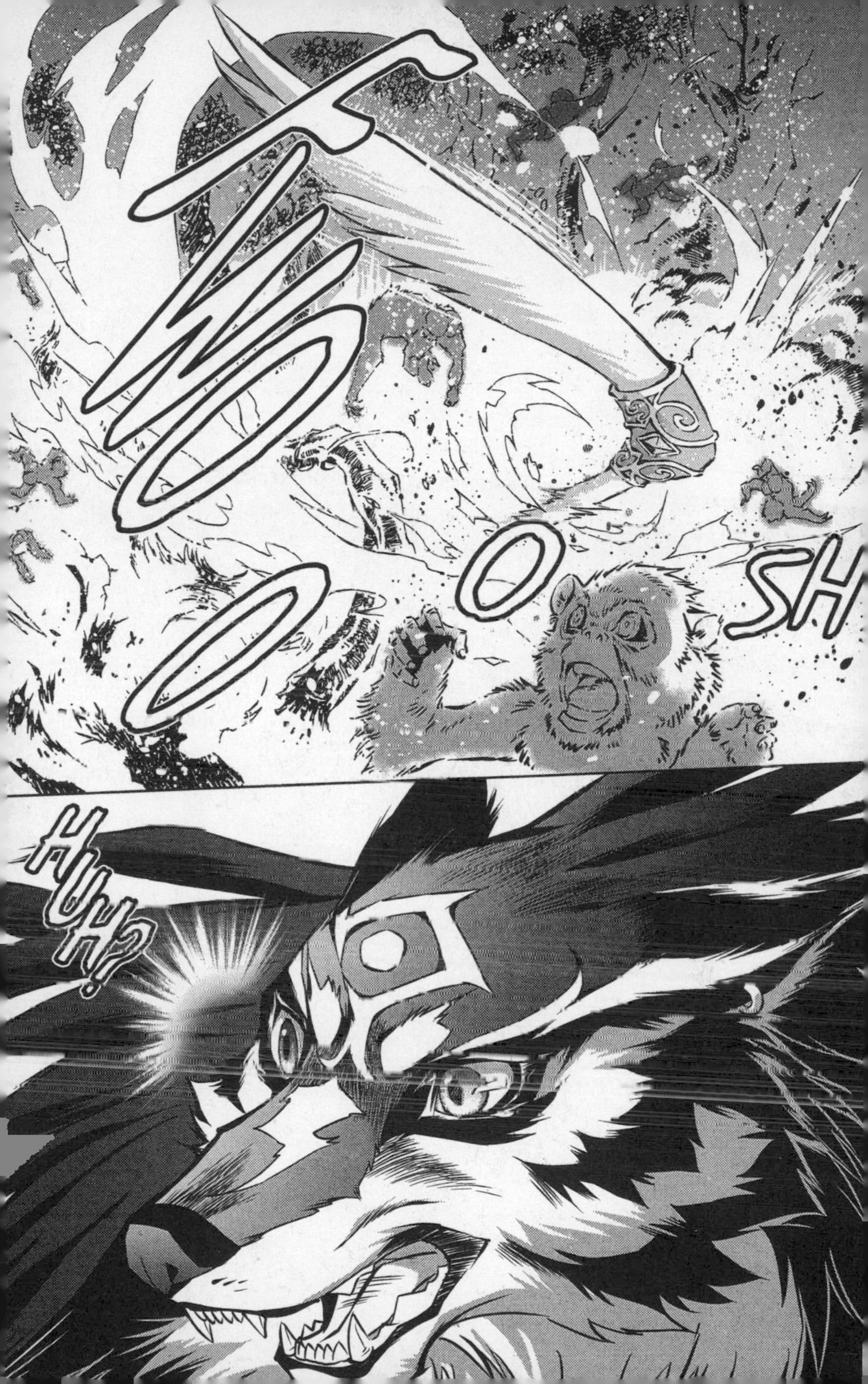
FWOOOSH
HUH!?

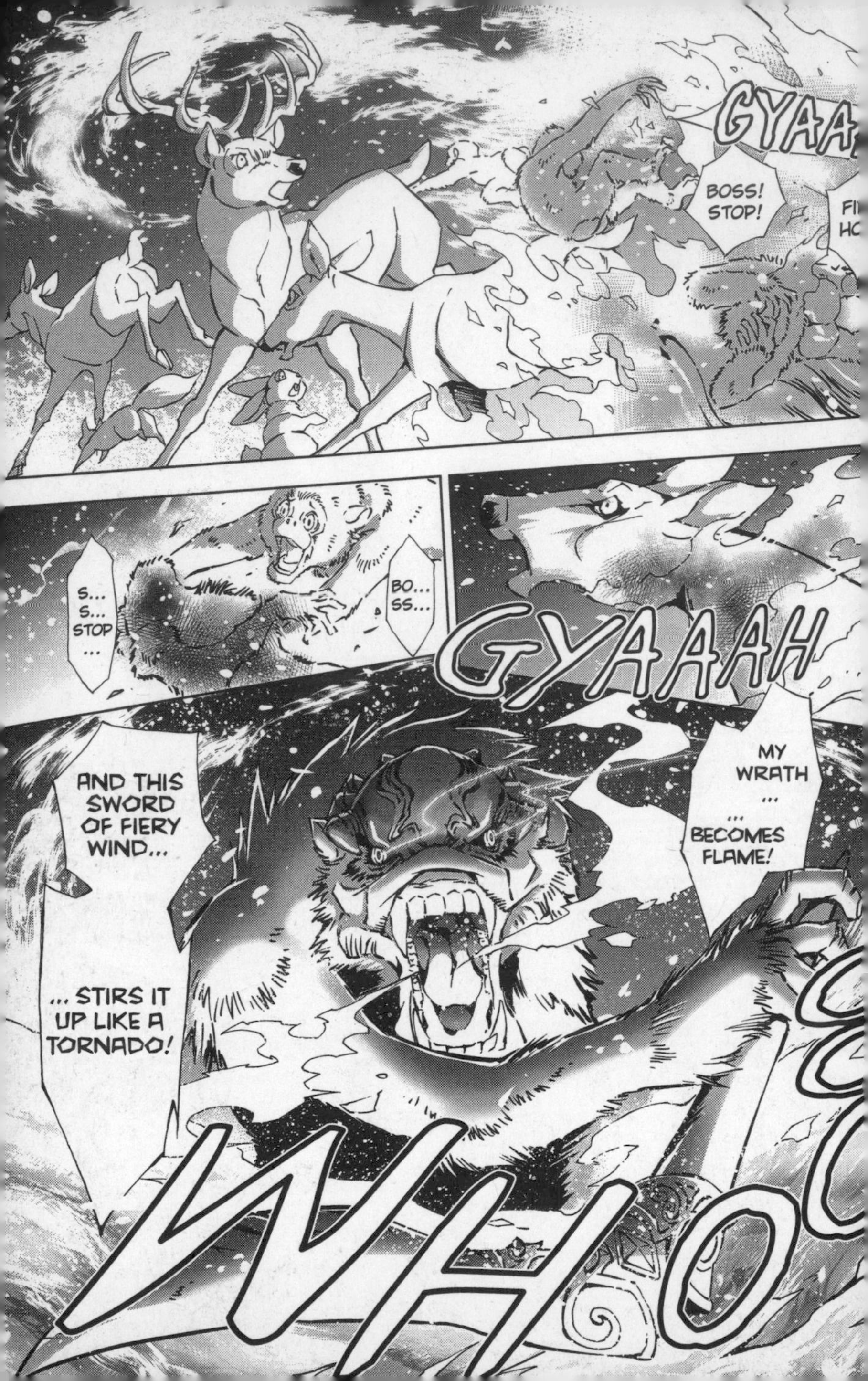
GYAA
BOSS! STOP!
FI HO
GYAAAH
BO... SS...
S... S... STOP ...
MY WRATH ... ... BECOMES FLAME!
AND THIS SWORD OF FIERY WIND...
... STIRS IT UP LIKE A TORNADO!
WHOO

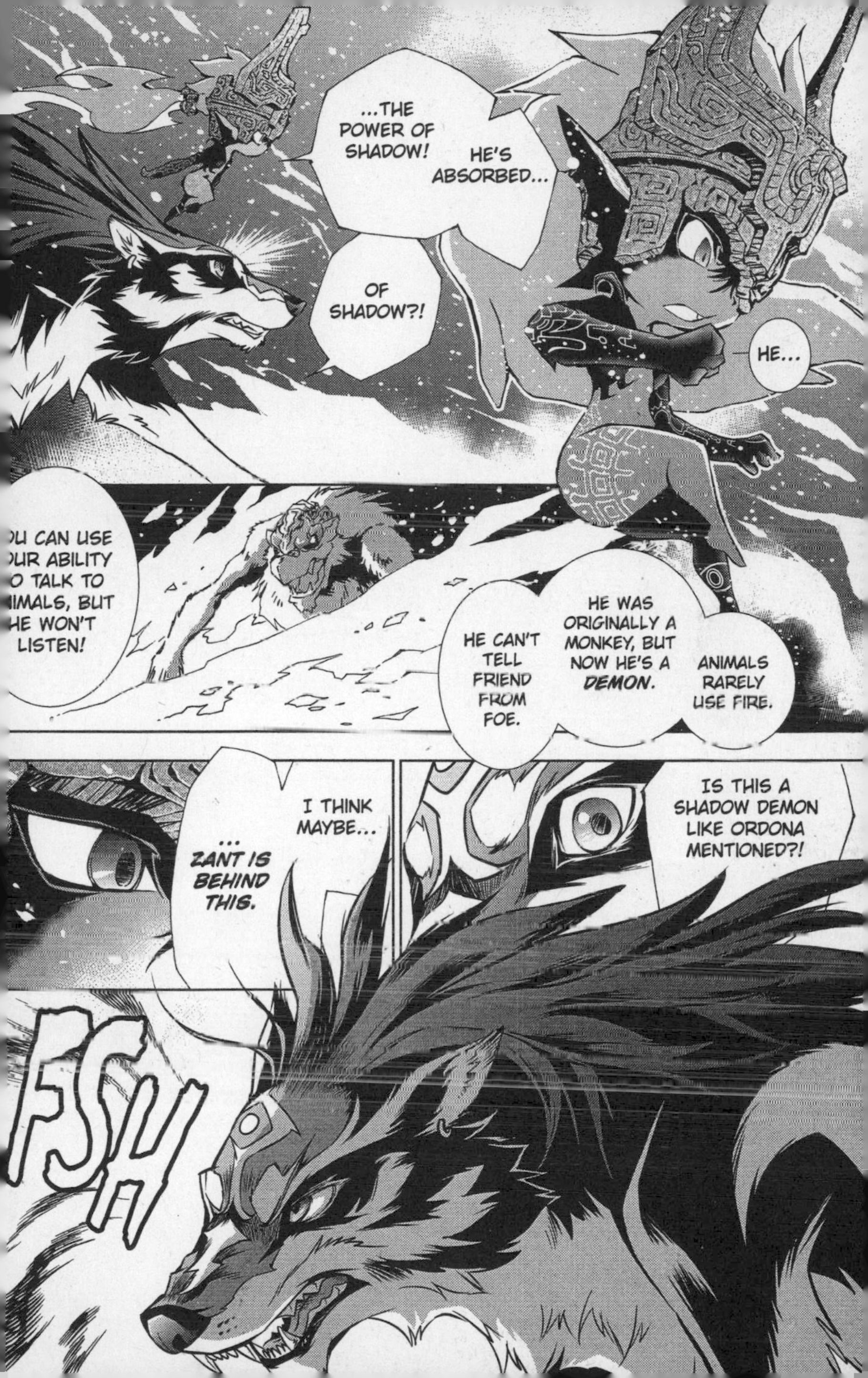
HE...
HE'S ABSORBED...
...THE POWER OF SHADOW!
OF SHADOW?!
ANIMALS RARELY USE FIRE.
HE WAS ORIGINALLY A MONKEY, BUT NOW HE'S A DEMON.
HE CAN'T TELL FRIEND FROM FOE.
OU CAN USE OUR ABILITY O TALK TO IMALS, BUT HE WON'T LISTEN!
IS THIS A SHADOW DEMON LIKE ORDONA MENTIONED?!
I THINK MAYBE...
...ZANT IS BEHIND THIS.
FSH

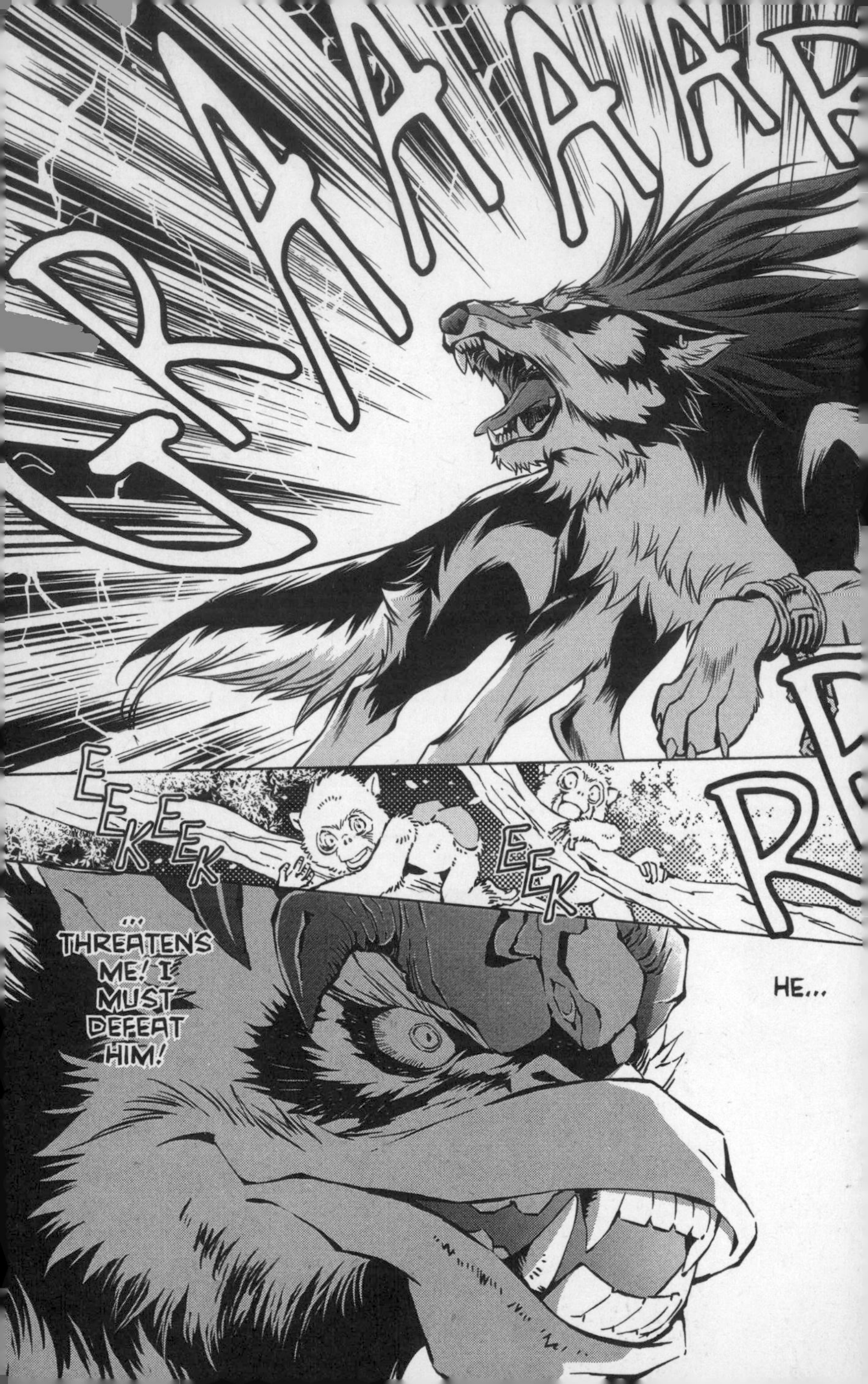
RAAAAR
EEEEK
EEK
HE...
...THREATENS ME! I MUST DEFEAT HIM!

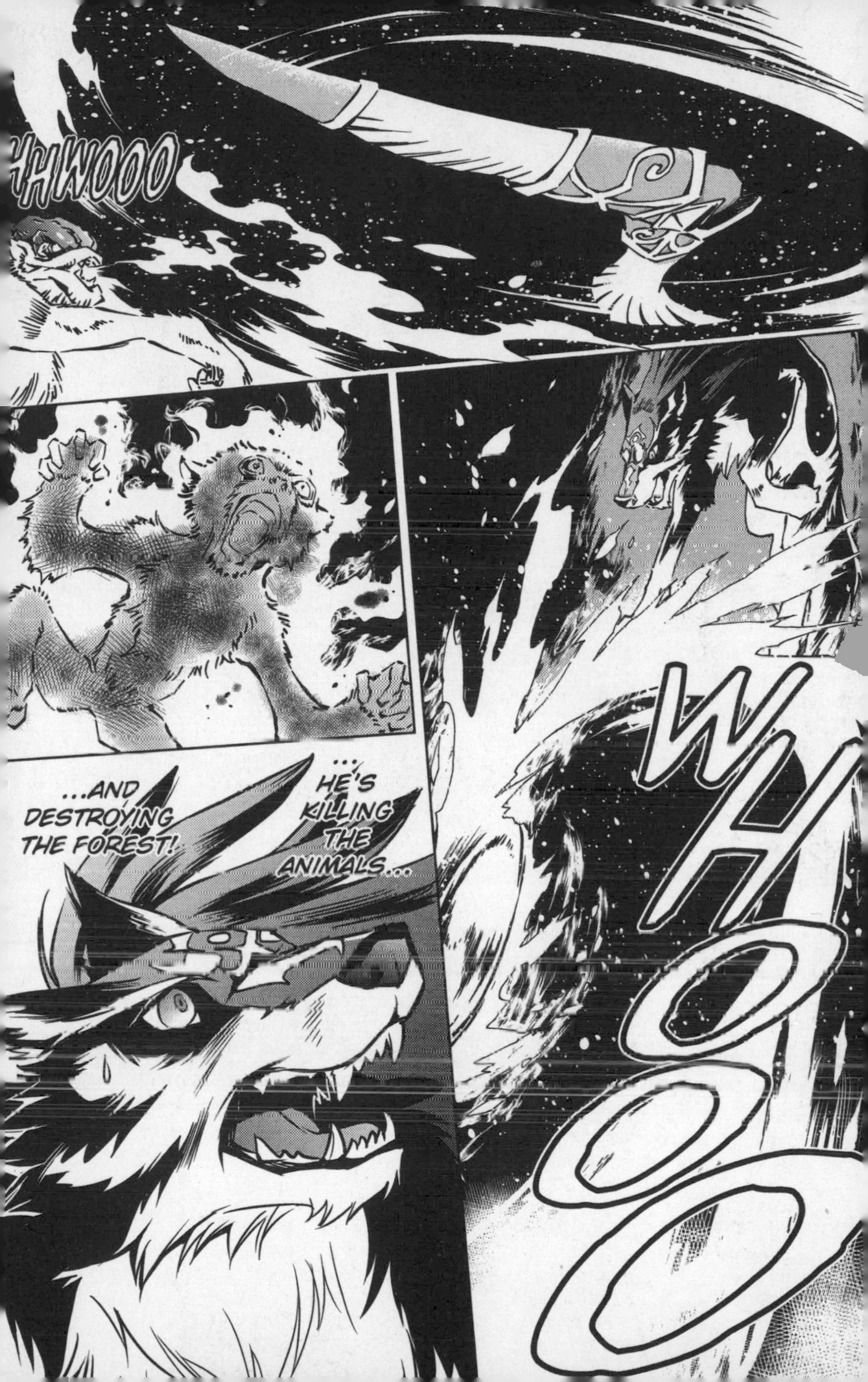
HWOOO
WHOOO
...HE'S KILLING THE ANIMALS...
...AND DESTROYING THE FOREST!

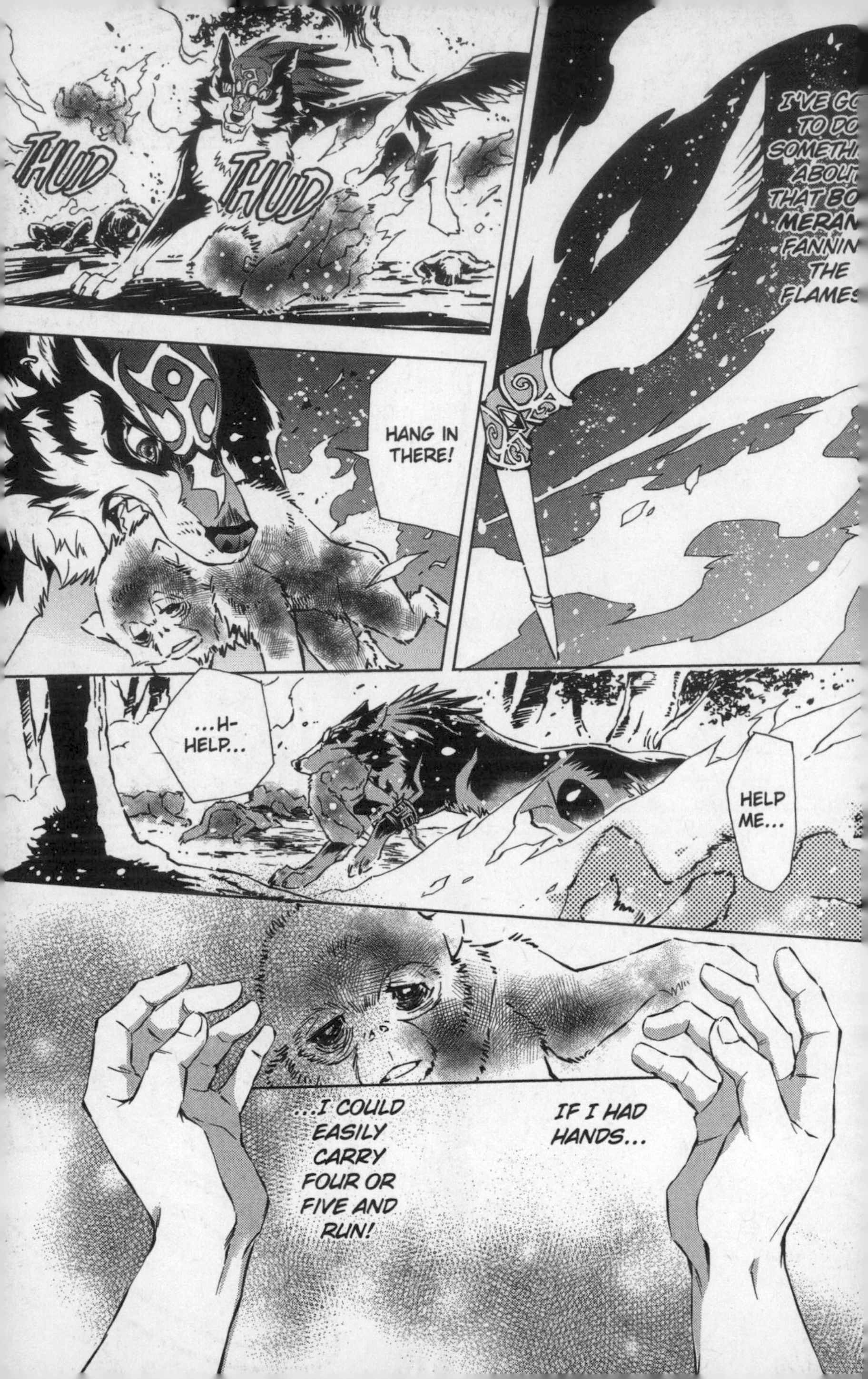

I'VE GO
TO DO
SOMETHI
ABOU
THAT BO
MERAN
FANNIN
THE
FLAMES
THUD
THUD
HANG IN THERE!
HELP ME...
...H- HELP...
IF I HAD HANDS...
...I COULD EASILY CARRY FOUR OR FIVE AND RUN!

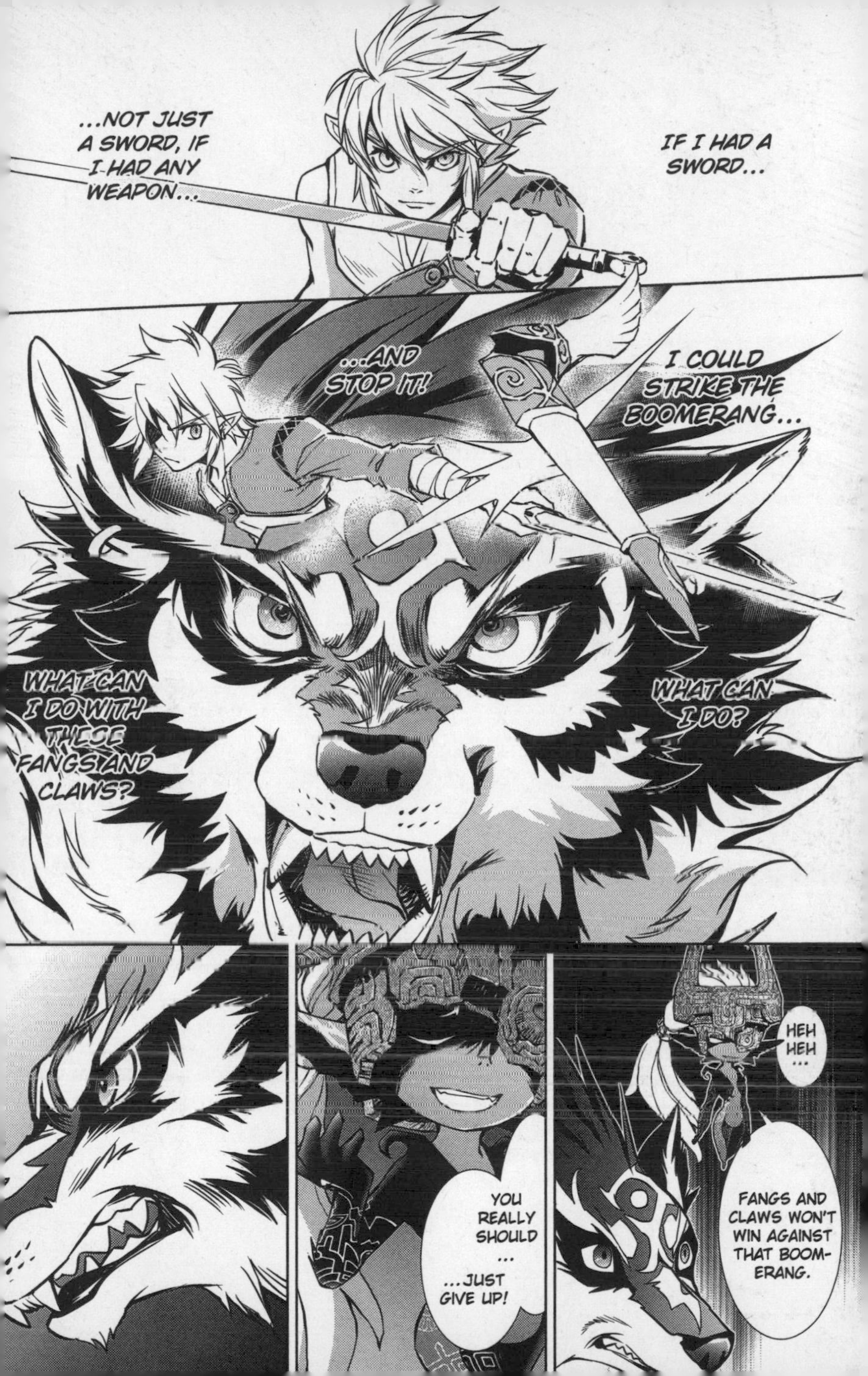
IF I HAD A SWORD...
...NOT JUST A SWORD, IF I HAD ANY WEAPON...
I COULD STRIKE THE BOOMERANG...
...AND STOP IT!
WHAT CAN I DO?
WHAT CAN I DO WITH THESE FANGS AND CLAWS?
HEH HEH...
FANGS AND CLAWS WON'T WIN AGAINST THAT BOOM-ERANG.
YOU REALLY SHOULD...
...JUST GIVE UP!

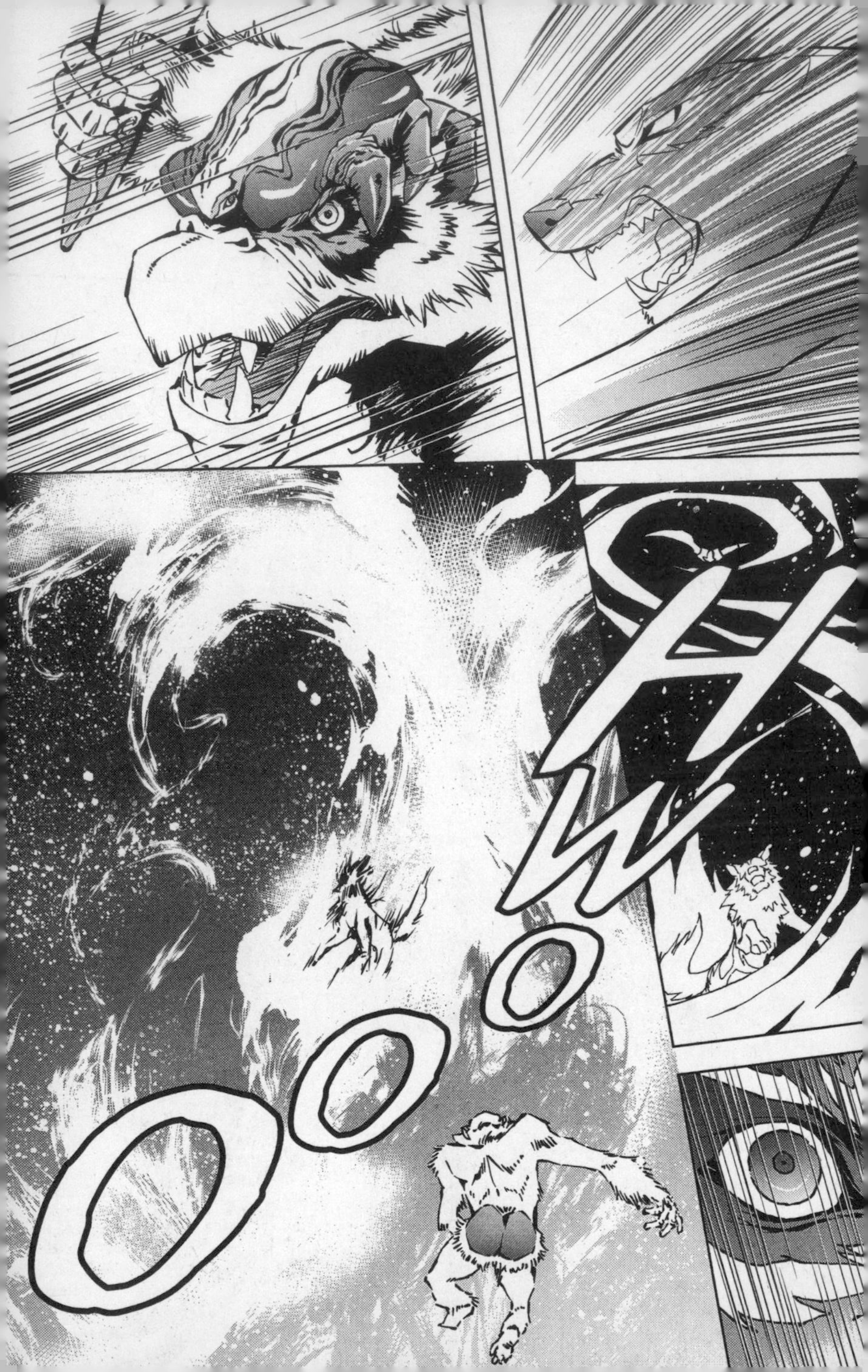
AWOOO

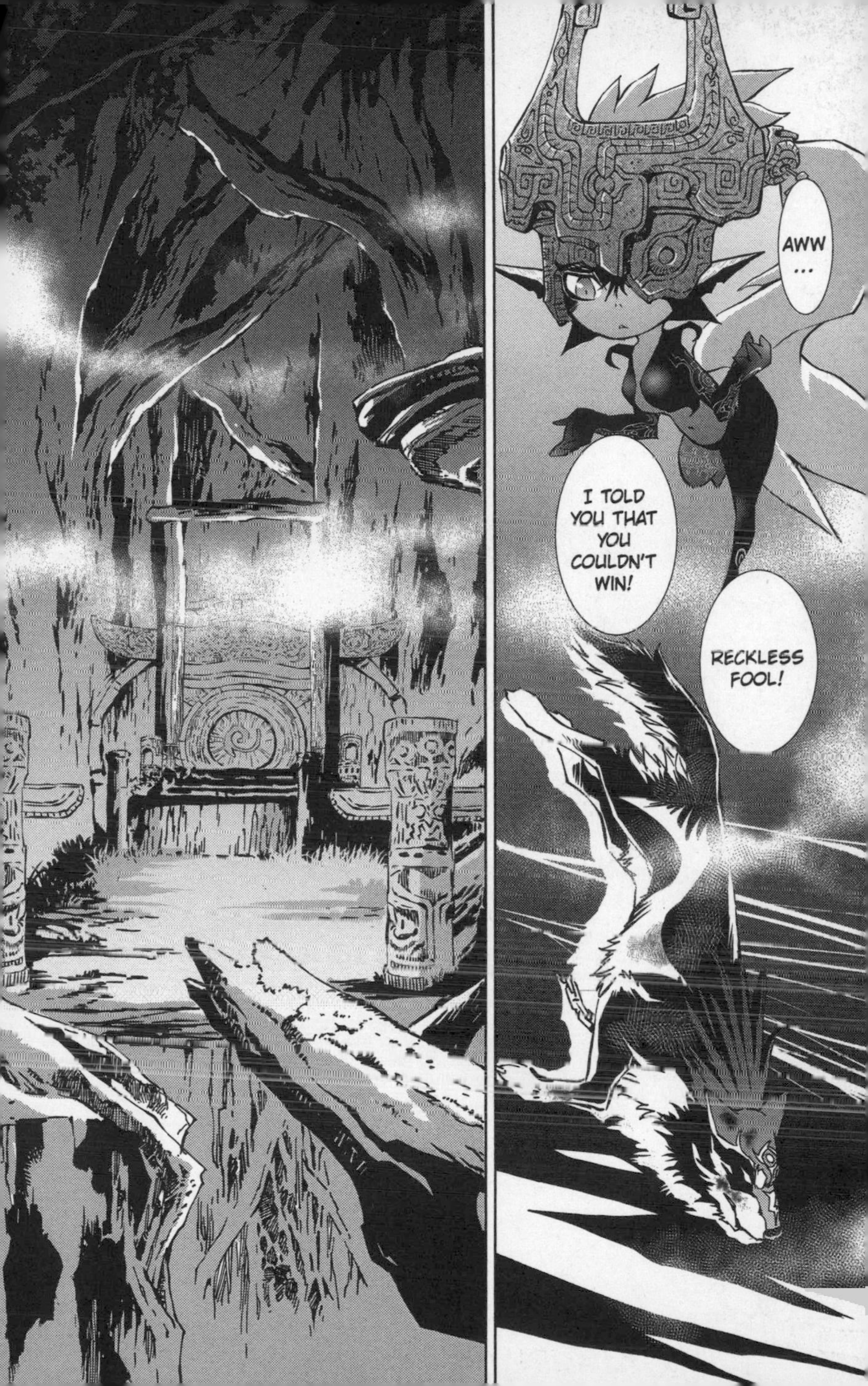
AWW ...
I TOLD YOU THAT YOU COULDN'T WIN!
RECKLESS FOOL!

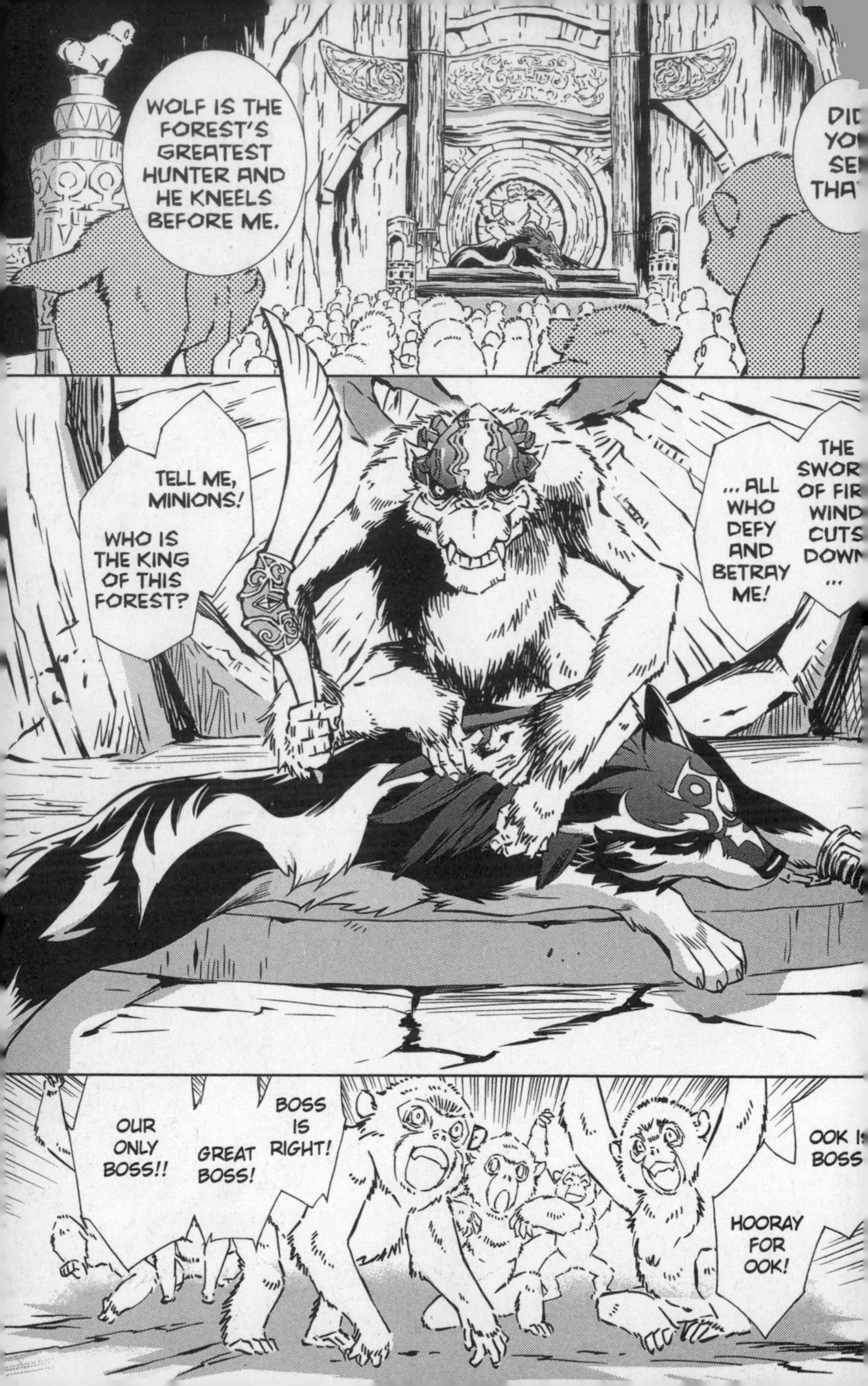
DI YO SE THA
WOLF IS THE FOREST'S GREATEST HUNTER AND HE KNEELS BEFORE ME.
THE SWOR OF FIR WIND CUTS DOWN ...
... ALL WHO DEFY AND BETRAY ME!
TELL ME, MINIONS!
WHO IS THE KING OF THIS FOREST?
OOK I BOSS
HOORAY FOR OOK!
BOSS IS RIGHT!
GREAT BOSS!
OUR ONLY BOSS!!

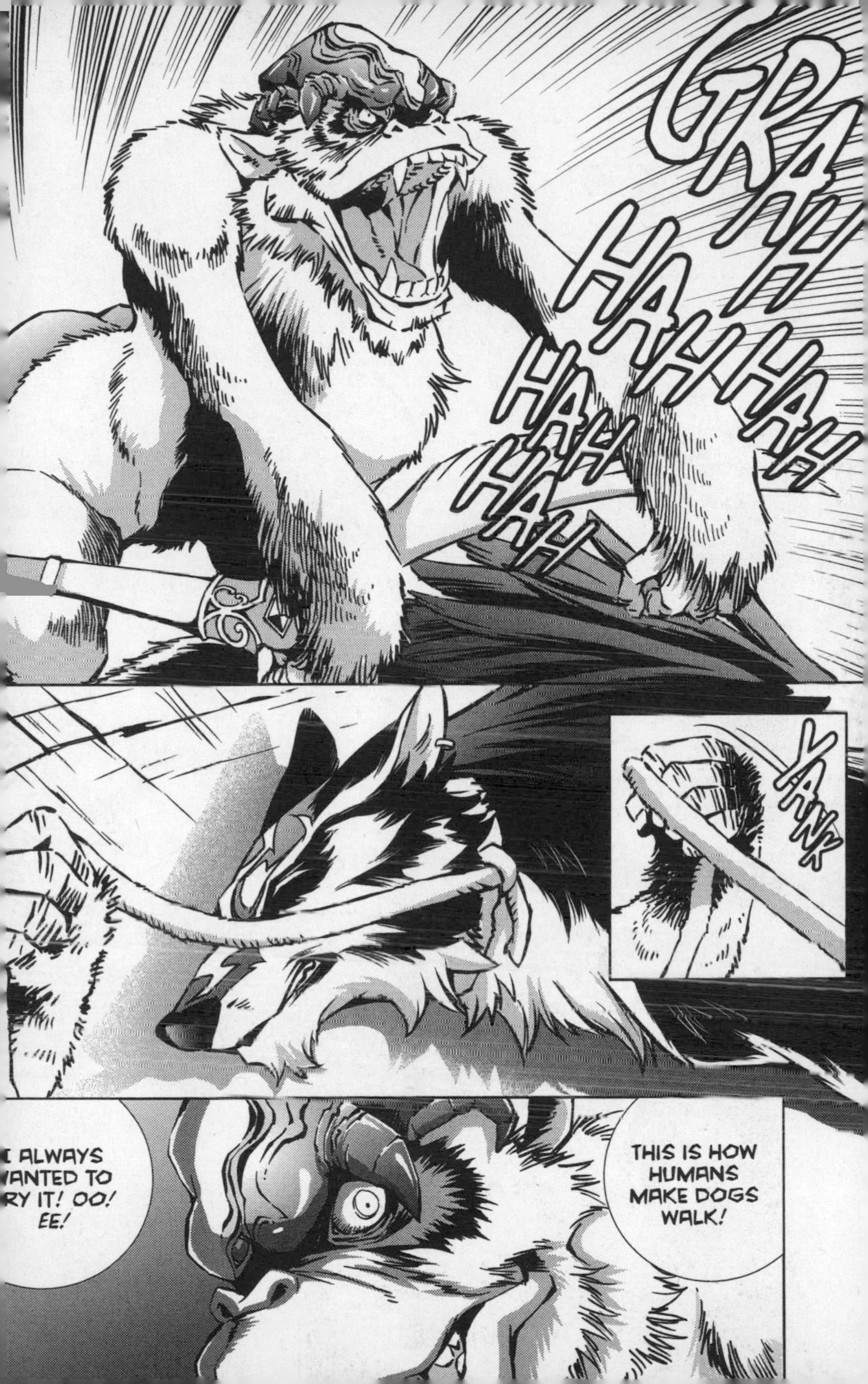
GRAH
HA HAH HAH HAH
HAH HAH HAH
YANK
THIS IS HOW HUMANS MAKE DOGS WALK!
ALWAYS ANTED TO RY IT! OO! EE!

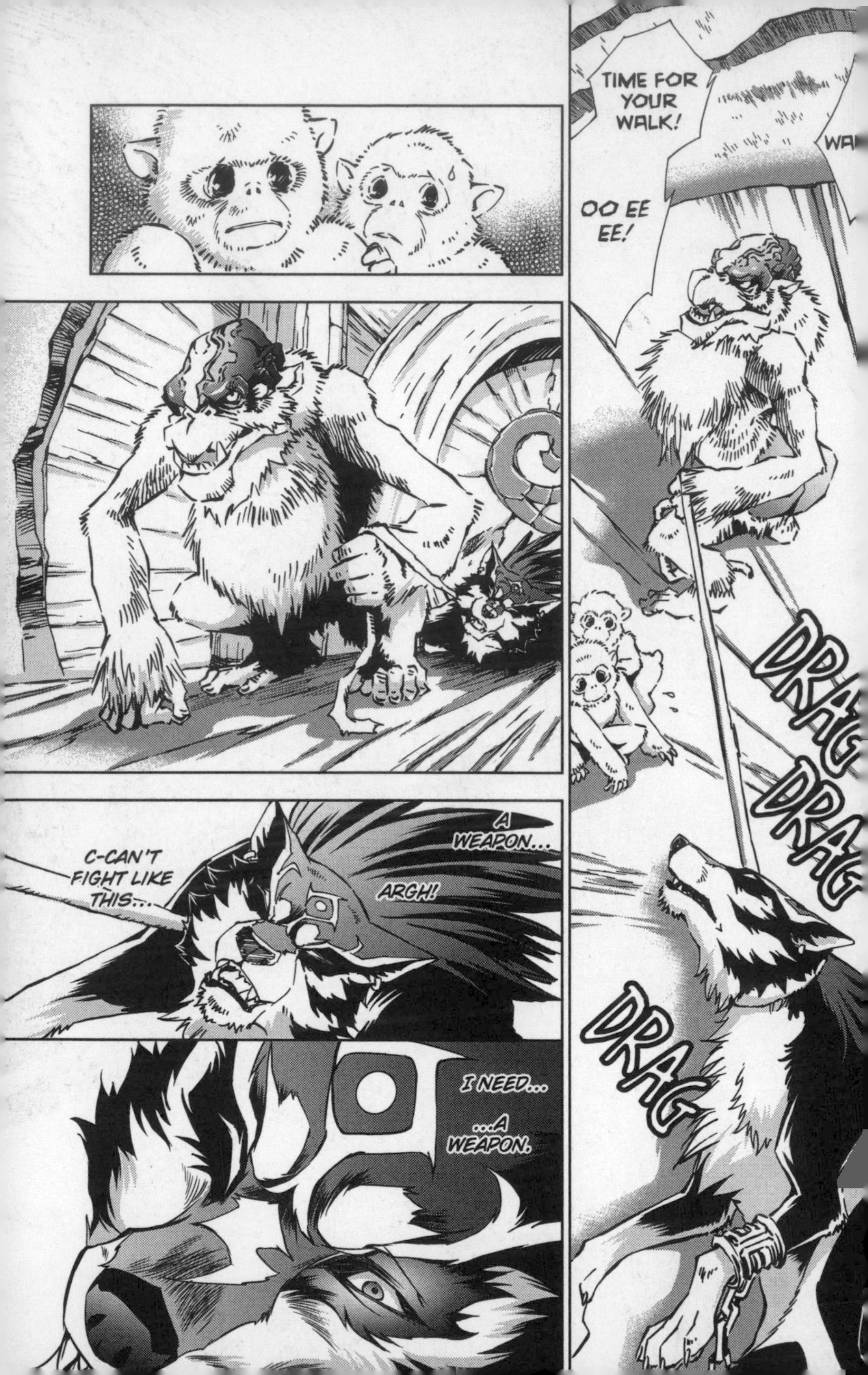
TIME FOR YOUR WALK!
OO EE EE!
DRAG DRAG
DRAG
A WEAPON...
ARGH!
C-CAN'T FIGHT LIKE THIS...
I NEED...
...A WEAPON.

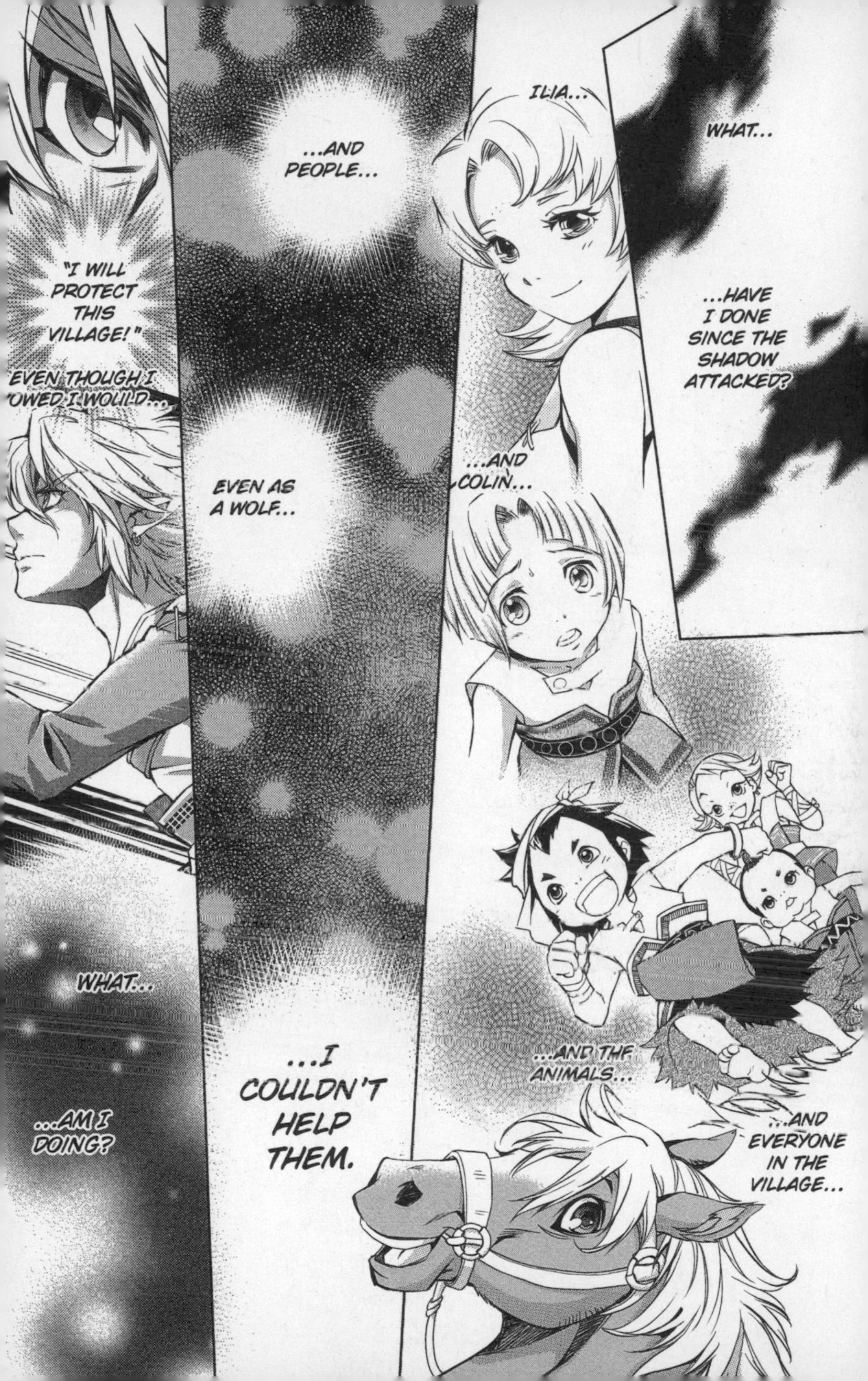
WHAT...
...HAVE I DONE SINCE THE SHADOW ATTACKED?
ILIA...
...AND COLIN...
...AND THE ANIMALS...
...AND EVERYONE IN THE VILLAGE...
...AND PEOPLE...
EVEN AS A WOLF...
...I COULDN'T HELP THEM.
"I WILL PROTECT THIS VILLAGE!"
EVEN THOUGH I VOWED I WOULD...
WHAT...
...AM I DOING?

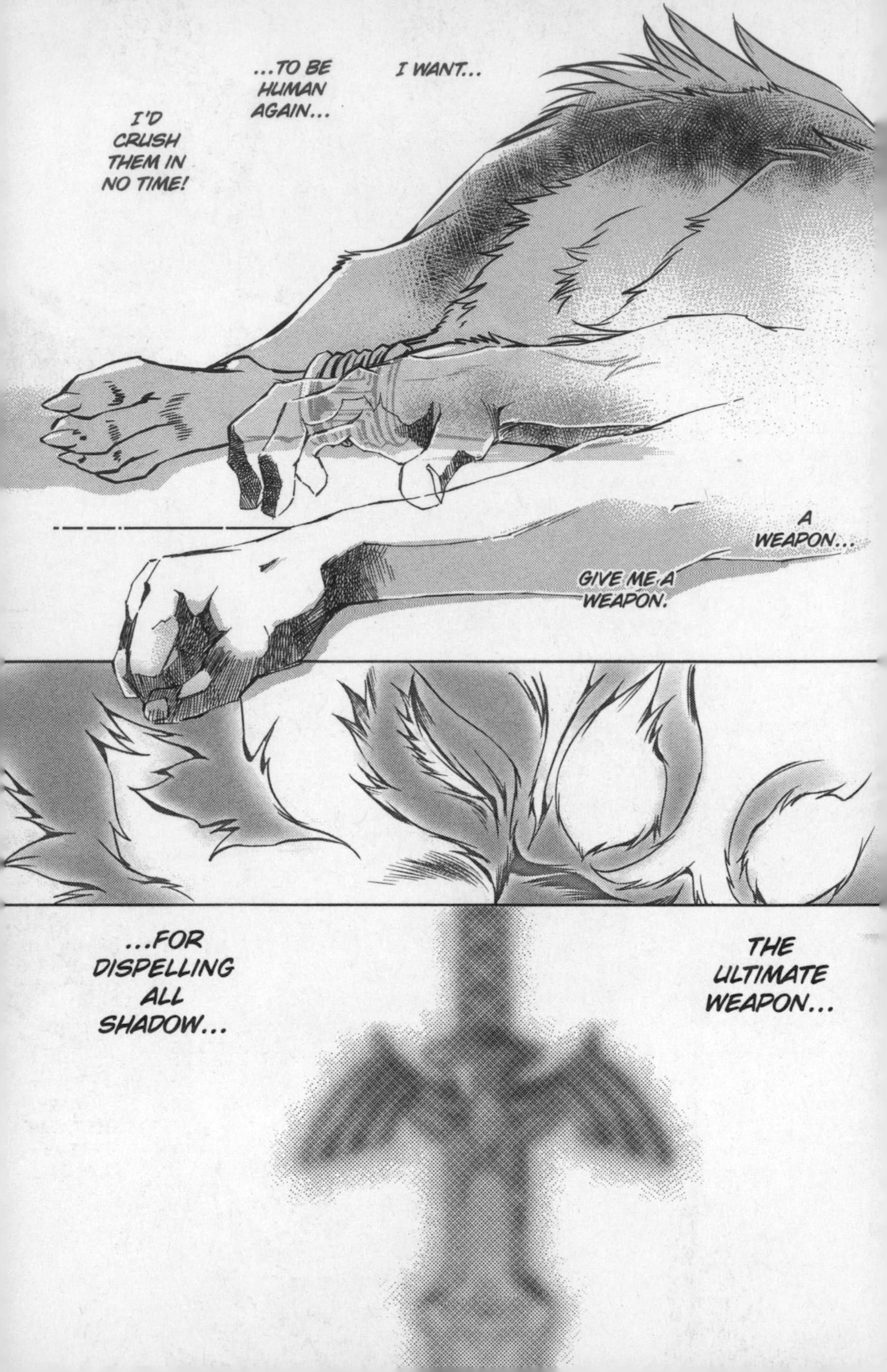
I WANT...
...TO BE HUMAN AGAIN...
I'D CRUSH THEM IN NO TIME!
A WEAPON...
GIVE ME A WEAPON.
THE ULTIMATE WEAPON...
...FOR DISPELLING ALL SHADOW...

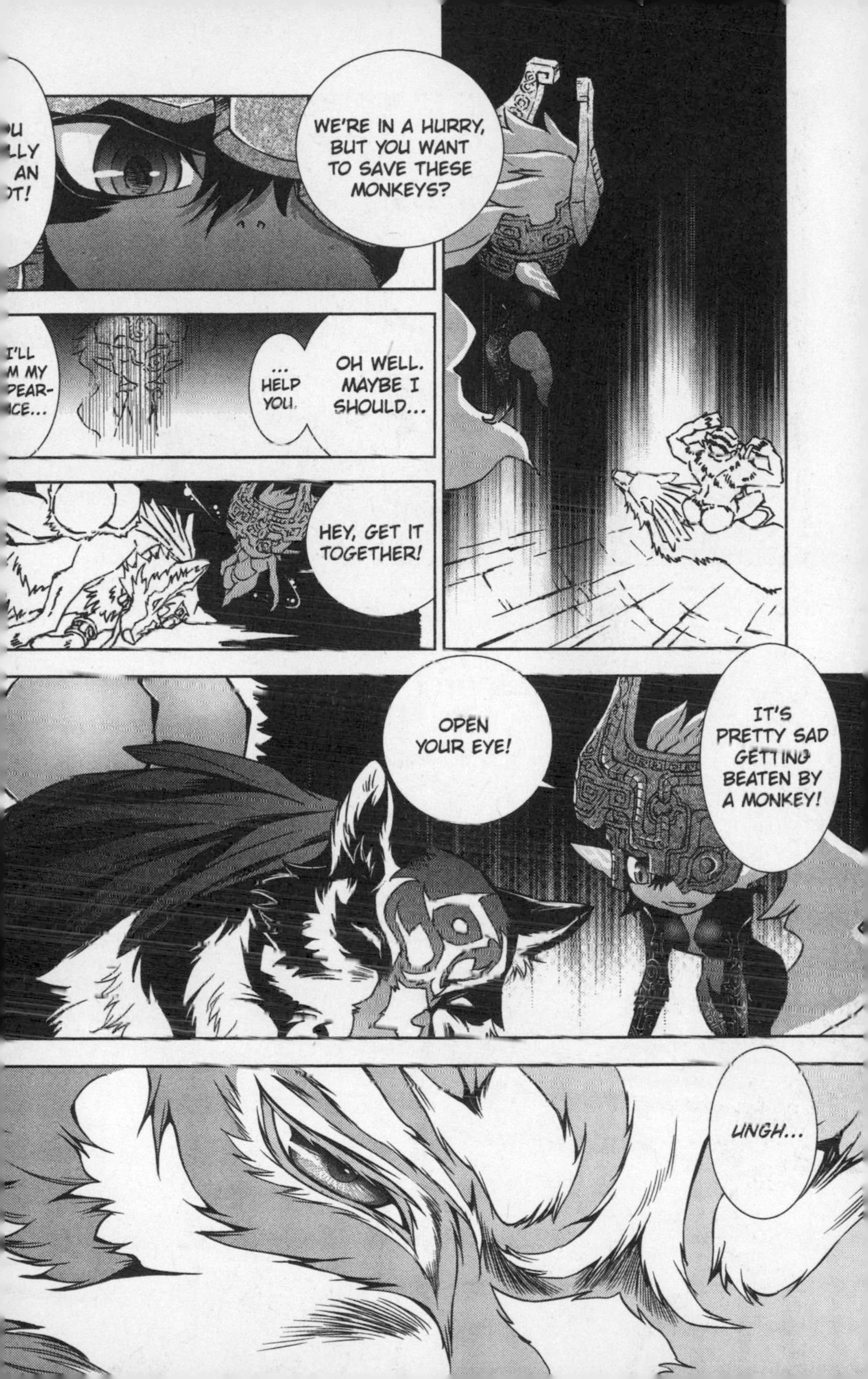
WE'RE IN A HURRY, BUT YOU WANT TO SAVE THESE MONKEYS?
OH WELL. MAYBE I SHOULD...
... HELP YOU.
HEY, GET IT TOGETHER!
IT'S PRETTY SAD GETTING BEATEN BY A MONKEY!
OPEN YOUR EYE!
UNGH...

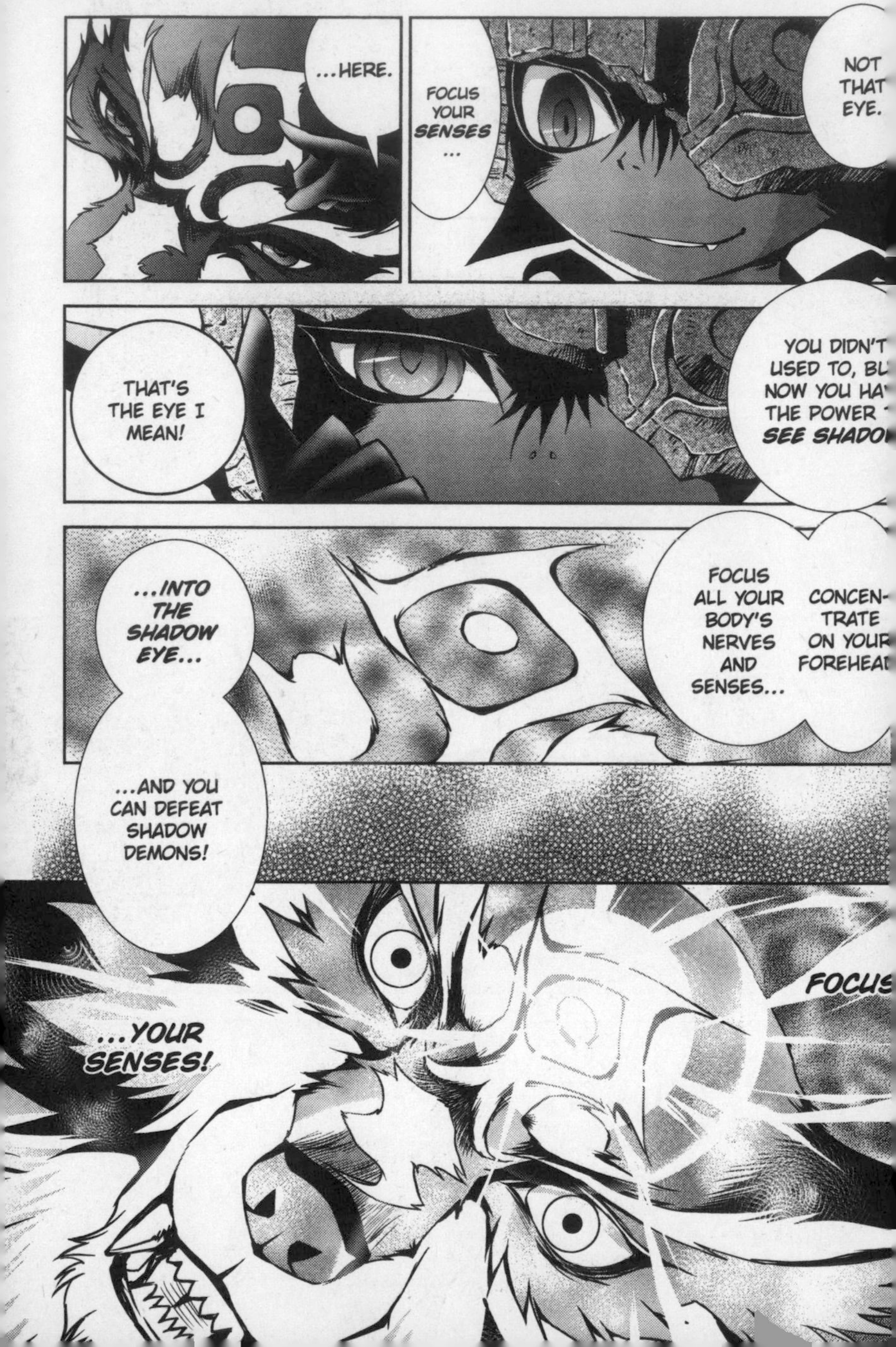
NOT THAT EYE.
FOCUS YOUR SENSES...
...HERE.
YOU DIDN'T USED TO, BU NOW YOU HA THE POWER T SEE SHADO
THAT'S THE EYE I MEAN!
CONCEN-TRATE ON YOUR FOREHEA
FOCUS ALL YOUR BODY'S NERVES AND SENSES...
...INTO THE SHADOW EYE...
...AND YOU CAN DEFEAT SHADOW DEMONS!
FOCUS
...YOUR SENSES!

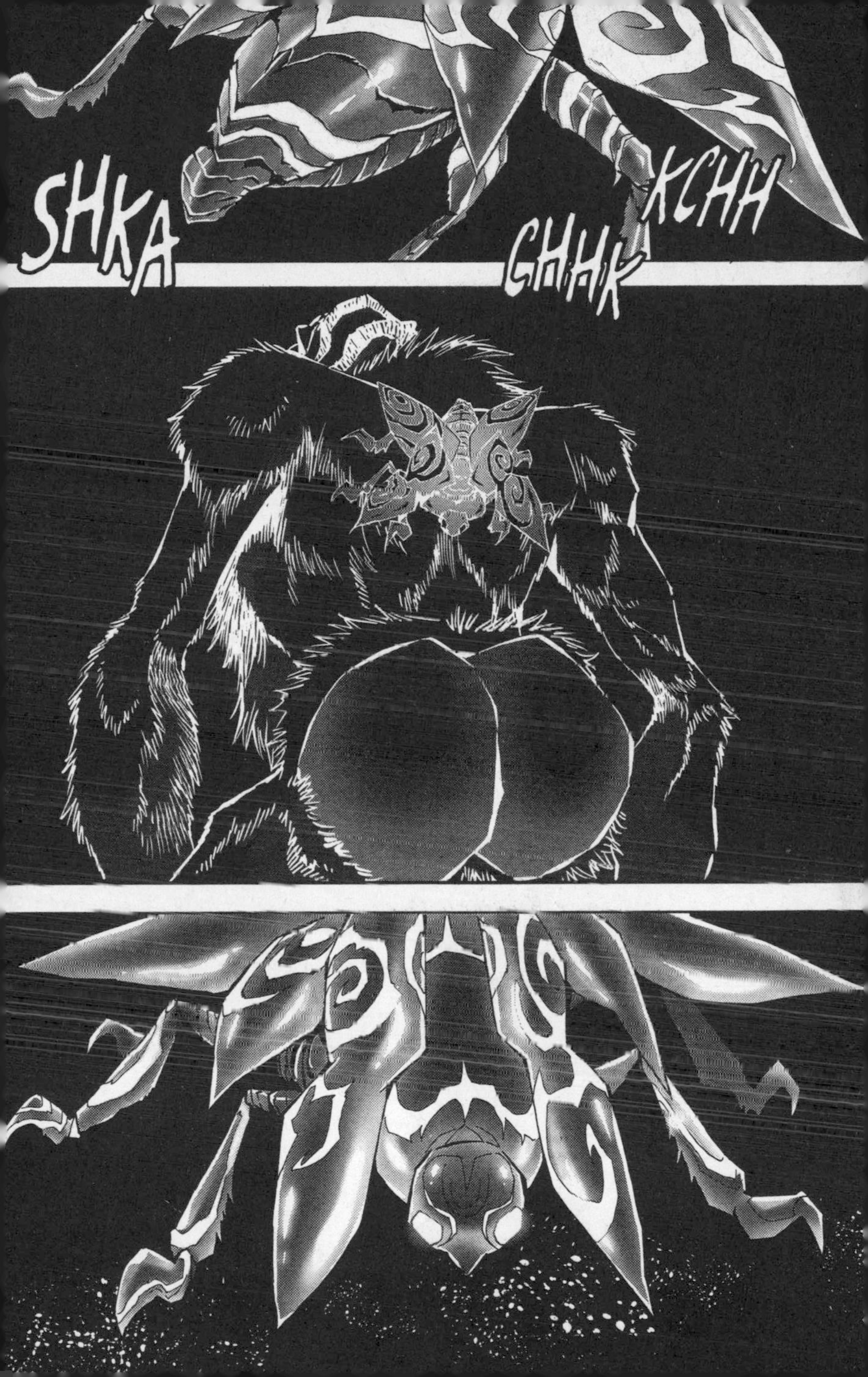
KCHH
GHHK
SHKA

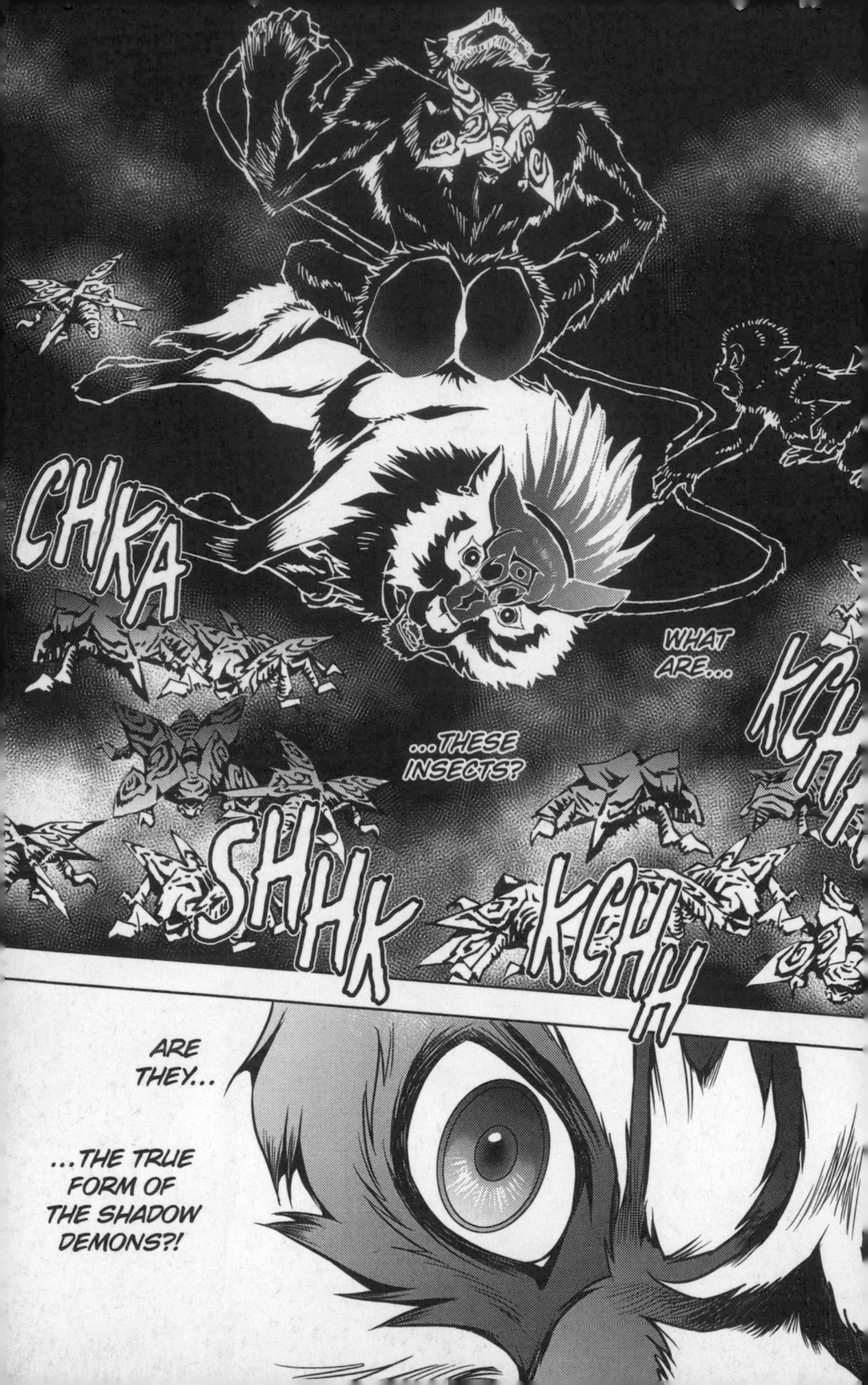
WHAT ARE...
...THESE INSECTS?
CHKA
KCHH
SHHK
ARE THEY...
...THE TRUE FORM OF THE SHADOW DEMONS?!

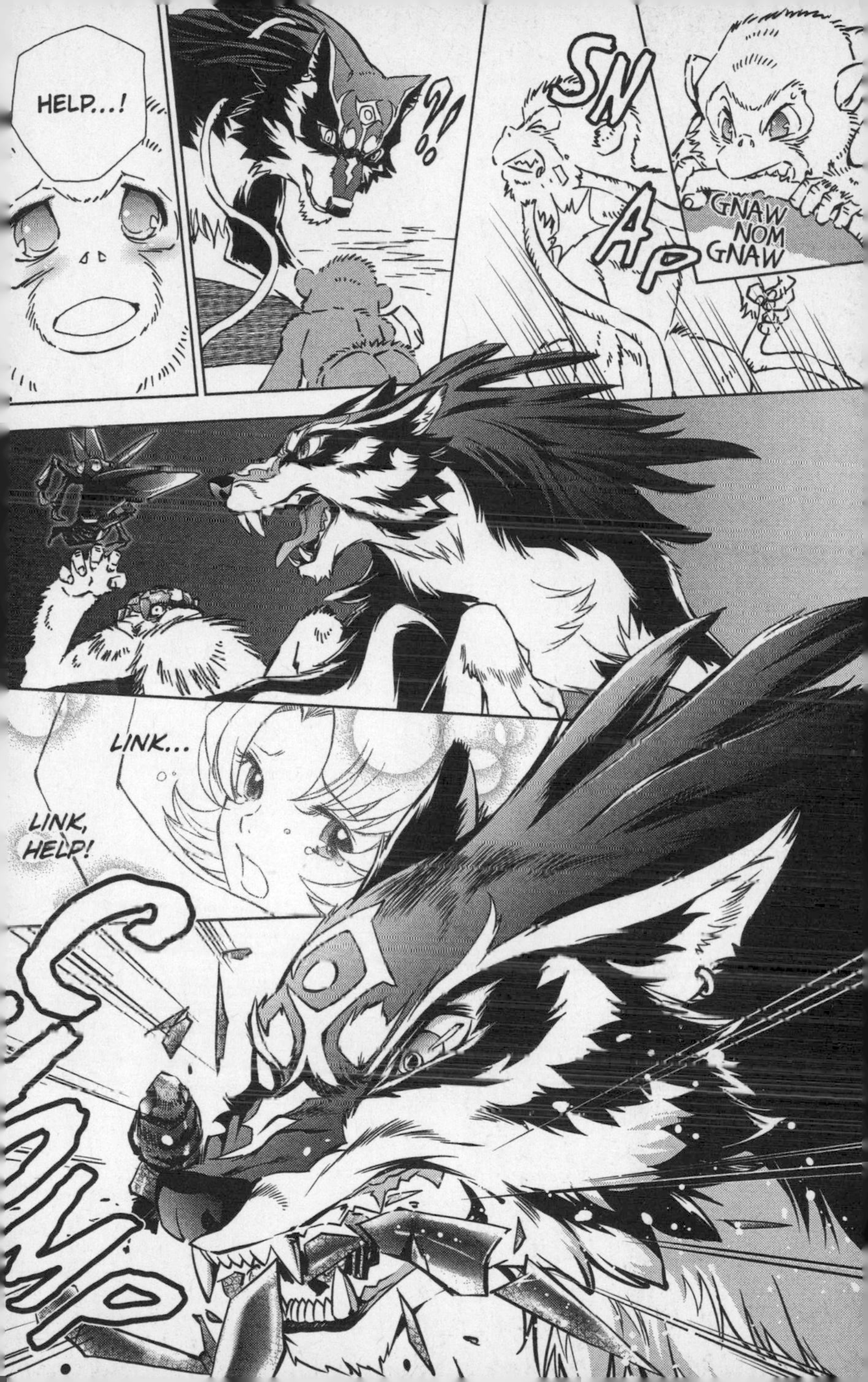
GNAW
NOM
GNAW
SNAP
?!
HELP...!
LINK...
LINK, HELP!
CHOMP

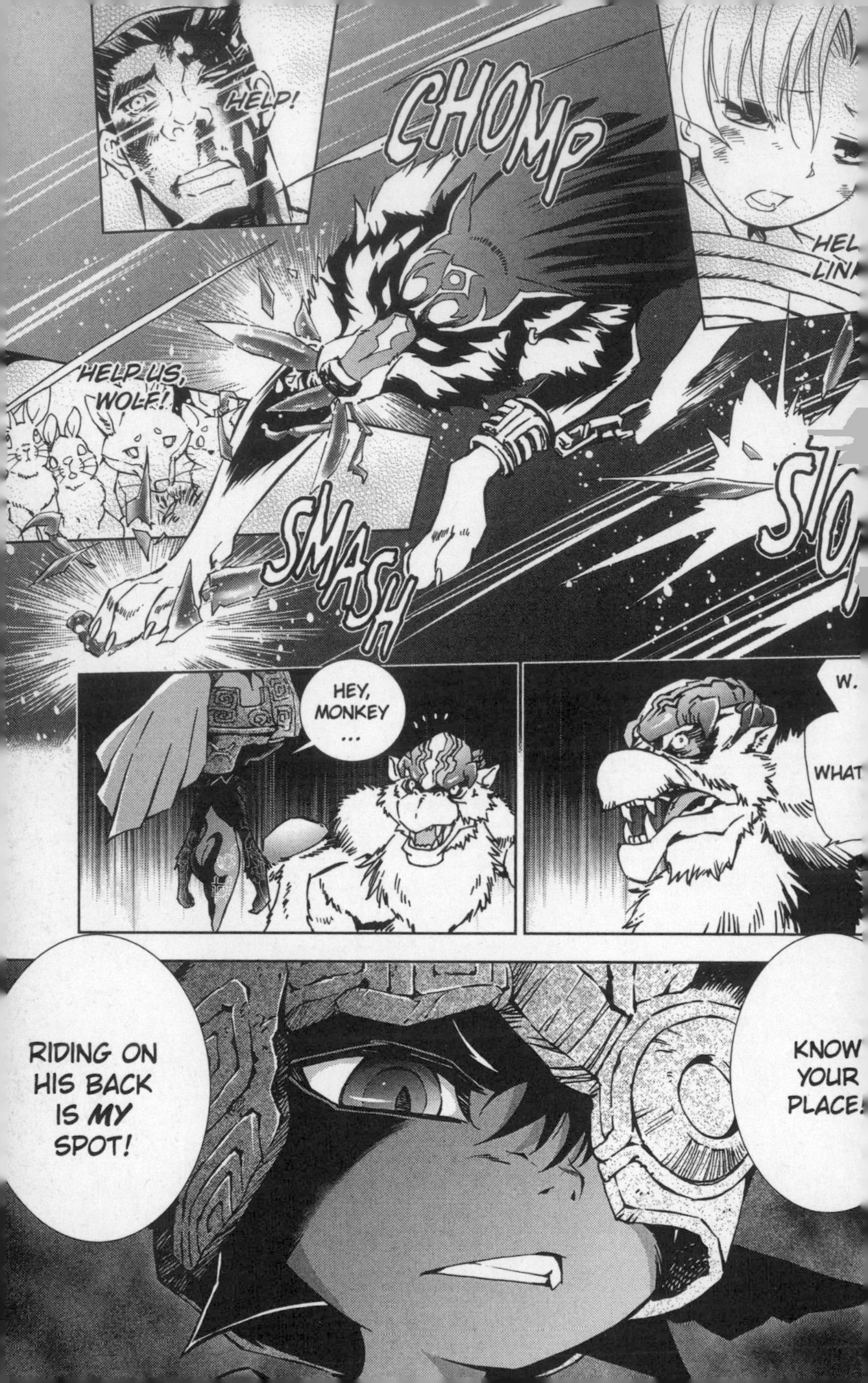
HEL
LIN
CHOMP
HELP!
STO
HELP US, WOLF!
SMASH
W.
WHAT
HEY, MONKEY ...
KNOW YOUR PLACE!
RIDING ON HIS BACK IS *MY* SPOT!

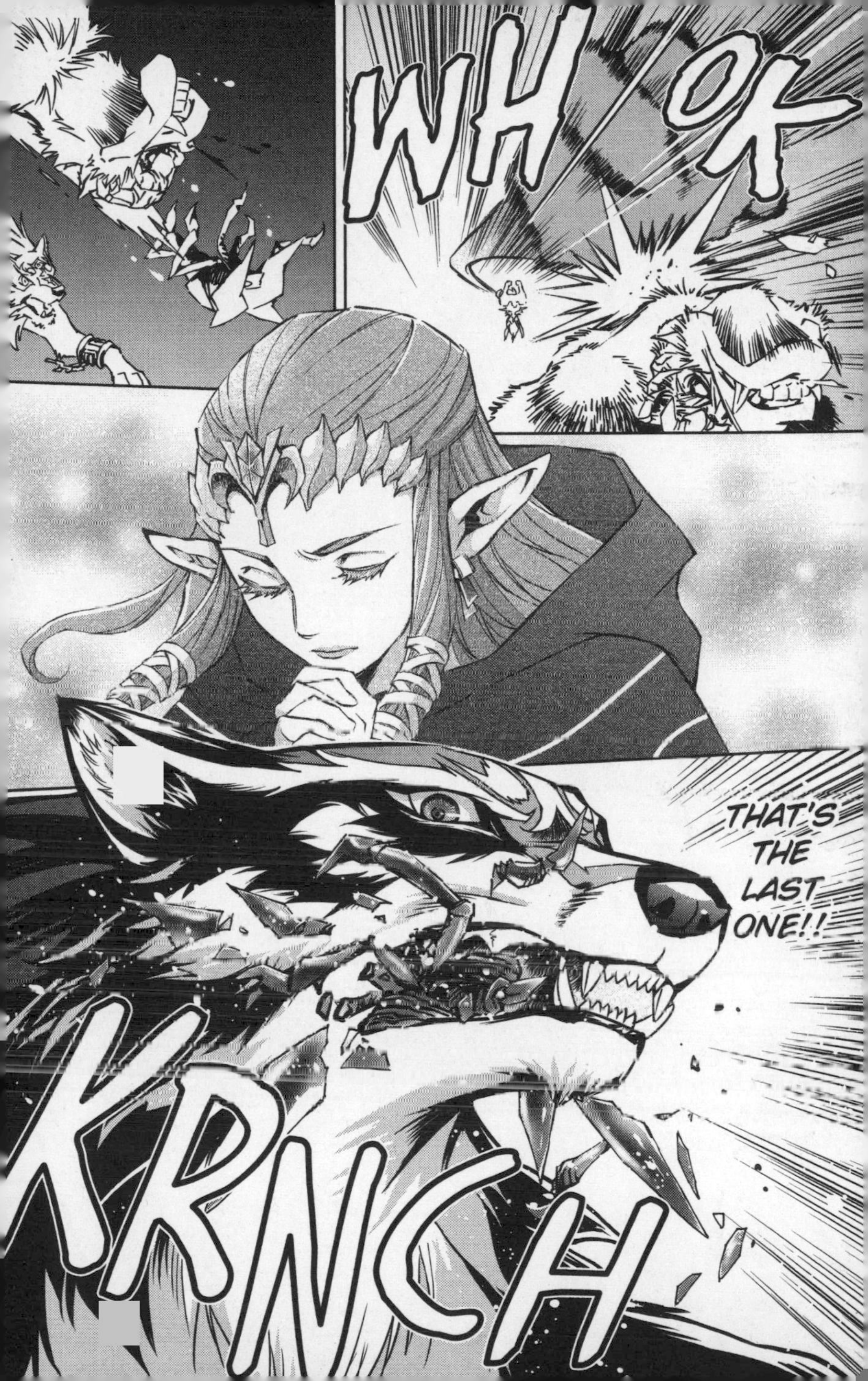
WH OK
THAT'S THE LAST ONE!!
KRNCH

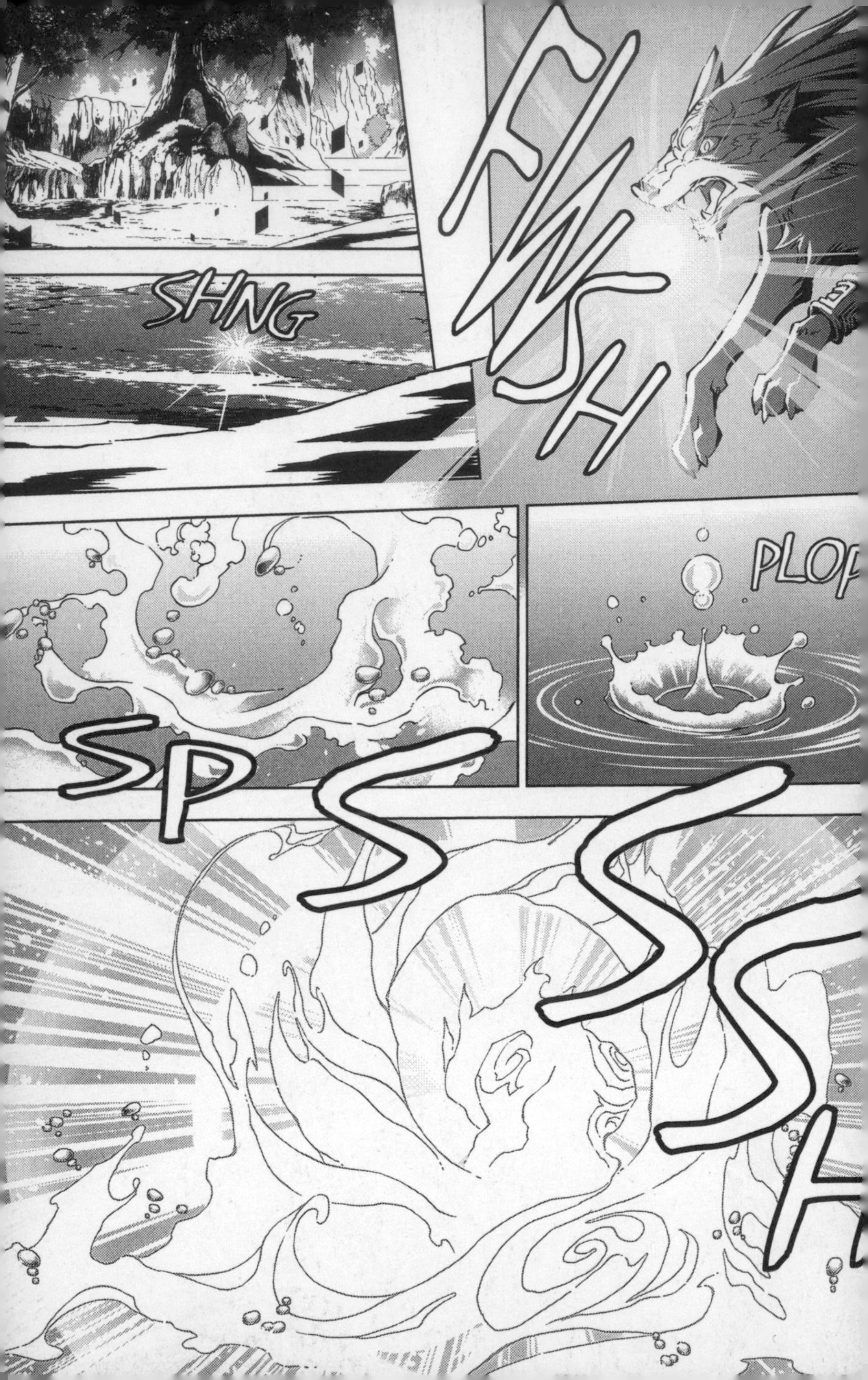
FWSH
SHNG
PLOP
SPSSSH

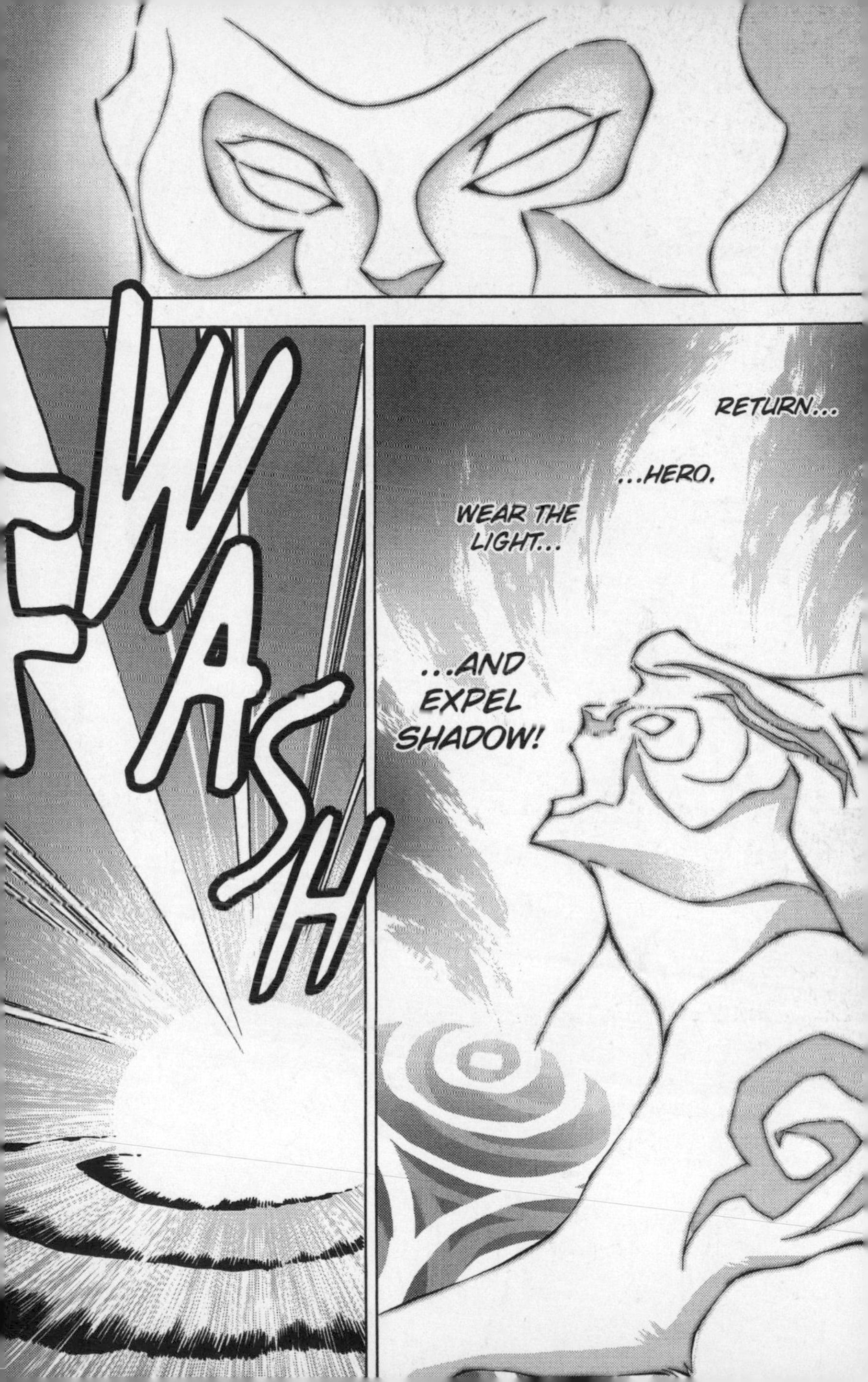
RETURN...
...HERO.
WEAR THE LIGHT...
...AND EXPEL SHADOW!
WASH

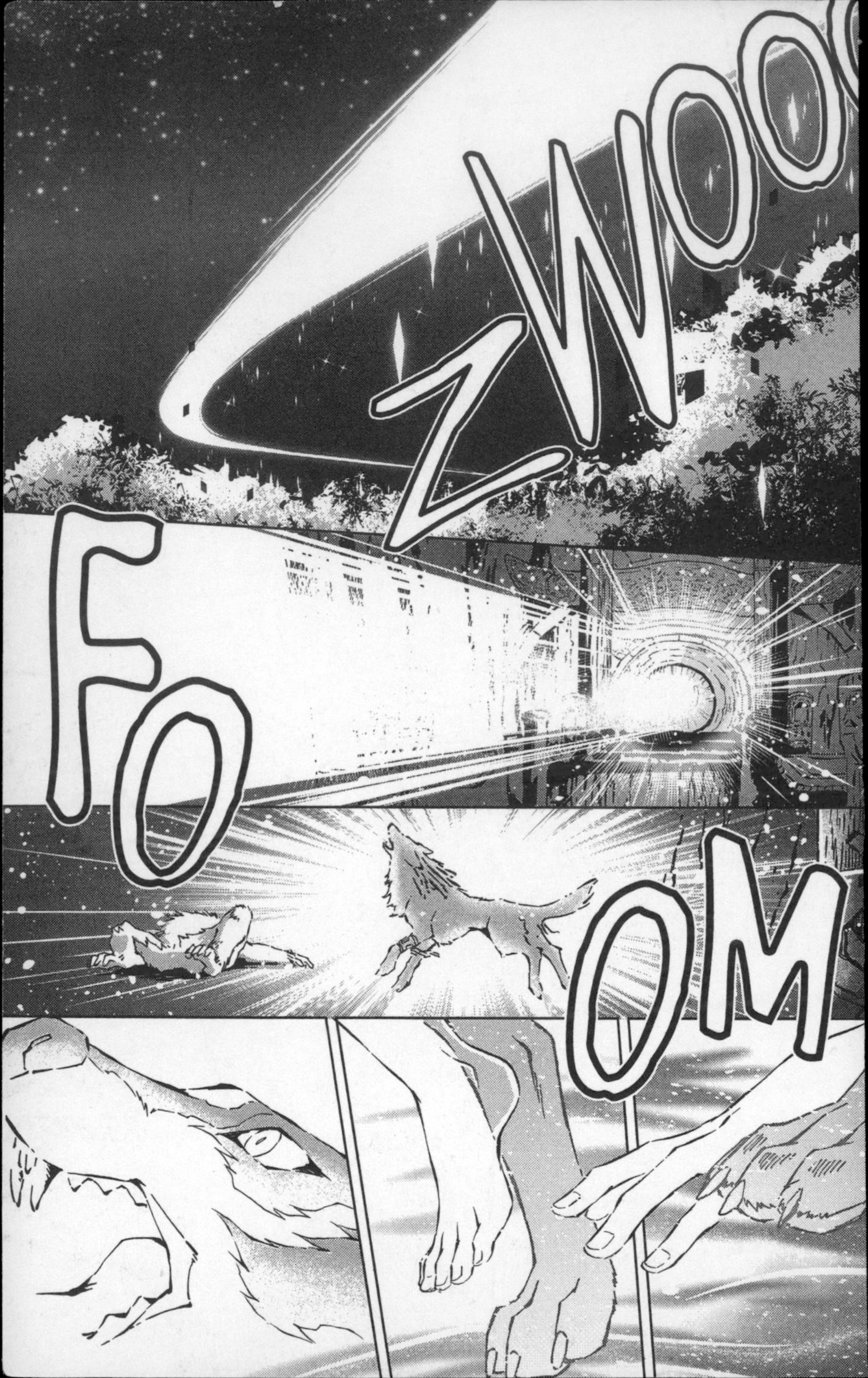
ZWOO
FOOM

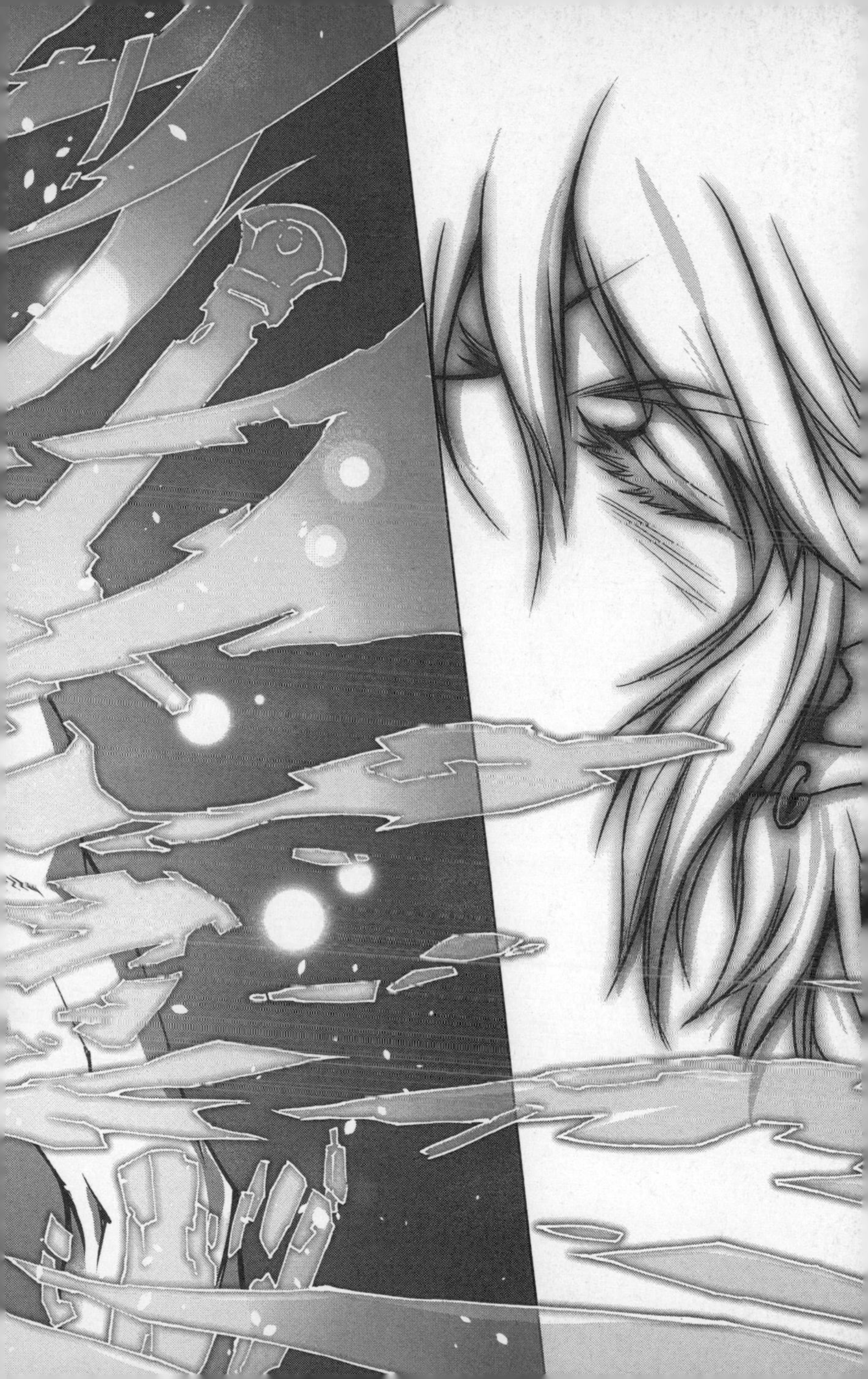

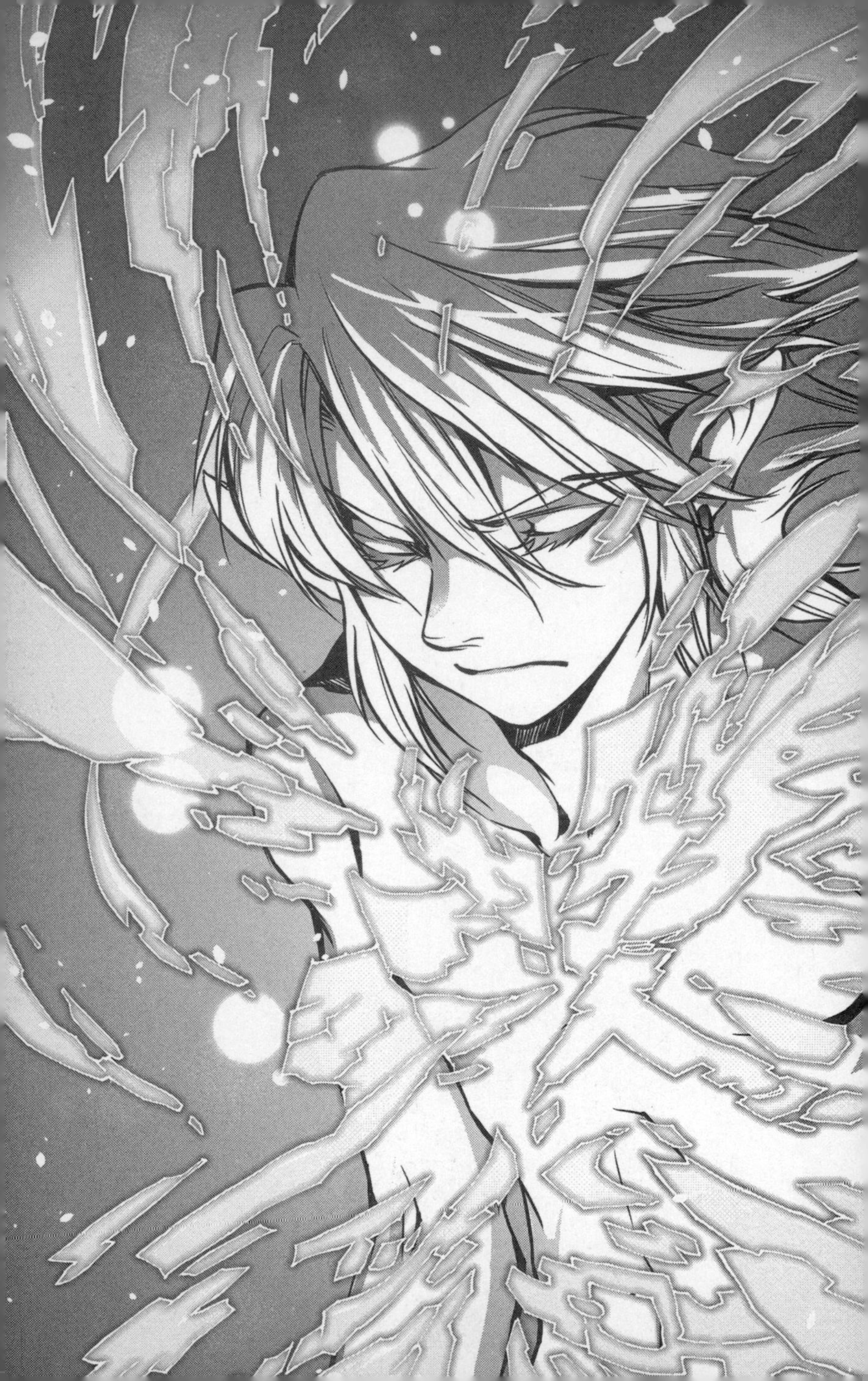

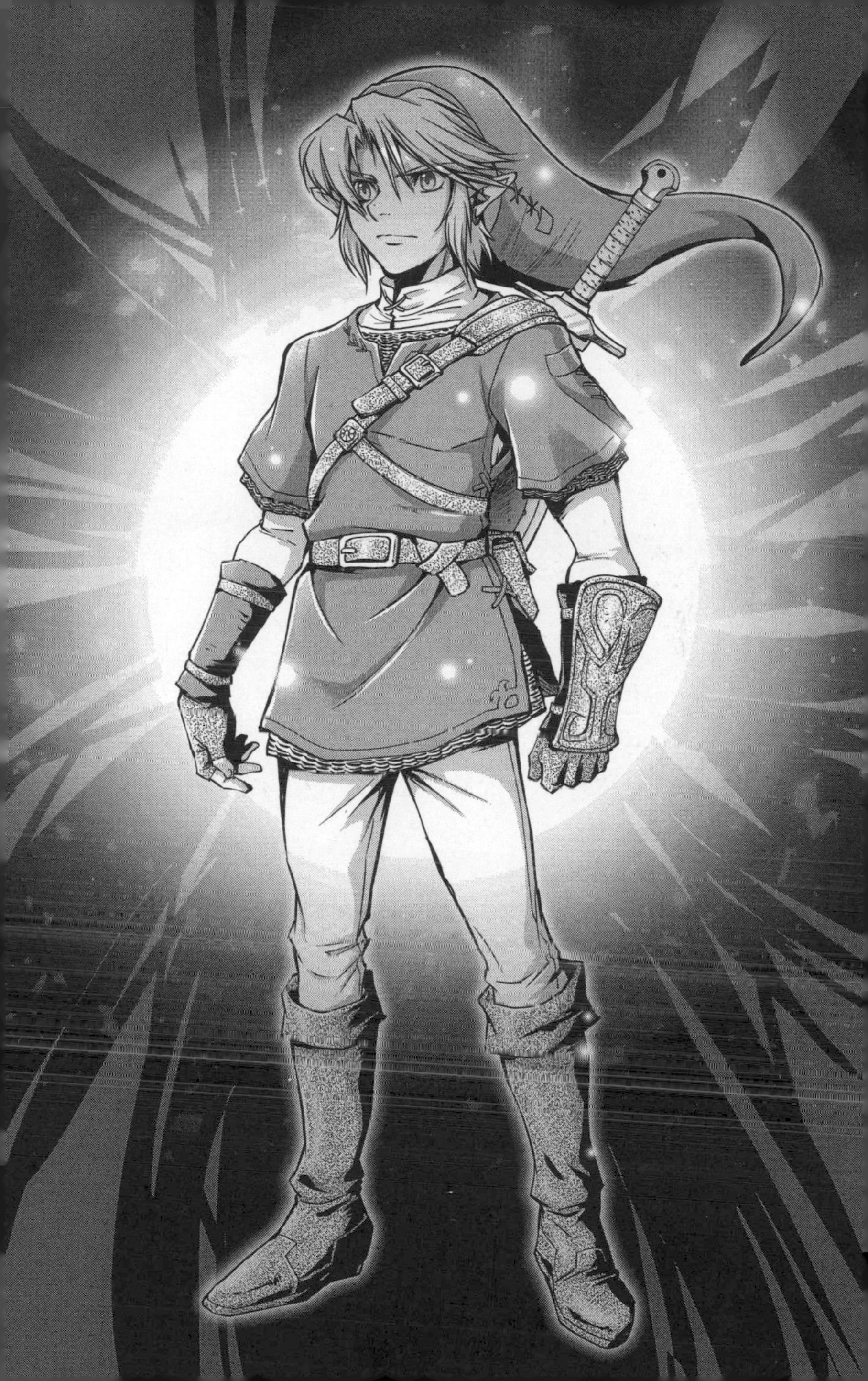

#16. HERO IN GREEN

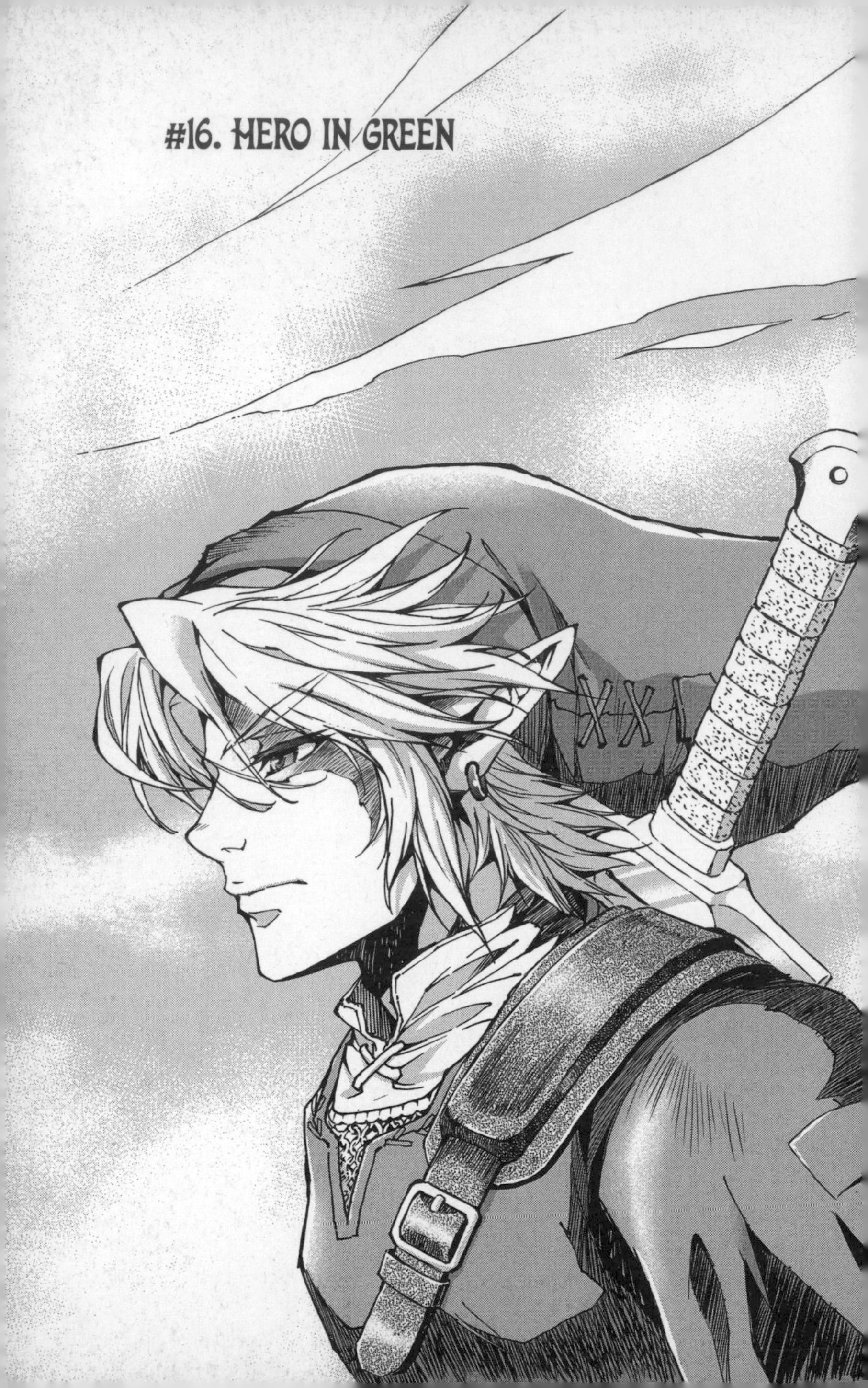

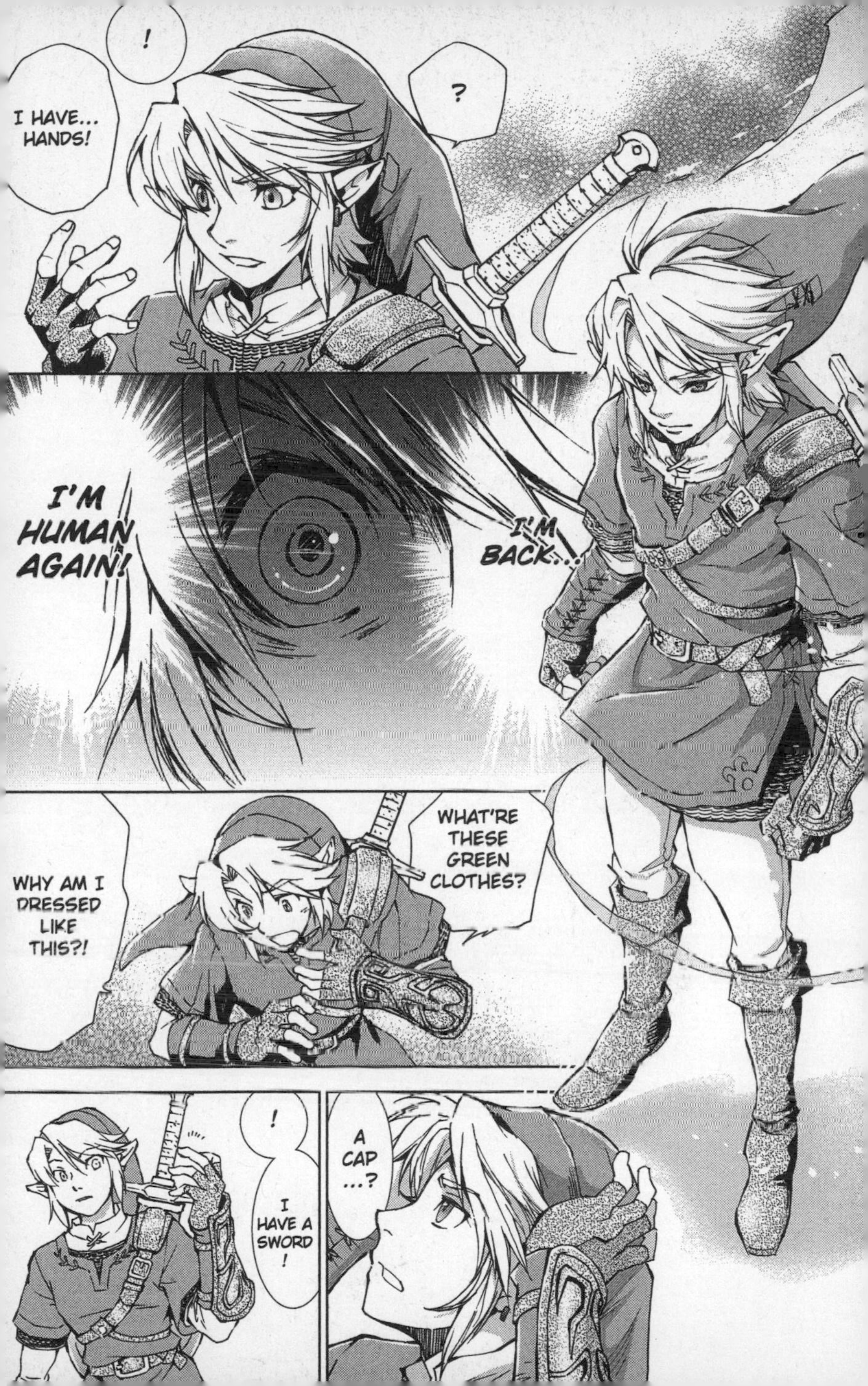

I'M BACK...
?
!
I HAVE... HANDS!
I'M HUMAN AGAIN!
WHAT'RE THESE GREEN CLOTHES?
WHY AM I DRESSED LIKE THIS?!
A CAP ...?
!
I HAVE A SWORD !

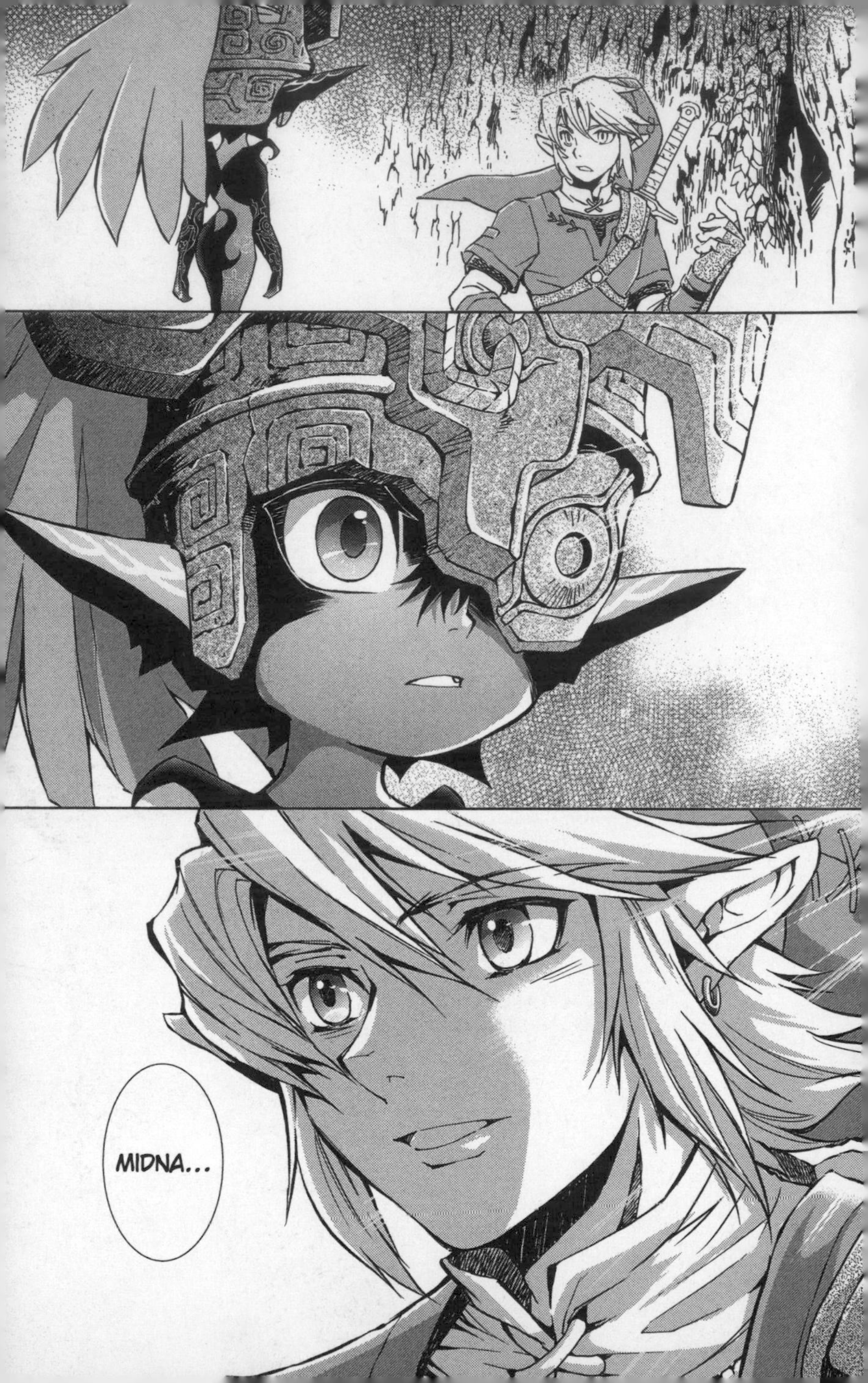
MIDNA...

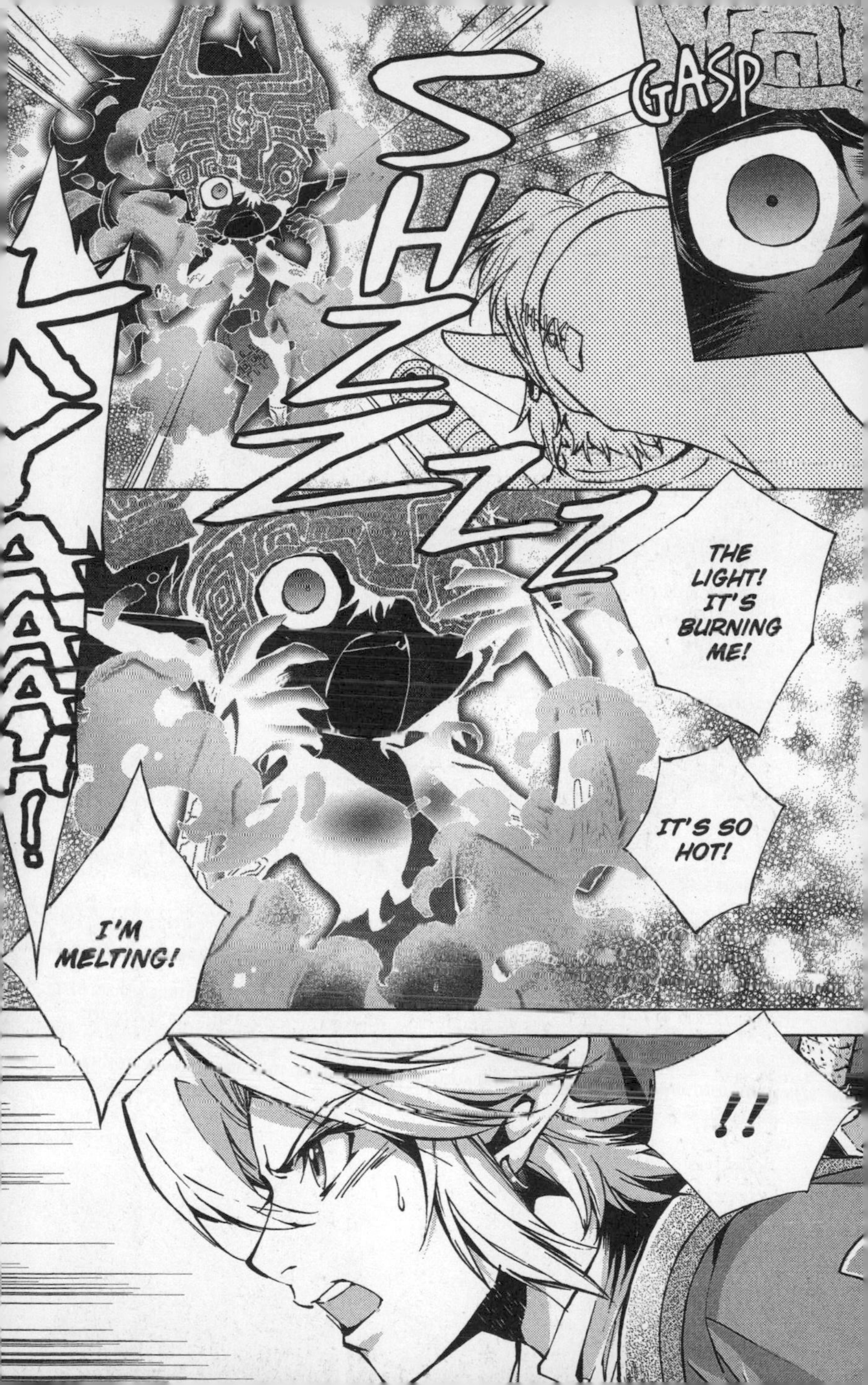
GASP
SHZZZZ
THE LIGHT! IT'S BURNING ME!
IT'S SO HOT!
I'M MELTING!
!!

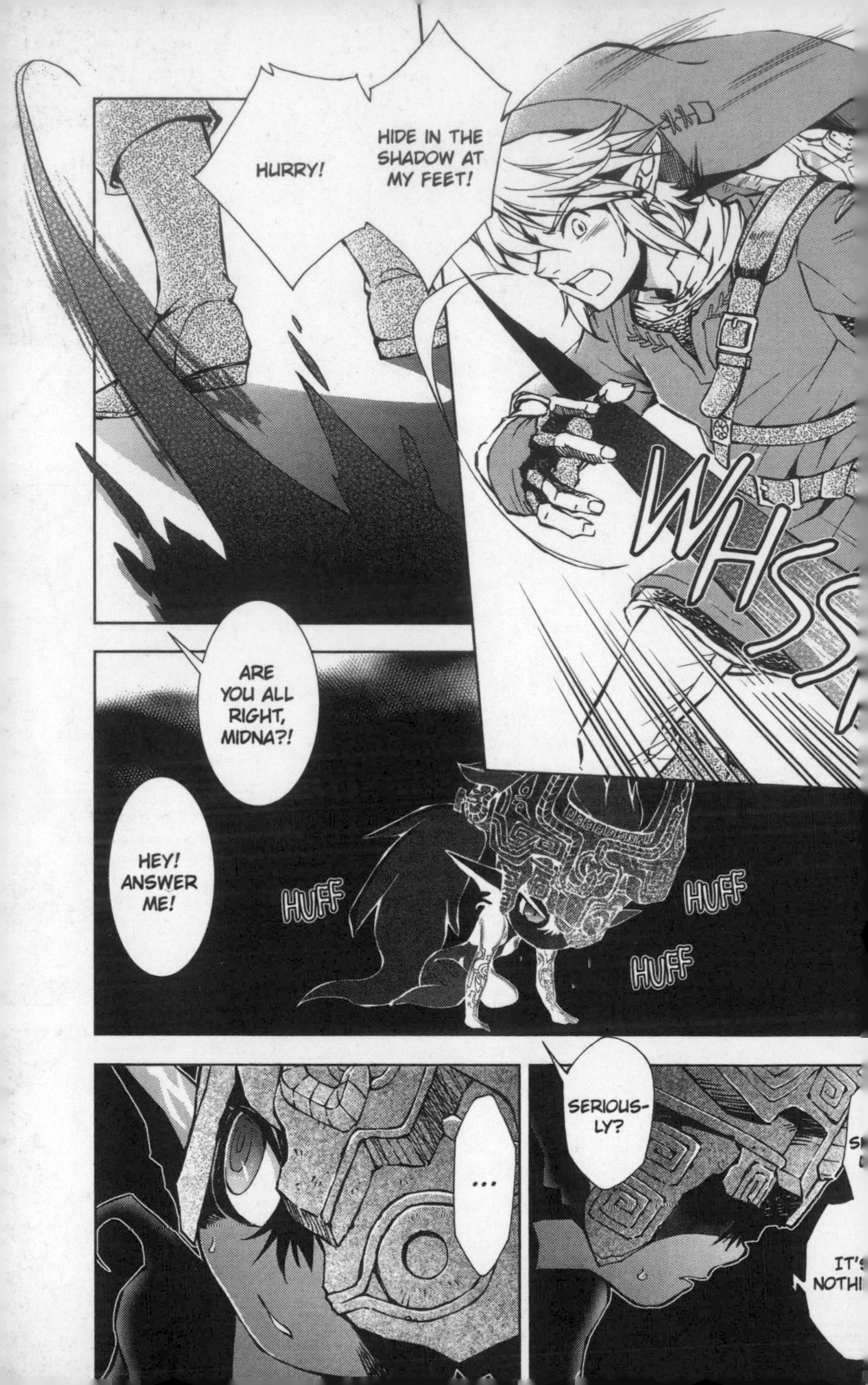
HIDE IN THE SHADOW AT MY FEET!
HURRY!
WHSS
ARE YOU ALL RIGHT, MIDNA?!
HEY! ANSWER ME!
HUFF
HUFF
HUFF
SERIOUS-LY?
IT'S
...

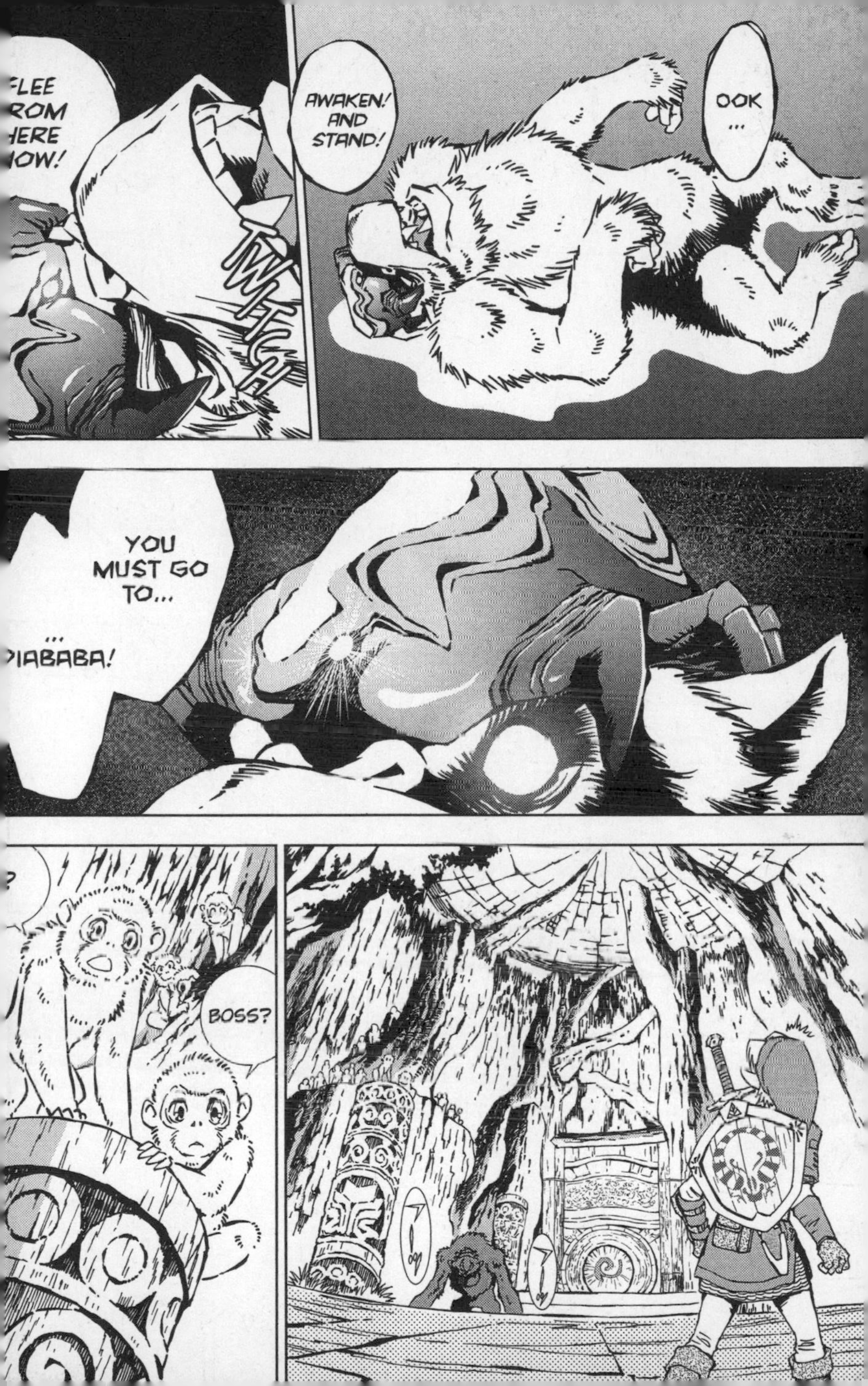
OOK ...
AWAKEN! AND STAND!
FLEE ROM HERE IOW!
TWITCH
YOU MUST GO TO...
... IABABA!
BOSS?

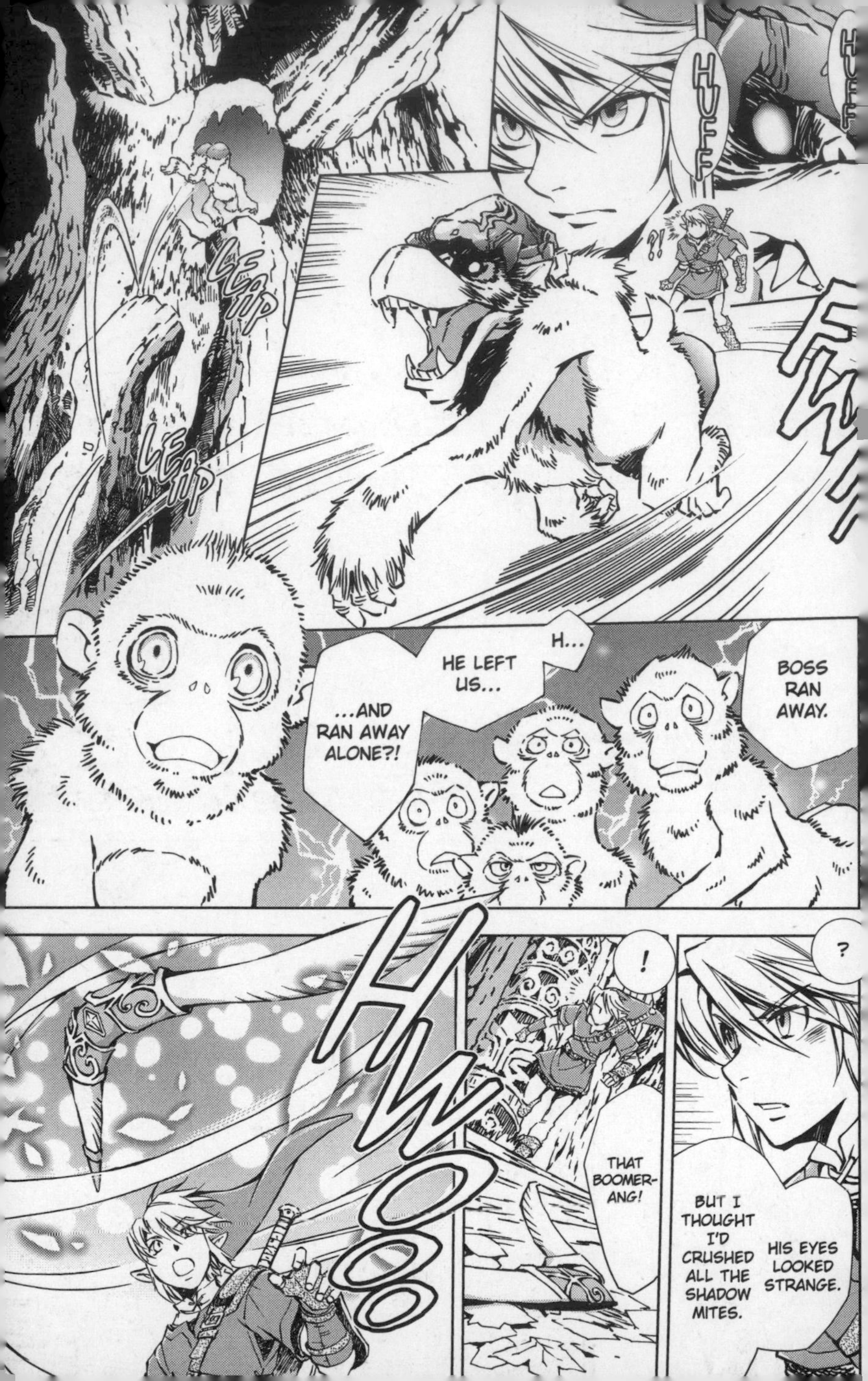
HUFF HUFF
HUFF HUFF
?!
FWIP
LEAP
LEAP
BOSS RAN AWAY.
H...
HE LEFT US...
...AND RAN AWAY ALONE?!
?
HIS EYES LOOKED STRANGE.
BUT I THOUGHT I'D CRUSHED ALL THE SHADOW MITES.
!
THAT BOOMER-ANG!
HWOOO

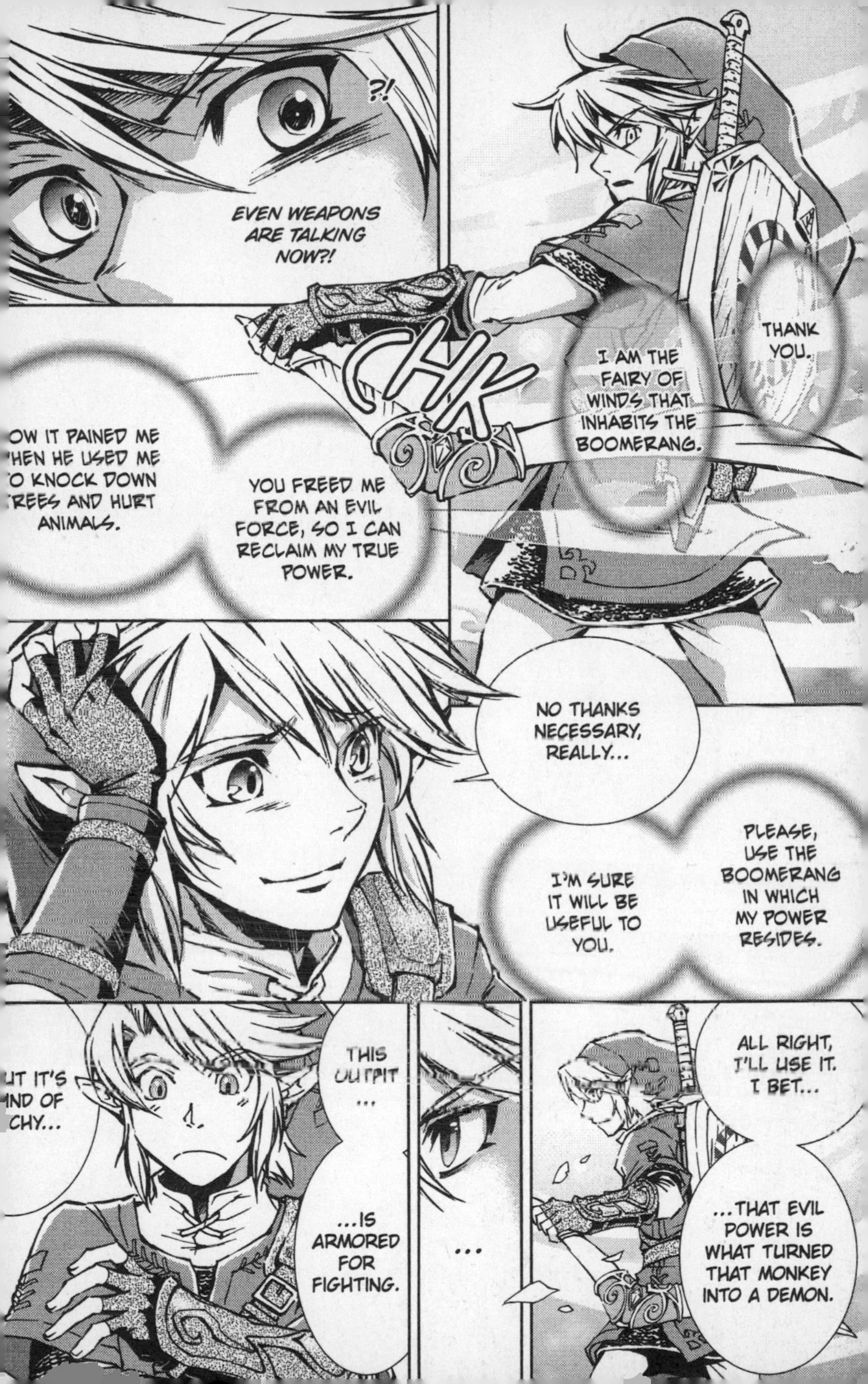
THANK YOU.
I AM THE FAIRY OF WINDS THAT INHABITS THE BOOMERANG.
?!
EVEN WEAPONS ARE TALKING NOW?!
CHK
YOU FREED ME FROM AN EVIL FORCE, SO I CAN RECLAIM MY TRUE POWER.
OW IT PAINED ME HEN HE USED ME O KNOCK DOWN REES AND HURT ANIMALS.
NO THANKS NECESSARY, REALLY...
PLEASE, USE THE BOOMERANG IN WHICH MY POWER RESIDES.
I'M SURE IT WILL BE USEFUL TO YOU.
ALL RIGHT, I'LL USE IT. I BET...
...THAT EVIL POWER IS WHAT TURNED THAT MONKEY INTO A DEMON.
...
THIS OUTFIT ...
...IS ARMORED FOR FIGHTING.
UT IT'S IND OF CHY...

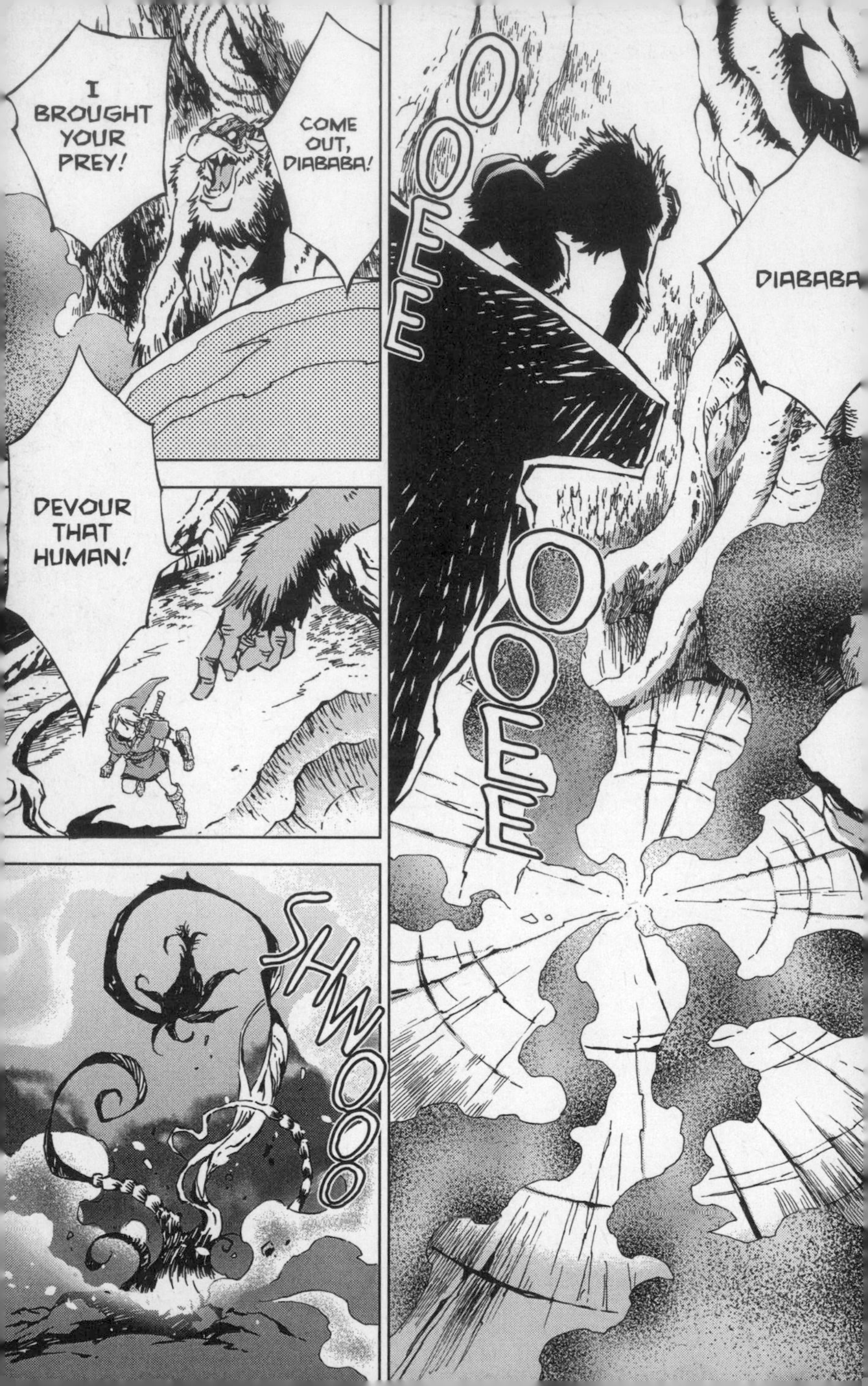

DIABABA
OOOEEE
OOOEEE
COME OUT, DIABABA!
I BROUGHT YOUR PREY!
DEVOUR THAT HUMAN!
SHWOOO

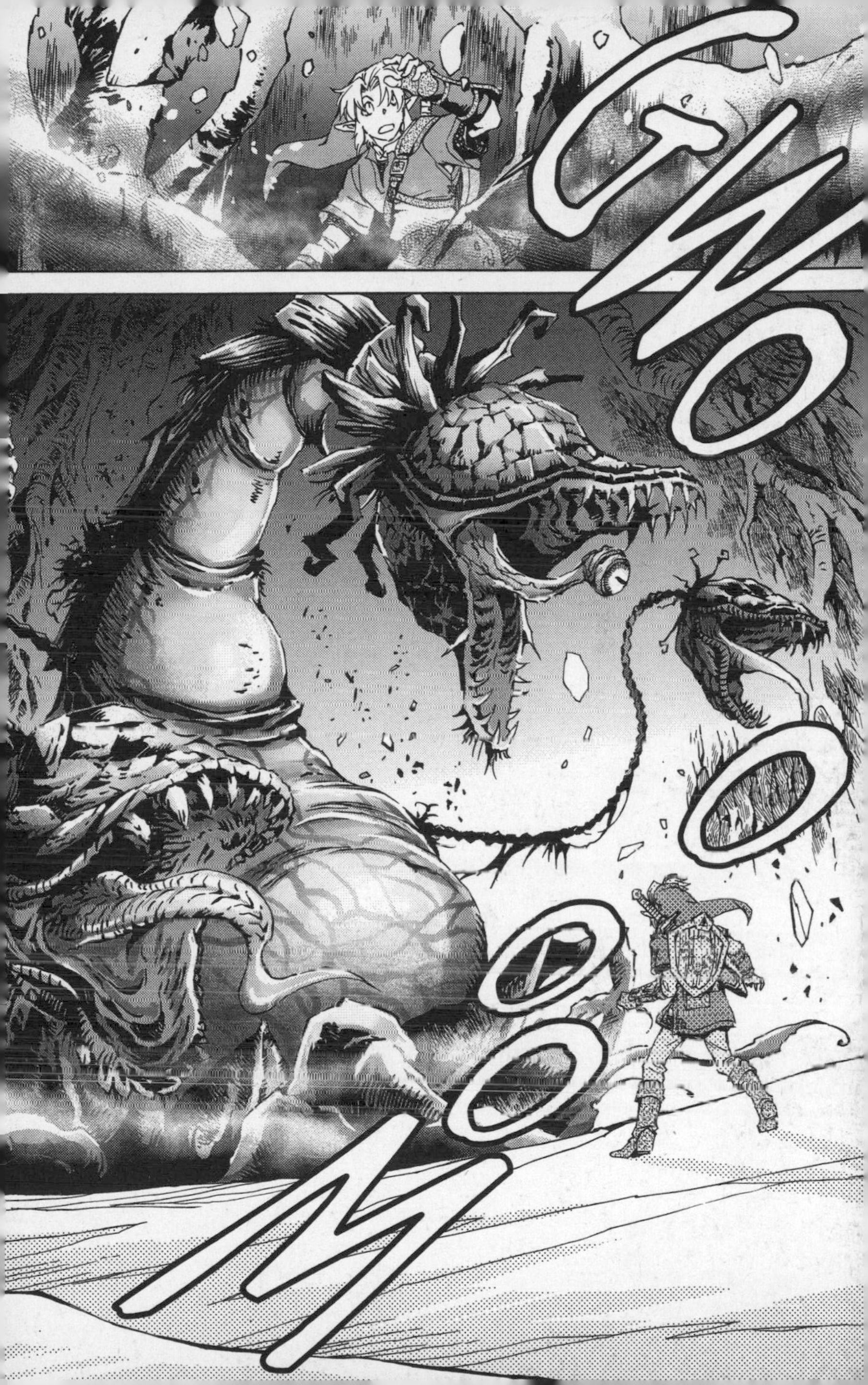
GWOOOOM

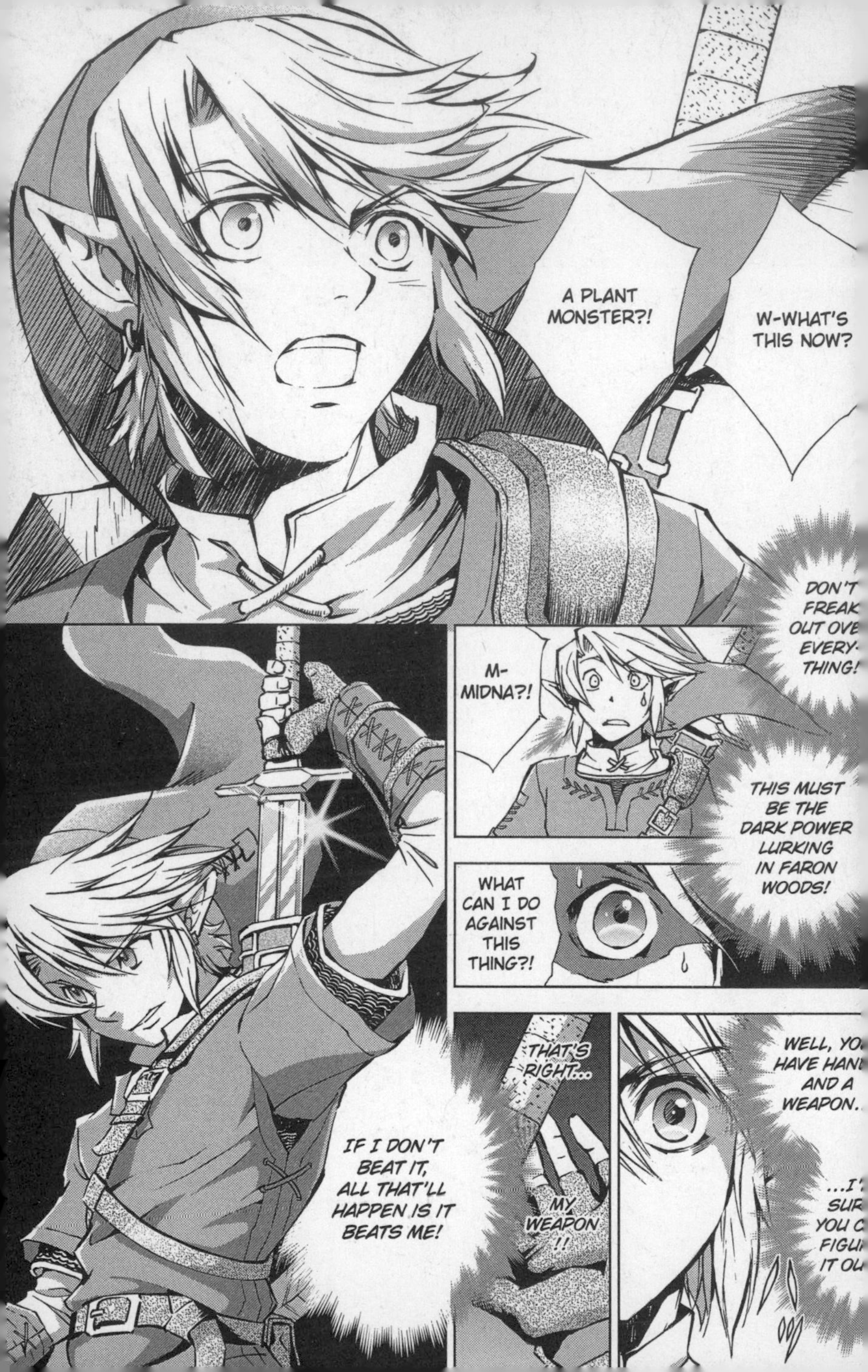
W-WHAT'S THIS NOW?
A PLANT MONSTER?!
DON'T FREAK OUT OVE EVERY-THING!
M-MIDNA?!
THIS MUST BE THE DARK POWER LURKING IN FARON WOODS!
WHAT CAN I DO AGAINST THIS THING?!
WELL, YO HAVE HAN AND A WEAPON.
...I' SUR YOU C FIGU IT OU
THAT'S RIGHT...
MY WEAPON !!
IF I DON'T BEAT IT, ALL THAT'LL HAPPEN IS IT BEATS ME!

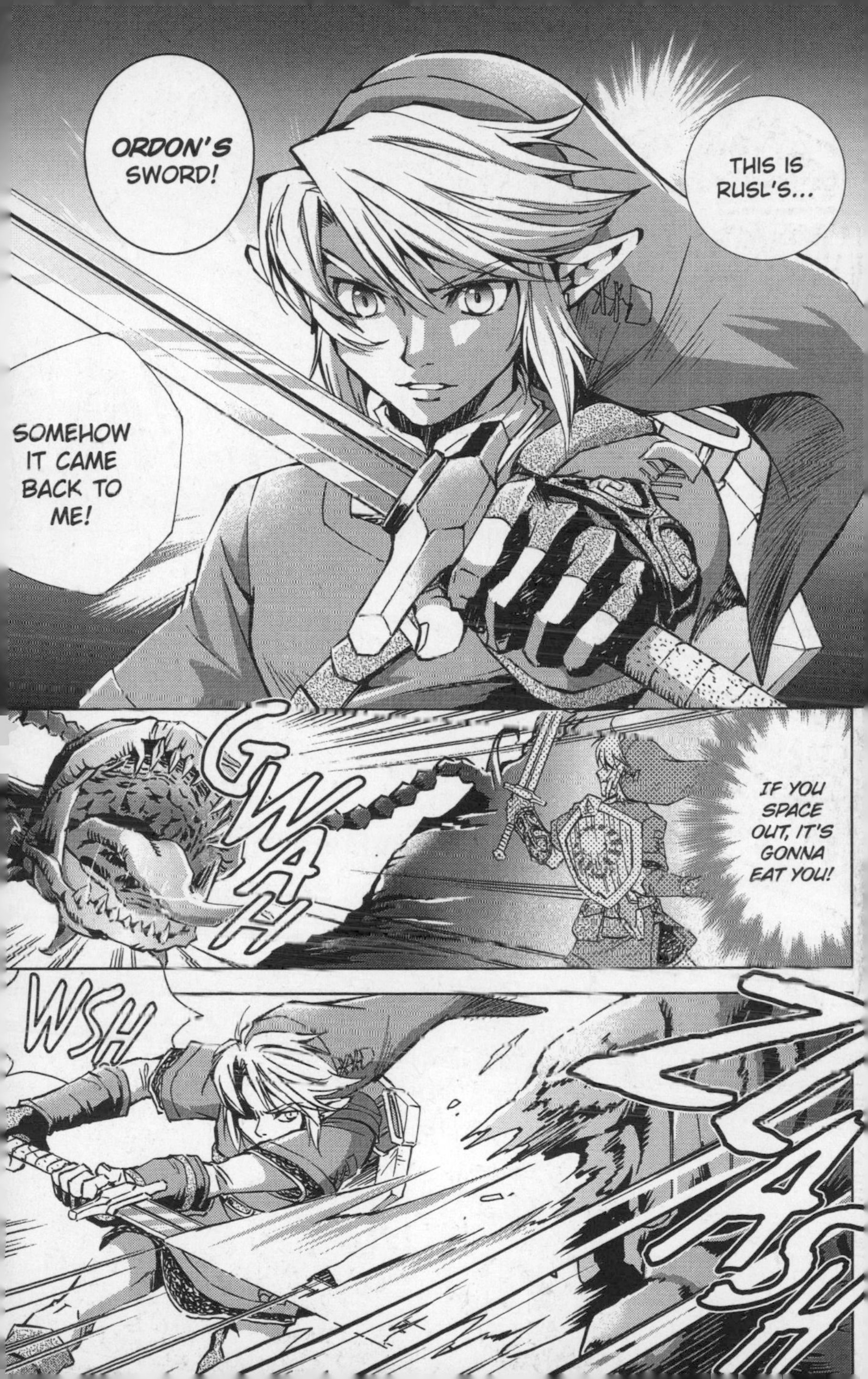
THIS IS RUSL'S...
ORDON'S SWORD!
SOMEHOW IT CAME BACK TO ME!
IF YOU SPACE OUT, IT'S GONNA EAT YOU!
GWAH
WSH

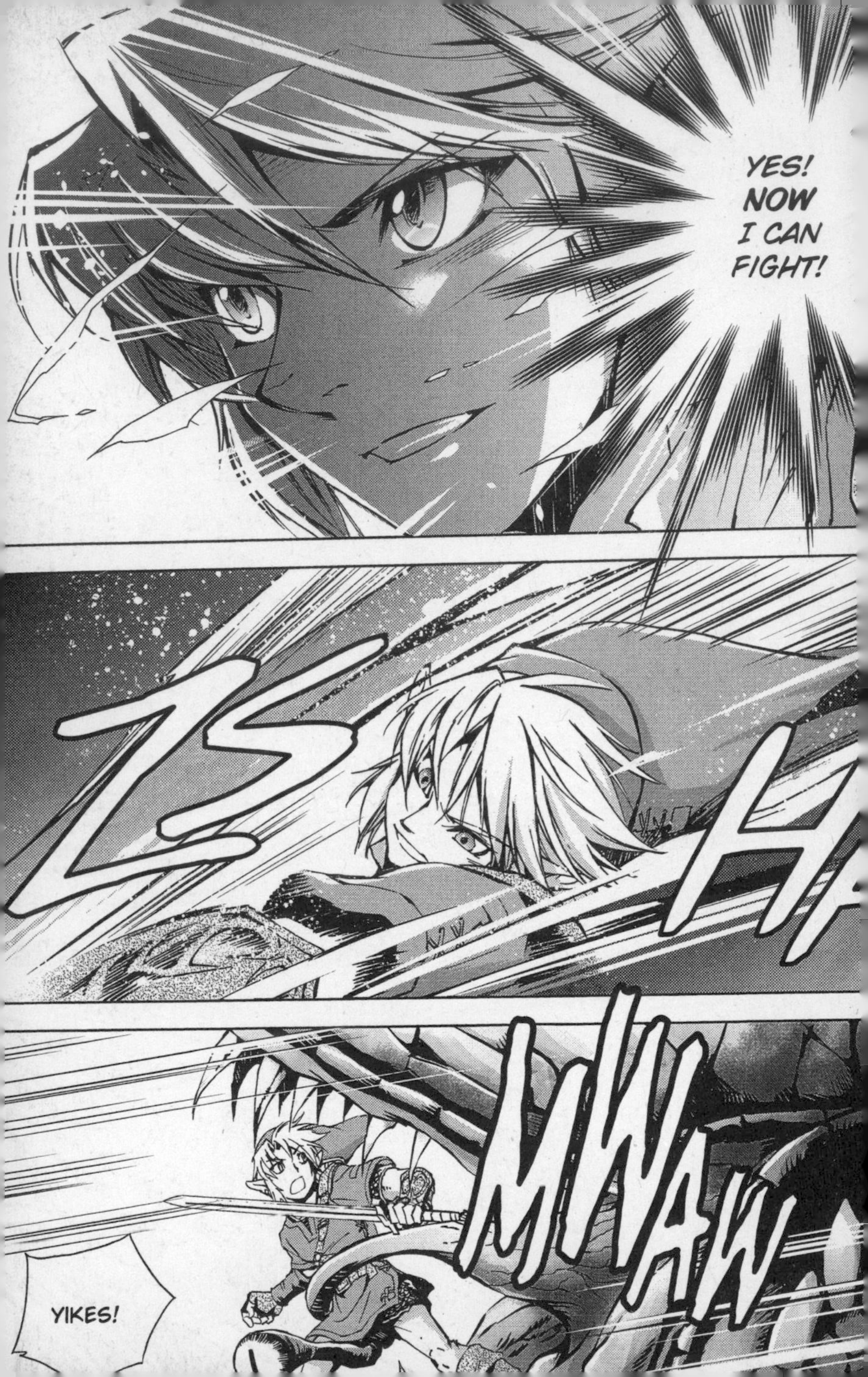
YES! NOW I CAN FIGHT!
YIKES!

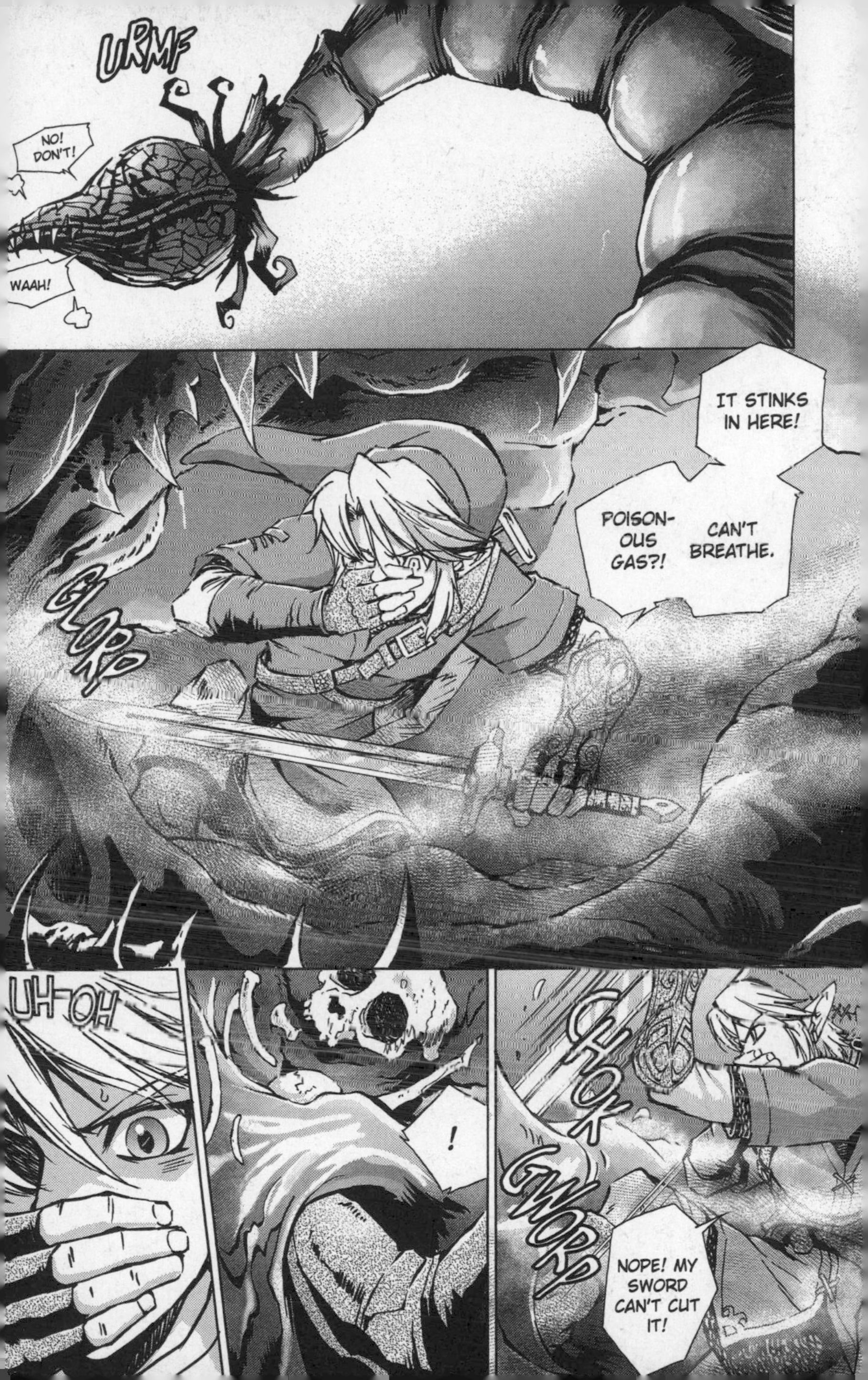
URMF
NO! DON'T!
WAAH!
IT STINKS IN HERE!
CAN'T BREATHE.
POISON-OUS GAS?!
GLORP
CHOK
GWORP
NOPE! MY SWORD CAN'T CUT IT!
!
UH-OH

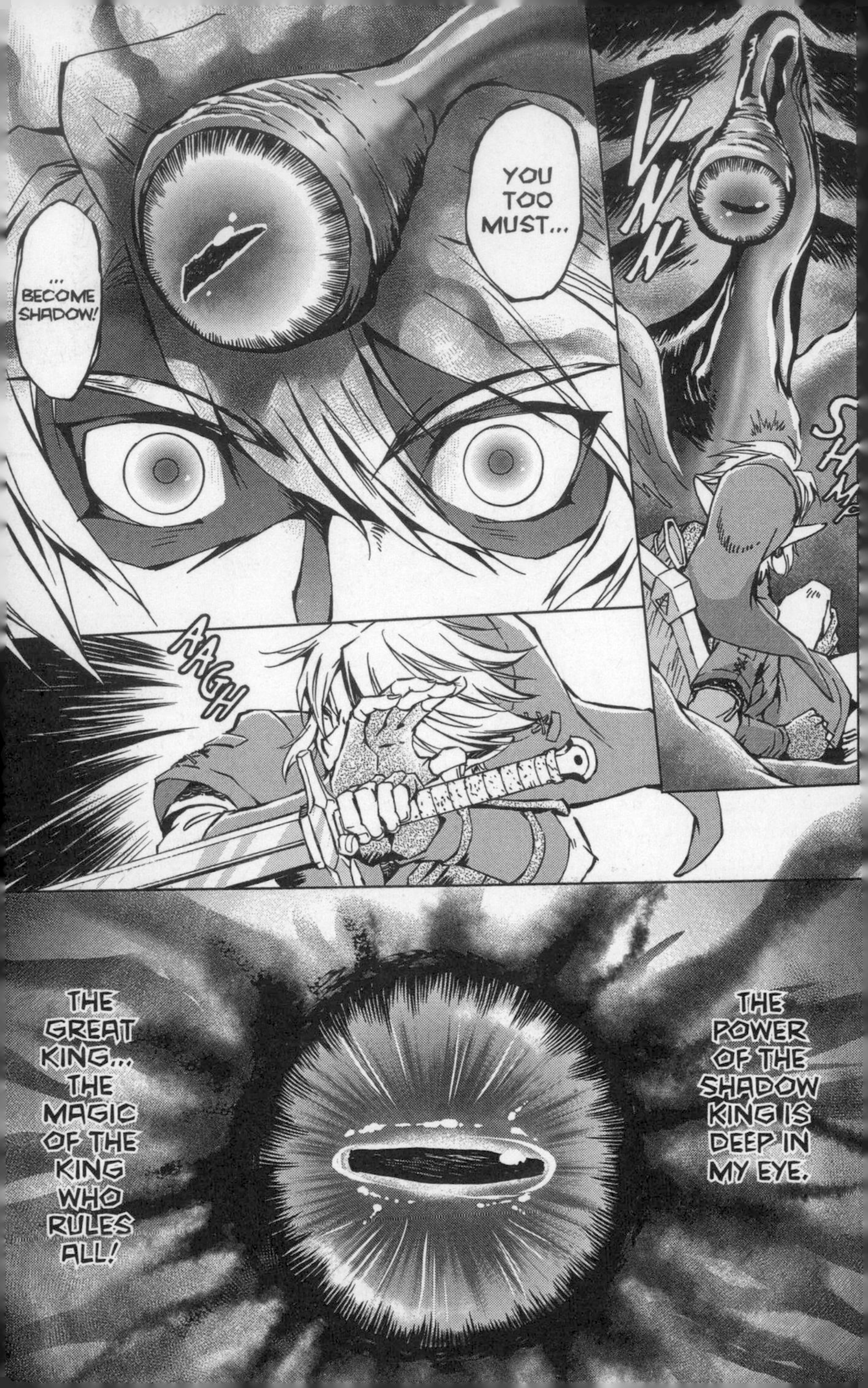
VNNN
SHMP
YOU TOO MUST...
...BECOME SHADOW!
AAGH
THE POWER OF THE SHADOW KING IS DEEP IN MY EYE.
THE GREAT KING... THE MAGIC OF THE KING WHO RULES ALL!

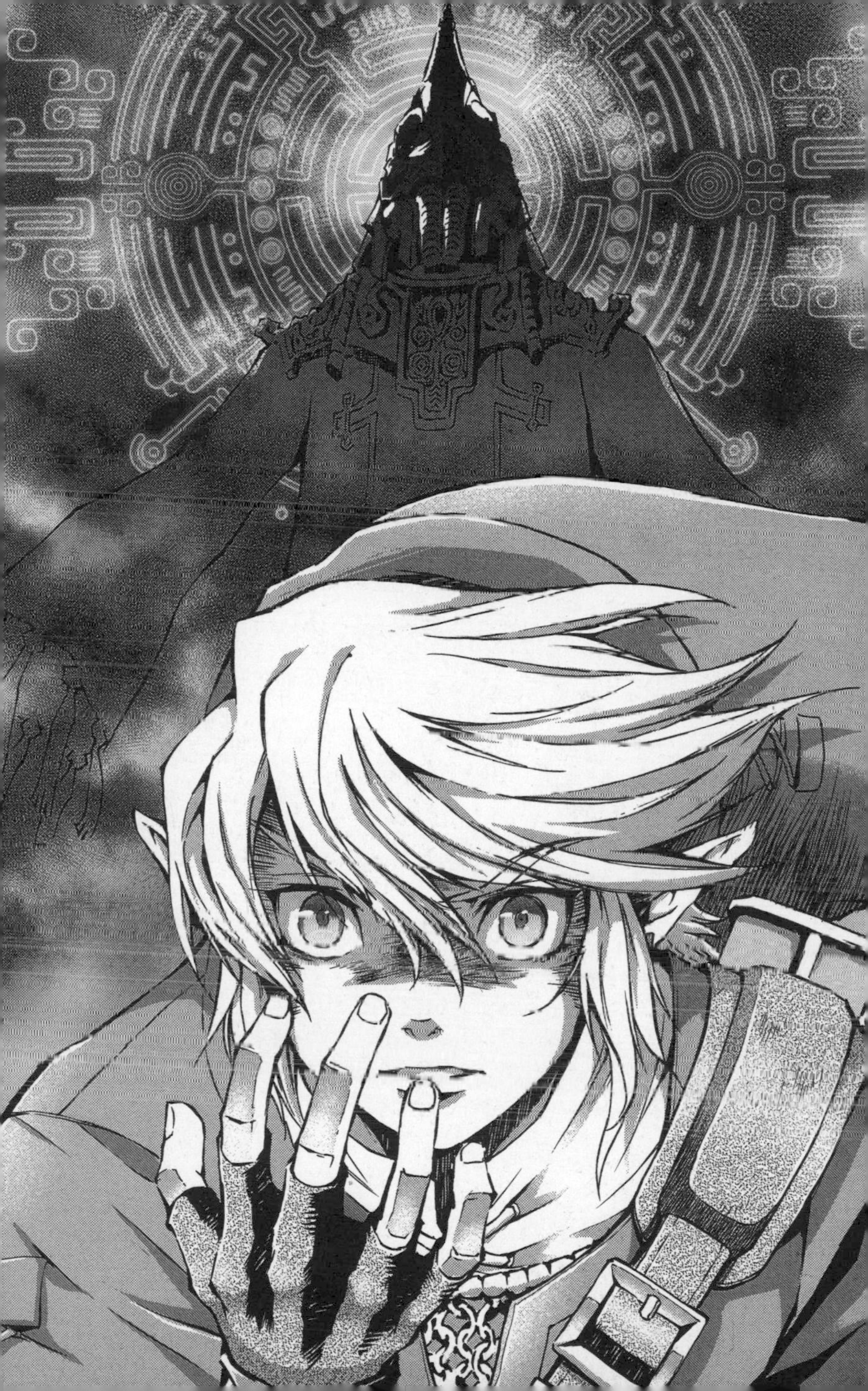

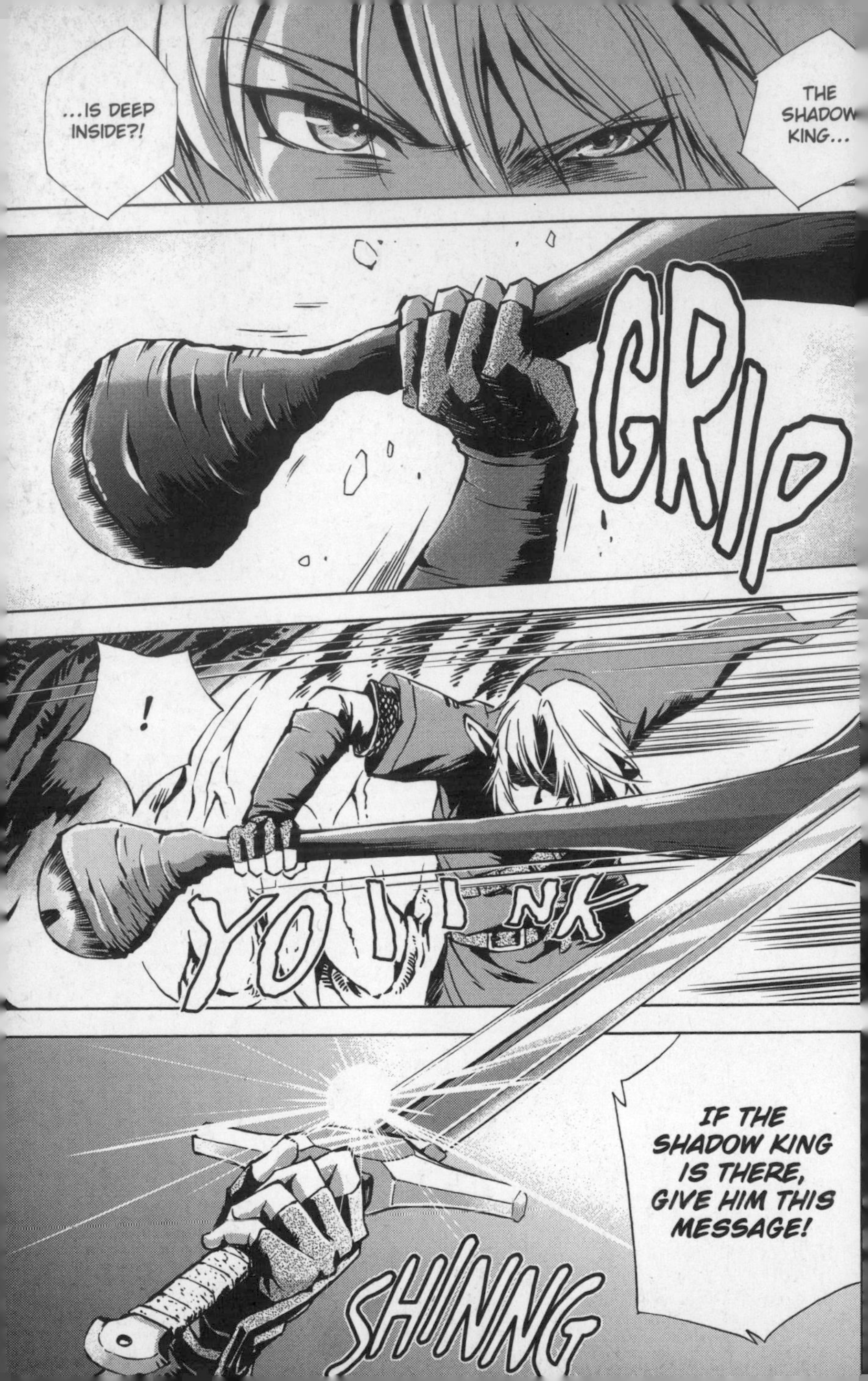
THE SHADOW KING...
...IS DEEP INSIDE?!
GRIP
!
YOINK
IF THE SHADOW KING IS THERE, GIVE HIM THIS MESSAGE!
SHINNG

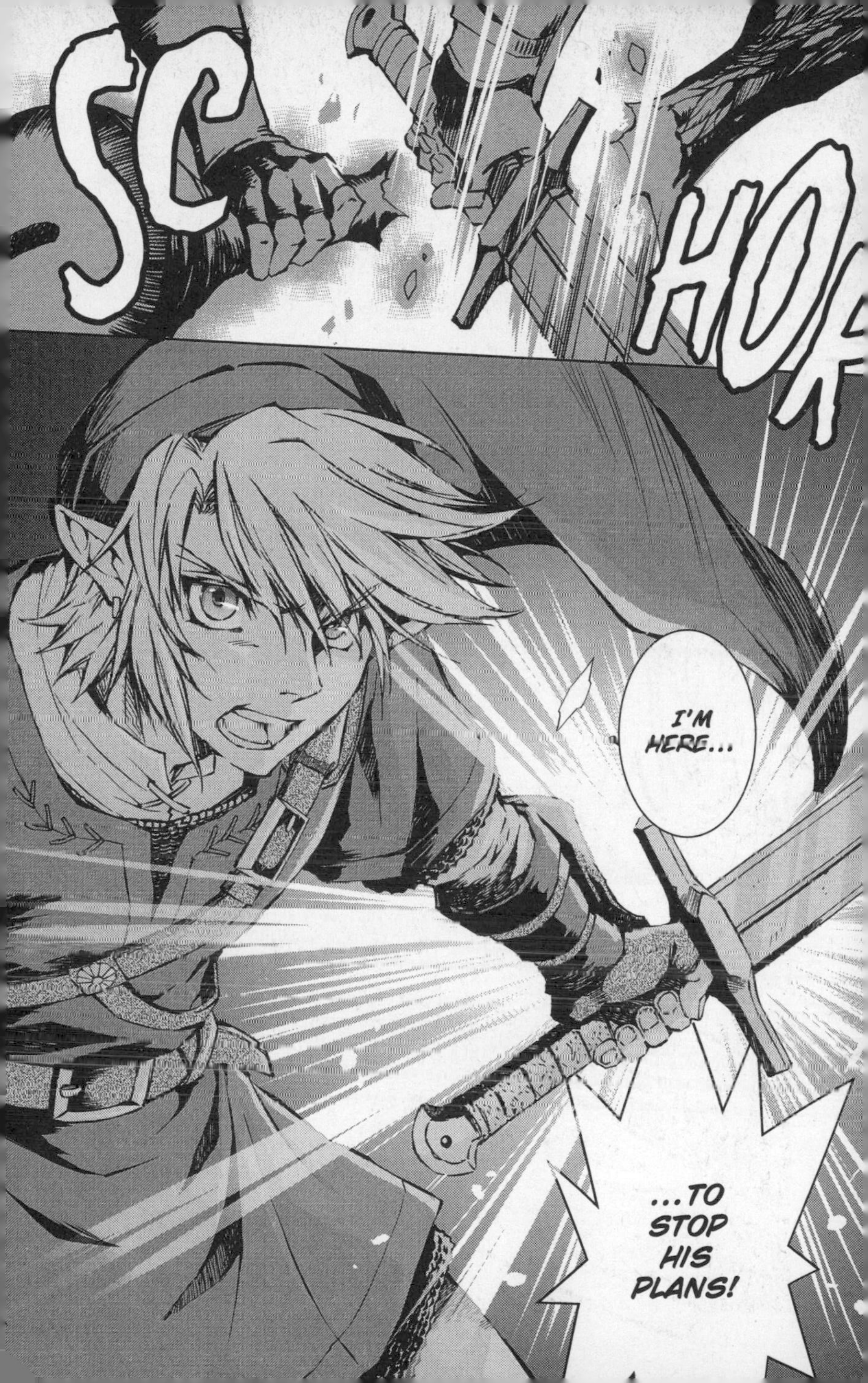
SC
HO
I'M HERE...
...TO STOP HIS PLANS!

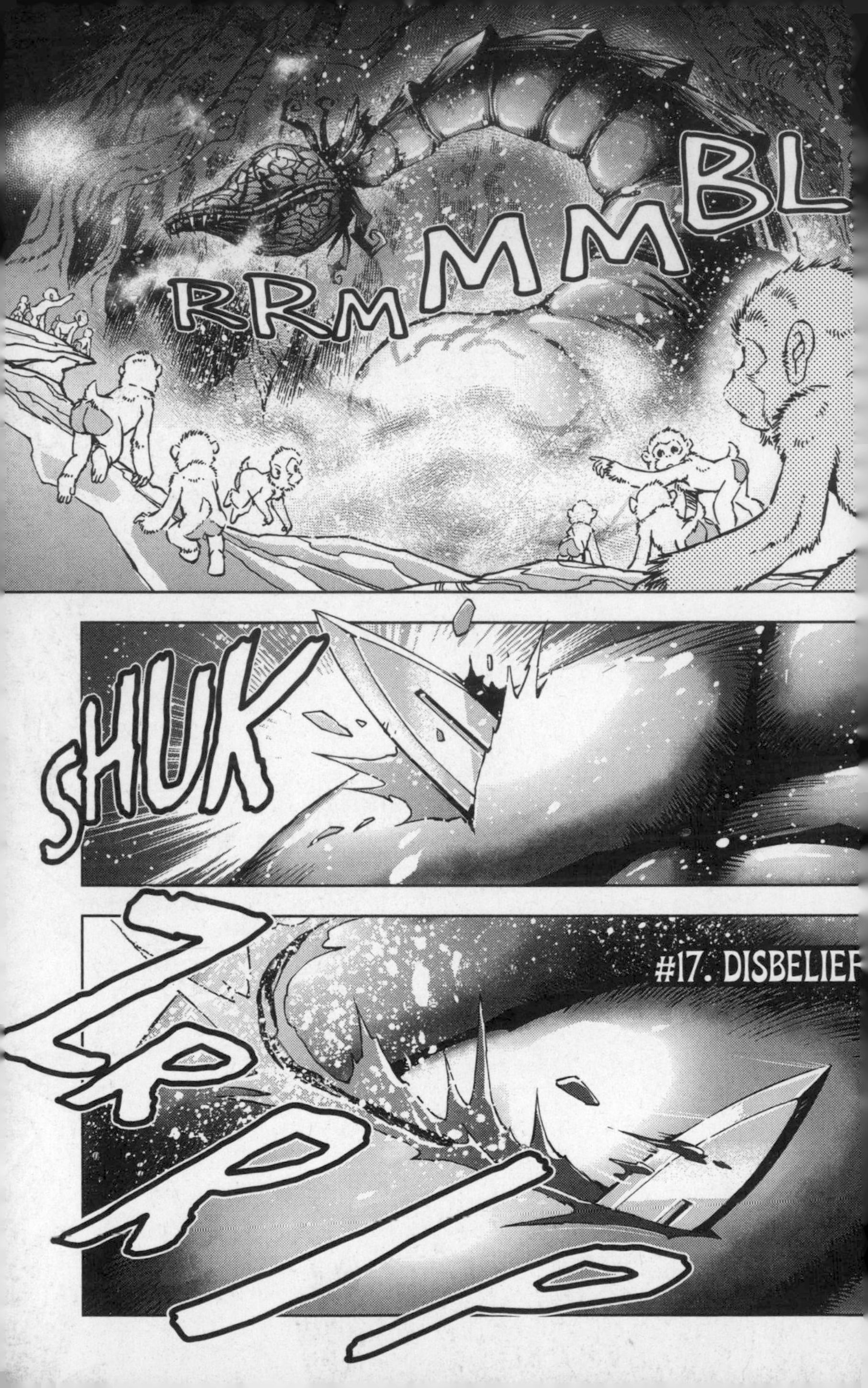
RRMMMMBL
SHUK
#17. DISBELIEF
ZLRRIP

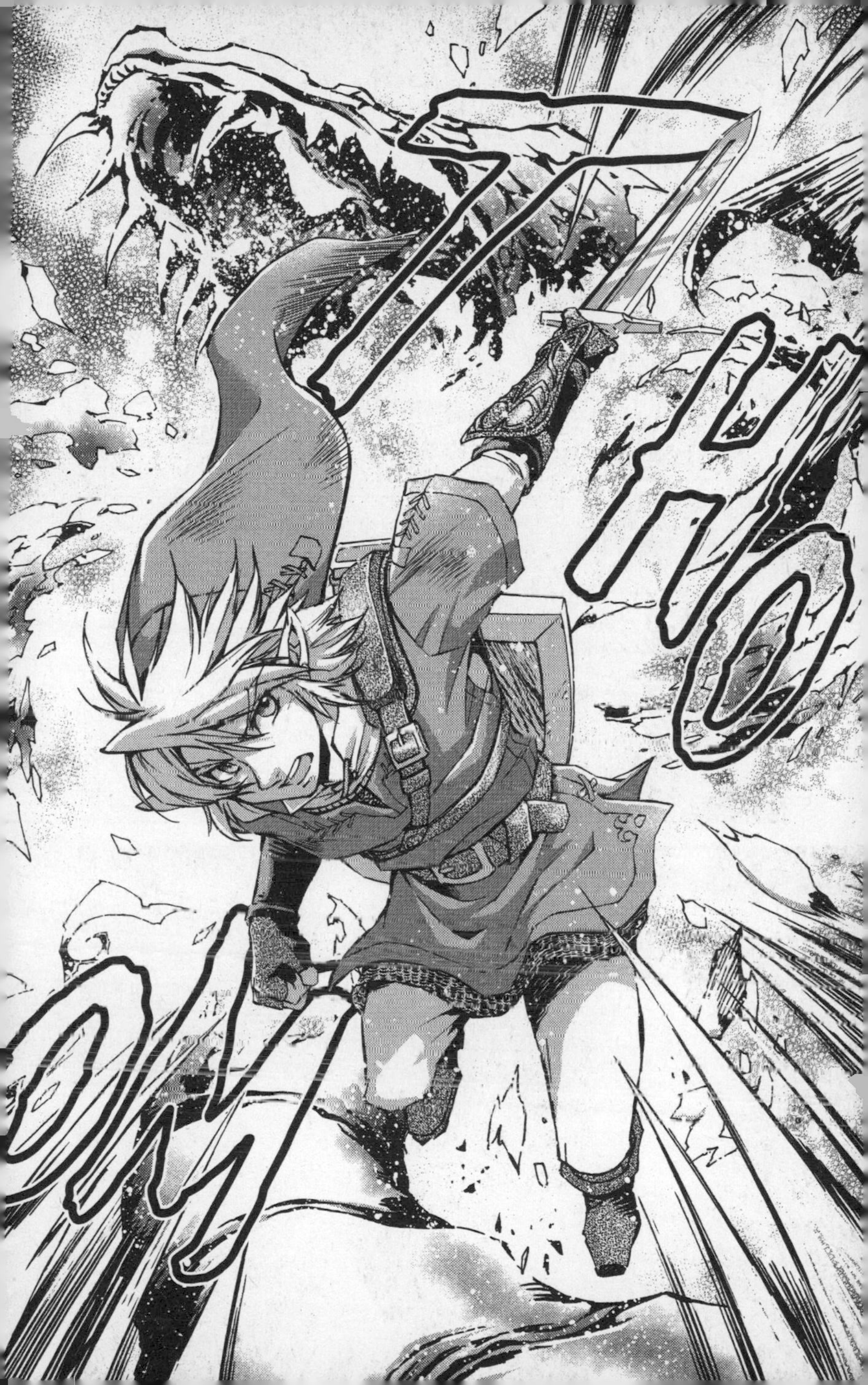

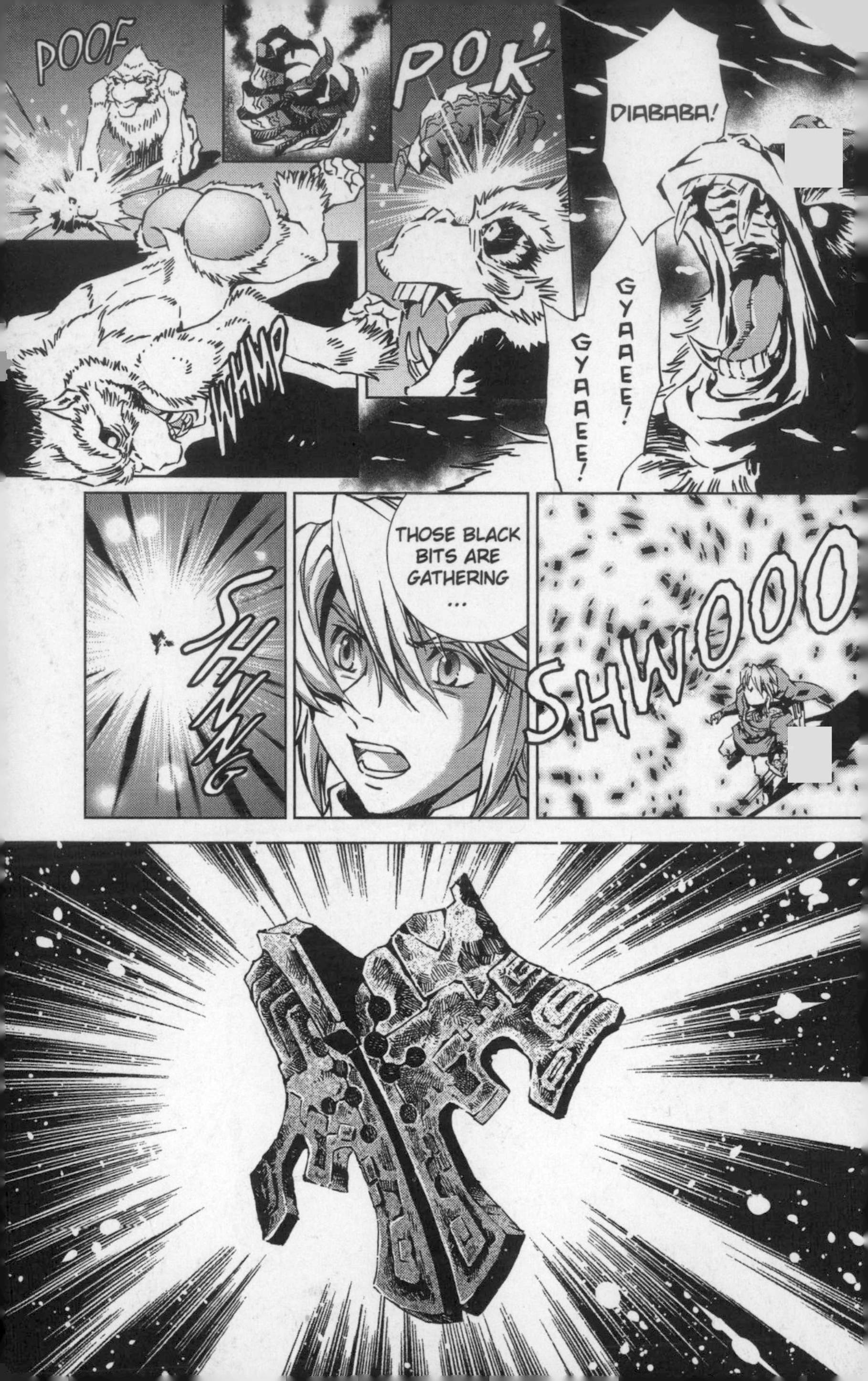
DIABABA!
GYAAAEE!
GYAAAEE!
POK
POOF
WHAMP
SHWOOO
THOSE BLACK BITS ARE GATHERING ...
SHWNG

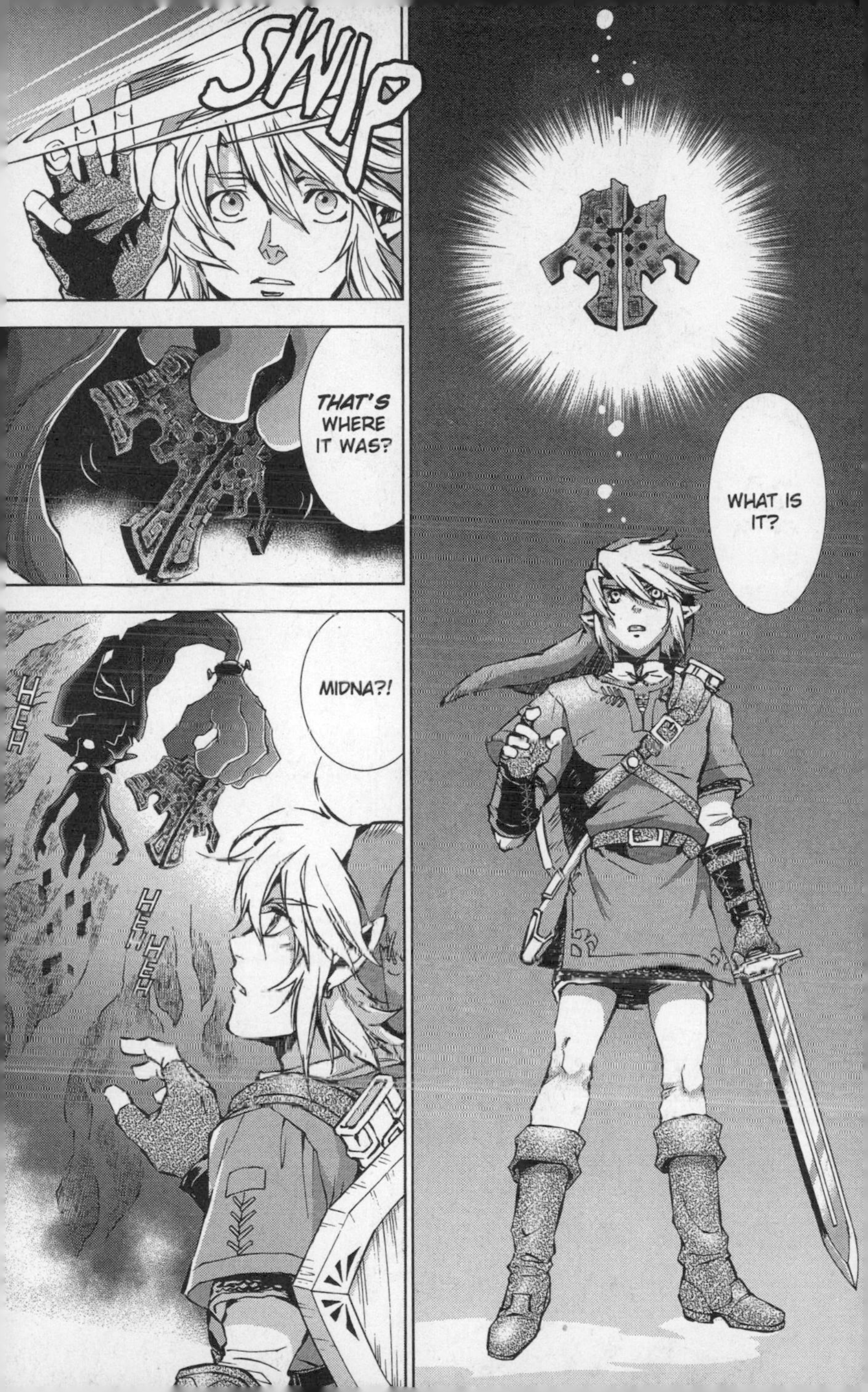
WHAT IS IT?
SWIP
THAT'S WHERE IT WAS?
MIDNA?!

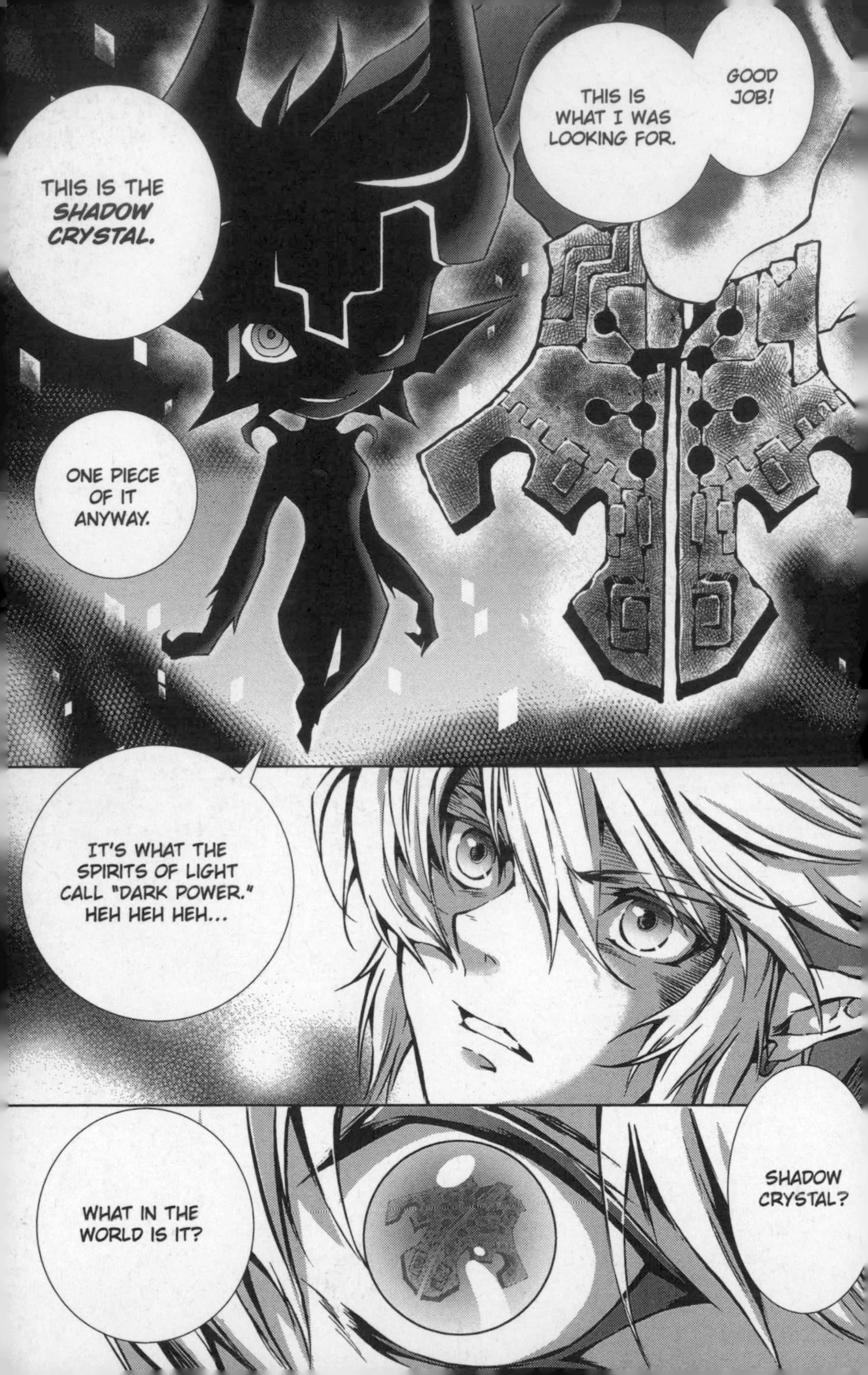
GOOD JOB!
THIS IS WHAT I WAS LOOKING FOR.
THIS IS THE SHADOW CRYSTAL.
ONE PIECE OF IT ANYWAY.
IT'S WHAT THE SPIRITS OF LIGHT CALL "DARK POWER." HEH HEH HEH...
SHADOW CRYSTAL?
WHAT IN THE WORLD IS IT?

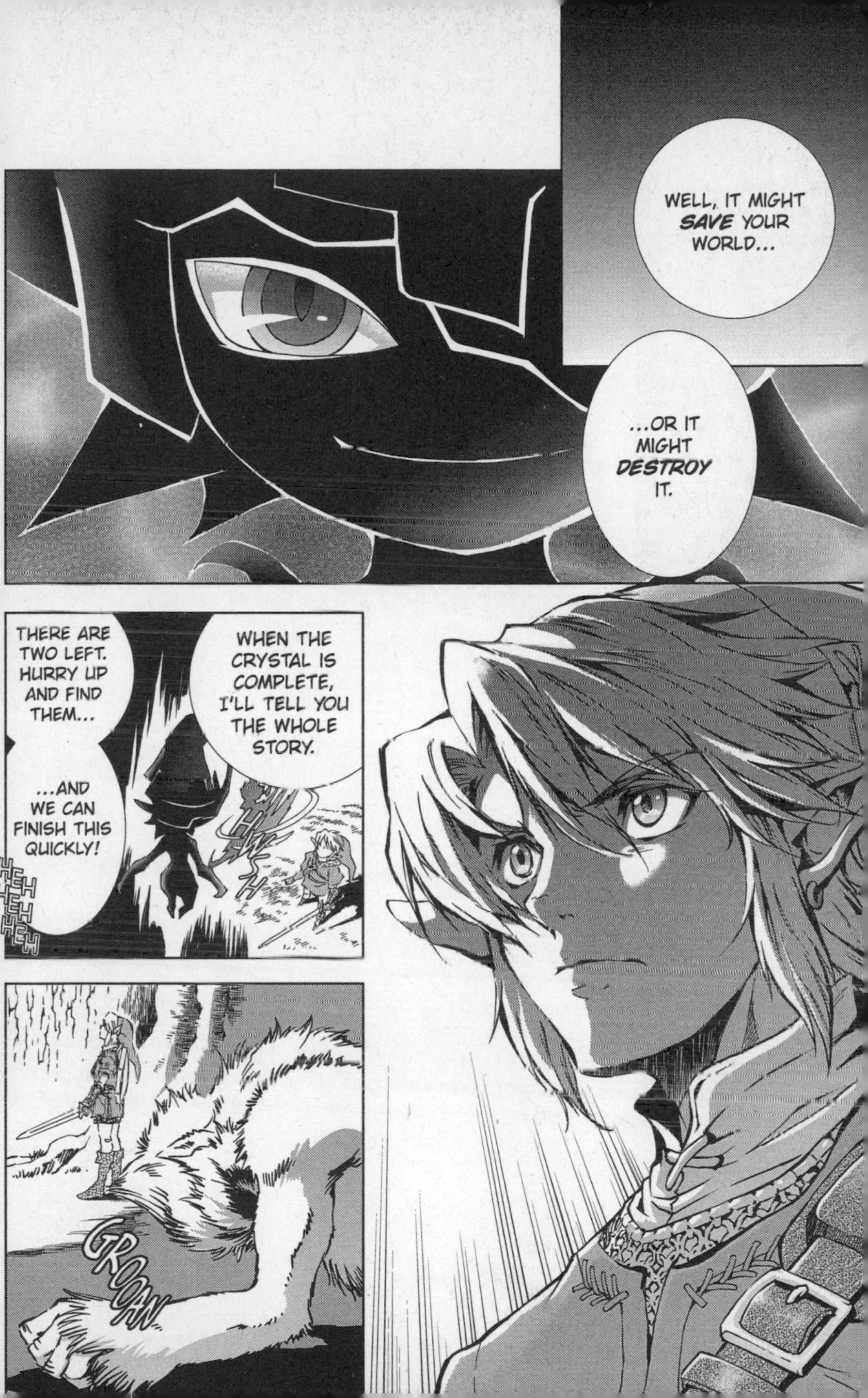
WELL, IT MIGHT SAVE YOUR WORLD...
...OR IT MIGHT DESTROY IT.
WHEN THE CRYSTAL IS COMPLETE, I'LL TELL YOU THE WHOLE STORY.
THERE ARE TWO LEFT. HURRY UP AND FIND THEM...
...AND WE CAN FINISH THIS QUICKLY!
HEH HEH HEH
GROAN

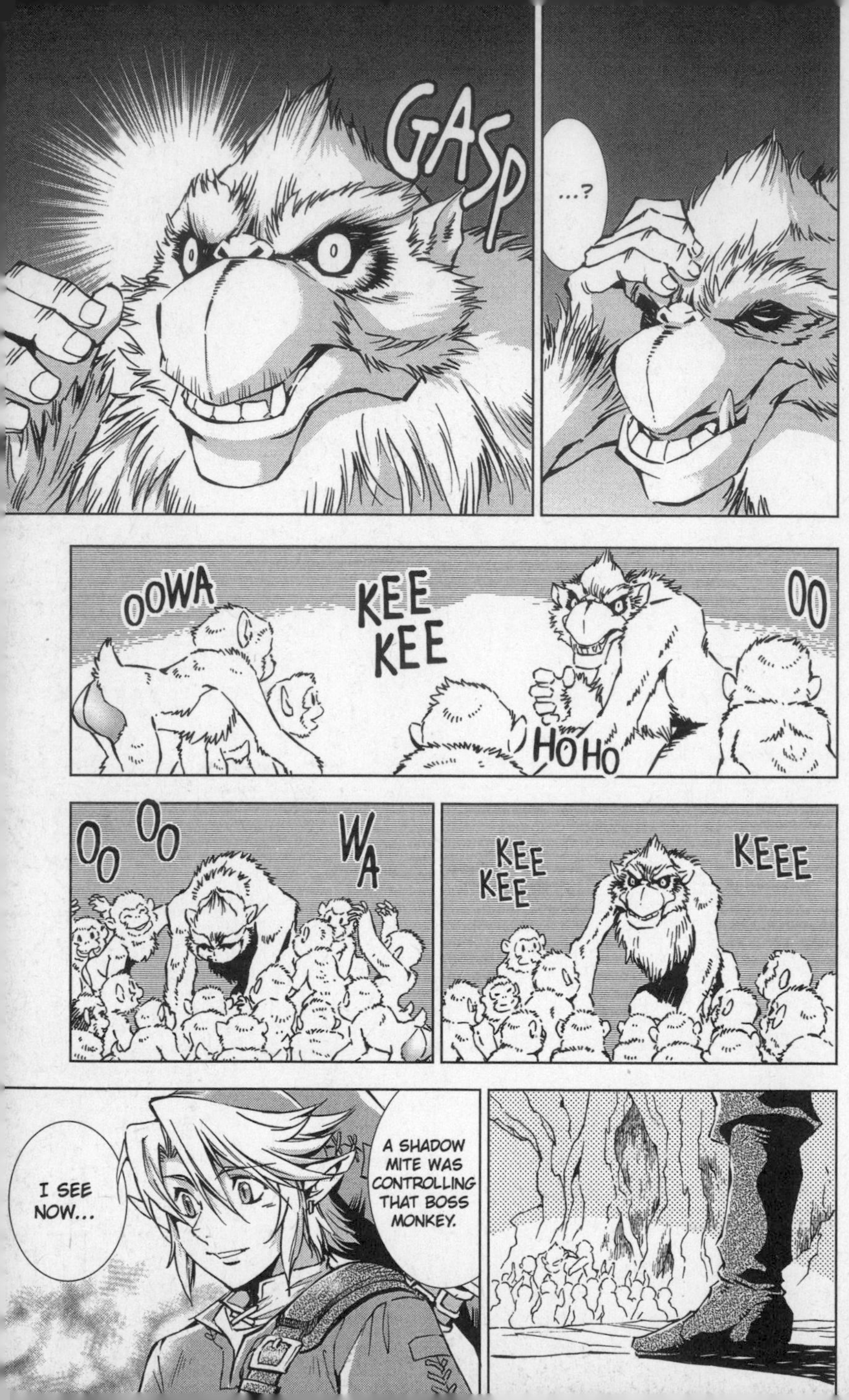
...?
GASP
OO
KEE KEE
OOWA
HO HO
KEEE
KEE KEE
WA
OO OO
A SHADOW MITE WAS CONTROLLING THAT BOSS MONKEY.
I SEE NOW...

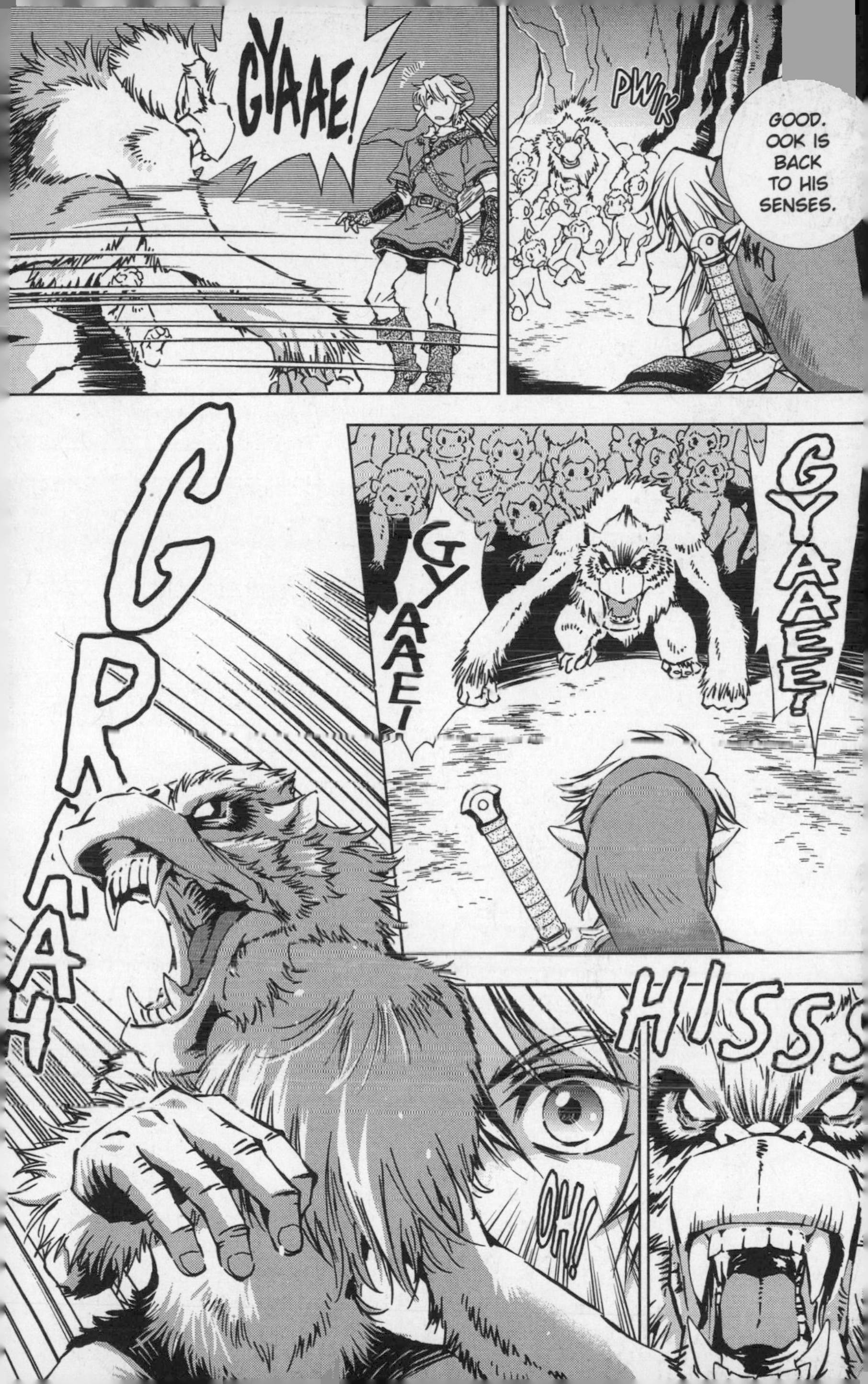
PWIK
GOOD. OOK IS BACK TO HIS SENSES.
GYAAE!
GYAAEE!
GYAAE!
GRAAAH
HISSS
OH!

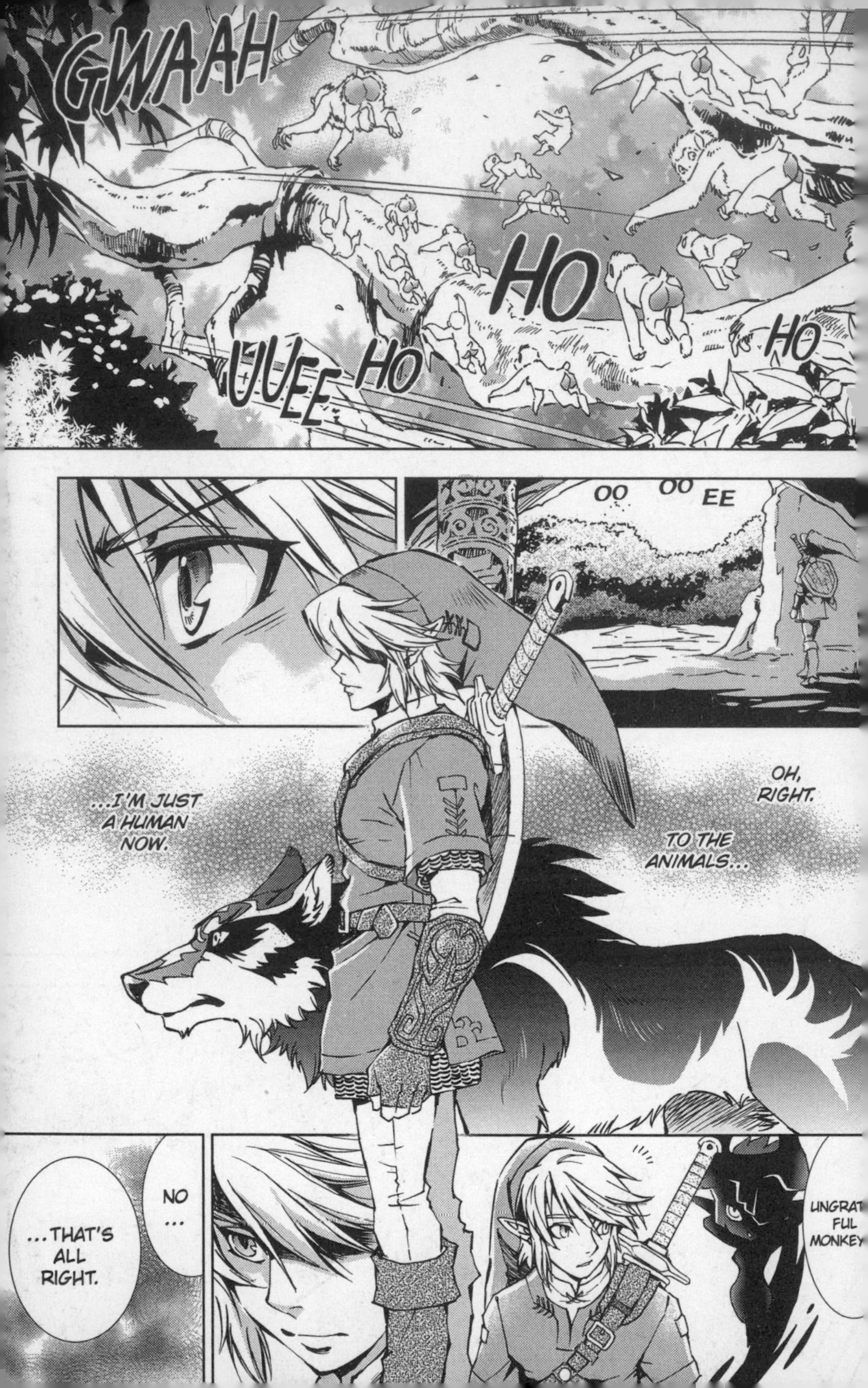
GWAAH
HO
HO
UUEE
HO
OO OO EE
OH, RIGHT.
TO THE ANIMALS...
...I'M JUST A HUMAN NOW.
UNGRAT FUL MONKEY
NO ...
...THAT'S ALL RIGHT.

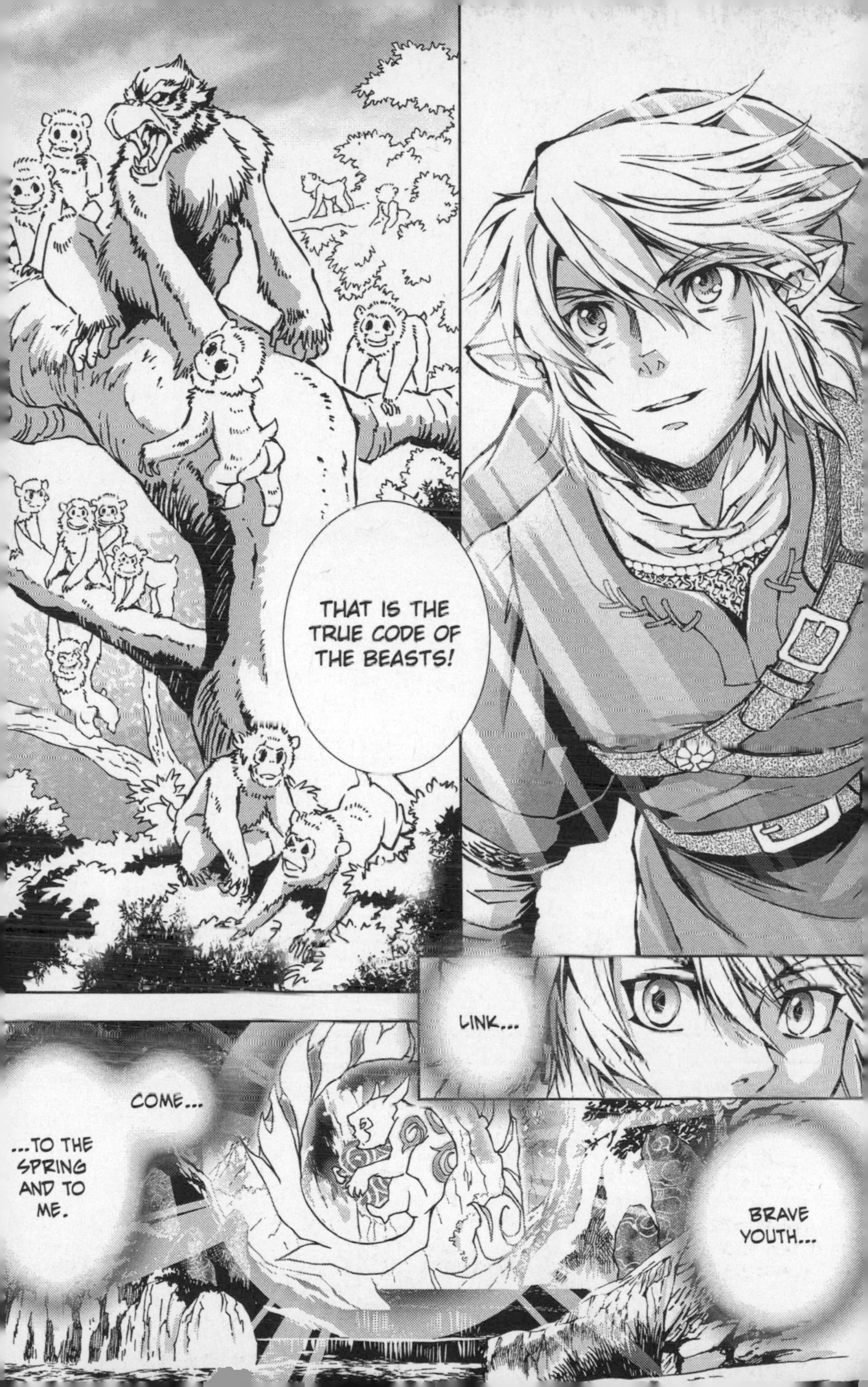
THAT IS THE TRUE CODE OF THE BEASTS!
LINK...
BRAVE YOUTH...
COME...
...TO THE SPRING AND TO ME.

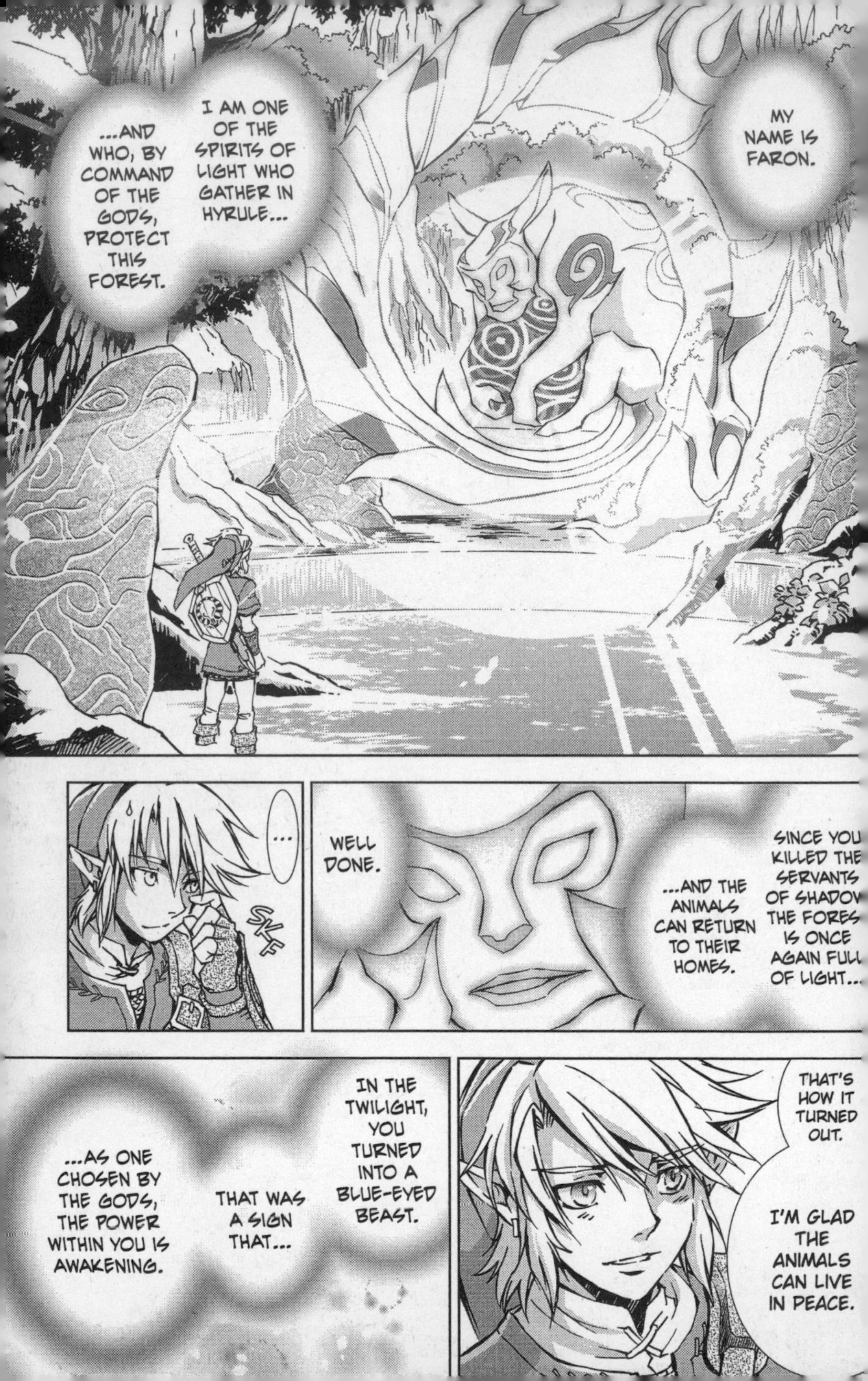
MY NAME IS FARON.
I AM ONE OF THE SPIRITS OF LIGHT WHO GATHER IN HYRULE...
...AND WHO, BY COMMAND OF THE GODS, PROTECT THIS FOREST.
SINCE YOU KILLED THE SERVANTS OF SHADOW THE FORES IS ONCE AGAIN FULL OF LIGHT...
...AND THE ANIMALS CAN RETURN TO THEIR HOMES.
WELL DONE.
...
SNIF
THAT'S HOW IT TURNED OUT.
I'M GLAD THE ANIMALS CAN LIVE IN PEACE.
IN THE TWILIGHT, YOU TURNED INTO A BLUE-EYED BEAST.
THAT WAS A SIGN THAT...
...AS ONE CHOSEN BY THE GODS, THE POWER WITHIN YOU IS AWAKENING.

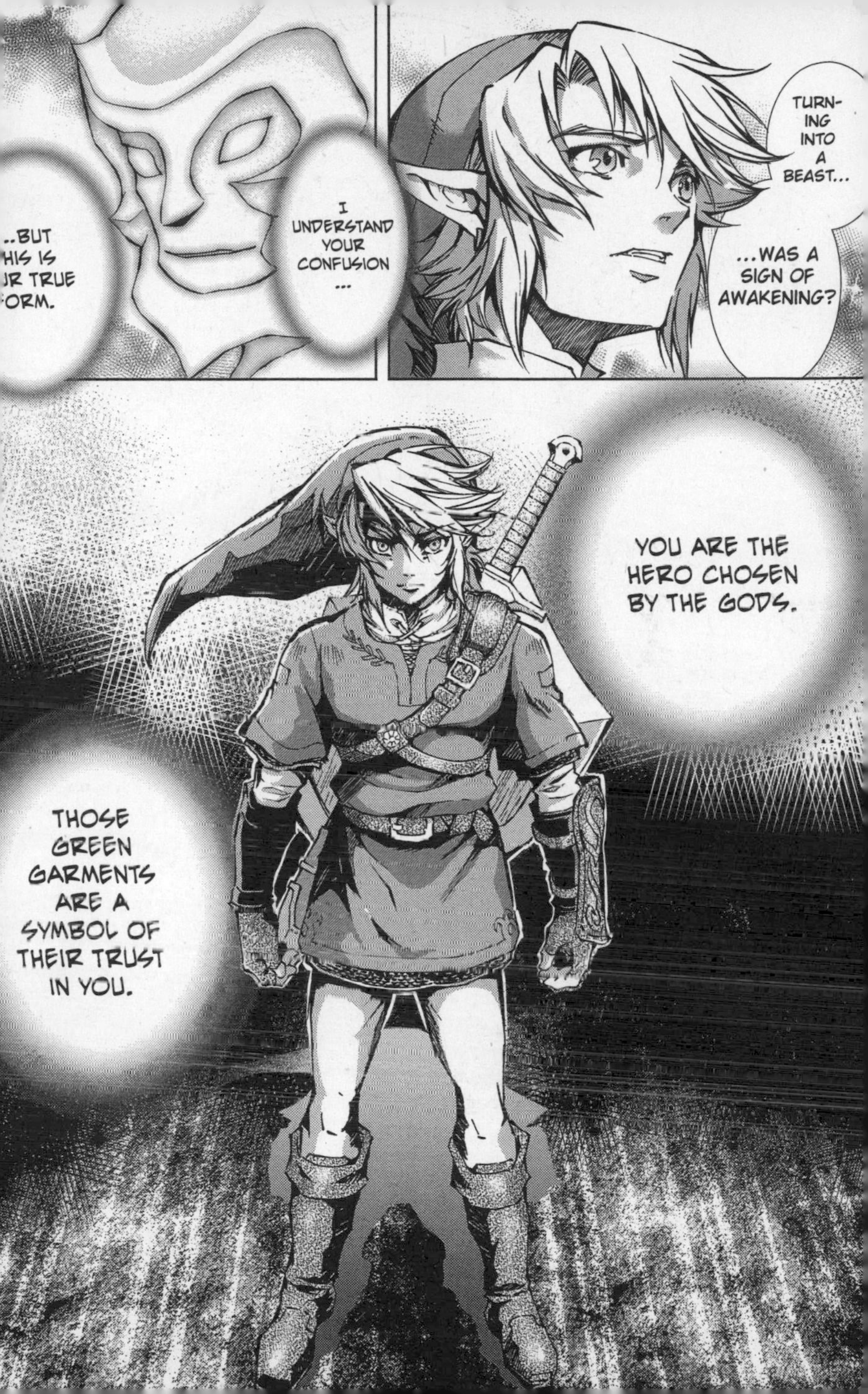
TURNING INTO A BEAST...
...WAS A SIGN OF AWAKENING?
I UNDERSTAND YOUR CONFUSION...
..BUT HIS IS R TRUE ORM.
YOU ARE THE HERO CHOSEN BY THE GODS.
THOSE GREEN GARMENTS ARE A SYMBOL OF THEIR TRUST IN YOU.

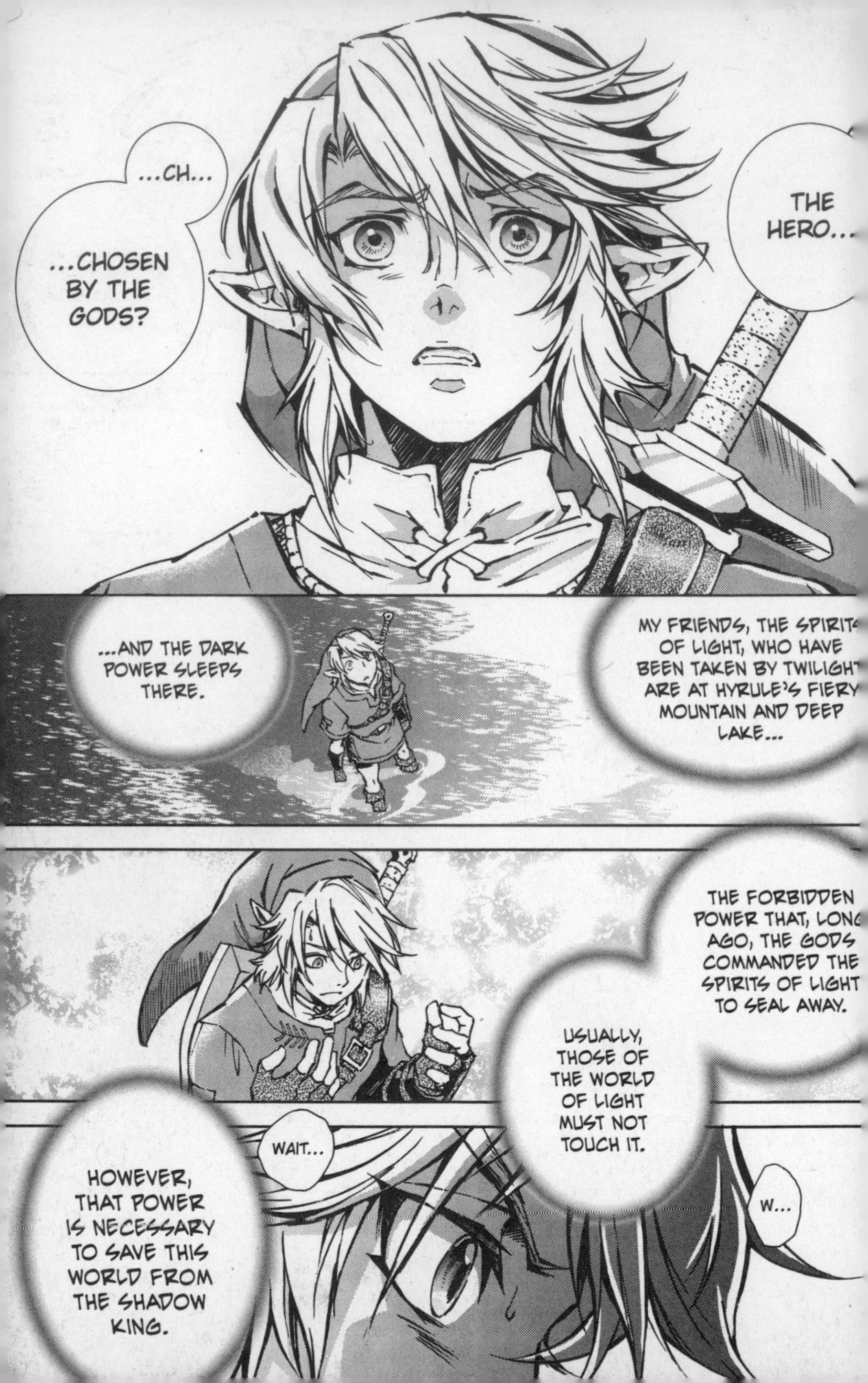
THE HERO...
...CH...
...CHOSEN BY THE GODS?
MY FRIENDS, THE SPIRITS OF LIGHT, WHO HAVE BEEN TAKEN BY TWILIGHT ARE AT HYRULE'S FIERY MOUNTAIN AND DEEP LAKE...
...AND THE DARK POWER SLEEPS THERE.
THE FORBIDDEN POWER THAT, LONG AGO, THE GODS COMMANDED THE SPIRITS OF LIGHT TO SEAL AWAY.
USUALLY, THOSE OF THE WORLD OF LIGHT MUST NOT TOUCH IT.
W...
WAIT...
HOWEVER, THAT POWER IS NECESSARY TO SAVE THIS WORLD FROM THE SHADOW KING.

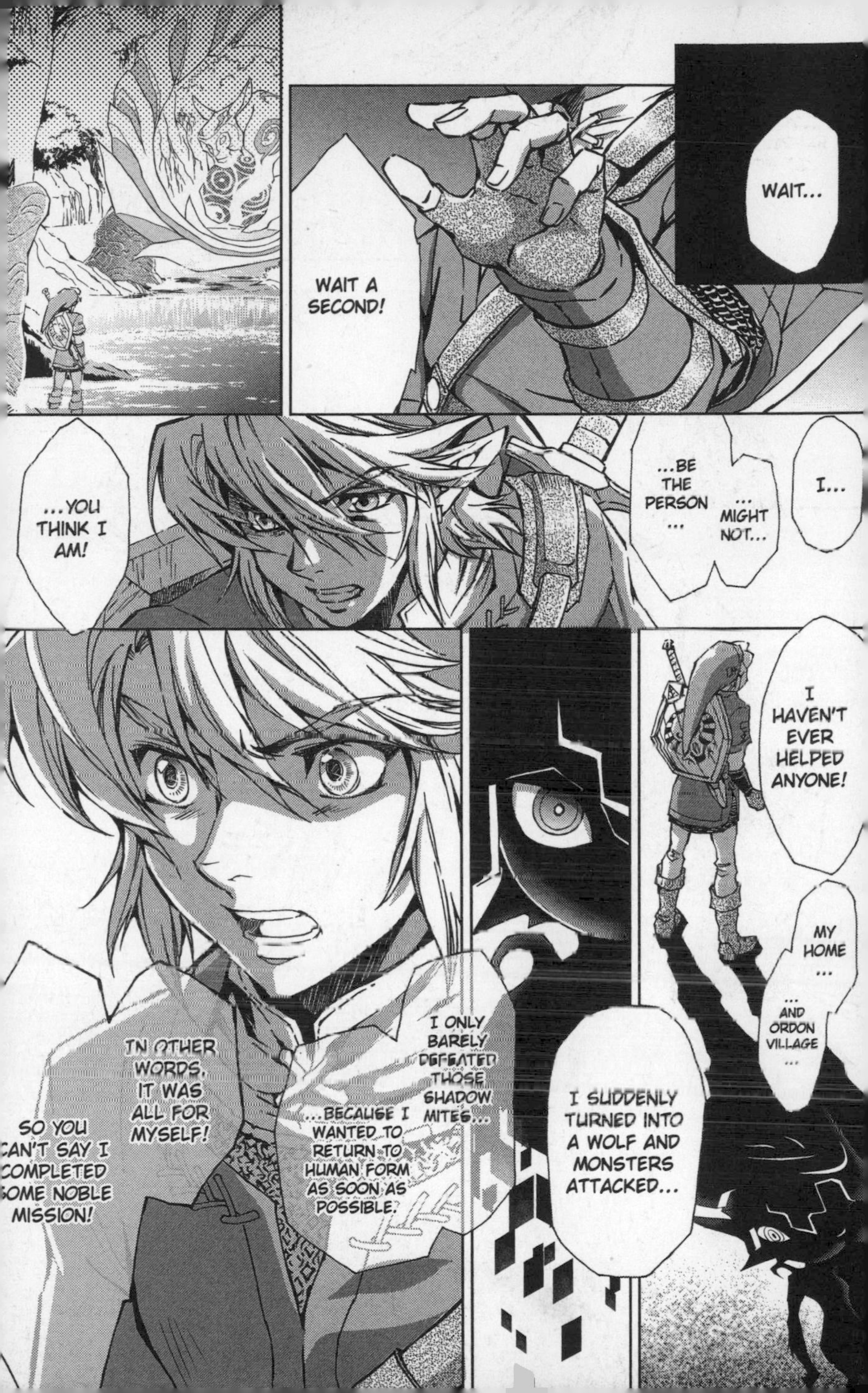
WAIT...
WAIT A SECOND!
I...
...MIGHT NOT...
...BE THE PERSON...
...YOU THINK I AM!
I HAVEN'T EVER HELPED ANYONE!
MY HOME...
...AND ORDON VILLAGE...
I SUDDENLY TURNED INTO A WOLF AND MONSTERS ATTACKED...
I ONLY BARELY DEFEATED THOSE SHADOW MITES...
...BECAUSE I WANTED TO RETURN TO HUMAN FORM AS SOON AS POSSIBLE.
IN OTHER WORDS, IT WAS ALL FOR MYSELF!
SO YOU CAN'T SAY I COMPLETED SOME NOBLE MISSION!

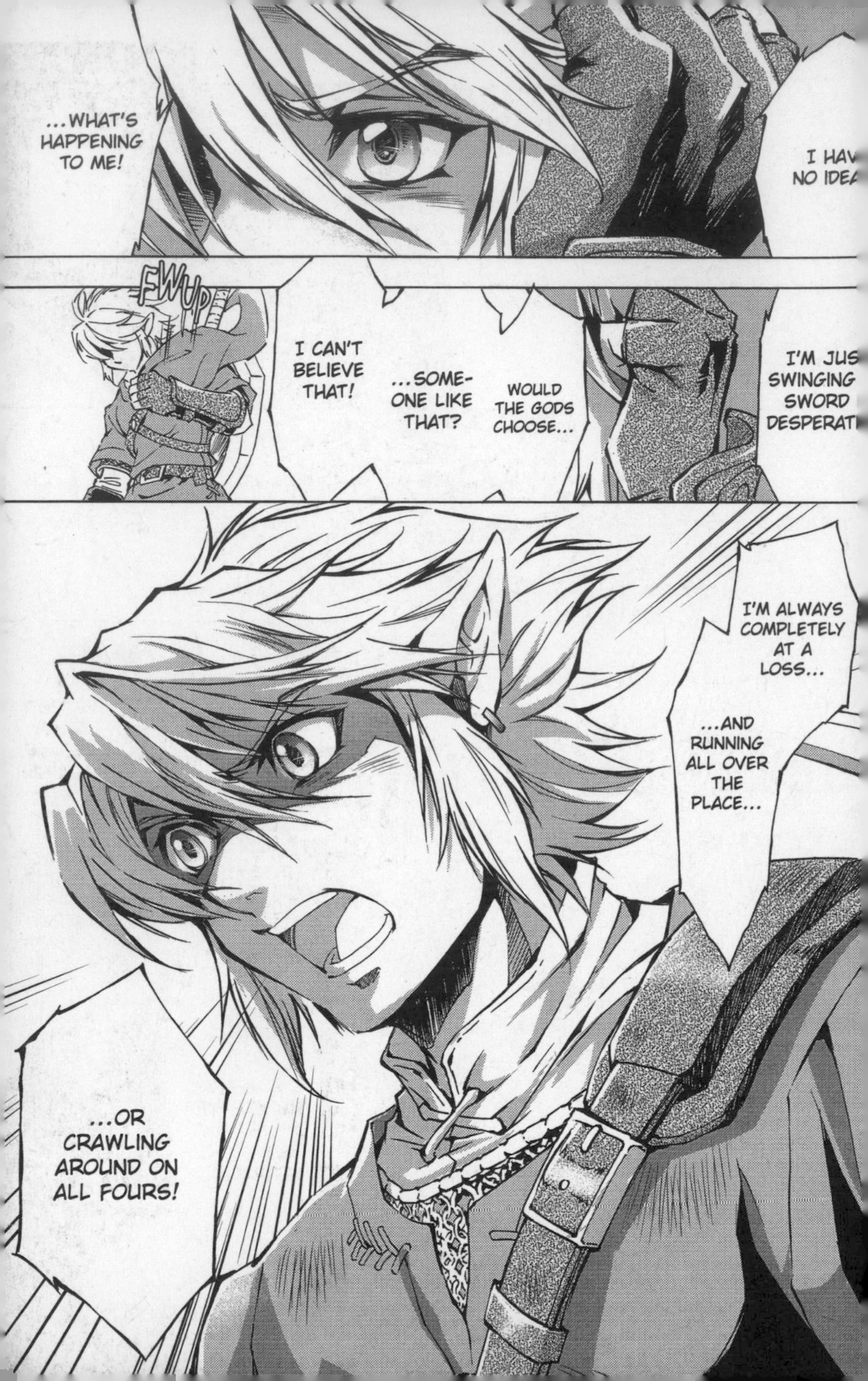
I HAV NO IDEA
...WHAT'S HAPPENING TO ME!
I'M JUS SWINGING SWORD DESPERAT
WOULD THE GODS CHOOSE...
...SOME-ONE LIKE THAT?
I CAN'T BELIEVE THAT!
FWUP
I'M ALWAYS COMPLETELY AT A LOSS...
...AND RUNNING ALL OVER THE PLACE...
...OR CRAWLING AROUND ON ALL FOURS!

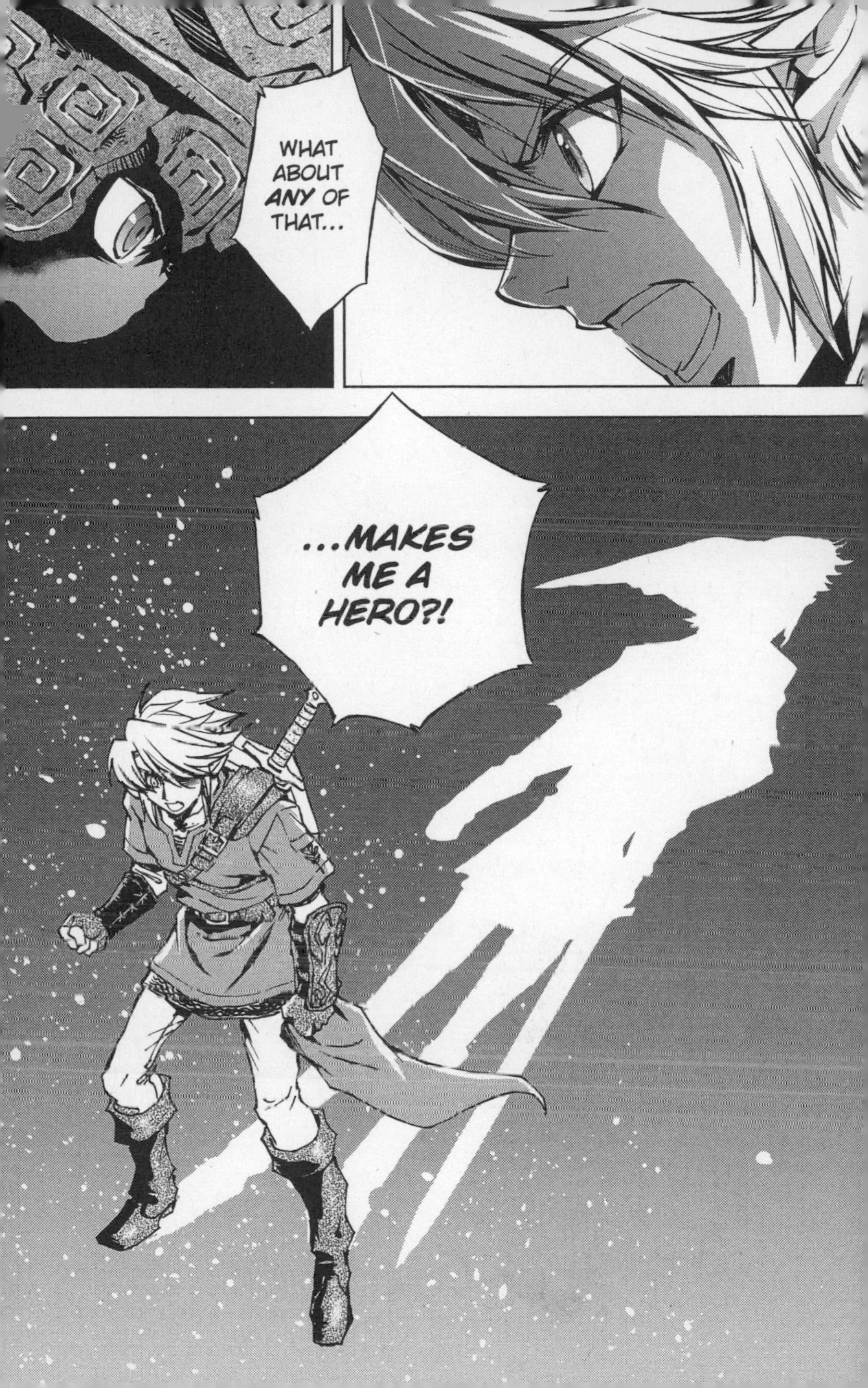
WHAT ABOUT ANY OF THAT...
...MAKES ME A HERO?!

Little Extra 1

Princess Zelda as a child

AS I WORKED, I THOUGHT THAT THE BRIGHT COURTYARD WITH WATER POTS AND BATHED IN LIGHT MUST BE ONE OF THE YOUNG PRINCESS ZELDA'S FAVORITE SPOTS.
05.2016

Little Extra 2

Heroes Pass the Baton

AFTER CHANGING HIM TO THE GREEN OUTFIT, I SUDDENLY REALIZED HOW I HAVEN'T DRAWN LINK AS A YOUNG MAN (CAN ADULT) IN MANGA SINCE *OCARINA OF TIME*, WHICH WAS 17 YEARS AGO! SO HERE'S A PICTURE OF THE HEROES PASSING THE BATON. LINK IN *TWILIGHT PRINCESS* MAY BE WAVERING AT THE MOMENT, BUT HE FIRMLY ACCEPTS IT. ^_^

AUTHOR'S NOTE

Volume 2 of *Twilight Princess* is out! This series once ran in a children's magazine and had to be complete at one volume, but this time is different. The story has progressed and, as of the second volume, Link finally has his green clothes! Please cheer for Link here at the beginning of his long and hard journey!

Akira Himekawa is the collaboration of two women, A. Honda and S. Nagano. Together they have created ten manga adventures featuring Link and the popular video game world of *The Legend of Zelda*™. Their most recent work, *The Legend of Zelda*™: *Twilight Princess*, is serialized digitally on Shogakukan's MangaONE app in Japan.

THE LEGEND OF ZELDA

·TWILIGHT PRINCESS·

Volume 2—VIZ Media Edition

STORY AND ART BY
Akira Himekawa

TRANSLATION **John Werry**
ENGLISH ADAPTATION **Stan!**
TOUCH-UP ART & LETTERING **Evan Waldinger**
DESIGNER **Shawn Carrico**
EDITOR **Mike Montesa**

Published by VIZ Media, LLC
P.O. Box 77010
San Francisco, CA 94107

10 9 8 7 6 5 4 3 2 1
First printing, August 2017

www.viz.com

Hey! You're Reading in the Wrong Direction!

This is the ***end*** of this graphic novel!

To properly enjoy this VIZ graphic novel, please turn it around and begin reading from ***right to left.*** Unlike English, Japanese is read right to left, so Japanese comics are read in reverse order from the way English comics are typically read.

1
2
1
2
3
4
3
5
6
4
7
8
5
9

Follow the action this way

This book has been printed in the original Japanese format in order to preserve the orientation of the original artwork. Have fun with it!

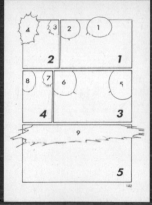